NEKORA

JASON SISSUNG

Copyright © 2021 by Jason Sissung

Paperback: 978-1-63767-404-8
eBook: 978-1-63767-405-5
Hardcover: 978-1-63767-532-8
Library of Congress Control Number: 2021915719

All rights reserved. No part of this publication may be reproduced, distributed, or transmitted in any form or by any electronic or mechanical means, without the prior written permission of the publisher, except in the case of brief quotations embodied in critical reviews and certain other noncommercial uses permitted by copyright law.

This is a work of nonfiction.

Ordering Information:

BookTrail Agency
8838 Sleepy Hollow Rd.
Kansas City, MO 64114

Printed in the United States of America

THE BookFest® AWARDS

Spring 2022

Nekora

Jason Sissung

Second Place

Fantasy

THE BOOKFEST
This award acknowledges your contribution to the world of literature and books.

Thank you and congratulations,

Desireé Duffy

Desiree Duffy
Founder

CHAPTER ONE

Aghram is an island with an immense landmass and a mountainous region encircling a vast valley spanning miles in every direction. The wood elves call this place home. In the central forest lies the wood elven Kingdom of Morhgrammir. King Kardin and Queen Arilana rule this Kingdom with fairness and kindness. Princess Nekora was adopted at birth by the King and Queen, or more so thrust upon them, but have always treated her with respect and love as if she were their actual daughter. Her brothers Meeka and Grogham are the biological sons of Kardin and Arilana and will always be the rightful heirs to the throne should anything foul succumb the King and Queen.

The mountain peaks range from several hundred to several thousand feet. The highest peak, due east of Morhgrammir, is rumored to house the infamous dark elves. There is but one small, hidden entrance on the top eastern side of the mountain known only by the inhabitants, hidden away from view by passersby. The top of the highest mountain harbors an immense crater, mimicking a volcanic opening, descending straight down several thousand feet to the dragons' lair. The sides are sheer due to the winds created by the dragons' descent, making any type of climbing impossible for anyone unless they are carrying rope that extends to the bottom. With seven pounds per ninety feet of rope, it is doubtful that anyone would carry over a thousand feet.

The black dragons' lair is located directly under the gigantic opening at the top of the mountain. Eight pillars several feet in height end in solid plateaus attached to the side of the mountain, creating a nook for the dragons to sleep unseen. They have made an agreement with the dark elves to conduct an amount of service in exchange for gold, jewels, and magical items. Dragons have a deep desire for such treasure. From each platform, there is a small, almost unseen climbable pathway. The pathway is used by the riders to embark and disembark their flights. Below the platforms is a jagged open area with a pathway leading to the additional side openings through the cavern.

The dragons normally emerge at night to hunt, hiding their presence and feeding on the ever-growing population of assorted creatures throughout the land. Some nights, dark elven dragon riders will mount to survey the lands, watching, ensuring no imminent threats exist. Dragon riders engage random encampments to solidify fear while maintaining secrecy.

Several tunnels to the south, east, and west lead deeper into the mountain, converging into one opening through the dragon's lair. The southern tunnel descends downward, zigzagging for another mile, leading to the bottom-most plateau, the Kingdom of Almaryha, home to the infamous dark elves. The eastern and western passages from the lair wind their way around seemingly for hours before they merge with the southern trail at the exit point. Deadly creatures roam these tunnel pathways as a last line of defense before the enemies battle the infamous Cerberus, the guardians of the city proper.

Cerberus are huge three-headed canines, brown, highly vicious, and roam the Kingdom grounds. They are trained to tear apart anyone or anything not belonging to the Kingdom. The exit marks the last chance effort of survival as it opens into a vast cavern with boulders and many Stalagmites and Stalactites, making a treacherous passage to the open grounds before the Kingdom of Almaryha. Driders are dark elven creatures in nature from the torso ending with a spider abdomen and eight pointy legs to effectively traverse any terrain with haste including webs and two arms to wield weapons. They control the outer regions of the hidden Kingdom.

Driders were developed when wizards attempted to fuse the potency and webbing ability of the black widow to the body of an elite guard. The dexterity and fluidity of the new guards coupled with grace and smoothness have opened opportunities. The guards are awe-inspiring indeed, and everyone moves out of the way when they approach. Deadly with the spear and precise web-shooting has made the Drider a fearsome opponent. They also control the Cerberus and patrol the grounds, keeping the Kingdom safe from intruders or escapees.

The northern tunnel winds toward the Minotaur lair and subsequently to the exit. The Minotaur lair is a gigantic maze with one way in or out to the north and south side and has a large opening in the center. Minotaur bodies are heavily muscled humanoids that are extremely strong with hooves for feet and a bull's head complete with horns. Large golden nose rings signify their rite of passage to becoming an adult warrior. Two horns protrude from either side of their heads, ending in sharp points to finish off weakened opponents. They wear leather cloth fashioned from the skins of their slain enemies. Their weapons are large, very sharp, Great Axes. One is wielded in each hand.

The Minotaur are the first line of defense against enemies traversing through to the dark elven city. So far, some have tried; all have failed. Each kill lies where they have been slain. Insects and other scavengers feast on the bodies leaving nothing but bones, weapons, and clothing behind. Jewelry and other items of high value, especially magical items, are collected and placed into the Minotaur treasury near the center of the maze where the Minotaur army resides. A food storage unit is kept in a large room close to the kitchen. Their food is supplied by their kills or the dark elves to keep them satisfied and buys their secrecy, allegiance, and protection.

The sleeping quarters and main hall are also located near a well, providing them with fresh water bucketed from a deep void into a hidden spring hundreds of feet down. Each side of the Minotaur barracks offers an entrance to the maze allowing quick access in any direction should they be needed. The walls in the labyrinth are several hundred feet high and smooth as glass to preclude anyone from climbing and running over the top of the maze. The cavern walls were the same, connecting to the maze's outer boundary, allowing only one entrance to the north. The only exit out of the maze is to the south through the dragons' lair.

The Kingdom of Almaryha is governed by King Bron and Queen Kardya, rulers with an aggressive nature yet just and fair. No one gets special treatment, not even family. The large castle is located at the rear of the city with the back against the sheer cliff with enormous protruding spires reaching high elevations for a clear view of the entire area. The castle is also where the royalty resides. Spreading outward is the market square followed by the rest of the inhabitant housing. The Kingdom itself covers over one-square-mile of the underground cavern. Slaves are always digging, expanding the Kingdom. They erect giant pillars at strategic points to prevent the surface world from falling through. Sporadic watchtowers housing expert bowmen ensure the population is controlled and protected. King Bron despises chaos.

The Kingdom contains dimly lit lanterns throughout the inner and outer territory to aid in vision. Though they are not needed for the elves, they are needed for the Cerberus and other non-elven creatures roaming the area. Shops are centrally located in the city, surrounded by housing. A wall has been erected to keep the Cerberus out of the city and in their own roaming zone. Feeding time consists of executed elven slaves, or a lunchtime arena disputation. Whenever an elf gets out of line, depending on the severity of the crime, the King will hold a special arena event to showcase the might and power of the Cerberus and instill fear by displaying what happens if the inhabitants get out of line.

Morhgrammir is situated under the immense treetops in the central forest of Aghram, masking their presence from any direction. The central mass of dense forest is where the tallest trees reside, mostly pine and oak trees, spanning hundreds of feet into the air. The surrounding trees are much lower, allowing a view all around without being spotted.

Guard platforms ascend just below the surrounding edge of treetops, so they can see for miles around without hindering their visibility and prevent detection. Occasionally, faint smoke can be seen, signifying Gnoll encampments, food cooking on the fire with the smell of roasting meat reaching the hungry guard's nose making for a long watch. Small smokeless fires were allowed and only for cooking in Morhgrammir. Smokeless fires were demanded to prevent detection.

The northern section of the Kingdom is where the barracks are located for the Morhgrammir army. The training grounds are situated next to the barracks, where duals are often conducted for training. Next to the training grounds is the archery range, where Nekora spends most of her time practicing and honing her skills. Her accuracy and speed are unmatched. The mage tower is located farther north, keeping a safe distance from the Kingdom while mages experiment with different spells. They share a building with the alchemists.

Magic is not allowed within the confines of the Kingdom, and those who possess the gift were secluded to the mage towers to the north for the safety of the Kingdom and themselves. Loud explosions were sometimes heard, though not often, from mages and alchemists experimenting or fending their territory from foreign intruders, namely humans and Gnolls. The humans from the eastern coast Kingdom of Haversmith occasionally wander into the elven zone by accident, scouting for new areas to collect resources and scout desired areas to expand their empire. If they have not been killed by the cyclops roaming the protective mountains or the ever-moving Gnoll camps, the elves will track and kill them.

The elven king has forbidden the knowledge of Morhgrammir to the humans, which would end in war. King Kardin would rather alleviate any possibility of war and sacrificing the loss of his society by ridding any intruders of the first opportunity, protecting their privacy and homeland.

The largest domicile within Morhgrammir exhibits a large base with heights close to, but not protruding from, the tallest treetops near the eastern edge of the tallest oaks. The topmost floor resides the King and Queen with windowed openings so they can keep an eye on their grounds as well as the outside world.

The view is spectacular, looking down at some trees, watching birds, as well as the mountains surrounding their land. The constant fresh air bringing in the strong smell of oak and pine from the outside. Even the stars at night are bright and peaceful to gaze upon. Ground movement is difficult to discern, but smoke and other dangers were easily spotted from the watchtowers before arriving at Morhgrammir. Outside the main residence lies the market square, an open area where celebrations, parties, and general mingling take place.

The dais is a large rickety platform the King and Queen utilize to make their speeches to the other elves and is found near the center of the market square. It is mostly used for the trial returnees to mark their official transition into adulthood. Special arrangements can be made by anyone with prior notification. Markets line the next area to surround the open area followed closely by housing and even a tavern. Regular elven dwellings are spread out for space making Morhgrammir seem huge by comparison.

Outlying walls protect the elves from free roaming creatures, especially the nasty Gnolls. Good thing the watchtowers are there since they have not entered or even came close to the boundaries. The only threats encountered now are the bird droppings from overhead nests. A small breeze is normally felt during the day, keeping the temperature at a near-constant eighty degrees throughout the year with the help of the giant pines in the surrounding area and some mighty oak trees shading the Kingdom from the overhead sun, keeping the temperature constant.

Upon reaching their eighteenth birthday, each male elf must attend and pass their trial. The trial consists of the elf providing notes on the migration patterns of the Griffins and cyclops that roam the upper mountainous territory. The Griffins would normally nest in one spot; unfortunately, the cyclops hunt the Griffin for food so they must nest in different spots each time. The migration patterns signify impending turmoil as the prophecies dictate, should they change outside the normal routine.

If multiple birthdays occur at once, each candidate must go in different directions. No one elf can aid the other in their trials. Once they set out, they cannot come back without the horn of a cyclops. Since they are trained in the art of war from childhood, they are lethal combatants. This test ensures they embrace and utilize everything that has been taught to them. However, it is no easy task.

The dense forest they must traverse to the mountains harbor Gnolls, Canine affiliates that stand upright. Gnolls are orange with black spots, full-body fur, canine face with sharp teeth, paws for feet, and hands for weapon-wielding. They have swift reflexes and are deadly in battle, making them ruthless and a fear in and of their own. Gnolls never stay in one spot, always following a hog herd making it tougher to be found.

Wild boars are known to kill with a charge, using their sharp tusks to impale their target. Giant birds known as Rocs that look like an everyday hawk but stand near nine feet tall with a twelve-foot wingspan and beaks that can cut a standard human in half with one bite have been seen near the mountain regions hunting for food.

If the potential elven warrior candidate survives the trek, they must survive the mountain climb. Since the mountains are huge, it will exhaust the candidate well before reaching the summit in their target area. Once on top, most go through an immediate melee as soon as they terminate their ascension. If they kill the cyclops, they must remove the horn and bring it back as proof of conquest. The horns are known for their medicinal value in healing compounds, and desperately needed in the Kingdom.

If they survive and return to the Kingdom on their own, they are ceremoniously promoted to adults with the mandatory army service. The minimum serving time is four years, after which they can resume or quit. If they quit, they would be taking on other tasks needed by the Kingdom like cooking, blacksmithing, and so on. If they fail or could not make it back on their own, the ceremony is canceled, and the future warrior must go back when they are deemed ready by the guards after extensive retraining.

Nekora's middle sibling, Meeka, traveled south a few years back during his trial. Unfortunately, he was caught off guard by a cyclops clan and killed during the fierce battle, so it was rumored. Meeka was far too good at fighting to fail otherwise. Grogham, Nekora's oldest brother, was more fortunate as he only faced one cyclops, which was slain.

While resting after the fierce battle, Grogham, Prince of Morhgrammir, had accidentally stumbled across the tunnel entrance by falling through the illusory entrance when attempting to sit on the side of the mountain to relax and take in the scene to the east. He had already recovered his horn from a cyclops, solidifying his success, but decided to explore the new and unknown expanse of the hidden alcove.

This hidden tunnel piqued his curiosity, and he decided to investigate his new find and report back to his father, the King, after any confirmation of locating the elusive, mythological, dark elves known as Drow. This new area was a significant discovery; he was determined to investigate and gather as much intelligence as he could collect, making him the hero of Morhgrammir.

Many creatures dwell in the tunnels. All of them are larger versions of their outside cousins; some were species he had never seen nor heard of—giant snakes with razor-sharp teeth slithering around looking for food. Occasionally, a snake would mistake the warrior for food only to fall to their demise. Spiders with crab claws roamed the larger tunnel's upper parts, descending from a thick web to unsuspecting prey. The deeper he descended, the stranger and larger they appeared, also more venomous. Some even provided a luminescent glow as he descended ever deeper into the cavern.

Many times, Grogham had to fend off giant spiders, scorpions, and a few large-sized snakes. These tunnels proved that one must be on their toes. Many hours had gone by, and he almost gave up until he entered a vast cavern. One small trail barely the size of mortal feet was seen winding down into a massive enclave before meeting with a maze of vast proportions hundreds of feet below.

From the top, he studied each twist and turn that led even farther into the darkness. Dimly lit lanterns were sporadic at best for minimal lighting. The other end of the maze was too dark for even him to see. Grogham decided to make camp and rest first. He backtracked several hundred feet to investigate a small nook he had seen earlier. After deeming all was clear, he squeezed through and rested.

Six hours later, Grogham woke. He carefully and silently made his way out of his hiding place and back into the tunnel. He retraced his steps back to the large opening toward the open cavern. He knew that his sister would love to hear about his triumphant adventure.

"I should come back after I turn in my prize. Take a band of warriors with me later to venture forth and investigate.

The intelligence alone on this is much too important, or I can investigate a little more and bring back news more noteworthy," he thought as he looked toward the exit. Grogham decided to keep going and see what lay beneath.

"Maybe something in the lines of the prophecies awaits here," he whispered to himself. "Maybe I can find a treasure for my little sister." Grogham smiled. He always loved Nekora, loved how she playfully fought, and her beautiful smile. He knew she would make herself great one day.

He slowly and methodically made his way toward the small path winding down, still smiling, remembering all the fun games he and his sister played throughout their childhood. It proved to be a slippery trek as he temporarily lost his footing on many occasions and luckily grabbed small protruding rocks on the cliff face to prevent falling. Grogham had to force his thoughts from memories of his sister to focus. Dangerous actions required full attention and focus on his current task. At the bottom, he viewed the immense walls. From what he had observed earlier, a maze of some sort, he remembered the outline well.

"Why is this here?" he thought as he moved toward the obstacle.

He continued to the large opening. Loud snorts, growls, and uneven hoof steps like a lame horse were heard from inside the maze. The darkness increased the pitch and volume of any sound, so he always had to be on guard. Grogham had his weapon ready, and his trophy slung over his back in case of a melee. From here, he could not recognize anything. The walls were massive and smooth, so climbing was not an option. The dirt pathway was littered with bones and spider webs; occasionally, finding an armored skeletal body with weapons still in place. The skeletons looked human with the full plate armor and a longsword with a shield lying by its side. Many skeletal armored figures lined the large pathway.

"What sort of creatures would leave armor and weapons behind?" he thought as he crouched to investigate the necklace on one of the skeletons.

He kept moving forward. He tried to remember the turns that led to the other side. Unfortunately, there was no path around. Just unclimbable cliffs forced a passage through the one entrance of the maze.

A loud snort was heard close by and sounded like a mad bull ready to attack from around the next corner. He peered around every corner before moving, careful not to make noise. Hoof steps were heard getting louder, closer. An awful sound like bones hitting stone followed by short bursts of roars and snorts, each second getting louder and nothing to be seen. He heard sniffing before each clack of the footsteps.

"What the hell is it?" Grogham thought, worried about his decision now to move forward.

He peered around the next corner to the left and saw an incredible creature. It stood about nine feet tall with hooves for feet, large muscular legs, arms, and torso, and had the head of a bull. Large horns protruded from the sides of its head, and a large golden nose ring looped into each nostril. The creature was dual-wielding great axes, sniffing the air, and making its way toward Grogham. Grogham quickly returned behind the wall, fear welling inside him.

"Shit, it knows I am here," he thought as he crouched, preparing for a battle.

The Minotaur smelled his opponent. It had picked up the scent of an elf not from this region.

"Another glorious battle," the Minotaur thought as it smiled.

It spied the elf peering around the corner sizing the minotaur. It smelled the fear and knew this would be a fun challenge. It stepped menacingly toward his opponent, hoping it would not run away. It was forbidden for any Minotaur to leave the maze, and the elf was still too close to the exit. Hoping the elf would not dash out, the minotaur increased its speed, then CHARGE! The minotaur was in full stride as it made a battle call, raising its axes.

Grogham quickly surveyed his surroundings. The only way back is to the entrance, leaving a wide-opened area to do battle and risk being surrounded or continue into the fray, taking on one creature versus many. He waited for the perfect time. If Grogham kept the battle inside the corridors, other Minotaur's could not surround him, leaving him the advantage. He listened and waited until he believed the minotaur was close before swinging his scimitars blindly to catch it off guard. As he went to swing, his instincts took over. He ducked just as a Great Axe came crashing into the wall where Grogham's head used to be, impacting the wall with a thunderous cacophony, causing a shower of sparks and rocks to fly in every direction.

Grogham tumbled sideways to get out of reach and reevaluate his tactics. No training he ever received prepared him for this. Time to improvise. He ducked, dodged, and tumbled out of harm's way, barely being missed, watching for some vulnerability, so he transitioned from defense to offense and vice versa. He could not find any weakness at all.

This thing is fast for its size and extremely deadly. What can I do to get it to open for an attack? Grogham thought.

This beast was a master of combat, highly skilled, and well-trained. Grogham's only survival trait was to be quick and agile, dodge until an opening was shown. The minotaur stepped back slightly onto a loose bone from a previous combatant and slipped just enough to be unbalanced for a moment, but it regained its balance quickly. The small stumble from the Minotaur gave Grogham just the opportunity he needed; Grogham sprang forward, feigning a thrust. The minotaur immediately raised his arms to block with his axes. Exactly what Grogham was counting on.

Grogham retrieved his weapon back to his body as he tumbled to the left side of the Minotaur and thrust his weapons as hard as he could through its sides. The muscle and bones of the beast made the attack problematic, but he landed his blow and caused it to stop its attacks. The Minotaur dropped its left Great Axe and roared in pain. This gave Grogham his opening; he dodged the second weapon swing and jumped up to slice its neck, opening a large gash that spurted blood. After a few seconds, the Minotaur fell to the floor in a giant pool of blood, breathless. The sounds of battle aroused the other Minotaur's inside the maze. Grogham had to get out and quick.

Grogham decided to collect the Minotaur's horns and put them in the bag with the cyclops horn as another trophy before he left the area, keeping an eye around him to ensure no surprises. He studied the body for future description and had to get as much detail as he could. Grogham heard the others, frustrated that they were not able to make the battle but getting nearer with speed faster than any elf could comprehend. He had to move through the maze swiftly if he wanted to get away.

Grogham quickly made his way through the maze, turning where he thought he remembered only to receive an occasional dead end. He was lost. Two more encounters with the Minotaur were more than he bargained for and almost cost him his life. The third encounter was made near the exit of the maze to the south. The last opponent was larger and stronger than the others. The body almost filled the corridor, no way to run past. It was fight or die time.

Grolf, the Minotaur King, successfully contacted with the elf, producing a large gash in his stomach as Grogham came running around the corner. A lucky strike with the right Great Axe made a connection before Grogham realized it was swung. Grogham's fatigue had caught up with him; he failed to tumble out of the way in time. The Great Axes carried by the Minotaur were sharper than they appeared. Both axes came crashing down where Grogham was previously kneeling. More showers of sparks and rock exploded from the ground. The deafening sound of the impact caused Grogham to hold his head straight from dizziness. Grogham used this opportunity to make quick slices across the Minotaur's chest. The cuts proved nothing more than a nuisance to the King of the beasts.

"Damn, this thing is strong. Stronger than the others by far," Grogham thought.

The King swung his ax horizontally to cut the elf in half as he was deep in thought. A quick back tumble followed by a forward step allowed him to jump on top of the ax, then another leap toward the head. When the ax impacted the wall, shattering stone and flinging debris down the hallway, it served as a platform to allow the tremendous leap. Grogham swung with all his might. The scimitars drove halfway through the King's neck, severing the spine, causing a near-instant death.

Upon defeating the monster, Grogham desired to find a place of solace and patch himself. He had hoped there was an exit to the south in the mountains so he could make it back home. His consciousness was failing. The cut was not as deep as initially thought, so he knew he had some life left. Unfortunately, a huge dark cavern leading south was all that stood before him.

Grogham had enough. He wanted to go home; he was exhausted and weak. To return through the maze would risk more fights with the abnormally strong minotaur—a jeopardy he could not afford. If he were rested, he might be able to escape. He decided to continue down the cavern in hopes of locating a resting spot.

"I should have turned around and brought an army instead of succumbing to bravado," he thought.

Within the southern cavern was a strong reptilian smell that practically made him regurgitate, let alone the overwhelming fear that succumbed him. He decided to find a safe place to rest. Huge columns streaked dozens of feet upward and appeared to end in a plateau at the top. Grogham decided to take out some parchment and a writing utensil and make notes with rudimentary drawings from the start of his adventure. He cursed himself for not being more proficient. He decided to look around and gauge the width of the cavern.

It was enormous, cold, and hard to see. He was not accustomed to darkness like this, but he did his best. Pushing his body with his wounds was not a wise idea. He could not take another battle just yet. He sat behind a boulder hidden behind a column and listened to every sound trying to make sense of everything while eating what few rations he had left.

Could this be the route to the elusive dark elves? Grogham's eyes went wide. "If so, I could still be a hero," the thought struck as he smirked. He decided to continue his trek after a brief rest and healing in hopes of finding the mythological Kingdom.

Grogham continued his journey. He remembered everything he was taught by the village healers and applied every technique imaginable. To his surprise, the healing was working. Slowly, but working. He got up and wobbled a little, steadying himself on the boulder until he regained his senses and continued. Dizziness overcame him as he stood. The cavern was vast and seemed to go on forever.

Grogham peered up and observed a partial night sky through a large hole at the top. It was too far to climb, and there were no footholds. Besides, he did not have the strength to make it, even if it was a viable solution. The only choice he had available was to continue and hope for another exit or risk more battles. He chose to push through.

"Oh, the celebrations coming up if I survive."

Claws scraping against stone were heard all around. He also listened to what sounded like wings fluttering above and behind him. He sensed danger, fear, the probability of imminent death. He looked back to see a large flying figure landing on top of the plateau above. The wings fluttered to slow the descent of the creature and knocked Grogham off balance. The force winds blew him southward as he tumbled through the jagged corridor. He skipped and fell over many rocks and bounced off the walls. A sharp pain sprang through him, and he lost consciousness.

Grogham woke moments later. He could not remember where he was or what he was doing. He tried to sit up, but the pain denied him. Farther down the corridor, he thought he heard growling and roaring, a barking sound but much deeper than the average canine. It sounded like there were many of them. He did his best to assess the severity of his injuries. He contemplated his options; he needed to get out of here. Grogham lay back down, ears ringing. His mindfulness varying.

A dark elf had dismounted his dragon and made his way down the embankment. He continued through the corridor and peered down at Grogham.

"What have we here?" A staff knocked him the head, rendering Grogham unconscious once again.

CHAPTER TWO

Nekora treated every day like any other day. Today seemed different. Something felt awkward and chillier than usual. Was it an alarm? She thought it was odd being the middle of summer. Nekora Mancer grew up to be a gorgeous elf with long wavy red hair flowing halfway down to her half-moon-shaped buttocks and above her deep blue eyes. Her appearance was flawless.

Her thin muscular body is toned from numerous hours of weapons practice, supple breasts that complimented her figure, and long muscular legs. Nekora is an excellent combatant, beating every soldier except the elders in sparring. Archery was her gift, but she spent most of her days training, honing, and developing new skills and maneuvers at the army training grounds.

She's also the pride and joy of the entire Kingdom. Always smiling and helping others around the Kingdom and in combat practice when they failed to learn how to read and counteract differing strikes. She's also gifted with the arcane arts but keeps her prowess a closely guarded secret lest she is shunned to the mage tower. Though she loves old books and scrolls, she could not imagine spending her life secluded from the Kingdom she loves so dearly. She constantly attempts to obtain more knowledge with her eidetic memory helping. She has better things to do for her curiosity's sake, which has always gotten her into trouble, so she cleverly hides her talent.

Nekora has always been an excellent archer. Her focus, doubled with magic, has made her one of the best archers in the Kingdom. Her bow was fashioned from the finest mithril threads melded with yew branches offering the strongest, yet lightest bow ever constructed. Only the strongest elves can pull back the weapon with moderate difficulty.

With the help of Thomas, her mage friend, she had runes imprinted on the upper and lower risers, each one signifying a different benefit. The topmost rune signifies power. It resembles a stick figure fish facing up with a vertical line from the nose down through its tail. The second rune represents calmness, resembling a plus sign with shorter concave lines passing just below the tip of each point. The third rune signifies success, resembling an arrow pointing up. The fourth and final rune is protection with a "Y" shape, but the protruding ends are one-third of the way down the vertical line. By muttering the rune names sequentially, the bow draw becomes light enough to use without sacrificing power behind the release.

She softly whispered her enchantment,

Puntera Di Sooth Gan Proto Niftus, Effis, Controlus,

meaning "Power of Calmness, Success, Protection, with Swift Effortless Control," would allow the runes to glow a bright blue and segment their power with the wielder. Due to the seclusion of magicians, Nekora must keep her bow wrapped in leather bindings to hide their glow lest it betrays her gift. Only she and Thomas are aware of the markings. No one else can touch her bow, the only object Nekora insisted.

Nekora is at her favorite place, the archery range. She is focused on her target, murmuring her secret magical words so softly, only she and her bow could hear. She lines up her shot to the target fifty yards away, going for the win at the annual archery event, ready to collect her glory and praise. Her father would be so proud of her. Feeling the gentle breeze flowing, adjusting her angle to hit the center of the bullseye.

She inhales deeply, closes her eyes, slowly exhales, opens her eyes, and releases the bowstring. The arrow flies straight and true to her mark. She knew she was going to win. The arrow was heading straight for the bullseye with a little bit of help from her enchantment.

"Nekora!" yelled her mentor to grab the attention of the daydreaming princess. "Pay attention; this is important!" he scolded.

"Yes, Loghan" she replied, tired of hearing about the same old prophecies. But to be a princess, she must be educated in all legends, myths, and foretold divinations. To her, it was a bunch of garbled fabrication and ramblings of old demented elves. Everything was in riddles and none of them made sense at all. She hated schooling and desperately wanted to go back to her archery and combat training. Eighteen years of age and she was still being treated like a child.

"Now, what is the prophecy of the heavenly fire?" asked Loghan.

"Flames from heaven raining through, on the coming of the second moon. From the ashes will eject a hero of which none shall expect. The wise and efficient hero shall lead, while the peril of others lies and bleeds." She answered more frustrated than intrigued. She knew all the proverbs by heart, but she did not understand their meanings. Whenever Nekora asked her mentor, he just replied with other questions and riddles of his own. Nekora felt the training was unnecessary since no one seemed to truly understand. It was then that the thought of the dark elves raced across her mind.

Is it true the dark elves exist? If so, what about the dragons rumored to be in their area? Where could they reside that they would be hidden for centuries, and no one knows of their existence? This was but a part of a long internal line of questioning Nekora wanted answers to. She decided to confide in Loghan once again, knowing he would not answer directly but shed some light in a new fashion that would make sense to her.

"I have a question Loghan, about the legend of the dark elves and dragons I've heard a lot about. If no one has ever seen them, how does the reign of power legend hold its legitimacy? It was coined by old elves many years ago. Also, the second moon is another cycle away and no reports or indications of our fate from the heavenly fires have been seen or documented. Surely, an outright catastrophe would have indications of pending arrival," she stated.

Sighing, Loghan closed his book. "I see this is going nowhere. All myths, legends, and prophecies, true or not, must be taken seriously. We must take every precaution to prepare for any event. The question you should be asking is, what if these old myths were true? If so, are we ready? No one really knows what truly lies ahead. The smallest indication could be the only clue or no clue at all. The answer lies in whether we see it, hear it, or feel it. Go now, frolic, play, do whatever it is young princesses do these days," Loghan said with a genuine smile. "Class dismissed," he finished.

Upon completion of her session, Nekora departed the building without hesitation. She went outside to enjoy the fresh woodland air that lacked the strong aroma of incense that filled the study room, giving her a headache. The air is clean out here, the sky is clear, and a slight breeze began blowing her long red hair in waves. Nekora pulled out a small willow bark to sooth her headache as she proceeded outside.

"How can anything go wrong on such a beautiful day?" she thought to herself. But the thoughts of the elusive dark elves and dragons stayed strong in her head.

Could this be a feeling of an oncoming disaster? She dismissed that thought completely and made her way to the village.

She was invigorated and desperately wanted to catch up with her friends about new gossip, her daily ritual. Nothing new was ever discussed, only the current migration sightings told to the women by trial candidates eager to impress them, how families are doing, and so forth, but it still felt comforting to be in a social environment.

Today, she thought, would be different. First things first, she rerouted her original plan and started making her way toward the market to help the villagers and satisfy her rumbling stomach with some fresh fruit picked by the farmers from the outskirts of the main square.

She desperately needed to know if there was any truth to the legends of the under-dark and dragons. The truth would be intriguing, and she would finally know for sure. Her fascination with the creatures has consumed her.

Someone had to have seen them, or how would the stories have spawned? She pondered as she bit into a large, fresh green apple.

She closed her eyes, drew in a deep breath, taking in the odor of the forest and the aroma of fruits all mixed, then exhaled as she opened them. Her curiosity was getting the best of her, so she decided to head for the mage tower the next morning where one of her good friends resided, Thomas, a magician she can trust.

She grew up with him and Thorn, always roughhousing and getting into trouble. The thought of Thorn, her best friend, always put a smile on her face. She loved being around him. He made her feel comfortable, not to mention an easy target for trash talking. They were always play fighting together, saying each one will be better than the other when they grew up.

Thorn is a thick, heavily muscled elf and very strong for his age. His short blond hair and penetrating blue eyes fashioned him as a pretty boy, a treasure for any single female elf. His gullibility always made him a prime target for Nekora. It pleased her to no end to make him blush or quick to anger. It made playtime that much more interesting.

"That reminds me, I need to train Thorn today," she said to herself and headed to the training grounds where they always meet before practice.

Thorn wandered the market square, contemplating on whether to ask the King for his permission to go on his trials earlier and return on his eighteenth birthday. It was two months until that day, the time he would become an adult. After careful consideration and pondering, he decided to ask the King. He brought along the notes he had been taking, surveillance of the Griffin migration, Gnoll camp movements, and, most importantly, the cyclops migration.

Notes serve as intelligence gathering for the King; every candidate must have them. They keep him posted and serve as an alert should any foul display go awry. With his sparring, practice, and meditation, Thorn was confident in his abilities. He had spent time in the watchtowers surveying, watching. He knew the migration patterns by heart. It was time to attempt the unthinkable, but he wanted first to run the idea through his best friend.

The idea of Thorn leaving early was toyed with during sparring. He chided Nekora about leaving early and coming home as the best hunter and fighter in the Kingdom. Both were laughing, though he was faking. Nekora laughed because she knew he would never be as good as her. She stopped and thought, "Why not?" The law says, "On the eighteenth birthday," but it doesn't specify the start or end of trials.

"I think you should go for it. Well, after a few more years of training you will be ready. You couldn't kill a field mouse!" Nekora prodded. She loved to push Thorn's buttons; it made life much more enjoyable watching him blush or flush with anger.

Thorn looked up, smiling. He knew he had Nekora believing it was her idea, not his. He was deep in thought as Nekora smacked him in the ribcage with the quarterstaff.

"Ouch! Not fair! You did that on purpose! You knew I wasn't ready," he accused, holding his side.

Nekora looked at him. "Maybe, besides, you are on the battlefield now. No time to reminisce!" She parried Thorn's continuous onslaught of would-be vicious blows. "Maybe I can go for you since you can't even beat a girl," she accused. She laughed harder and almost caught a blow to the side.

Blow by blow, Nekora and Thorn squared off, striking only to be parried by the other. They paused for just a moment.

Nekora coached, "Okay, you need to keep your knees slightly bent. It allows for more fluid movement and quick reverse moves should an attack come from a direction you are not anticipating. Also, use your peripheral vision and watch for movement. That is your best defense against a myriad of opponents. Try again. This time, the attacks will be from random directions."

Thorn did just as he was told and even impressed Nekora with his modification. The whistle blew; practice time was over. Both walked toward the village square.

"Nek, you going to the feast tonight?" Thorn asked.

"Maybe, going to hit the range first to release some stress." She turned and looked at him. "From dealing with your lack of combat abilities." She turned back around and continued down the pathway. Thorn readied his notebook and threw it at her, hitting her in the back.

"Ow!" she exclaimed, still walking away rubbing her back where the notebook had impacted her. Thorn went to pick up his things.

"Only wussies fight with arrows!" he yelled to her.

"Not maximizing your combat skills will be your downfall. But, meh, your choice, Nekora yelled back.

Thorn had dressed in his finest attire after the practice session. He had brought them from home, hoping the King would hear him out. His mind was made up. The sound of the trees slowly and gently swaying with a slight breeze had Thorn relaxed. He loved it here and could not imagine living anywhere else.

As he walked by the archery range on the way to meet the King, he witnessed Nekora readying for her shot. As he glanced downrange, he saw what had to be the tightest group of arrows in the center of the target he had ever seen. He was amazed at the gift this woman had. Nekora grabbed an arrow, knocked it into place, and pulled back on the string. He was mesmerized at the perfect silhouette and tone muscles flexing as she pulled the string back for another shot. When she was about to release her arrow, he faked a loud sneeze.

"ACHOO!" The unanticipated loud noise caused Nekora to flinch and miss her shot. She turned around and scolded Thorn.

"You asshole!" she exclaimed, but he just smiled as he kept on his path.

"Excuse me!" he yelled back. Thorn could not get Nekora out of his head. Her beauty did not compare to any living soul. Her long red flowing hair, flawless body, and beauty he could not comprehend. She was a model of perfection.

"How can anyone be so damn perfect?" he thought. It's not possible." He pondered the latter. How is it one person can be flawless? He did not know the answer, but he knew in his heart that he must be with her somehow.

He soon realized that he had fallen in love with her. Her smile, constant yet irritating positive attitude in anything, their training, the way they got along, he loved being with her all the time. Unfortunately, she was the princess, and he was just a regular elf.

Just another Elf trying to become an adult. He had to push the thoughts out of his head if he was going to confront the King. He needed every ounce of concentration to try to persuade the King to allow him to depart early. Besides, the earlier he left, the earlier he would return to Nekora.

I hope I can focus on my trials he thought, knowing Nekora would jump back into his thoughts. He briskly walked to the castle.

The King allowed an audience from Thorn. He knew that he and Nekora were best friends and questioned just how close they had become.

"Your majesty," Thorn said, "I will try to make this brief. I know you are occupied with more important matters for the Kingdom. I have been doing a lot of research and studying in the Griffin migration patterns." He handed the squire his notes. "I have been practicing daily to hone my skills in combat and have become quite experienced. I would like, with your permission, to start my trials one month early ending with my arrival on the day of my eighteenth birthday." The King looked upon him questioningly. As the King stood, Thorn bowed.

While his eyes were averted, the King motioned a guard to strike. The movement was from slightly behind Thorn, where he was caught in Thorn's peripheral. The guard was quiet, flowing, and graceful. The quarterstaff came down unexpectedly and easily dodged by Thorn as he saw it coming. Thorn rolled away from the guard, causing the quarterstaff to miss, then rolled closer to the guard and dropped him with his foot slamming into the guard's shin knocking him over on his back.

"Damn, the peripheral works better than I thought," Thorn mumbled and immediately hopped up and on top of the guard, quickly disarming and pinning him. Thorn was far too strong as the guard could not move at all.

"Enough," exclaimed the King. "Based on your reaction, your steadfast notes, and ability to disarm my guard so quickly, I will allow your request. Be that as it may, you must not return until the day of your birth, no earlier." Thorn again bowed.

"Thank you, your majesty." The King dismissed Thorn and he exited the chamber hall with haste and excitement.

"You think he is ready?" inquired the King's adviser after Thorn departed.

The King replied, "He has been trained by the best, including my daughter. He is more than ready."

King Kardin looked over Thorn's notes.

"This is interesting," the King stated. He read one page, then turned back three pages. He turned back to the original page and pointed.

"This shows the Gnolls moving forward as they always do. Here," he flipped back three pages, "shows the Gnolls in the exact spot from a few days earlier. They have never backtracked, let alone camped at the same spot twice." The King examined. "We must keep vigilance in the Kingdom. Something may be coming our way," he continued.

"Yes, your majesty," came the reply of Captain Luka. Captain Luka was not only the captain of the guard but also the head of the elite soldiers. He was responsible for ensuring the safety and security of the Kingdom under the scrutiny of the King. Luka sought out sergeant Poko in the training field to formulate a plan to increasing awareness and security in the Kingdom.

Two weeks passed, and Thorn was constantly trained and studied. He knew how long it would take to reach the mountains. He timed where the cyclops encampment would be when he got there. Nekora helped him every step of the way. She had ideas he never thought of and filed the ideas away for later. Thorn was becoming stronger each day, both mentally and physically.

"Your father has granted my request to go early."

Nekora looked away saddened, then turned to Thorn and spoke in a serious tone, "You are the best warrior I have seen, a bitch to train, but I know you have the strength to be successful. You will be in the history books if," she paused, catching her error, "when you succeed." She tried hard to keep up his spirit; it was what friends did. She did not want to be responsible for his failure. She took pride in teaching her friend, a friend she had grown very fond of.

Thorn looked at her with passion. "I have you to thank for this. My confidence has grown tenfold with you as my mentor. But now, I have a lot of work to do before the week's end."

Day after day, Thorn and Nekora squared off. Thorn was starting to feel better about himself as it took longer for Nekora to take him down. The notes kept coming, and he addressed concerns for some of the migrations he noticed. He needed to address this to the King as well before he departed on his journey.

Three days before his departure, Nekora and Thorn squared off in the training grounds. She had to take it easier on him. No injuries before leaving as it was bad luck.

"It looks like I may beat you after all," Thorn chided as he thought he had the advantage over his friend. Thorn had improved; he was stronger and faster than ever.

Nekora smirked. "You will NEVER beat me in combat."

Thorn looked at her questioningly. "What makes you so sure?"

She smiled. "I still know tricks that you don't. I taught you, remember? I know all your tricks."

"Okay, a challenge then. Full out battle. Loser buys dinner."

The halt in practice caught the attention of Sergeant Poko. He started to say something when he realized it was a dual. He motioned the soldiers to watch. Leron started a bet. Half the soldiers bet on Nekora. The other half bet on Thorn.

Sergeant Poko whispered, "You guys will see something absolutely grand. I have only witnessed it once." He looked to the contestants. "During a solo dance."

Nekora stood straight, closed her eyes, and barely whispered in a foreign language. Her lips barely moved. No one could see or hear her.

Tegata ni Sharnye

She slammed the butt end of her quarterstaff to the ground, opened her eyes, and looked at Thorn.

"You ready for the ass whooping of your life?" Nekora asked.

"Bring it on," replied Thorn.

Thorn came in with a barrage of blows, easily blocked by Nekora. They danced as he attacked, and she parried.

Thorn commented, "What's wrong, Nek? No time to strike?"

With that, she dodged the next blow with ease and hit Thorn seven times before he could bring his staff back to position. Nekora was a blur to both Thorn and the audience. Her grace and precision were impeccable. Another shot from Thorn. To her, he was slow. Nekora struck him another eight times before he could bring his weapon back. Thorn was lying on his back, bruised and sore. Nekora helped him up.

"You had enough yet?" Nekora asked as she offered a helping hand.

Thorn yielded. "How the hell did you move so fast?"

Nekora shrugged "Practice."

She was not going to let him know that she cast a haste spell on herself. Haste allows the target to move at double speed. Had she cast a slow spell, everyone would know what she did and realize she had the gift of magic. The slow spell halves the movement speed of the target.

"Looks like dinner is on you," Nekora commented.

"I guess so," he replied.

Two days before departure, Thorn went to each watchtower to take some last-minute notes before addressing the King. He took time to ensure the irregularities in the migration patterns were noted. King Kardin looked upon Thorn with admiration. He had by far taken not only the best notes than any other candidate but also noted all the irregularities the others lacked. The King had no doubt Thorn would be successful on his trial.

The day before his departure, Thorn walked around the Kingdom. He took in every detail. A memory he was storing to keep him strong and encourage him to return safely, especially Nekora. He spied Nekora talking with her female friends in the marketplace. He took in her silhouette, soft red hair, and fluid movements. He wanted this memory to last forever, and he knew the task set before him was not going to be an easy one, a definite trial of his desire to succeed and return to her.

He felt both invigorated and scared at the same time. He was lost in thought and did not notice Nekora sneaking up on him until the last second. He turned, grabbed her arm, and flung her on her onto the ground.

"What the hell was that for! I was trying to give you a hug since you decided to leave early. Damn, you're a selfish wench," Nekora stated.

With that, a bird landed droppings onto Thorn's head. Nekora rolled with laughter. She laughed so hard her sides felt like they were splitting.

"What the hell you laughing for? That's disgusting!" Thorn exclaimed as he attempted to wipe off the bird droppings.

Nekora regained her composure. "What are you worried about? That's a sign of good luck!" she exclaimed, laughing hard again.

"How do you know it is not a sign of impending doom?" Thorn asked sarcastically.

"Because you are still standing," retorted Nekora, laughing again.

Thorn looked at her on the ground. "I am sorry, Nek. You told me to keep on guard. So, this is your fault!" he accused.

He reached out a hand in gesture to help her up once she calmed down a bit. She obliged, taking his hand, and pulling him forward and off balance. She reached up, planted her foot into his abdomen, and flipped him on his back then jumped to her feet.

"I also told you to expect the unexpected." She helped him up. He laughed.

"So, you did, and I failed." They smiled and continued walking around the market, chatting about current events and the forthcoming trip.

The day arrived. Thorn wanted to get an early start. If his studies were correct, he would need to be at the farthest point of the mountainous region to the east in one week. As he crept to the door and opened it, he was startled to see his friends waiting for him to depart. Nekora stood in front of everyone. She gave him a peck on the cheek.

"For luck," she said. He said his goodbyes and started his trek to adulthood. Thorn walked through the forest as the villagers watched him go, wishing him luck. He touched his cheek where Nekora had kissed him and headed off toward the east, tears starting to well up.

"I really hope I can make it back to you, Nekora, my love," he thought as he was out earshot, thinking everyone would hear his thoughts. I already miss you, and I love you so much. He did not realize tears had been flowing down his cheeks. He was not sure if they were from leaving Nekora or fear of what awaited him in the unknown. Time would tell.

CHAPTER THREE

It's Thorn's birthday. He turned eighteen and had gone in pursuit of his adulthood trial a few weeks ago to bring back proof of killing the infamous cyclops by returning victorious with its horn on this day. If successful, Thorn would be the youngest elf to ever complete the trials. Nekora anxiously looked in the direction of the eastern mountains.

"Please come back to me safe and alive," she whispered.

From the tallest trees, elves kept watch in anticipation for signs of his return in hopes they can celebrate. There was much food and wine to be had with music and dancing. Tables were in place with cloth held down by rocks or tied to the legs so the breeze would not blow them away. A definite stress relieving event all elves looked forward to.

Nekora headed to the nearest eastern lookout post prior to entering the market square.

"Any sign of Thorn?" she asked the guard looking out toward the mountains. He turned to face her.

"Nothing yet, Princess, but I am sure he will be along soon. Thorn is strong and tactful."

She had an inkling that something was amiss. Patience was not in her vocabulary. Her eldest brother Grogham had set out for his trial four years ago and has yet to return; he is presumed dead. Her middle sibling, Meeka, set out three years ago and is also presumed dead. This was not a good outlook for the King and Queen's heirs. The only heir to the throne now is Nekora. She kept her hopes up but feared the worst.

"No, no, no," she thought as she started for the market. "I cannot think like this. I trained him. He will succeed." She did her best to hide the remorse from her facial expressions.

On her way to the market, she saw the banners and other decorations being hoisted. Due to past failures, the food was prepped and stored until the hunters' arrival. If everything is good, the food is cooked and set out on tables, covered to prevent insects from contaminating the food. Between the rigorous Kingdom upkeep and the trial for the new warrior, the event was used to celebrate and relax, to forget woes, and be with friends. They also love hearing tales.

The warriors compared stories to their own and others. Their trials dictated how much mocking the new recruits would receive once they were cleared by the healers to attend basic training. Nekora was a visitor, a friend to everyone. Since women were not allowed in the trials, she insisted on at least attending practice.

Nekora knew how good her friend Thorn was in combat. She helped train him, and she personally made him stronger than he should be. It was her dedication never to lose him. She thought this trial would be a cakewalk for him. She knew in her heart that he would make it back to her alive. Yet she still worried. Something was nagging at her, telling her something was wrong.

"Your friend's life is in the balance. You must get to him, help him, or he shall perish like the others," the voice in her head was so real, but she ignored it. Nekora pushed those thoughts out of her mind. "If lesser trained elves can go out and come back, he would walk through this with his eyes closed" she kept telling herself. It calmed her nerves as well. But the nagging feeling was ever present.

King Kardin walked along the main dirt pathway in the village inspecting everything as he always does during such an event. Queen Arilana, walking by the King's side, smiled at all the villagers.

"It looks like the elves are outdoing themselves this time. I am surprised we do not run out food with as many birthday trials there are throughout the year," Arilana stated. The King looked at her and smiled.

"They try to outdo each other at every event. Besides, Thorn will make history if he succeeds. It is nice to have so many festivities throughout the year, but I think the families are planning to have more each year. It is amazing to see the responsible parents of the future adults make this event their own. It brings a sense of family to the warrior and relieves a little stress and anguish most of them go through. Besides, I would have thought Thorn would have shown by now. He is stronger than any other participant I have seen yet, and very smart." Both were gazing around the market when the guard in the eastern watch post shouted, "Smoke a hundred yards to the southeast!" Everyone looked in that direction and saw smoke rising in the distance above the tree line. Smoke usually means one of two things; someone is seriously injured or there is a camper on the verge of intrusion. Either way, guards were on alert.

Nekora heard the shouts and started running in the direction everyone was looking. Her father immediately grabbed her arm. "You stay here," he insisted.

"But, father, I can help! What if it's Thorn?" she retorted. The King turned to his guards.

"Sergeant Poko, I want you four to check it out! Be careful it could be a trap." He turned to his daughter. "Get back to the main hall. I want you out of harm's way, just in case. I may need your archery skills." He turned to his squire who was never too far away from the King. "Escort the princess back to the main hall."

"Yes, your majesty," was his reply as he escorted the princess back to the quarters. Once they reached the quarters, Nekora rested in her ornate chair fashioned from an oak tree with red silk linings and soft cushions. Jewels outlined the rim of the chair giving off sparkles in the light. Despite the comfort, she was frustrated. She had to help. But how? The voice in her head was right, she just knew it. She could not rest so she stood and headed to her window and watched the smoke billowing from the trees.

She could not leave Thorn alone. She knew it was him. She thought, "What if the guards fail? I could help protect them. What if they are too late?"

Nekora sprinted to her armoire only ten paces away, hastily dressed in her dark green hunting leathers, and stuck both her scimitars in the sheathes behind her back that were specially designed and given to her on her thirteenth birthday as a gift from her father. She slung her bow, clipped her full quiver, then snuck out the window, descending on a rope tether she had fashioned to escape the madness of being in her room without being caught.

She had the rope hidden under her armoire so as not to be found in case someone decided to snoop around. She started in the direction of the smoke taking care to be hidden among the trees. Her movements were fluid and silent as she quickly made her way through the dense trees and brush. She was behind the guards by ten minutes at least and needed to catch up quickly.

After about twenty minutes, she caught up and observed the guards cautiously approaching the campfire. She shadowed them, taking every precaution to not be noticed. She glimpsed the camp and viewed but a small fire and fixated on a figure holding a bulging bag. She immediately recognized the bloodied and marred face.

"Thorn!" she inadvertently screamed as her eyes went wide with terror and quickly covered her mouth. Tears immediately poured down her face. It was too late. She had given herself away. The four guards immediately turned and saw her.

"Princess Nekora, what are you doing here?" exclaimed Sergeant Poko, questioningly but in a cautious whisper. Sergeant Poko was Nekora's mentor. He taught her how to wield her scimitars in a deadly dance of power and grace. The King wanted his daughter to protect herself should she be in trouble when no one else was around to protect her.

It was a decision proving to be a bad idea as she constantly gets into trouble with her confidence.

The King knew his daughter would be safe under the mentorship of Sergeant Poko. In fact, she almost beat Poko in battle during their sparring sessions. He was very proud of her accomplishments and how fast she had learned the art. It took her twenty days to master what took two months for the other guards. She is well gifted. Practicing in her room everyday helped.

She looked to the sergeant with watery eyes. Nekora could not control herself; it appeared her best friend may be dead or dying, a thought she desperately needed to force out of her mind.

"I thought maybe I could help you should you guys need it." Worried about the turn of events, he looked at her.

"Just what do you think will happen when your father finds out?" Poko responded.

"Please do not tell my father. I only wanted to make sure you guys were protected," Sergeant Poko sighed.

"I know you wish everyone to be safe, but what if this was an army? Huh?" Nekora sighed.

"I understand," Nekora responded. Poko smiled.

"Get back to the castle, and I will not say a word to your father." With that, Nekora sprinted back to the main hall, crying. She owed everything to Poko. He'd been more secretive to her actions than anyone in the Kingdom. She would help him out every chance she got and earned her trust fully. A feat hard to come by.

One hour passed since the guards went to check out the smoke. The King was getting worried that something dreadful happened. He looked at the captain and told him to ready his men for action. The captain immediately rounded up his troops and put them on alert. Forty swordsmen took their places hiding behind the local trees while archers took up rear defense. The archers would be the first to act, drawing attention to them while the swordsmen waited to spring a surprise attack on the unwary intruders once in view. The other three hundred soldiers of varying specialties took their place behind the archers, ready to run forward at a signal.

"Your majesty," Captain Ghallis said. "The units are in position and awaiting your command."

"Good," the King replied. "Have a small regiment standing by to help clear..."

Before he could finish, an elven "all clear" whistle sounding like an owl was heard coming from the forest to the southeast. Everyone, even the King, looked in that direction. The army relaxed a little but remained aware in case of trickery or the possibility of an enemy tracking their movements. The King's four guards returned carrying a body on a makeshift bed. One of the guards was carrying a large bulging sack. The King immediately made his way to the guards.

"Your majesty, it is Thorn," Sergeant Poko said. "He is alive but badly injured." The King motioned them to take him to the healers immediately. The immense bulge in the sack the elf was carrying caught the King's attention immediately.

"What is in the sack?" he asked in a demanding tone. Everyone halted their movements. The guard lifted the sack.

"There is a problem your majesty," he said, then dumped the contents.

"Get him to the healers immediately," the King demanded as he kept an eye on the contents. "This is a story I must hear. Corporal, return the contents into the bag and DO NOT let anyone see them."

"There is something else, your majesty. We thought we heard flapping of a very large predator to the south. We think it may have been a Griffin, but it was too dense to see. We did not want to waste time investigating so we brought Thorn home and to report what we heard," the Corporal responded as he was refilling the sack with the spilled contents.

The other guards were out of earshot while quickly getting Thorn to the medical building. His blood was pouring out of his forehead, slow, but not stopping. The gash was deep and long.

"Thank you," replied the King. "You did perfect." He walked off pondering all of this. His Kingdom may be in danger. He made it a point to talk with Poko to hear what has transpired during their journey after he came out of the medical building. Sergeant Poko recalled the events, leaving out Nekora entirely as promised but exaggerating the intensity of the bird flying off. Griffins have never entered the valley, nor were they speculated to. Their food and homes are in the mountains.

Something was off. As offbeat as it sounded, he believed they heard something out of the norm, which wasn't good. He motioned for Captain Luka to come forth. He instructed him to gather the four troops and get a written testimony so he could make a tactical decision on how to approach the potential threat. He ordered the troops to be cautious, report everything, and keep on extra alert.

The King made his way to the divination building in hopes of retrieving answers. Though he hated it in there, he had to get a clear vision. He sided with Nekora that the immense aroma of incense was far too potent, giving way to massive headaches.

Nekora came out of the main hall to see what all the commotion was, acting innocent. The King, already in his throne, was deliberating with the wise men when he spied his daughter coming into the room. Upon seeing her entering, the King got up and approached her.

"It is Thorn; he was badly injured but is currently in the care of the greatest healers around. I have postponed the celebration until he is well enough to attend and tell his tale." Nekora faked surprise with wide eyes filling with tears. She had to practice this just in case such an event called for it. She could not let her father know she already knew. She darted out of the room, wiping tears away as she went. The King frowned.

All day, Nekora sat beside her best friend, tears flowing. "Happy birthday, Thorn. I am sorry for your troubles, but I am glad it is finally over. You are back with me," she whispered as she wiped the blood from his wounds and hair from his face. "Thank you for still being in one piece." She would keep him warm by placing the blankets back on him when they fell off.

His face was pale, and he appeared to be dying. So much blood was lost from his wounds even before he was found. She watched the healers do their work, learning their trade in case she needed that skill set sometime. Then a thought occurred to her, and she ran off to the mage tower.

"Thomas!" Nekora yelled as she ran into the tower and down the hall. "Thomas, I need you." Thomas, a slender built elf, came out of the far room into the hallway where Nekora was running.

"What's wrong, Princess?" he asked. She updated him about Thorn looking the worse for wear.

"The healers may be failing him. Too much blood was lost; he might be dying." She was tearing up again. Her words staggered as she could not control her grief. Thomas thought for a moment.

"I'll be right back as quick as I can." He dashed out of the room. A few minutes later, Thomas came back hiding something in his satchel. He handed a small black vial over to Nekora.

"I have been cross studying the healing arts with the alchemists. We developed this potion that may or may not help him. It has not been tested yet, but I can assure you, it will not hurt him. I snuck this from the lab. We have many so one will not be missed. See if you can get him to drink this. And please let me know how it worked." Nekora took it questioningly, but she trusted her friend.

"Thank you, Thomas. Now I owe you one," Nekora said gratefully.

"Don't thank me yet. Not unless it works." She hugged him and ran out the door back to the healers building. Thomas sadly watched her depart.

Once she arrived, she looked around to make sure no one was watching. She pulled the small black vial from the satchel and opened it, smelling the contents. It smelled rank, like rotten vegetables in a stopped-up outhouse. She gave a disgusting look and gagged, then peered around the room.

"I am sorry, Thorn. I hope this works." She slowly poured the contents into his mouth, ensuring he swallowed it. After the contents were emptied, she waited. Color came back to his face immediately. But that was all that she could see. Shortly after, Thorn started breathing easier. The potion was working! A huge smile of elation came across Nekora's face.

The next day, Thorn was awake and feeling better yet aching. He looked the worst for wear, but all in all he could slowly move and speak. After relieving himself in the bowl, he made his way back to his bedside when the King entered his room.

"How are you feeling?" the King inquired.

"I am doing well, your majesty. I am sorry, I have failed in my quest. I was supposed to return on my own," Thorn replied wincing in pain. The King regarded him with a soft smile. He had always looked at Thorn as if he were his own son.

"Do you feel up to telling me the tale?" the King asked.

After Thorn finished his story about the travel, the fight, and the travel back, the King became more concerned. Not just for Thorn, but in the sudden change in events. Too many changes were occurring for his liking.

"I will allow the dinner ceremony tomorrow evening. I would like you to tell the tale to everyone in the village."

"So does this mean I have passed my trials, your majesty?" asked Thorn expectantly. The King looked upon him.

"I will make my decision in the morning. Get some rest, tomorrow is going to be a busy day."

Thorn addressed the King before he departed. "Your majesty, a Gnoll said something to me, and now I am confused. Do you know what it meant by "You smell of royalty but not from this region." Do I have royal blood?"

The King paused then looked at Thorn. "Ask your father. It is about time you knew your real past." He departed the room and headed to the market square, where he made the announcement about a "special" celebration to all but Thorn.

The next day, quick preparations were underway. The way the King sounded about this event, the "special" celebration, each villager had to make sure everything was in perfect order and only the best of the best decorations, food, and wine were selected. Gossip and rumors flowed like wildflowers across the village. No one really knew what happened and whether the King would allow Thorn to become an adult or try again the following year.

The sun was directly overhead when Thorn finally came out of the healers building. He was slow and a little weary but doing great compared to how he arrived.

The healers at Morhgrammir are impressive indeed, thought the King and Queen. Thorn looked about the village as the preparations were underway. Everyone was smiling and greeting him but unsure whether to congratulate him. This made Thorn nervous. He was not looking forward to a retrial. Thorn could not think of doing the adventure again.

The pressure was on to make this the best celebration ever, as demanded by the King. Nekora came up to him and hugged him tight as he winced; she was happy he was back and alive.

"How are you feeling?" she inquired.

"Not as painful as your lessons," came the breathless mocking reply. She laughed and slugged him on the shoulder. Thorn shouted in pain.

"I am so sorry. Consider that a lesson," she said and laughed as she walked, aiding Thorn through the market.

"Do you know why the King would hold a celebration? I failed in my task, but he has not mentioned anything or answered when I asked," Thorn inquired. Nekora thought for a moment, her spying and attempts to listen to gossip.

"I have not heard anything, actually; usually I know before anyone else. I hate surprises. This one he kept silent," Nekora answered. "I wonder if my mom knows anything?" she continued. "I will be right back and see if she knows anything." Nekora went running off toward the castle where the Queen spends much of her time.

The Queen was in her quarters getting her formal dress ready for the night's event when she heard a knock on the door.

"Enter," the Queen said.

Nekora slowly opened the wooden door. She peered into the room only to find her mom looking at her with a smile. Nekora could not help but smile back.

She entered the room and closed the door finally making her way over to the Queen.

"Mom, I haven't heard anything about Thorn. Is dad going to advance him to adulthood? Have you heard anything at all?" Nekora stopped, knowing she was asking too many questions at once. She grasped her hands in front of her body and tilted her head down. "I am sorry. I am just aggravated that I know nothing of these events and yet the celebration is going on without word."

"The Queen looked accusingly at Nekora. "And how may I ask do you know of the others then if you cannot stand the waiting?" she inquired.

Nekora's face turned red. She was now caught. Her secret inadvertently came out.

"I spied when Dad was reaching his conclusions," Nekora confessed. "But this is different, this is Thorn, my best friend," she stated defiantly. "If he did pass, then the celebration makes sense. If he did not, then why the celebrations? He failed in coming home of his own power. Is Dad going to forgive the law this once? Is he going to promote my best friend?" Nekora asked, confused.

Queen Arilana sat on her bed and patted a space next to her. "Your father does what he does, he is the King," she started.

"Sometimes, there are special events that take place that may warrant overlooking. But I do not know in this case since he would not even confide in me," Arilana stated. "What he has planned, I do not know, but I know there is something special in that boy your father sees. Like he knows something but will not say it. It is not my place to ask. If he tells me, that is one thing, but to ask, that is another. You will learn someday when to ask and when to keep silent. Let us see how this turns out. I am dying to know as well," Arilana said, the latter with enthusiasm to get her daughter to smile as she grasped Nekora's hands and raised them in glee to forget about the woes in life even if for just a bit. She also hated seeing Nekora unhappy and always did whatever she could to cheer her.

Nightfall was fast approaching and the entire Kingdom, minus the watch, was in attendance to hear the news. There was about an hour or two left of daylight. In the center of the stage in the middle of the market square, were three cloth-covered, box-shaped items sitting upon three large pedestals. One box, in the center, was significantly larger. Guards were posted to ensure no one sneaked a peek. A few minutes passed, and all the villagers were getting antsy when the King, Queen, and Princess finally arrived on stage in their formal wear as appropriate for these occasions. The Queen and princess took a seat on either side of a larger chair where the King sat.

The King stood, and villagers bowed in respect as he walked forward to the center of the stage and addressed them.

"Elves of Morhgrammir, we all know the rules of the trials. One must depart and return on their own," the King specified, "with a horn of a cyclops as a trophy proving their triumph and strength. Yesterday, Thorn returned with aid from our fellow guards thus disregarding the rule of returning on his own and has failed his trial."

The crowd let out a disappointing groan when the King finished. Thorn put his head down in shame and embarrassment, eyes filling with tears just thinking of the retrial. He was reliving his travels in his thoughts, wincing from the re-imagined battle he was living once again. The King continued, "Each trial only necessitates a single horn from a cyclops." He lifted the veil that covered the two smaller boxes revealing two cyclops horns. The crowd gasped and looked upon Thorn in admiration. The other box, much larger in size, remained covered.

"Thorn," the King called out, waking Thorn from his thoughts, "would you accompany me upon the stage?" It was more of a demand than a question. Everyone turned to look at Thorn as he slowly, painfully, stood and made his way to the stage with help from his army friends. The King continued as Thorn made his way through the crowd.

"There is a problem we must address immediately. The wise men and I have counseled on the matter and agree that there must be more vigilance in the Kingdom."

Thorn arrived next to the King and did his best to bow professionally. The depth of pain still resided, and it hurt to do anything, even with his rapid healing.

"Thorn, would you mind removing the cloth from the third box?" As he lifted the cloth, the villagers immediately gasped at the sight. The third box housed a horn twice the size of the other two. Muttering was heard from the crowd. The King continued his speech.

"It takes a tremendous amount of skill, tact, and cunning to down just one cyclops; Thorn has returned with three," The King said three louder and more pronounced while extending his right hand with three fingers up. "Not to mention, the immensity of the creature that harbored this horn would have been extremely difficult for even an army of elves. Lieutenant Thorn, would you like to tell the tale of your heroic encounter?"

The crowd went into hysterics, and mass cheering erupted. It was hard enough to get into the army as an adult, but to be ceremoniously promoted to lieutenant had never been done before. This truly was a "special" celebration.

The King sat as Thorn recounted the days of observing the Griffin migration and preparing himself for battle by practicing combat techniques every day, and highly praised Princess Nekora for her help as he continued.

"There I was…"

Chapter Four

Thorn walked briskly along the narrow path. Dense brush separated enough for someone to walk between without damaging the plant life. He had a long way to go, and he did not want to chance an accidental encounter with a Gnoll camp. He heard tales of their speed and intelligence from army members that had encountered one or more during their trials. He also did not want to arrive at his destination injured; he needed all the strength he could muster for the final battle with the infamous cyclops.

Gnolls are intelligent for canine hybrids and are difficult to track since they are random in their encampments. Nearest he figured, they should be well away from this area during his adventure through the zone. Since he only has a couple days to get through, he decided to chance it. The first day was uneventful as he set up camp exactly where he planned. His timing was impeccable thus far, and he hoped his luck remained.

It was about midafternoon the following day and halfway to his next rest area when he heard bushes rumbling off to his right. Thorn stopped and slowly put down his pack, then crouched behind a large bush and listened intently for movement. The foliage was dense, easily masking his presence as he eyed the small clearing in front of him. He was upwind from the clearing and cursed himself for the bad decision-making. If the noise did not come from a Gnoll, he would not be noticed. He looked intently in the direction of the rustling. A rabbit scampered out of its hiding place to feed on some wild grass.

Relieved and reminded of hunger, Thorn started working up a quick snare as quietly as he could. He finished the snare and tossed it near the rabbit. The rabbit stopped eating and started smelling the air. Figuring there was no threat, it started eating again, slowly getting nearer the snare.

Just as Thorn was about to pull the small string and capture his late lunch, a large spear abruptly landed, instantly killing the rabbit. The turn of events frightened Thorn, and he jumped back as a Gnoll came into view.

"Ah, a wandering delicious elf. Have you come to feed my family?" asked the Gnoll in a throaty, growling voice. "Perhaps a poacher, here to steal our food?" Thorn was taken aback by the immense size of the creature. It must have stood about eight feet tall, with orange-colored fur and black spots. The creature stood on its hind legs as if it were humanoid. The Gnoll sniffed the air then looked in Thorn's general direction.

"You must be a spy for the Queen of Almaryha. Yes, you have scent of noble but not from this region. A most delectable treat, yes?" The Gnoll looked as if it was smiling, baring its teeth in a menacing fashion.

Gnolls were not supposed to be in this area for another week, he thought, a detriment to him for being random.

Thorn gasped. "You have it all wrong, creature!" He walked out, proud, brave, scimitars in hand, yet scared.

"I am Thorn from Morhgrammir. I am just passing through and do not wish any harm to you or your pack." The Gnoll looked at him laughing, mouth drooling with a voracious appetite.

"Just stay right where you are young elf." With a swift motion, the Gnoll knocked an arrow and let it fly. The swift action took Thorn by surprise. Expect the unexpected. Thorn rolled out of the way, barely missing the arrow as it whizzed next to his left ear. He raised his scimitars and rolled forward to plunge them into the beast. The Gnoll flipped backward with inhuman speed, evading the impending attack.

"Challenge accepted!" it growled, dropping its bow, and grabbing its spear. The fight was on.

The creature's movements were fluid and specific. The Gnoll always seemed to move out of the way just in time. Thorn finally understood why they practiced so much with a heavy emphasis on dodges and parries. The Kata, a form of battle slow dance to mimic movements in slow motion, suddenly came to realization when he used it to evade an incoming fatal attack from the spear. It was in that moment he realized the importance of muscle memory. Thorn watched the Gnoll with anticipation of finding its weakness, a flaw he could use to down this creature. Unfortunately, this creature was a fighting machine.

"Just like sparring with Nekora," he thought. At the same time, the creature was getting frustrated. It appeared as if Thorn was reading its every move and counteracting with fluid motions. To the casual observer, it would appear the two were in a hypnotic dance. The Gnoll changed it up and feigned a normal thrust with a parry move that was expected. The Gnoll quickly brought the spear back, twirled it behind its back, then brought it forward in a twirl that caught Thorn off guard. The spear was leveraged behind the Gnolls back as it twisted with great speed and power. It had contacted Thorn's face knocking him down. With quick reflexes and agility, Thorn was back up and in the fight.

Thorn had always reminisced how he could best Nekora at a fight. All the what if scenarios played through his head as he dodged and countered. He needed this thing off balance to end the dual. Strike after strike, dodge after dodge, each combatant showing no signs of stopping or tiring.

"Thank you, Nekora, for the stamina schooling," thought Thorn as he nearly dodged a head thrust.

After five long minutes of dodge, parry, and attack, Thorn found what he was looking for. A pattern of strikes the Gnoll used was now clear. The Gnoll always made two swipes, thrust, spinning spear for parry, then forward thrust again. An occasional block move when warranted, but the attack sequence was clear. It was just difficult to get close without impalement.

He needed to wait for the next thrust. When the Gnoll did his second thrust, Thorn dodged the attack and jumped over the Gnoll with a flip and buried his scimitars into its back. The Gnoll was not expecting the move and yelped as it went limp and fell lifelessly to the ground.

Tired and weary, he gathered up his belongings and the Gnoll's spear and resumed his trek, traveling farther ahead of his planned stop so as not to be found by other roaming Gnolls. They are much harder to defeat than previously anticipated. The stories held no merit from his friends in the garrison that had the unfortunate fate of dealing with one. He felt as if they downplayed their adversary, yet he now felt a whole new admiration for the creatures. Recounting the dual, he saw a similar pattern from Nekora.

Did she know the Gnoll movements? Did she purposefully train him for this moment? Too many questions needed answering. He made a mental note to ask her when he returned from his trial.

Thorn finally found a promising rest spot, set down his pack, and closed his eyes in the afternoon shade of the forest.

Thorn was in the sparring pit with Nekora. Both were lashing it out when he found her pattern. She thrust her staff toward Thorn when he dodged with a flip over her head and slammed his staff into her skull, accidentally killing Nekora. He became deeply saddened. "No!" he exclaimed as he held Nekora in his arms, tears flowing down his cheeks and blood flowing down his arms. He was crying, "I am so sorry, Nek!" The guards immediately took him and threw him in jail. The next day, the King had him bound and hung in the market square.

He awoke with a start the next morning at the end of his fall with the rope around his neck. He was sweating, tears flowing. "Oh, thank you for only being a dream," he thought as he prepared to depart. "It was just a dream. I would never hurt her," he whispered to himself repeatedly until he started making headway. He soon realized that he was far behind where he was supposed to be. His encounter with the Gnoll followed by a much needed but far too long of a restless rest had taken up valuable time. The ground was extremely hard and uncomfortable to sleep on. Thorn had quickened his pace to catch up so he could be back on track.

"I must be successful," Thorn thought as he hurriedly made his way forward to reach his goal.

He arrived at the base of the mountain six days later. He had run across a couple Gnoll camps and had to circumvent them quickly. Many small river crossings and a small ditch also slowed him much more than he had initially presumed. The time lost was too much to make up. His only hope to make it back on his birthday was to quickly dispatch a cyclops and leave swiftly.

He was deep in thought as an unusually large spider leaped out of the ground bunker it had made as a trap to the unwary traveler. Thorn saw the creature leap at him with his peripheral vision and rolled forward to evade the attack. The gigantic spider was now facing him, crouched, ready to strike at any moment.

"No one ever said anything about giant spiders!" he yelled more out fear than anything.

Thorn dodged a lunge from the spider's forward legs as he drew his scimitars. The spider reared back, showing its fangs. The fangs were large and menacing, glistening from poison. The spider itself was fifteen feet long and five feet tall. It was black with a small body and large abdomen. The fangs were sprung out menacingly, looking to be two feet in length each. It dropped down on all eight legs and ran toward Thorn and great speed. Thorn swung one scimitar, contacting the forward leg chopping it off. The spider retreated to assess its next attack. It moved sideways left, then right, looking for an opportune moment to attack and minimize its own damage.

    The spider raised it back legs and faced its abdomen forward. Knowing what was happening, Thorn rolled to the right quickly. The web was shot, which impacted Thorn's feet wrapping them tighter as he rolled. The spider ran up on Thorn using its good leg to attack and bring him toward its fangs and mouth. Thorn dodged the attacks as best he could. He swung his scimitar many times but missed from the speed. The spider pinned Thorn down and moved forward to eat. Thorn used his last ounce of energy and cut the front leg that was pinning him down. The spider retreated to gauge its next attack. As the spider retreated, Thorn used his scimitars to cut the webbing from his feet, freeing him for a second before the spider attacked again.

    This time, the spider jumped into the air landing on top of Thorn, wriggling to get its meal into place. A few moments later, the spider slowly moved. It went sideways as Thorn used the scimitars to move it. He had lunged them into the main body when the spider descended, killing the creature on landing with fangs impacting the ground on either side of his head. Thorn retrieved his blades and sheathed them after wiping off the muck.

    He made his way to the nearest river to rinse the bile and blood from his body and clothes. Any predator with a good scent would pick up on the scent and attack, thinking him to be easy food, a fight he was not ready to contend with now. Once he was cleaned, he proceeded toward the mountain base. He had brought out his sharpening stone and started sharpening his blades as he assessed his travel up the cliff's side.

"The mountains look so much smaller from the Kingdom. Not as treacherous either," he mumbled to himself. The cliff's side was steep and appeared difficult to ascend. A quarter of the way up, he saw a small alcove.

"Perfect place to rest." Thorn had put away his weapons and stone, satisfied with their sharp edges, then began his ascent. His arms, legs, back, and stomach were sore. He felt like he just sparred with his best friend, again.

"Oh, Nek, if you only knew the pain," he said and paused, then started laughing, rekindling his pain. After about an hour of rest and satisfying his thirst with water, he continued his ascension.

I wish I were with you, Nek, instead of this. But I will only be gone for a short time. He pondered as he sat on the ledge eating some bread and cheese, he brought with him. With renewed strength and ambition, he continued his climb.

He arrived at the top of the mountain around dusk. There was still some light left, but he needed to rest for the final combat. The climb had almost killed him as he struggled to keep hand and foot holds along the cliff's edge. He met with a lovely couple of rattlesnakes along the way.

His quick reaction allowed him to dismember the two and save them for food later, changing from the same bread and cheese spread. A rattlesnake sandwich sounded good when it was safe to make a fire. As he peered over the cliff's edge, he realized he was exactly on his mark, but had quite a bit of travel left to reach the campfire he saw in the distance.

He was not that far off. His calculations were right on the money. He looked over where his Kingdom should be and realized he was exactly where the cyclops camp is supposed to be. But why were the cyclops so far ahead? It did not matter. Thorn grabbed his supplies, relieved that the top of the cliff was easier to traverse than the side.

The top was a flat plateau, appearing heavily worn through the years. Massive boulders jutted into the large pathway hindering his view to clear his approach to the cyclops. There were many dangerous ledges leading straight down from where he was, but he did his best to avoid the cliff and boulders and used every sense he had to clear his path forward.

He looked to the east and was awed at the view, the gentle breeze blowing his hair around him. He took in as much as he could to recount the view to Nekora on his return. She would love to hear this. The majestic beauty of lush grasslands, a deeper, denser, forest farther out. He could barely make out the silhouette of the human Kingdom off in the distance.

That must be Haversmith. I need to make a trip after this is over. He pondered the idea then brushed it off. Too many tales were overheard about how evil the humans were against other races. He dismissed the idea.

Thorn slowly and quietly made his way to the campfire. After another hour of rest, he felt balanced. He hid behind a large boulder and peered around the corner. A single cyclops was tending a Griffin rotisserie oblivious to its surroundings. Thorn knocked an arrow, took steady aim, and was flying over the cliff's side. His vision was in and out, but he felt himself falling. With a thump, he lay unconscious on the cliffs edge a quarter of the way down. Thorn, the mighty would-be warrior, did not expect the unexpected.

As he was taking aim and about to release, a second cyclops batted him with a tree-sized club. It was more silent than thought possible for the immense size of the creature. It watched as the elf flew and furious because it hit him so hard, he flew out of reach. The cyclops turned toward the campfire and saw that his female companion was dead. An arrow through her eye, piercing her brain.

The eye oozed aqueous fluid, a thick opaque fluid found in the eyeball, and the eye itself appeared to be melting as it drained. The cyclops was angry and ready to torture the elf, but it could not get to him. Watching the unmoving form, it gave up and went to its mate. There he sat, grieving. Tears welling down his eye. His hunger was no longer an issue.

Thorn woke hours later, battered and bleeding profusely from his head. He had no idea where he was. After a few minutes Thorn had realized that he was ambushed. He cursed himself for believing it would be so easy and letting his guard down. But he had to succeed in his mission. He slowly, painfully made his way back up the cliff after wrapping his head in a bandage to stop the bleeding, his head was swelling and vision swirling from the pain.

After reaching the summit he viewed the boulder he was behind and his bow laying on the ground. His head was spinning and almost vomited, his vision bouncing from blurry to focused and back to blurry. He quickly checked for his arrows. They were still secured on his back. He looked upon the dead cyclops.

"Now how the hell did I get flung over the side?" He was bewildered. He made his way back to his bow when he suddenly saw what happened. A second cyclops he never saw coming was posting watch. Damn my foolishness. I will NOT make that mistake again. Thorn grabbed his bow as it wobbled in his hand. A quick survey revealed it was snapped in two. The other cyclops was sitting behind the rock, unseen from Thorn's point of view, but he sat there grieving. It almost made Thorn cry for he could not fathom losing Nekora. No time to ponder, time to act, and act fast.

"Curses!" He hissed to himself. As he had no idea how to down the second beast. A thought occurred to him as he crept along the backside of the boulder.

Thorn found himself behind his new nemesis. When he was in range, he jumped up on its back and drove his scimitars deep into the back of the cyclops' neck. It struggled to get the Elf off but to no avail. It ran backward, slamming Thorn into the large boulder he was once hiding behind, smacking his head once more driving his vision and consciousness to come and go in waves. It also drove the scimitars deeper, causing severe fatal lacerations. After a bit of a fight, the cyclops keeled over, dead.

"Woo hoo! That's TWO horns for the celebration!" The elation was over quickly when his head spun, and he almost vomited. The pain was unbearable. He doubled over on his knees. Thorn was injured badly. He had no idea how, or even if, he was going to recover from this. His thoughts quickly became dismal, realizing his body was in immense pain and had to urgently return to the Kingdom on his own.

He had to suffer through it; success was number one. He needed to retrieve his trophies and head back to the bottom of the mountain. He would recover from there in the safety and security of the forest. Luckily, few animals if any traverse the forest edge.

Thorn started hacking away at the first cyclops' horn, gagging, almost regurgitating from the sharp, acrid odor from the oozing eye fluid. He felt a deep vibration from the ground and quickly halted his actions. His internal alarms were warning him of danger. He looked around. Another thump, then another. The small water casket was rippling from the vibrations.

This must be huge. I cannot see it yet, but I feel its foot stomps. Thorn was sweating; the thumping became louder and the vibrations stronger, but he could not see it yet.

He hid behind the large boulder next to his first victim, his scimitars at the ready.

I cannot keep doing this. My body cannot take much more. He waited. The thumping stopped next to the boulder. A Griffin, even larger than the one on the spit, thumped to the ground next to him, lifeless. Its head was as tall as Thorn with a massive beak. The talons could grip a full-grown horse with ease. The claws on the lion half of the body were huge and sharp. It was a weird mixture of eagle and lion. He started wondering how the animal would taste—chicken or beef? He quickly dismissed the thought and focused on his new opponent.

He heard sniffing followed by a roar so loud he thought his ears would explode and increased his headache tenfold, fluctuating his vision. He took the opportunity and rammed his scimitars blindly. They connected to the calf of the large cyclops. The cyclops roared in pain as it swatted at Thorn. Thorn dodged the blow by rolling away. His scimitars were not so lucky. The swat snapped them in two. It was then, Thorn realized, he was in more danger than he could comprehend. At around twelve feet in height, he realized he was in immediate danger. The only weapon he had left was his trusty dagger and the Gnolls spear.

"I love you, Nekora," he whispered before springing into action.

Thorn thought quickly, he had to grab the dead cyclops' club and pry the boulders apart at the right time so it could squash the cyclops. The club was so heavy he could barely lift it; the spear was too flimsy for this job. He dashed behind the rock where he was formerly hiding. The cyclops quickly followed, fierce, anger in its eye. Thorn used the club to attempt to dislodge the smaller boulder supporting the gigantic one. The smaller boulder was not budging. The cyclops swatted at Thorn, connecting to his side. He quickly recovered from his stumble and ran to the next rock, trying to figure a way to defeat it. A worthless gesture in his mind. He had an idea.

Without weapons in his immediate grasp, how could he defeat the giant beast? He found his pack and removed his rope. It was a preloaded lasso he was going to use to wrap around the boulder next to him. He ran, dodging the cyclops blows to the other boulder where he got one wrap in. He had no time to tie the rope. Tripping the beast was his best option. He ran away from the cyclops to the other side of the boulder and pulled his dagger. For a split second, he looked at the dagger and laughed.

The cyclops was slowed from exhaustion, he presumed from fighting the huge Griffin. This gave Thorn the advantage. He ran around the boulder away from the beast. He saw his moment when the cyclops neared the edge of the cliff, sniffing for his nemesis. Thankfully, their vision was poor, but their sense of smell more than made up for it.

Thorn came around the back. He swung his dagger into the calf of the giant cyclops. The dagger connected and sliced its tendon. The move caught the cyclops off guard as it stumbled back on the club wedged into the smaller boulder. The larger boulder came loose and hit the cyclops, knocking him forward, off the cliff. The blood curdling roar was deafening as it descended the mighty cliff. The cyclops landed with a huge thud and died instantly. Thorn felt the vibration of the landing from where he stood.

After a quick search, Thorn found that no more cyclops were around. He sat and ate some of the Griffin on the spit, regenerating his energy.

"Yep, tastes like chicken," he laughed. After detaching the horns from the first two, he gathered his things and descended the cliff to his lifesaving ledge and rested for two days, examining his broken weapons, and laughed as he thrust them into his pack to show the elves. After his rest, he realized he had to make up more time.

Thorn descended the cliff as fast as his aches would allow. Once he reached the bottom, he found the giant and removed its horn. The rotten decomposing smell made him vomit more than once, but the importance was too much to let go. The last horn was abnormally heavy.

Three horns in his bag, a sure blessing into adulthood. He recounted what he could remember. The combat, the Griffins, anything, and everything on his trek. Adrenaline kicked in, dulling the pain if for a short time. Thorn made his way back home. Once the adrenaline wore off, his pace slowed dramatically, causing a loss in his final stretch.

"Will I make it back in time?" he asked himself as he looked to the sky, trying to gauge how much time he had left.

A day away from home. His body still aching, the wounds were healing, yet he still had a hard time walking. He made camp. Looking at the stars, tomorrow was his birthday.

"Please, help me make it back," he prayed. He realized he had to make up more time if he wanted to be successful. He stopped constructing camp and repacked. He headed toward the Kingdom to be closer throughout the night and into morning.

"Oh, what a bad idea," he thought as he heard more rustling off to his left. He was scared now; he had no weapons except for his dagger, and the thought of another Gnoll frightened him. He had lost the spear in the mountains somewhere. He could not defeat another Gnoll without weapons.

As the thought finished, a boar came charging at him full speed. He was nicked by a tusk to his right calf as he jumped. The boar turned and charged again. Thorn drew his dagger and squared off. As the boar just passed him,

Thorn jumped on top of it, grabbing the head while lying on top of it. The boar reared its head back, attempting to gouge the threat upon its back as it flattened to the ground from the sudden shift in weight. Thorn moved his head but not fast enough. He received a large gash on his forehead from the sharp tusk. His instincts kicked in and swiped his blade across the boar's throat. After a few failed rolling attempts, the boar stopped moving.

"I cannot rest with this blood loss. I am getting weaker by the moment." Thorn pushed and pushed as hard as he could. The slow walk turned into stumbling. He could not think anymore; his vision was lessening, and pain was increasing. The cut in his calf slowed his progression even more, causing a major limp. He was too weak to press on and barely able to keep his eyes open as he kept falling to his knees. He mustered as much strength as he could to keep upright and make it back to the Kingdom.

Too much blood was lost. He made the decision to make camp. He got out his essentials and put his trophy bag on his lap, close but too weak to move any more. He started a campfire signal. He could not return on his own accord. Thorn, the mighty warrior, collapsed.

CHAPTER FIVE

Eyes were wide and frozen in awe. The villagers were taken aback by the recounted story Thorn gave. Most of the villagers were on the edge of their seats. Some thought he fabricated the story quite a bit and mocked that he was defeated by a lesser beast. Those were his Army friends joking with him. The King saw the confusion and tension in the crowd. A new look of admiration came from most. They now understood that the ceremonious promotion was warranted. A look of relief overcame them after the King spoke again.

"This is definitely new information; a threat not to be taken lightly. However, the cyclops remain roaming their own territory, so we decided that no direct threat to the Kingdom is imminent. We can proceed as normal. Let the festivities begin!" the King shouted as he waived his hands in the air. Everyone scrambled this way and that, no one really knowing where to go next. Some made a beeline to be the first to congratulate Thorn on his victory.

Everyone moved about, hustling to get the final details in order. Music was playing, elves were dancing, drinking, and eating. Everything was good in the city. Nekora helped Thorn off the dais.

"Happy birthday, Thorn, and, most importantly, congratulations! How are you feeling?"

Thorn was appreciative. "I am actually feeling much better than I thought I would in such short time, and its lieutenant," he said sarcastically.

"We either have the best healers in the world, or I heal quickly," Thorn stated. Nekora smirked.

"We have the best healers in the world," Nekora replied. Thorn put his hands on her shoulders and looked into her eyes to show the seriousness and urgency of the matter at hand.

"I have to talk to my father about a most urgent matter. Please excuse me and I will fill you in later," Thorn said.

"Of course, Lieutenant," she said mockingly. He laughed and winced. She smiled and looked in the direction of the mage tower, her smile grew wider. As he departed, she made way to the tower to let Thomas know about how their concoction, she called a healing potion for lack of a better name, worked before attending the rest of the festivities. She had to be back before the archery contest, so she made haste.

Thorn looked about and found his father in the crowd.

"Father, I must speak with you," Thorn said urgently.

"Ah son, I could not be prouder of what you have become. You are, indeed, my hero."

"Thank you, but I have to know about my real parents."

Thorn's father, Lord Granther, looked about ensuring no one overheard his question. "Come with me, and I will tell you who you really are."

Lord Granther sat him in a quiet location under a tall oak tree away from the beaten path so as not to be overheard. Lord Granther looked down the pathway a moment before facing Thorn.

"The King told me you inquired about your heritage. We have decided it was about time you knew," he began. "Thirteen years ago, my son Burgen went on his trials."

Burgen, son of Granther, made way for his trials. He headed toward the eastern edge. He was a short but strong elf with a promising future in the guard. He did not see it that way. He only wanted to be a master blacksmith. He trained daily with the local blacksmith and was surprised at how many friends they have.

The day was young, the air was fresh and a little brisk for an early winter day. He had his route planned from the start and wanted to ensure that he destined for the eastern mountains. Considering how tall the mountain was, he wanted a good view at the presumed human Kingdom of Haversmith.

What makes the humans so special? They are just another line of beasts desiring to conquer the lands. He pondered, but quickly dismissed the thoughts when his father came by to wish him luck.

Burgen went over his notes or at least a copy of them before he left. No notes were allowed on the journey. Memory was also tested during these trials. He was scared; he did not want to go through the trials but knew he must if he wanted to grow and work anywhere.

Those who refused to go on their trials were immediately cast out of the Kingdom. No one has ever refused since

Chroonin over ten years ago. Everyone watched him leave the Kingdom in disgrace and shunned from ever returning. No one knows what happened to him.

Burgen set out, leaving his notes with the king. It was a fresh semi breezy day filled with promise.

The trek to the mountains was uneventful as he avoided many Gnoll camps by paying attention to signs and indicators. Most of it was hearing but also smell as they emit a foul stench that would cause a troll to vomit. Luckily, he was downwind as they would not smell him making his trek easier to navigate.

Days later, he had arrived at the cliff's base at the eastern mountain range. He carefully climbed to the top and slowly peeked over the edge. The wind was at his back, so he had to be extra cautious. No cyclops in the immediate vicinity, so he traversed the ledge and sat behind a large boulder obstructing any view from potential dangers.

Burgen heard flapping and looked upwards toward the sun only to catch a glimpse of a giant flying creature coming at him. He dodged the attack by rolling and went around the boulder he was hiding. He scanned his immediate surroundings and found no general danger, so he carefully scanned the sky, using his right hand to shield the sun. He saw it, a large birdlike creature, on the front half of its body. A lion's body filled in the last half.

GRIFFIN! His internal alarms went off. He had heard of them being a vicious creature killing anything that lives or breathes. He knocked an arrow and shifted positions to put the sun out of frontal view. The Griffin came into view from around the rock and started its attack run toward Burgen.

He quickly raised the bow, pulled back the string and let loose the arrow. It impacted the Griffin in the eye instantly killing it as it fell lifelessly to the plateau.

If there is one, there are more. He thought to himself. Usually, a cyclops band is not too far behind either. Burgen set out to investigate his landing. So far, only a dead carcass of a Griffin was found, so he inspected it. He jotted down some detailed notes about the beak and claws, which were the main weapons—the outline, and the wingspan compared to the body was abnormally large. He figured it was to counter the weight of the lion half of the body.

He took a couple feathers and put them in his sack. He also inspected the area and found a nest with no eggs. It must have just finished the nest building for breeding, which meant the cyclops were not close yet. He pondered his options and opted to make his way to the north toward the eastern peak. He had found the cyclops camp on the northern side of the peak. There were four of them. One of them caught a whiff of something and looked in his direction. He realized he was upwind from the creatures.

"Curse me for not paying attention." Burgen quickly made his way to the south where the peak of the eastern mountains had started as the cyclops let out an angry roar and charged him. He turned and let fly an arrow, impacting the cyclops eye and penetrating its brain, killing it almost immediately.

He quickly cut off the horn and headed to the base for descending. He heard a voice behind him. He quickly turned, expecting a fight but found a pale elf holding a bundle.

"Please!" he pleaded. "This child is Queen Kardya's son. He is also mine. If the King finds out this is not his, he will die a horrible death. The King will feed him to the dogs alive. Please, I beg of you, take him with you," the elf implored. He reached the bundle of blankets toward Burgen, and he took it. He investigated the bundle and viewed a baby elf.

"So cute!" he whispered and started down the base. He turned to ask why, but the elf was gone. It was as if a Griffin swooped in and swallowed him whole, vanishing without a trace. He had no time to search; the rest of the cyclops would be upon him within minutes, so he had to disappear.

He found a small pathway, making his ascension quicker but no less threatening. He was now in a race against time. He did not know what babies ate. Upon reaching the bottom, he made haste toward the dense forest to hide from incoming dangers.

He picked up speed but kept the noise level down as he was taught. This used a lot of stamina, but he needed to make it back and fast. By the time he got to his first camping site, his legs and arms were cut from the thorny bushes he ran into along the way.

As he rested, he peered into the bundle again and gazed upon the baby elf. His thoughts wandered as to whether he would find the love of his life and start a family of his own. The baby started to get restless.

"No, no, no, do not do this to me right now. Just a few more days," he frantically whispered. "I cannot keep you safe if you start rustling!" Burgen was getting worried. He decided to make for the Kingdom in one straight trip.

He successfully averted Gnoll camps and wild boars as he arrived at the Kingdom exhausted. Lord Granther was there after being summoned. He made haste to get to his kid. Burgen explained the story of the baby as he handed it to Lord Granther before collapsing from exhaustion. Burgen slept for three days.

"He was successful. I took you to the King immediately and recounted what he had told me. The King gave you a name, 'Thorn', from all the thorn plants that cut him up." Lord Granther gave a quick chuckle. "You truly were a thorn in his side."

Thorn did not look amused. "Since it was my son who found you, the King entrusted me to your upbringing. I oversaw raising you as my own. Burgen died three months later from a Gnoll army that attempted to attack the Kingdom. I know the burden of Gnoll fights firsthand. You are extremely lucky to have survived your trial."

Lord Granther was looking down as he finished. He then looked to Thorn. "Please do not be upset with us for hiding this from you. We were going to let you know when the time was right. This is now the time. I have conversed with the King and figured since you accomplished what no other elf had done, and are a prince, he thought it was only right to promote you to lieutenant so you would not be treated as a regular soldier but rightfully as a royal figure. Do not betray his trust in judgment. Being an officer is a huge burden and you will carry a lot of responsibility, especially the lives of younger warriors trying to rise in the ranks. They will take care of you, of course, but keep using your head."

Thorn teared up and hugged his father.

"Thank you, Father, this is the best news I have ever heard, and I am grateful for everything you have done," he said, thinking about Nekora. Thorn looked away. He had to tell her, but how could he break the news? Would she still be his friend or turn her back on him? He could ask her to marry him; that thought brought a sense of warmth throughout his body. He had to plan that part later.

For now, there were too many things to consider, but he understood. He also had to get back to the ceremony before he was missed, and a search party was sent for him.

How can I tell her? She must know. As Thorn and his father departed, heading back to the ceremony, he was looking for Nekora. He was happy he was a prince but confused about his heritage.

"Am I really a prince since I am the son of the Queen of Almaryha, or am I just another woodland elf out of his realm?" Time and fate will decide. For now, he just wanted to bask in the ceremony, answer questions from the villagers, and be a part of what he felt—his true home of Morhgrammir.

"Thorn!" Nekora was coming from the north. "Ready to be star for a day?" she mocked as she hit his shoulder as she always does.

"Yeah, I hope to be a star forever," he answered.

She looked at him quizzically. "What do you mean?" He was about to tell her when other elves were descending upon him to greet and congratulate him.

"I will tell you later; now is not a good time," he whispered. Nekora stopped and stared at him as he continued.

"Something is wrong," she thought. Has he changed since his promotion? Will he no longer be my best friend? Does he think he is too good for me now that he is a lieutenant? The thoughts killed her inside. She had to know and had to know now. But she remembered something from years past, and it finally made sense.

"Let's see how long it takes," she whispered when he was out of earshot with a smile.

The wild hogs burning on the spits were filling the air with a delectable aroma; it was time. The fruit, vegetables, cheese, and soft bread were fresh, the wine was of the finest available, and the decorations were perfect. Things could not be any better. Nekora rushed to the archery event that was about to start.

Nekora and the rest of the archers were the first to eat so they could put on a show as the rest of the villagers ate, a common practice to keep them entertained. Nekora always won. The tables were finally being filled, and the musicians picked up the pace and changed their tune to signify the start of the archery event. It preceded the melee demonstration and mock fighting of beasts, which were elves in costume.

There were three targets paralleling the feast tables. Arrows flying in front of the patrons always gave them a surge of energy as they ate. The tension was always tight.

The first three were new archers in the group, followed by the intermediate, advanced, and professional archers. This was so the audience could see the progression of training. Nekora was in the advanced group, hoping to progress to professional after this event.

The first group took their places, knocked their arrows, aimed, and let fly all in unison. Two hit the third ring; the third one was in the second ring. The intermediate group took their places. Same show. Place, knock, aim, shoot. Two were in the second ring and the left end was dead center.

The advanced group took their places. Nekora was the center shooter. She preferred that spot since it gave her a better sense of aiming.

She whispered her words, breathed outward, and all three released. Both ends were second ring; Nekora hit dead center. The last group, the professionals, took their places. All three archers hit center. As always, the ones who hit center advance to the finals. A fourth and fifth target was brought in for the five finalists. This time, the targets were half the size in diameter, and all were attached to a swivel. This way the crowd must wait until the judging was finished since no one will see where the targets were hit. To top it off, they were swinging. The archers had to anticipate where the target would be when the arrow gets there. Place, knock, aim, shoot.

Four of the five targets fell backward. The fifth one, the contestant from the intermediate stage, barely missed his target. He was not accustomed to moving targets just yet but good to get experience. The judges circled the targets and talked among themselves. Once they determined the order, they went from last to first as they lifted the targets so the crowd could see the shots. As each target was, there was clapping and cheering.

The first target was Granger. He had been off and on training and thought archery was far too easy. He skipped lessons as he saw no use for it. He was by far the hardest elf to motivate. The second target was Prin. A friendly beautiful elf who made as much time practicing as Nekora. She was the newest up and coming champion and hit a solid second ring. Nekora was proud of her. The last two targets were simultaneously brought up. A first in Morhgrammir history. Nekora turned to see her opponent and was surprised to see Thorn standing there. She did not recognize him earlier. He smirked. "Uh oh, looks like a new champion is about to be recognized." Nekora was upset but impressed at the same time.

"I thought you said archery is for wussies?" she inquired.

Thorn regarded her. "It was until my last battle."

The judges conversed and decided that one shot, one target would signify the champion. A target even half the size of the movable ones was put in place. A coin was tossed, Thorn won. He decided to shoot first. Thorn took aim. Nekora was right behind him awaiting her turn. Just before release, Nekora feigned a rumbling noise that only he could hear. He missed the center by less than an inch and turned around and whispered, "That wasn't fair." She smirked.

"Paybacks, my friend," she teased and took aim. Nekora hit dead center of the target and was crowned the champion.

"Well played, Nek," Thorn whispered.

"Why, thank you, my Prince," she whispered, feeling embarrassed.

Thorn looked around; no one seemed to have heard her.

How does she know? The rest of the challenges left the crowd nothing short of entertained. Everything went off without a hitch. Everyone was having the time of their lives.

The festivities went through nightfall. It was dark and no stars shined. There was much laughing and dancing when a guard came running to the King.

"Your Majesty," Hicka said, out of breath. "The night is covered with clouds. We could see nothing but thought we heard the flapping of heavy wings. It sounded close, almost like Griffins. We thought it suspicious but wanted to give you notice and await your command. We do not know if there is a credible threat; otherwise, we would have rung the gong." The King rose from his seat and set out to investigate. He went to the highest tower, looked, and listened.

"Send me an archer!" the King demanded. Hicka more than obliged and grabbed one quickly, returning for further orders.

"If it flies, it may be a danger or food, but the sound is too loud to be food. Whatever it is, it is camouflaged by the night. I want you to shoot at the sound. Bring down whatever plagues our festivities."

"Yes, your Majesty," the archer replied. He took aim and listened. He lit his arrowhead and adjusted his bow to follow the flapping sound and gaged its speed. He released. The arrow was true, but it barely missed the giant beast when it quickly altered direction. The fire lit upon the arrow allowed the elves to get a quick glimpse, and the Kings eyes went wide with fear.

"Dragons!" he whispered harshly.

Nekora was watching her father depart the festivities with Hicka, the guard second in command, when Thorn snuck up and pulled Nekora aside.

"What have you heard? What do you know?"

Nekora looked at him. "Years ago, I overheard my father talking about you. I heard your name in the conversation, so I naturally stopped and listened."

Thorn nodded. "Of course."

"Well, I overheard something..." The warning gong stopped everyone in their tracks. Everyone looked at each other and ran for cover, or defensive positions. Nekora quickly grabbed her bow and arrows as did Thorn. They raced to where the King had gone. He was running quickly to his daughter.

"Listen, I need you guys to follow the flapping sounds and shoot down..." Fire rained from the heavens. Nekora tumbled and ran for cover; Thorn by her side. She counted eight pillars as she looked back while running. She quickly found cover and started flinging arrows into the air.

"Flames from heaven raining through, on the coming of the second moon. From the ashes will eject a hero of which none shall expect. The wise and efficient hero shall lead, as the peril of others who lie and bleed," Nekora recited as her face flushed pale. The prophecy! Her Kingdom was doomed. She watched as her Kingdom was quickly destroyed.

A hail of arrows went up all at once. Hundreds of arrows, causing the dragons to scatter. Morhgrammir was up in flames. Villagers by the dozens came out of hiding to help put the fires out. Another hail of arrows followed by a loud screech. A dragon was hit, but how much damage could arrows do to the heavily armored dragons? They were mythical, Godly.

Nekora witnessed a flurry of fireballs and lightning from the north as they slammed into the nearest dragon, screeching as it fell. The amount of damage the dragon sustained was immense but necessary to help her Kingdom.

"Thank the heavens for mages!" she thought as she ran to Thorn.

The screech was getting louder until Nekora realized the dragon was falling toward them. The dragon came in sideways, hitting the ground near them and bounced once before sliding and settling in the middle of the market. Nekora ducked when it bounced but not fast enough. It caught her along the side of her head and body, knocking her unconscious. Fire was burning everywhere. Lights out.

The next morning, the wood elves were wandering their burnt city. The King and Queen lay dead, burnt from dragon fire as well as hundreds of villagers. Nekora, practically suffocating under the ash, woke and attempted to rise. The pain in her head was great. The ash had sealed her wounds and stopped the bleeding, thus saving her life. After a brief vomiting period and dizziness, she rose, dusting off the ash. Villagers saw her and came to her aid.

"Your highness, don't you realize? You are the prophecy." Nekora paused and thought. Out of the ashes will eject a leader of which none shall expect. She looked down at her ash-covered body. Her clothing was mostly destroyed by the fire, baring her body, with burn marks and sealed gashes. Other villagers had the same burns; most were naked from the destroyed clothing but bared char marks on their skin. "Could it be? I could not be the leader in the prophecy. I am just a young woman, not ready to lead. But they are right, I must be strong for these people."

Thorn rose next to her, groaning in agonizing pain.

"Not again," he groaned. Nekora helped him up.

"I am so confused," she whispered.

She surveyed the group and counted half of the population.

"Where are my parents?" she demanded as tears flowed down her cheeks, expecting the worst. She started to run though the village and find them, but the pain kept her in one place. She was more scared than she had ever been in her life.

"Your highness, the King and Queen are dead. Burnt by dragon fire. They lie over there." He pointed to the west.

"No, no, nooooo!" she yelled, running to her parents. "Who would do such a thing?" She found her parents and cried as she knelt, tired and exhausted. She was hurting from the wounds she had received during the night.

She immediately went into action, talking to the villagers after a brief reconcile with her lifeless parents. She was choked up and hoped she could talk.

"Villagers of Morhgrammir, I am Princess Nekora. Hear me out." Nekora started violently coughing from all the ash she inhaled. Thorn broke through.

"If I may, your highness?" She allowed Thorn to speak.

"I would like to formally introduce myself. I am Prince Thorn, son of Queen Kardya of Almaryha. I just found out yesterday afternoon, but I am a wood elf like you. It is a saddened day indeed about the deaths of our loved ones and our beloved King and Queen. It is therefore my duty to advise you that the princess here is no more."

Every villager gasped and could not believe the blasphemy coming out of his mouth. Nekora even looked at him with fierce apprehension, ready to kill him.

"She is the sole heir to the throne and shall be henceforth recognized as Queen Nekora Mancer." Thorn made a gesture with an open hand pointing in Nekora's direction. Every villager looked to her and mumbled among one another.

Everyone looked blankly, then understood. She was the only heir and with the King and Queen gone, she was now, by law, the Queen of Morhgrammir whether she liked it or not. They turned their gaze toward Nekora in unison and bowed to show respect to their new leader, their new Queen. Even Nekora was taken aback by the salutation.

"Your highness, what is thy bidding?" Thorn asked. After her bout with a coughing fit, she addressed the Kingdom.

"I need every able body to round up the dead for a funeral ceremony. We will honor those who sacrificed their lives to protect the Kingdom." An unexpected cough interrupted her speech. "We will then rebuild and seek revenge to those who have declared war." Queen Nekora was lightheaded from the earlier blow and fumbled. Thorn caught her before she fell. Thorn, holding his Queen, looked deeply into her eyes.

"I love you, Nekora," he said.

"I know," she smiled and replied, "and that's QUEEN Nekora."

"Forgive me, my Queen," Thorn replied. She desperately wanted to grieve for her parents, but now was not the time. The Kingdom needed her now more than ever. They needed guidance, a leader. Thorn aided her in standing.

"Now, let us rebuild," she commanded.

Nekora and Thorn walked to the dragon that fell. Upon it was a saddle.

"Dragons can be ridden?" she asked.

"Apparently," Thorn replied. "But where is the rider?" A quick search of the premises resulted in the finding of an elven body. Very pale for an elf, almost white.

"Drow!" the Queen whispered. He was more muscular than Thorn. "They never see daylight, which is why they are so pale, but look at the features. They are very strong. Must take an immense amount of strength to mount a dragon," Nekora stated. She motioned to Poko, who was close by.

"I need our entire research team to go over this dragon. I want to know everything there is to know about them."

"Yes, your highness," Poko replied.

Nekora recollected her memory. "I thought I saw eight pillars, so there may have been eight dragons, minus this one." Nekora turned to face Thorn. "They know where we are." She paused and looked to Thorn. "These dark elves will soon learn that they have dealt with the wrong Kingdom. Thorn, see what you can find from this thing. I need you at the head of the investigation."

"At once, your highness," he replied.

"I will return shortly. I need to gather my thoughts and a plan of action." She turned and headed to the north, staggering to the mage tower.

The mage tower seemed intact. It was a good thing her father insisted they were away from the Kingdom. Inside she immediately met Ghorn, the Kingdoms master mage.

"Ghorn, so good to see you again. It's been a long time."

He replied, "Yes your highness, and I am truly sorry we were late. We had no idea what was going on until Thomas came in out of breath declaring the Kingdom under attack by great beasts."

"That is okay; your fire and lightning scared them off before they could finish their attack. We owe you our lives. For now, I need a favor."

"Anything for you, your highness," he replied.

"Thank you. I need to know all the magics you can do, even the ones being researched. We are going to war, and we desperately need your help."

"As you wish."

"Oh, and Ghorn?" Nekora called.

"Yes, your highness."

"I need to learn those spells as well. I am gifted in the arcane arts after all." Ghorn's eyes were questioning.

"And you hid this talent because you did not want to stay here forever?" Ghorn commented. Nekora's eyes looked down.

"Yes, and we can talk about changes to make life easier for you," Nekora stated, looking at Ghorn. "We will start by allowing the mages in the city at all times, maybe even moving your tower. But we need to set ground rules, which we will talk about later." Ghorn smiled, almost chuckled.

"Of course," Ghorn replied with a smile.

CHAPTER SIX

Baern, Prince of Almaryha, was on night patrol heading to the northern flats on his black dragon. He peered to the southwest and saw smoke rising from the forest floor. "Those pesky humans are at it again. Damn them!" He circled his dragon and headed for the smoke. His night patrol just started, so he had time to check it out. He landed his dragon in a small clearing just south of where the smoke was coming from and dismounted.

"Hunt, my friend, feast then, return here." With that, the dragon made its way to a clearing so it could stretch its wings and lift off. It roared into the air and circled, looking for food. Baern quickly but quietly made his way to the campfire. As he peered into the clearing out of sight, he beheld an elven figure holding a bag in his lap, unconscious from his wounds.

An elf, out here? Is he one of ours? After careful investigation, he realized that he was not a dark elf. A wood elf! His Kingdom must not be far away. He heard a shout.

"Thorn!" It was a female voice. More figures cautiously approached the figure. He counted four but did not want to take any chances and stepped farther back to watch the events unfold. From the looks of it, warriors.

This kind of information would be more valuable to the King. He stepped back and out of sight and earshot. Moments later, his dragon reappeared, and he headed home to report his findings after the elves departed the scene.

Baern was deep in thought during his travels home. So, the wood elves exist. How is it possible we have not seen them in all these years? How well armed and trained are they? Would our warriors have any problems wiping the scum from the face of Aghram? "These are questions I must find the answers to." Before long, he realized he was landing.

The dragon landed at the base of its nest, allowing the prince to disembark at the lower level. After the prince jumped down, the dragon lifted to the raised plateau, did a quick self-cleaning, then roared into the air to hunt again on its normal grounds. As he passed the guardians of the city, the growling Cerberus attempted to attack the intruder until they realized it was the prince. They settled down and cowered; he continued to the castle to approach his father. A smile crossed his evil face.

"Father, we have a problem." He recounted the events leading up to the potential discovery of the wood elves; the King's smile grew ever larger.

"At last, the wretched wood elves have been found. Show me where on this map."

"I can do you one better," Baern replied.

Baern took his father to the exit of the mountain peak and pointed. The smoke was barely visible. It seemed the guards have extinguished the fire to protect their location.

"Ah, that means their Kingdom is somewhere near that area. I want double patrols flying that sector until they are found. I want a full outline of their location by weeks end," the King demanded. "I want them eradicated from existence."

"Yes, Father," the prince replied.

Prince Baern quickly made his way to the guard shack and demanded to see Kith, the head guard.

"Yes, my Prince?" Kith asked.

"The King demands double patrols in the western valley." He took out a map of the valley and pointed to the sector in question. "Report anything resembling a dwelling in this area." Baern circled the western section where he had found the fire in red.

"Yes, sir, I will make that happen starting tonight," Kith replied. The prince turned and walked away. The prince decided to check with the historians while his dragon was hunting and the other guards were patrolling.

"Your highness, what brings the honor of your visit?" inquired Lago.

"I want to know everything you know about the wood elves," demanded the prince.

Lago, the historian, immediately jumped up and searched the clutter for any information on the wood elves.

"We do not know much about them, my Prince. All we know are rumors." He was looking through the back of a shelf when he grabbed a rolled parchment. "Aha, here it is." He brought it back to the table and unrolled it. "Says here that rumors of a new generation of elves known as top-siders, or sun bathers, have made camp somewhere in the land of Aghram. Kingdom unknown, Royalty unknown." He spoke in softer tones, saying, "it says here, last paragraph, that any ruthless violent gesture against them would result in their annihilation. Why would it say that I wonder?"

Baern looked most displeased.

"Is this it? Is this all the information you have?"

Lago thought for a moment. "Hmm, allow me to check another spot. We may have more information." The prince was enraged. He had no time for useless opinions or garble. "Ah, this one was way in the back. It is a log of some sort. Dated two hundred years ago." Lago cleared his throat. "The King is too ruthless. I must depart and find my way elsewhere. I will build a great empire. I will be fair and just and make the elven nation feel safe and content. Prince Bron threatens everyone who gets near him. If he is going to be the next King, I will not be here." It is signed by Prince Kardin.

"Who is this Prince Kardin?" asked Lago.

"I don't know, but my father would. Let me have that sheet." Lago obliged for fear of reprimand. He handed over the parchment and retreated, scared of being punched or even killed.

Baern moved quickly to ask his father about this new-found prince. Since he was part of this movement, there was some information he was either withholding, or forgot. Either way, his father was the key. He quickly moved about, looking to the guards at their station to ensure they were doing their job. He finally arrived at his destination. The King was busy looking through paperwork when Baern stepped in.

"Father," he greeted with urgency.

"What is it, Baern? I am busy and in a foul mood this moment."

The prince cautiously approached as he inquired, "Do you remember Prince Kardin?"

The King slammed the table with his fist and yelled, "What do you want with that garbage?" Baern produced the writing to his father.

"Apparently, he was afraid of you and grandfather. He made the decision to leave two hundred years ago. He may be what we need to find. If we knew where to find him…" The King cut him off.

"He left, and the guards went after him. They lost him to…" the King tapered off and eyes grew wide. He read the rest of the note and whispered, "Could it be?" "Baern, if he is alive, I want him here. He may be the reason the wood elves exist. I want Grogham interrogated again, and Kardin here for treachery."

He could not believe it. No, it could not be true. He looked to his son. "We may be at war with your uncle." How could he survive the surface world? If he has a Kingdom, then others followed suit. The King decided he must remember the events that unfolded that day. It was dark as it always was in Aghram. The dimly lit lanterns gave out just enough light for other creatures since Drow are accustomed to darkness. Their night vision was unrivaled. Bron and Kardin were at the dinner table with their grandfather at the head, stirring up trouble with drinking and women. Grandmother could only look the other way, disgusted that her husband had the audacity to do that in front of her. "So, what shall we toast tonight?" King Furit stated in a drunken slur. The women were giggling and all over him, looking at the Queen to make sure she was still troubled at the sight.

"I know," said one of the wenches. "How about we start a new contest for the troubled? Make an arena for everyone to gather and witness your power?"

"What a grand idea!" Furit stood and demanded an arena be built in the town center. "We will take prisoners and have them fight for their lives!" he said with a great smile.

"With each other? Or with the "dogs?" another maiden asked with laughter.

"That's it! We will have the contestants fight the mighty Cerberus. If they live, they may or may not get a pardon." The King roared with laughter.

"Bron! Start the design on the arena immediately! I want to watch this action in my lifetime!" the King demanded.

"Yes, Father. It will be a glorious moral boost for the citizens," Bron responded as he got up and left the table.

"Kardin! Why are you still here? You will never be as great as your brother if you mope around all day," the King stated. He then took a huge bite of a leg, gave a large, hefty kiss to the maiden's cheek, and smacked the wench's ass. Grandmother was truly annoyed.

She left the table the same time Kardin did and followed him out the door.

"Kardin?" Queen Elsbit called after her son. "Kardin, wait up. We have a lot to talk about, and I will meet you in your bedroom post haste," she stated softly so as not to be overheard and made a left at the corridor corner. Kardin kept walking straight for his room.

Ten minutes later, the Queen arrived. "We must get you out of here, sweetheart. I can see you having issues with your father; believe me, I have a much stronger hatred for that man. I have a plan that will get you out on your own, take some slaves with you, and start anew. Make your own Kingdom, prosper, and be kind to your citizens since they are the ones who will take care of you," she started.

Prince Kardin looked her mom in the eyes. "I hate him, Mom. I hate this place! I hate that you must suffer with his antics. Was it always like this?" Prince Kardin asked.

Elsbit frowned, "No, sweetie. This used to be a prosperous place. Everyone was kind and happy. Your grandfather ruled with fairness and had a kind heart. Your father saw that as weakness and decided that this place needed a ruler, not a babysitter. He killed his three other siblings so he would be the only heir to the throne." Elsbit continued, "There was a time that they all got along."

Prince Kardin sighed. "Why does Father have to be such a monster? Doesn't he see that he is ruining this Kingdom? His marriage? His family?" Tears welled in his eyes, but Kardin was strong. He kept them from falling in front of his mother. He wanted to show her he was strong but had a heart. He was not a monster like his father or brother.

"I know, sweetie. I believe Bron may be planning your demise as we speak, which is why the urgency on getting you out of here. I have gathered a dozen or so slaves to accompany you and get you out. Slaves that I can trust and hate your father as much as we do. Come to think of it, I think everyone would fit that boat.

Either way, these handpicked slaves each have a specific gift that will help in building your empire. We do not know what awaits you outside these caverns; hopefully, nothing bad. I want you safe," she commented.

Kardins tears came down uncontrollably. He could not keep them back anymore. "What about you, Mother? Are you coming with us?"

Elsbit shook her head. "Unfortunately, no. My place is here. My job is to distract your father while you escape unnoticed. Go while you can. Everyone is meeting behind the church after curfew," Elsbit finished.

Kardin got ready and took only what he needed to survive the outside world from what he had heard in stories.

That night, all the slaves promised by his mother were waiting behind the church, each elf itching with anticipation to leave this dreadful place, to run out and be free.

Lights out was ordered. Kardin took the lead as they snuck through the city proper to the outside walls and scaled them.

"Okay, the Cerberus are going to challenge us. Look fierce and stay strong. Show no fear, and they will leave us alone. They discern enemies by smell," Kardin whispered just before scaling down the outside wall. The others followed.

After they all gathered at the bottom, Kardin led them with purpose. He took the front and told the slaves to let him do the talking if anything arises. Off to the north they headed.

Cerberus challenged the group on multiple occasions but backed off. Upon reaching the large, cavernous opening to the north, two Drider guards blocked their path.

"No one leaves the confines of the city proper," one guard stated as he pointed a spear at Kardin.

"Do you really want to challenge the order of the King?" Kardin stated in a demanding tone. "He has ordered that these slaves be executed by Minotaur immediately for conspiring to overthrow the King." As if on cue, the slaves looked down in shame.

"I will have to clear this. No one leaves unless we get word. We have not received any word, so your word is useless!" the guard challenged. Kardin smiled and produced a rolled parchment with the King's seal keeping it together.

"Here are your orders, guard" he stated with authority while handing over the parchment. "How dare you talk to me in that fashion. I am Prince Kardin, son of the King, and you WILL show me some respect." With that, the guard snapped the seal and looked over the papers.

"Very well. You may pass." The guard showed the order to the other. Both Driders stepped away. Kardin and the gang of slaves passed point one.

"Okay, the minotaur lair will be a different story. We will need to traverse the top of the maze if we are to make it out alive." Kardin headed to the right side of the maze and found what he was looking for. Small footholds that would otherwise never have been seen marked the edges to the top of the maze. Each one was careful in where they stepped and made it to the top. Granther helped each individual up the ledge.

"From here, we need to sneak by quickly but silently. We do not want to awaken the Minotaur. They will sound a bell that will alert everyone in Almaryha," Kardin whispered. As fast as it started, the trek was over. They shimmied down the opposite side and made way toward the small pathway leading to the mountain's eastern exit.

Bron woke feeling like something was wrong. He checked on his brother and found an empty bed. He searched the castle to no end. He decided to confront his father. As he entered his parents' room, the King was busy fornicating with the maiden and wench. Oblivious to his surroundings, Bron found it offensive. His treacherous brother had escaped the city, and he was here fornicating.

"Father!" Bron shouted. The shouting startled his father and stopped mid stroke, got out of bed, and pulled up his pants.

"What is the meaning of this outburst!" the King demanded.

"While you are in here indulging in the sexual fantasies of these whores, Kardin is missing," Bron retorted.

The King was furious. "This better not be a joke!" he stated and woke the entire guard to look for him. The King was going to hang him for causing his encounter to be shortened.

The warning bell sounded, and all guards came to the courtyard. The paperwork was hidden from view just in case.

"Where is Kardin?" the King demanded. "He should be here at my side!" he bellowed. The two guards from the gate looked at each other and knew they'd been had.

"We saw him running toward the exit, and we went after him. He had a long head start so we could not catch him. He entered the Minotaur lair. He is dead, your worship."

The guards quickly lied. The King looked at them with fierce anger in his eyes.

"For your sake, he'd better be dead." He scowled. "I want his body right here," the King demanded as he pointed to the front of his feet.

The body was never found. The two guards were slain for incompetence. The Queen smiled internally. She knew he was safe; she felt it. That was all she ever wanted for her son. Bron killed his parents shortly after and took control of the Kingdom. He made the Kingdom believe he was a good person while he always had evil and selfish intentions.

It was at that moment, King Bron realized that his brother must have escaped the city all those years ago. He did very well in hiding, indeed. He turned to his son. "Baern, I want to know all the intelligence on this forsaken island. I want to know what beasts reside where. We are going to have to make alliances if we are going to kill your uncle," Bron stated.

Baern looked quizzically to his father. "Drow with allies? That is unheard of, preposterous."

"Did I say we were going to remain allies you Cerberus dropping?" the King retorted. "They will be dead after they do our bidding."

A servant hiding in the corner overheard the entire conversation. When everyone was gone and it was all clear, he left to tell the others. He, as well as hundreds of others, were tired of living in fear. They had to escape. He went to whom he trusted and whispered everything he overheard. The rumors spread quickly to those who warranted it. They secretly gathered and devised a plan to escape.

"We need to somehow provide a distraction so the guards will be preoccupied. Otherwise, we will not make it out. This may be our only opportunity to leave this horrible place and acquire solace."

"Leave that to me," said an old scrawny dark elf. "I have lived my life. You need to find yours."

"The distraction is covered. If there is any hope to a happy life, we will find it there." The younger slave produced a map as they were in dialog. He unrolled it and pointed to the area of concern. "That area may be their home. We can finally be at peace."

Another elf looked up. "Do you think they will be receptive to a band of dark elves?" one slave mentioned. All of them looked at each other with apprehension. It was a good question and should be further investigated. All of them agreed to keep their ears open, especially since their livelihood was in jeopardy.

"This is the only chance we have. They will either receive us or we die free. Either way, we win." They pondered the options and did not particularly care for the latter. A slumber of looks was discernible, but they knew those were the only options. Or they can die in this terrible place. The slaves disbursed. It was known that any gathering was met with force, so they went their separate ways before they were caught. Now they just needed the time. The meeting place was established.

Throughout the next few days, a plan had formed and came together. Soon, hundreds of dark elves had something they never had in their lifetime—hope.

Two more days passed. Prince Baern had finally found the hidden Kingdom of Morhgrammir. Plans were in place to attack immediately, to finally rid the land of their filth. They were an embarrassment to the elven name. All day, the King and his advisors were up organizing the attack.

"Sire, what if we hit them with a couple dragons, do a couple flybys burning them to the ground?" The King looked at him and shook his head.

"No, I want every available dragon ready. We will take them by surprise. Tomorrow night, there will be complete cloud coverage. They will not see us coming." After the deliberations, the meeting was concluded.

The attack will happen tomorrow night. Prince Baern smiled a deep smile, "Finally, something worth flying for," he said aloud so the King would hear.

The next morning, Baern held a briefing. The world map was on the wall with a large-scale map of Aghram. An X depicted where the Kingdom resides.

"Here," Baern pointed, "is where those wretched scum have made their Kingdom. They have plagued this land for far too long, and it is time we seek restitution for their crimes." The dragon riders were all smiling. It was finally time to witness the destruction a dragon can produce.

Prince Baern continued, "Two hundred years ago, my uncle escaped with a multitude of slaves into the open forest. They have made their camps and grew their Kingdom illegally. Population and size are unknown so we will start here." The prince pointed slightly south of where the Kingdom was found.

"Their Kingdom resides below the dense forest, which is why we have never found them before. They have let their guard down, and we now have their location. Yes, the wood elves are real, and they will be annihilated tonight under the cover of the dark clouds." The prince looked at the map once again, then back to the riders.

"We will go in at a hundred feet so they cannot hear the flapping of the wings. The dragons will let loose their fire along the route here, here, and here." Baern pointed to three different spots and swiped up, covering as much land as they could. "No one alters the course unless directed by me, is that understood?" Baern stated more than asked.

"Yes, sir," was the only reply.

The prince finished up the briefing, "The outcome of their judgment has been ordained as death by the King. We will need all eight dragons on this one since we do not have an accurate size of their territory. It could be the whole damned forest.

Now, get some rest for the nights attacks."

All the riders disbursed to their quarters to get some sleep. Some were antsy, including the new rider Tragu. He had very little experience but showed promise. Nightfall soon arrived. The clouds were dark and seemed on the verge of thunderstorms.

"Should we wait until it is a little clearer, sir?" questioned Chelan. "What if lightning strikes our dragons?" he inquired.

"What if I slam my scimitar across your neck, Chelan?" Baern retorted. Chelan immediately backed down and readied his dragon for flight and combat.

All the dragon riders were readying their mounts for the night's mission. Each rider prepares their dragon in the nest prior to launching to their meeting point on top of the ridge. They knew exactly where the attack would happen after yesterday's successful reconnaissance flight. Eight dragons in all, ready to combat the wretched wood elves.

"Sir, we are ready. Any other directions prior to flight?" asked Gainly, second in command to the dragon knights.

"No, do exactly as we have planned."

Ominous clouds were over head as predicted. A perfect attack and run scenario. All eight dragons and their riders met at the top of the mountain, finalizing plans, ensuring everyone knew their orders. Once they were complete, they took off into the night air. It was chilly, and the adrenaline of overrunning a Kingdom washed that sense away. Everyone was ambitious for the new mission.

As they neared the location, they heard music. Prince Baern smiled, your festivities have just given away your position and sealed your fate. Time to die, wretched scum. Each dragon took position. Chelan was lower than what they briefed and knew the elves would hear them. Prince Baern yelled at him for his stupidity and would aptly punish him when they returned. An arrow of fire went up, narrowly missing Chelan. The time to attack was now. A gong was heard. They were spotted.

"Fire!" Baern screamed. The eight dragons released their fire breath in unison, raining into the Kingdom. Elves were running around on fire, buildings burning and collapsing, all put a big smile on the prince's face. A barrage of arrows went up, bouncing off the prince's dragon. His dragon roared a triumphant roar. He smiled even bigger, enjoying every minute of torment.

"I hope you enjoy the last seconds of your miserable lives." The prince laughed. A scream caught the prince's attention as Tragu, the least experienced dragon rider, was hit with a barrage of exploding fireballs and lightning. His dragon went down immediately.

"Mages! when did they get mages? Back to the cavern, now!" the prince commanded.

The dragons immediately and willingly obliged after seeing the demise of one of their own. Before long, all dragons disappeared.

After they landed, they walked back to the Kingdom in silence. We lost one of our own; the mages will pay for this. But how do you defeat mages? Myriad thoughts raced through the prince's mind as he made his way back to the Kingdom.

"Father, we were mostly victorious," the prince commented.

"WHAT! What do you mean mostly?" The King slapped his son across the face. "I do not tolerate failure!"

"The Kingdom is protected by mages, a bit of missing intelligence, I would say. However, we burned down their Kingdom, but the mages came out of nowhere and killed one of our dragons in one barrage." The King was not happy at all.

"Anything else I need to know?" the King demanded.

"Yes, sir. Chelan came in low, giving away our presence before we could set up and strike as planned. He will be punished for his stupidity".

"Is that so?" The King looked at Chelan, who bowed but trembled in fear. The King raised his crossbow and fired. The bolt impacted Chelan through the top of his head and into his throat, killing him on the spot. "Consider him punished," stated the King as he reloaded and put his crossbow away.

"Feed him to the Cerberus!' the king yelled. "If anyone else decides they want to make their own rules, say so now!" he threatened as he reached for the crossbow grip.

"Let that be a lesson to those who do not follow orders around here. You think I make orders for fun? This is what happens! If any are alive, they will take years to rebuild. Since they have no idea where we are, we can train harder. DO NOT fail me again! Where are my advisers? I want to know why they did not warn us of these mages!" the King yelled.

"Yes father." The King looked at them "Dismissed!" The prince hopped on his dragon and flew to the top of the mountain, watching the massive fires burn in the distance.

Now, where did your mages come from. I will make this my life goal to find and destroy all of you.

Grogham heard footsteps coming down the stairs. The shackles on his wrists were the only thing holding him up. His legs were too weak to stand on his own. The King entered the dungeon.

"Grogham, I have great news for you. We have found and destroyed your Kingdom. Isn't that great?" Grogham looked up weakly.

"And how is this great news?" he asked in a rasping voice.

"Why, we have need of another dragon rider," the King responded as he threw a grape into his mouth. "Since you have no home, you can now join us. Being that you are a prince, I will offer this to you once. Or you can rot in this dungeon. Quite frankly, I am surprised you are still alive," the King mentioned as he wiped the grime from Groghams shackles.

With that, the King started walking out. Before he exited the dungeon, he turned to Grogham. "Your choice, of course." The King departed with an evil grin. "Beat him to an inch of his life, but do not kill him," he whispered to the jailer. "We may need him yet."

King Bron figured the prince would not take him up on his offer. Giving him an offer would made him look good to his people, and he would not be lying for extending the invitation. A gruesome fight will be just the moral lifting event this city needed. He started practicing his speech on the way back to the main entryway, whispering as he walked the hallway.

"Ladies and gentlemen, we have an exciting event for you today. A prince from the outer city has come by to sabotage our beloved city. We have captured him before he could accomplish his treacherous intentions. But, with the grace of my heart, I have offered a place in my military to give him a second chance at life. He violently refused and thus has been chosen for extermination. We will see how he fares during this extraordinary battle against our beloved Cerberus," he recited softly. Pleased with his ad-hoc speech, he smiled and continued his merry way.

Grogham dropped his head, tears welling inside.

What can I do? What should I do? Join and be strong, or sit here weak and dying? Did my family survive, or did they truly perish? The stress was too much for Grogham to bear. The jailer was smiling as he entered his cell. Grogham welcomed his imminent death.

Almaryha was alight with celebration with the victory over Morhgrammir. With them out of the way, the elves of Almaryha remain the dominant force. King Bron surveyed his minions, as he thought of them. It gave him a sense of power. Queen Kardya was just as cruel. She reveled in the suffering of others. Prince Baern at their side watching, ready to punish anyone who got out of line. That happened a lot in this Kingdom, but force kept them at bay.

"What's the next plan, Father?" the prince inquired.

"We shall interrogate this Grogham for the whereabouts of the mages. If he cooperates, we will keep him alive a little longer. If he does not, then he will face off with the Cerberus in the arena." The king laughed at his idea since he knew the prince's answer already. It helped further the validity of his speech.

The prince interjected, "What about sending him to the Cerberus with or without cooperation? He is eating our food."

The king brought his finger and thumb to his chin. "Good point. We will stop feeding him."

King Bron was already ahead of his son. His plan could not flow any smoother.

CHAPTER SEVEN

Queen Nekora looked to the eastern mountains. After consoling with Thorn, they narrowed the location of the entrance to the tallest peak. At least seven dragons, and an entire Kingdom of dark elves, the widest base and highest peak seemed the ideal location. She talked with her advisers and concluded that a scout and eight warriors would check out the area and attempt to find the entrance and the city and map every detail down to the residential creatures and bring back detailed information.

No fighting was allowed unless it was self-defense or protection of the scout. She browsed the history books at the mage tower, she talked with other military elves who scouted to the east, and none of them mentioned an entrance of any sort. The only clue is in the story Thorn just heard from his father. These are desperate and frustrating times now.

The Kingdom is in the process of rebuilding; fortifications receiving upgrades with help from the mages. She went through the spells and alchemy they had completed or were still in research. Queen Nekora ordered hundreds of healing potions from the mages. She even kept her training up to stay sharp and focused. She also aided in training. She wanted the strongest, sharpest, most lethal army in the land. After that night, she had to be prepared for a pending re-attack.

Their army was down by ten percent, not bad considering what they just went through. All in all, a plan was slowly forming. She just needed time and sleep. Running a Kingdom was much harder than she thought. She missed her parents badly, but knew they were watching over her.

Thorn came in tired. He was up just as much as Nekora, helping her plan, train the units, and keeping up morale. He was beat. Queen Nekora told him to get some sleep; she needed him fresh and alert.

"I will if you do, your highness," he responded. Nekora thought about it. He was right. They both needed rest. Thorn walked the Queen to her room.

"Sweet dreams, your highness. See you in the morning," Thorn said as he turned to walk to his room.

Nekora called to him. "Thorn, would you stay with me? I can use the company right now." Thorn stopped and turned to face Nekora, standing by her bed. She slowly removed her shirt and pants to bare her perfect body. Thorn smiled as he willed for this day for a long time. He shut the door and went to her; both laid on the bed. They looked deeply into each other's eyes. Thorn brushed the hair from Nekora's cheek. They went into a long passionate kiss.

Thorn took off his clothes to match Nekora's outfit. His hand slid down her arms with his nails barely touching her skin. The feeling gave her goosebumps as she longed for his embrace. He slowly went back up her arm and to her chest, where he thumbed her nipple, causing her to be aroused. Her body moved with erotic desire. They were still kissing; he moved to her cheek then down to her neck. Softly kissing her skin and caressing her chest with tender love.

She moved her arm down his chest, farther down, and stroked him gently, causing him to squirm with delight. His arm gently caressed her stomach. His mind was racing at how magnificently smooth and hard her body was. He reached down and rubbed her inner thigh until she was ready.

Thorn rolled on top of her and slowly made love to her. Both were in a deep trance as they passionately looked into each other's eyes.

"I love you, Nekora," Thorn softly spoke.

"I love you to, Thorn," she replied as her eyes rolled back and she arched back.

The lovemaking lasted for an hour. Both Thorn and Nekora were not only exhausted from their love but from the day's events as well. They quickly fell asleep in each other's arms, a smile on their faces.

The next morning came quickly, and both Nekora and Thorn felt refreshed. They were more than content and smiling. A quick bath refreshed their spirits and aptly woke them.

Life was finally turning for the best, Thorn thought as looked upon Nekora. He still had the fresh memory of her silky-smooth body, and how she felt during sex was heavenly. He was very much in love with her and would die protecting her.

They both got out of the bath and dressed for the new day of rebuilding. Nekora had fresh ideas about the city and embarking on the path to repay the Drow in kind. After dressing, they kissed and walked down the hall together.

Nekora turned to Thorn before they entered the great room. Ashes still littered about but was mostly clean with fresh wood nearby, ready to be used in the rebuilding of the walls. She looked at Thorn with pure love and asked him a question.

"Thorn, every Kingdom needs a King as well as a Queen. In this time of sorrow and grief, the Kingdom needs to be rebuilt and governed," she paused a moment, "probably not the best time to bring it up…"

Thorn took Nekora's cheeks into his hands and looked into her eyes passionately.

"If you are going to ask me to marry you, I would be elated and want nothing more. I just want to be with you. You are all I have ever wanted in life. I know it sounds cheesy and not because you are a Queen now…"

Nekora took a step back with a surprised look. "You thought I was going to ask you to marry me? Are you mad? No! I wanted you to find a suitable King for me," she said with disgust.

Thorn was confused, embarrassed, and ready to commit suicide. Nekora, receiving the response she was looking for, slugged him hard on the shoulder.

"I was kidding. Yes, I want you to be the King." Nekora was laughing now and reached in to kiss him. "This Kingdom needs you. I need you," she continued as she looked upon him with seriousness. Thorn sighed a huge relief. He was breathing now as if he had just run a marathon. His heart shattered into a million pieces, and he was waiting for it to come back together. His brain was finally able to process again.

"Damn, Nekora, you scared the shit out of me!" he exclaimed.

"I thought you were used to that after all these years," Nekora replied innocently.

Thorn bent over with his hands on his knees and concentrated on his breathing again. Nekora watched him and laughed.

"I guess I got you good on that one." She continued laughing. Once they were stable again, they walked up to the mighty doors that signify the entrance to the great room.

At least they were in good spirits, and they had each other. They had one final kiss before entering.

"Shall we get married before or after the raid?" Thorn inquired as they stepped through the entryway.

"After, just in case you don't make it," Nekora chided.

Lord Granther greeted them at the podium. He was in deep sorrow for the loss of his friend, the King. Too many lives were lost that day, and it brought memories back that he had subdued all those years ago. With all the grief, he managed a smile to the Queen of Morhgrammir, a woman he always treated as a daughter out of respect to his friend for all he has done for him.

The villagers all gathered around for the prayer of the fallen. Every corpse was laid to rest and prayed upon individually. The King and Queen were buried in a tomb specially designed by Queen Nekora. She insisted they get recognition for the hard work and dedication they put forth in the Kingdom. The tomb was erected in the courtyard behind the castle. In the market square, all villagers were in attendance. Nekora stepped forward.

"Elves of Morhgrammir. We are here today to pay respect for the fallen. It is my duty to remind all of you, the hard work and dedication of King Kardin and Queen Arilana, my parents, that built and harnessed this Kingdom to where we were before the attack. We were harmonious and peaceful. I will do my very best to ensure we remain that way. But this is not just about my parents; it is about all the loved ones we have lost during the attack, and all of you sacrificing your time to recreate this great Kingdom better than it was before. Let us pay homage. Let us remember them for who they were—loyal, honest, friendly elves. They have touched our hearts in different ways. Let us make a grand comeback celebration honoring every elf that had given their lives to protect this Kingdom."

The Queen continued, "The unwarranted attack on our Kingdom will not go unpunished. Plans are in the works to repay the dark elves in kind." The audience was quiet.

Nekora paused for a moment to gather her thoughts, then continued, "We, as a population of warriors past, present, and future, will grow stronger. We pulled out of the ashes, and now we will show our enemy that they have trifled with the wrong elves. Please give a moment of silence as we honor our fallen." The Kingdom was quiet. Each elf lowered their heads praying to the dead, asking the gods for the dead to be protected, and to watch over the Kingdom. Once they concluded, every elf was wrought with renewed energy and continued to rebuild.

Days later, no imminent threat was discernible. Guards were watching the eastern territory for any sign of impending re-attack. The Kingdom was weeks away from being rebuilt. With the buildings separated as they were, most of the structures remained intact. The elves worked quickly. She spotted Thomas and approached him.

"Thomas, would it be possible to put up some sort of magical barrier to surround the Kingdom?"

"I don't know, your highness, we never even thought about it. I will check with the master mages and see what we can do."

Nekora smiled. "That is all I can ask. Thank you."

Thomas bowed and headed for the tower. Most of the mages were in the village; the masters were in the tower researching spells Nekora had asked for.

"Your highness!" It was Thorn calling to Nekora as he approached. He had to be respectful in the company of the villagers.

"Any news from the scouts we sent?" Nekora asked.

Thorn replied, "No, but it takes about a week's travel just to get there. The cliff's side is steep and treacherous. Not to mention the cyclops that inhabit the area. If they encounter no resistance, they should be back short of three weeks. That is including about a week of investigating the mountainside. It is a lot larger than it looks from here."

Thorn remembered his trials and touched his head without noticing. The long trek to and from the mountains. The battle. Nekora looked saddened. She could not imagine what he went through. But right now, his expertise is the best knowledge they have so far. She made him write about the valley and mountains after his return, so they had records.

Thomas returned later in the day after conversing with the master mages. Thomas ran to the mage towers. Tired of being so far north. At least it kept him in shape. He entered the tower in search of Ghorn.

"Master Ghorn?" Thomas called out.

"In the study," was Ghorn's reply.

Thomas made way to the study and found Master Ghorn with a stockpile of scrolls at his desk as he unrolled each one. He also had a dragon scale mounted in a holder with a bow and arrow propped up.

"What is it, young Thomas?" Ghorn asked as he hastily went through the ancient writings.

"The Queen has asked if there was a way to put a barrier up around the Kingdom," he replied.

"I figure there would be, give me a second," Ghorn trailed off as he was reading through the scroll. "Grab that bow and arrow and stand right here." Ghorn pointed to a fixed spot twenty feet from the large scale. "I want you to fire that arrow at the scale."

Thomas did as he was told. He fired the arrow, which bounced harmlessly from it.

"Just as I thought," Ghorn stated.

"He grabbed the arrow and made a magical enchantment causing the arrow to levitate. Orange, red, and yellow magical fields surrounded the arrow, spinning it in all directions. The arrow came to rest back on the desk. It was straighter than normal and more solid.

"Try it again," instructed Ghorn.

This time, Thomas fired, and the arrow stuck to the scale, protruding one inch from the backside.

"Hmm, as expected. The bows our army are wielding are much to soft. This arrow is magically hardened and straighter than our normal arrows, so it is not the arrow. The bows need more power," Ghorn explained. We need Nekora's bow to make certain. We need to test the theory since she has the strongest bow in our Kingdom.

"She does not let anyone near her bow; it is the only thing no one is allowed to touch," Thomas explained. He helped her make that bow so he knew the power and secrecy behind it. Even the master mage did not know.

"Then please tell her to bring it so she can fire it at the scale. We need to test this theory," Ghorn replied.

"Yes, sir," Thomas replied as he headed off to find Nekora.

Thomas found her walking through the central market. He quickly caught up with her. "Your highness, it may be possible to protect this Kingdom, but they ask for your audience." Nekora nodded.

"Tell them I will be there shortly. I have another task that needs overseeing."

"Yes, your highness. Master Ghorn requests you bring your bow for a test," Thomas replied as he bowed and ran off to the north. Nekora continued to the training grounds and searched for Poko. He was quickly found talking to the units when she approached.

"Sergeant Poko," she called. He came running and bowed low.

"Yes, your highness," he said as he stood upright once again.

"I need a chain of command. You are the best warrior out here that I know. You are now hereby granted the rank of lieutenant. It will be your responsibility to ensure we have the best garrison in the land. Since you know the expertise level, it will be your duty to assign duties and ranks to those whom you think is qualified. I also want documentation outlining the structure and have each elf aligned with their expertise. How many warriors do we have now?"

Lieutenant Poko thought for a moment. "We have about three hundred fifty, your highness. Sixty being expert archers."

"Good, for now I want three units. Split the archers evenly. I need one unit especially strong. They will be our special tactics unit, or elite guard. The rotation will be one day aiding the village, one full complete day of training, and one day of rest with guard rotations from the resting unit. I will help oversee the training as I will need them soon." Poko thought about it and smiled.

"A most impressive thought, your highness. I will see to it immediately."

Nekora smiled, thanked him, then continued, "I also need the archers as strong as the warriors. There is going to be some drastic changes and I need them ready soonest."

She continued toward the courtyard to find Thorn. She needed him to oversee the strength training as well as learning how the Kingdom works together so he has a better understanding.

"Thorn, I have an urgent matter needing my attention. You need to come with me so you will understand. I need my bow first." The encrypted yet vague command left him confused, but he obliged. She led him to the north, toward the mage towers after they stopped and grabbed her bow and quiver of arrows.

During their walk, Nekora chatted with Thorn. "I need you to oversee the strength training of the archers. You are the strongest elf here, and I need you to get them where you are."

Thorn responded, "Yes, ma'am." Nekora hit him for his mockery.

Upon arrival at the mage tower, Thomas was waiting for them at the entrance. He spied them coming up the road and wanted to greet them personally.

"He looked Thorn up and down. Nekora told him he was with her and that he needed to understand how the mages intertwine with the Kingdom. Thomas smiled and led them in the tower.

"Nek, I already know about the mages."

She smiled. "Yes, but do you understand their entire roll in the Kingdom?"

Thorn thought about it. "I guess not."

They passed a multitude of beakers, fire pits, scrolls, books, and unidentifiable objects. Thorn was impressed. He had no idea what they did, and this really surprised him. Ghorn, the master mage, was up ahead with scrolls laid about on the desk in front of him.

"Your highness, I am pleased to make your acquaintance."

Nekora replied, "Master Ghorn, good to see you again my old friend. What news do you have for me?"

"We have analyzed the dragon. The scales are too thick for mundane arrows to pierce. That is why your archers were unsuccessful in bringing them down. The teeth are so sharp it would chomp an Orc in half like a sword through warm butter."

Nekora looked jumbled. "Orcs? What are Orcs?"

Ghorn explained as he passed a detailed drawing to Nekora.

"Orcs are humanoid creatures with a large muscular body mass. Tusks grow from their jaws like oversized teeth. They usually have one to four tusks depending on their genetics. Each one is different according to our scouts. They reside outside the mountain range to the south and are extremely dangerous. Their diet consists of unclean water and meat, which has caused their skin to have a greenish hue. The depth of hue varies individually. They have no regard for any life but their own. The humans have been at war with them for years."

Nekora had a surprised look on her face. "What do you mean scouts? Did my father secretly send you guys out to spy on the land? Why wasn't I told?"

"No, your highness. We are inquisitive and would prefer to know about our enemies. We send our own out into the lands and report what they see. Like your trials. How do you think your father knew about all the creatures in the land? He most likely kept you in the dark so it would not scare you. Since they do not leave the confines of their area, they pose no threat to this Kingdom. Your Kingdom now." Ghorn smiled.

This was all new to Nekora; she was fascinated now and even more curious about what is out there beyond their lands. Ghorn continued as he pulled out an arrow, "A well placed shot here." He drew the wings where they connected to the body of the dragon as he spoke. He pointed to the joint connecting the wing of the dragon to the body. "Will ground the dragon making them prey to soldiers on the ground. Make no mistake, from what we understand, they are just as ferocious on the ground as they are in the air. But it will give you a better advantage in defeating them with more elves to combat the creature. Now for the bad news," Ghorn continued.

Nekora looked shocked. "You mean the news gets worse?" she interrupted.

"Yes, the soft spot is in the mouth. From there, it appears the brain is unprotected. That is how you can kill them." Ghorn took the arrow and showed a rough angle and impact point for the arrow to penetrate the brain.

Thorn stepped in this time. "Or with magic, right? How are we supposed to hit the inside of the mouth with sword or arrow?"

Ghorn looked at Thorn. "This is what we have from the short time in our research. We are diligently working as hard and as fast as we can to find answers but thought we would update you on our progress," Ghorn finished.

Ghorn looked to Nekora. "Thomas told me you tested a vial for us. You called it a healing potion? How did it work? Who did you test it on?"

Nekora was embarrassed. Thorn angrily spun around to look at Nekora; she would not look back.

"And you were going to tell me..." demanded Thorn.

She recounted the tale and apologized to Thorn. He was not supposed to know. Ghorn recognized the tension and quickly changed the subject.

"This arrow is streamlined and specifically designed to puncture the dragon scales. But there is still a problem."

Ghorn produced a scale they removed from the dragon with an arrow stuck through it. He continued, "As you can see, it will only penetrate this much at close range."

The arrow protruding from the scale had, in fact, gone through, but only an inch came out the other side.

"So, we need stronger bows?" inquired Nekora, understanding and had a plan in place to rectify that shortcoming. She touched hers.

"Yes, but the amount of strength needed is greater than your strongest archer. Your archers need more strength; they are too frail. One of your warriors may be able to succeed." Ghorn looked to Thorn. Nekora thought about it.

"Okay, I can fix that. I have a plan in place already to overcome that barrier," she stated.

"Good, now, may I ask you to shoot this particular arrow at this scale?" Ghorn asked as he removed the arrow from the scale with moderate difficulty.

"Certainly," responded Nekora.

Ghorn set up the scale on the mount and handed the arrow to her. She asked everyone to stand back so she could concentrate. Actually, it was so they would not hear her incantation. She muttered her words softly, aimed, and fired. The arrow went through the scale and sunk deeply into the solid wood on the farthest wall.

Ghorn could not pull it out. Thorn could not remove the arrow. The test was a success. It was a shock to see what her bow could do, but a success, nonetheless.

Nekora saw the results with her own eyes. She was flabbergasted at the outcome of the test. She knew her bow was special but not like this. Thorn commented that they need bows exactly like Nekora's. She slipped the bow over her head so it hung along her side.

"That's exactly what we need!" Thorn said excitedly. Nekora did not say a word. She was caught between making something stronger or telling them the truth. The truth would prove she had been cheating, so she has opted to go with the former and make stronger bows.

Ghorn continued, "Here are some potions I believe will prove useful. This one," he picked up a red tainted bottle, "will explode on impact if thrown or dropped. It is very dangerous. This one," a white tainted bottle, "will produce a light so bright, you will be blind for a couple minutes. This one I am sure you are familiar with." He picked up a black bottle.

Nekora looked at Ghorn and took the red bottle. "Ghorn, would it be possible to mount this exploding liquid on arrow heads without premature explosions?"

Ghorn did not even realize it. Yes, it was so simple. He produced a huge smile.

"Yes, yes, of course. We just have to work on the stability of the liquid."

Nekora asked, "So how many can be made and how fast can it be done?"

Ghorn thought about it. "We can make five hundred in a month, but we need certain ingredients that grow far from this valley."

"Good, get it done quickly please. After this is all over, we will talk about some much-needed changes as promised. Thank you, Ghorn."

Nekora and Thorn departed the tower.

Thorn took Nekora by the shoulder and spun her around. "You used an unproven potion on me? What if it killed me? How can I trust you anymore?" Thorn was irate. Nekora forcefully removed his hands from her shoulders.

"I did what I had to do! The healers were failing! You were dying! Using that potion was a last-minute decision that was not taken lightly, and I was desperate. I could NOT sit there and watch you die. Making you the test subject killed me, but I had no other choice! Besides, you're still alive, aren't you?" she yelled and stormed off. Thorn was again belittled.

"I'm sorry, Nek!" he yelled, trying to catch up to her. He felt bad for exploding without first reasoning.

Nekora made straight for the blacksmith. "Duma!" she called. Duma was a burly elf, muscles ripping from all the metalworking. He was clean shaven but covered in ash and soot.

"Yes, your highness," he replied.

"I need a favor, and I am going to ask the unthinkable of you. I need harder metal. And a resupply of scimitars. Can you make this happen?"

Duma pondered the question. "The only metal harder than what we have is steel, but it is very heavy and would make the scimitars more difficult to wield. We do not have access to steel. We would have to steal it from the humans."

"Okay, I need you to make the best possible scimitars you can with what we've got, but they need to be solid. Ones that aren't as brittle as to be broken from a swat of a cyclops."

Jangir was walking by when he overheard the conversation. "Your highness, my name is Jangir. I am the head alchemist at the mage tower, and I believe I can help."

Nekora smiled. After a brief description, the blacksmith and alchemist came up with a solid plan to produce deadlier scimitars.

"We have concocted a polymer that when added to a metal at specific periods and pressure will bond and contract the metal, making it denser. This would strengthen the metal to be much harder than the current iron we are using now. However, the process will need a Mithril alloy, which is rare in these parts to make the metal tougher than steel yet remain as light as or lighter than the current scimitars now. Iron is far too brittle as we have discovered. I have a Mithril shipment coming in tomorrow, actually."

"That is indeed great news!" Nekora responded. "We will need enough Mithril to arm our warriors."

"When I placed the order, I foresaw that, so I took the liberty of obtaining enough Mithril for testing and arming. I was on my way to find you to let you know about our discovery. Good thing I found you here since we will need the talents of our most excellent blacksmith. Give us a week to test out the mix ratio, and we will get moving on the blades as soon as possible," Jangir finished.

The process was a lengthy one as everything needed to be in exact proportions. Dwarven Adamantine would be the best, but they are not found on this land. They could only be reached by boat, which adds too much time to their clock. Plus, the additional weight would make the weapons unwieldy except for the mightiest of warriors.

The new scimitars would be able to cut through armor with ease. The old ones would be used in training. The Mithril blades would be awarded upon graduation from training. Additional magical enchantments allow the wielder to easily swing the blade in every direction with zero effort, making them feel lighter than air. The edge will always remain razor sharp adding vorpal to the mix and never dull thanks to a magical enchantment discovered by the mages. Cost was the problem but was settled prior to Nekora departing the blacksmith. Everything was coming together.

Thorn made for the bowyer when Nekora departed for the blacksmith and inquired about stronger bows. The master archer replied by saying the bows they make are tailored to the individual and their strengths. Thorn was adamant about the stronger bows. He would work with the archers personally.

"If we had metallic threads we can interweave into the fibers of the yew, we can control the strength required to pull the bow back, making them stronger and faster," the master archer stated.

"We need to at least reach seventy to eighty pounds of pull on the strings," Thorn responded. "This is mandated by the Queen. The archers are going through rigorous training as we speak and need these as soon as you can get them," Thorn finished.

"The strongest bow in this Kingdom is Queen Nekora's. I do not know who made hers, but the arrows coming from her bow are straight and smooth. If we can get who made her bow, we can make similar ones which will increase the accuracy in any archer," the master bowman responded.

Thorn did not realize it until now. Her arrows do fly straight and fast. She does have a powerful bow, and he made a mental note to ask her about it later. He desired a similar bow; his was weak but workable.

Another deal struck. The alchemist was going to work with the blacksmith to make the perfect scimitars, the bowyer is going to fashion the strongest bows they can make, and the mages are looking into fashioning exploding arrows and magical barriers.

Nekora headed for her room, exhausted from the day's work. Her thoughts were going from one place to another, now to wait to hear from the scouting party.

CHAPTER EIGHT

The scouting party departed early. They wanted to get a good head start and scour the area for an entrance to the famed city of Almaryha. The scout would skip ahead of the sentry to find a path. He was silent and fast, yet fragile. The lighter the scout, the more silent the travel. The first day proved uneventful.

At night, the scout would check his surroundings to ensure there was no threat so the group could make camp and rest for the night. The next morning, they packed up and continued their mission. It was about midafternoon when the guards heard a call for help from the scout. They rushed to the scene, following the cry. They found the scout wrapped in a net with a Gnoll holding it.

"Drop him!" yelled the first guard.

"Ah, more food. We will be eating good tonight." The Gnoll dropped the net just as four arrows landed hitting their mark—one in the head, one in the neck, and two in the center of its chest. The Gnoll could not react fast enough and dropped to the ground quickly. The scout was thankful.

"I had no idea they were that fast."

The lead guard mocked, "I thought you scouts were silent?"

The scout peered at him. "Have you ever thought of smell? As he sniffed by the guard." Laughter erupted from the rest of the party as they kept moving.

"I guess the jokes on you," the guard mocked. The rest of the party laughed harder at the jest.

No more incidents occurred. They made the cliffs edge in five days. They had found the large cyclops Thorn was talking about still in place. The beast was immense, and they were shocked that Thorn was successful at all. The amount of stench from the giant cyclops was overwhelming. The rotted flesh was almost gone from critters, but it still smelled vile. The story he told left him no justice.

They made it to the base of the mountain, and looking up the cliff, the entire party sighed.

Two of them gag laughed. "Yep, just like old times." They started their ascent up the cliff. As they progressed, they noticed semi fresh tracks.

"This must be where Thorn climbed. According to his story, there should be a rest spot halfway up," the scout commented. Sure enough, the ledge was there, but there was only room two elves. Another ledge was seen to their left; it looked larger so the other three made way to that spot. After fifteen minutes of agonizing side swiping, the three made it. There was enough room for ten elves, so they made themselves comfortable. Some dark spots were seen near the edge where blood had dried.

The guard looking at the spot said, "I guess this is where Thorn landed," as all three looked up, amazed that he even survived the fall.

"From this day forth, this ledge shall be called, wait for it, Thorn's Landing," the scout joked, making quotations with his hands. They all laughed then threatened to throw him over the ledge.

After a few hours of rest, they continued their trek up the cliff. Upon reaching the ledge at the top, a strong aroma of death filled their nostrils. One quick heave to the top and a quick heave to relieve themselves of their consumed rations. The half-eaten bodies of cyclops were seen with two Griffins.

"Yep, Thorn was here." They laughed and covered their faces to hide the stench.

As they surveyed, north was the route they agreed on since the next mountain was taller than the others. They made their way quickly to get away from the overwhelming stench. Night fell, no cyclops or Griffins to be seen or heard. They made a quick camp with no fires lest they give away their position. Now was the time to be extra cautious. The watch was set up, so each had an equal turn. It was around nightfall when flapping was heard. The scout, having the first watch, woke the guards. They sat still and observed. Nothing could be seen, but the flapping was loud. After what seemed like an eternity, nothing else happened. The watch and rest resumed.

The next morning, they made the next base of the mountain. They were in awe with how tall the mountain really was. They gathered around to decide.

The scout asked, "So, do we start at the base and work our way up in hopes of finding the entrance?"

The lead guard asked, "What about the top? Wouldn't you think the top would have an entrance?" The other guards pondered when one of the other guards countered.

"What about that section? If you look closely, you can see a small ledge and what appears to be a not so well traveled trail." Everyone looked to where he was pointing. The scout was the one who broke the silence.

"Sounds like a good starting point. I will go check it out; keep me covered."

"We always do," laughed the lead guard. The other seven joined in his laughter.

"Ha, ha, funny," was the scouts only reply. He made his way to the foliage-covered hidden trail and started upward. The trek was not easy. Loose gravel gave way, causing him to almost roll back down the mountain. He was at the ledge in about an hour surveying the area. There was no entrance. The scout scanned and surveyed the entire area inch by demanding inch.

Nothing. The scout went to pick up a rock and throw it out of rage, but his hand passed through the rock. There it was, the entrance, an illusion placed to camouflage it and hidden so well that he would have easily missed it. He made notes and headed back down the trail.

"Okay, so the entrance is definitely there. It is small and well hidden by an illusion spell. I almost missed it."

The lead guard pondered, "If it is that small, then we need a single file march.

I will be in the lead, you second, then Krit, followed by you and Jamis in the rear." Krit was the scout and Jamis, second in command.

Leron, the lead guard continued, "If anything should happen, take up staircase firing positions. Krit, you take cover, get as low as you can so we can do our job. Remember, our job is to locate the city, then return and report. Everyone understand?"

They replied, "Yes, sir!" Off they went to the entrance.

The climb to the ledge was just as Krit remembered. He wondered how the guards were doing with all their gear. A quick peek back showed they were keeping up just fine. "Maybe the extra weight helps?" he thought. They got to the ledge unscathed. All of them took a moment to view their surroundings. The foliage was dense, and they could barely see the human Kingdom off in the distance. It was a beautiful scene to take in.

"Okay, guys, let's roll," Leron commanded. The tunnel from the entrance was small. One elf nearly fits in a one-by-one march. After about two hundred feet, the tunnels opened a little wider. They could finally breathe a little. The tunnel wound around in a downward direction for close to an hour.

"Keep a lookout for any rest areas, we may need to backtrack," Leron whispered.

Only one fitting to the left was seen just prior to their entering a large cavern. Krit was busy drawing his pathway and making notes, not realizing the front guards have stopped and bumped into them.

"Sorry," he whispered.

The tunnel opened into a massive cavern, and the ledge was large enough to allow all of them to spread out and survey the area.

"Krit, check out the opening we passed," Leron whispered.

Krit was busy sketching what he could see of the maze and did not hear him. Leron tapped him on the shoulder.

"Sorry, what?" said Krit.

"Check out the opening we passed a couple minutes ago," Leron repeated.

"I am trying to sketch the maze. We may need it to get through; send a guard," Krit retorted. Sighing, Leron told the youngest guard to check out the opening, which he obliged.

Darin, the youngest guard, did as he was told. He backtracked until he found the opening Leron mentioned.

"Fairly tight fit but should be doable," he whispered to himself more for notes than anything else.

He took a dimly lit light and shined it when he saw something sparkle. He squeezed through and checked out the area. He found a ring that had the symbol of Morhgrammir. He picked it up and pocketed it for further investigation. All nine of them could fit, but it would be snug. A cramped rest spot indeed. He departed the alcove and returned to the group. He gave the ring to Leron explaining where he had found it.

Leron asked Krit how they were doing on time.

"Well, we were given three weeks, provided no setbacks. We are currently ahead of schedule by at least two days." Leron pondered for a moment.

"Okay, Krit and Jamis, I need you to find a way down and investigate the entrance to that maze. I figure that will slow us down considerably. Finding a way around is paramount," he stated.

Krit and Jamis did as they were told. The only way down was to jump or follow a small path winding downward barely the size of feet. They chose the path. After a grueling battle with the slippery footpath and short breaks to fill in the missing gaps for the maze drawing, they finally made it down to the bottom where the ingress to the maze beckoned entrance. They followed the large walls, hundreds of feet tall to the cliff's face. There was no way around. The cliff face was smooth just like the walls.

"It appears the only way past this, is through that maze," commented Krit.

Jamis did not like it one bit.

Krit said, "I'm going to look, not far into that entrance. See what I can see so we know the terrain."

Jamis looked at him. "Just be careful. Do not go far and run back here or scream for help if you are in any trouble. I don't want to lose my head if you die."

Krit smiled at him. "Thanks for the vote of confidence, but I feel this is necessary, and we may find something that we can use to our benefit."

After a couple minutes of searching, Krit returned pale and shaken.

"We must go, we must return now!" Krit yelled. He ran for the pathway back up. Jamis looked confused with a hint of fear on his face. He looked at the entrance and wondered what could possibly spook him so bad.

Was it a dragon? The thought sent a chill up his spine as he followed.

Ever since the dragons attacked, Jamis had nightmares. He will never forget that unfortunate day, and his memory will forever haunt him. Jamis looked back one last time to see a beast of immense proportions looking at him. A large muscular torso, arms, and legs wielding large great axes was staring and appeared mad. Jamis stopped.

"Why is it standing in the entrance? Why doesn't it come to battle?"

A thought he meant to take up with Leron upon their return. Krit barely made it up the pathway, out of breath.

Leron commanded, "Report!" Jamis was not far behind.

Krit took a drink of water and sat to relax a little. His nerves were on edge.

He looked to Leron and explained, "Good news, bad news, and worse news. The good news is the maze is large enough for three of us to traverse side by side. The bad news is the walls are slick and smooth, rendering climbing non-traversable. The worse news is there are skeletal bodies, human in nature, lying around the dirt floor. They looked like warriors wielding this." He produced a steel longsword. "Not to mention giant beasts. Extremely muscular, dual wielding great axes with a bovine head with two large horns protruding from the sides."

Jamis interjected, "I have seen the creature. It was huge, almost filling the entrance. It refused pursuit and stood at the entrance, watching with an evil look. I think it wanted to kill us."

Leron thought a moment. He heard of such creatures but in myths and legends. The identification eludes his memory. Either way, he looked at the drawings made by

Krit. He studied the maze and looked down to get a sense of size.

"If that maze is as large as we predict, then there may be a large group.

Protectors to the under city, no doubt."

Leron thought a moment. "Okay, the plan is to return after a short respite. We will not risk a battle and need to return home to report the news. This intelligence is far too important should we fail."

Leron knew it was a failed quest, but his orders were to observe and report the location of the city; do not risk battle. Everyone rested while they could.

The plan was to double haste back to the Kingdom. Vigilance was necessary to elude the Gnolls and return as quickly as possible. They climbed down the cliff's side and continued toward the Kingdom. Once they entered the woods, they heard snarls and growls. A multitude of them. A quick feel of the breeze allowed them to relax a little since the Gnolls were upwind. The foul stench overwhelmed them, but they held their positions. Leron tapped Krit on the shoulder. Krit turned to see Leron pointing at his eyes, then pointing at the noise signifying for him to get a look. Krit obliged and was quickly off. He returned a short time later holding up nine fingers. A family, he thought.

A fire signal was given by Krit, meaning they were setting camp. Leron quickly got the attention of the others and signaled to backtrack and walk around. Once they were clear, Jamis asked why. They could let them pass on through, then keep going. This is adding time to their travel. Time, they did not have. Leron explained that Krit saw them taking up camp, which meant patrols were soon following. So, this roundabout is saving time. Jamis understood.

Jamis was just promoted to second in command and had more to learn. He was quickly picking it up, and Leron knew he would be a leader in no time. He just needed more experience. Most of the trip was left unhindered.

Two days before arrival, and the group was exhausted. They pushed more than they rested to get home as fast they could while keeping alert and ready for battle. Everything was going smoothly. Leron was woken by Krit, who had his finger up to his lip, signaling to be quiet. Leron understood. Krit led him to the small clearing, where they witnessed Gnolls setting up a large net and burying it under loose dirt and leaves.

"What kind of food do they think they will catch necessitating that large of a net?" Kit whispered softly.

Leron looked at the net while watching the Gnolls and replied, "Us."

They made their way back to the campsite and woke everyone. Leron explained to the group what they saw.

"The best chance we have is to split up. I want you and Jamis to round to the left. You and I will go to the right. Krit, you follow whichever group gets through.

Stay behind and watch. Those notes are high priority."

Once everyone knew the plan, they dispersed. Krit started up the middle to listen and watch before deciding on the direction to take.

Leron took lead and slowly made his way to the right side to get around the trap. They were moving slow and silent. After about ten minutes, three Gnolls jumped out of the brush, spears in hand.

"Ah, and where do you think you're going?" it growled. "We need to get back home and wish no trouble with you," was Leron's reply.

"But trouble you found it seems." The Gnoll laughed. His demeanor quickly changed to that of anger; the orange turned to red.

"Your kind has killed my brother. We found him with wounds from your weapons. Prepare to die!" accused the Gnoll.

The Gnolls lunged forward to the elves. The elves jumped back and readied to fight. "Left!" Leron yelled. Krit heard Leron's deep voice "Left!" He immediately took that route. As he turned to leave, he heard Jamis's voice yell, "Right!" Could it be the Gnolls set the trap and planned on the group to go around? An ambush?

"Shit, now what?" he thought.

He waited, listening to battles on both sides. Which way to go? He decided to wait. Five minutes later, he heard both sides coming in his direction. He climbed the tall tree to his left to see if he could get a better view. His head was going from left to right, and he knew he would see them soon. At that, both groups came into view and headed in the direction of the trap.

"They are luring them into the net!" he said in a harsh whisper.

He was about to yell "Trap!" but it was too late. Both sides were herded into the net when spears hit the ground just behind the elves, counting on them to tumble backward.

Both sides tumbled into the net. The net was quickly hoisted, trapping the guards. One immediately started to cut the net with the knife he retrieved from his belt. A spear was thrown and landed square in the back of the youngest guard. Krit was taken aback by the sudden turn of events.

"Any more movement from any of you and you will end up like your friend there." he Gnolls laughed.

"Drop weapons or die!" demanded the head Gnoll in a growly voice.

All the weapons were dropped. Krit thought quickly. He attempted to make the sounds of dragon wings flapping, a sound he practiced since that horrible day. Leron looked at him, moving his fingers and demanding Krit to depart and get to the Kingdom. Krit knew the importance, but he also did not want to leave his friends behind. He started in a low voice until he got it. Slowly, he increased volume, tricking the Gnolls into thinking the dragon was coming closer. The Gnolls peered in Krits direction but looked up. Frightened, the Gnolls panicked.

"Griffins!" one shouted.

The Gnoll who appeared to be their leader yelled, "Come back for them later.

Scatter!"

They disappeared. Krit quickly followed the line to where it was tied. He dashed to the tree holding the knot and cut the rope in one swing. The net crashed to forest floor. All the guards picked up their weapons and made quick headway toward Morhgrammir.

Leron stopped the group. They had a half day's travel left to go. The run made up time. They were amused at just how far one could run when scared. Jamis put the body of the fallen guard on the ground. He picked him up prior to leaving the trap, not wanting to leave any elf behind. They were out of breath. As they ate the last of their rations and drank water, Leron spoke, "Krit, that was very brave and quick thinking. I will ensure you are rewarded for your heroism and bravery. Most of all, thank you."

The rest of the group gave thanks to Krit. He did not want recognition, and he did not feel like a hero; he just did what any other elf would do. Breathing starting to come back as they kept listening, no sounds were heard. Everyone was safe. Once they were rested, they made the rest of the trek home.

Leron gave an owl's whistle, declaring their arrival. The eastern watchtower sent a runner to fetch the Queen. A short time later, the group showed up.

Queen Nekora greeted them "Welcome back. I am antsy to hear your story, but first eat, drink, and rest up."

"Thank you, your highness." Jamis brought the fallen guard to Poko, who started the preparations for the funeral. A couple hours later, they assembled in theaudience chamber. Nekora, Thorn, Poko, Krit, Leron, and Jamis were in attendance as well as the Queen's advisors. Leron started to speak. "Getting to the mountain, we encountered minimal intrusion. As Prince Thorn previously explained, the cliff's side was a treacherous climb. We saw the results of your trial and are impressed indeed," Leron said to Thorn.

Thorn smiled.

Krit continued by summarizing the notes, "We searched the mountain and found the entrance. It is located on the eastern face up a steep and slippery slope. The entrance itself is small and camouflaged by an illusion spell; only one elf will fit at a time. After a couple hundred feet, it widens a little allowing breathing room. It winds downward for about hour or so before it widens into a cavern too enormous to gauge the size."

He continued, "A small alcove was found just prior to entering the large cavern."

Krit handed over the notes and drawings. Leron explained, "The alcove was barely big enough to hold the five of us. This was found inside." Leron placed the ring with the Morhgrammir symbol on it on the table. The symbol was that of a large oak tree and crossing scimitars.

Nekora gasped and put her hand to her mouth. "That's Grogham's ring!" she exclaimed. "He was my brother who set off to the east for his trials but never returned. It looks like he may have stumbled on the city." She gasped.

Meeka went to the south. Could they still be alive? Is it possible Grogham found Almaryha? Tears welled on her face at the thought of it. After a moment, Krit continued, "A large plateau at the entrance to the cavern is wide enough to hold an army. Unfortunately, the pathway down is very narrow as described in the book. From the top, you can barely see what looks like a maze. I have drawn the maze in my book so you can see." Krit continued to describe the creatures found inhabiting the maze that he thought were guardians to the underground city.

Nekora knew who they were instantly from her teachings. "Minotaurs," she murmured. Leron remembered that name from before. He scouted inside just to see and make note of the terrain. Krit described the maze.

"The walls are unclimbable, standing over a hundred feet and smooth as glass. The dirt floor looked used. Bones were found littering the area. I grabbed the weapon left behind by the previous owner, that was when the 'Minotaur' saw me and charged."

Krit continued to explain how he ran out of the maze and made way to the guards. Jamis picked up from there.

"As we left, I looked back and saw that the minotaur would not come out of the maze. It halted at the entrance and looked livid."

After a quick discussion and the description of events that took place on the way home, it was understood that the dark elves must reside in that mountain. The Queen dismissed the group, thanking them for the intelligence, and talked with her advisors; she needed a plan and fast.

"We cannot go on this information alone, your highness" her advisor said.

"For all we know, they may be the only creatures residing in that mountain."

Nekora was perplexed. "Look here, if these notes are accurate, then the entrance to the city should reside through here." She pointed to the opening on the other side of the maze. "But what is through there?"

"I cannot send another party. Too much time is wasted." Thorn looked to be deep in thought. Finally, he addressed the court.

"What about a small regiment? One unit to go check out the area."

Nekora smiled. "Of course, I have been training a special unit. This will be their first mission." The court continued as they made final plans.

"Lieutenant Poko!" yelled Nekora. Poko came running to greet his Queen with a low bow.

"Yes, your highness," he replied.

"How is my special unit doing? How long until they are complete?"

"They are in practice tomorrow, your highness. They have been doing well, but I am not sure how far they need to go for I have not trained a unit like this before."

Nekora sighed. "Very well. I will be back tomorrow to gauge their abilities. I need you on the team as well, leading them and showing them the way to be their finest yet, Captain." Nekora turned and walked off. Poko looked confused, captain? Then he smiled.

She is getting used to being in charge. She found it invigorating and frustrating at the same time. But she was quickly learning the ropes and becoming more proficient.

The gong rang again. "Oh no, now what," thought Nekora. Her first instinct was to peer upward. No dragons in sight, so she quickly rushed to the east where the gong was heard as the watch sent his message.

"Your highness, the watch reports several figures heading this way. He counts roughly one hundred and fifty." Nekora called upon her guards to dispatch the group quickly. There was no time to mess with side acts.

The small regiment quickly made their way in the direction of the interlopers. They contacted the band minutes later.

"Halt! Who goes there?" Jyan yelled. At the first shout, numerous armed guards came out of the foliage, surrounding the pale elves with their spears drawn.

"Unclean and ripped cloth with no weapons," Jyan thought. "Who are you?" he demanded.

"Please, we have escaped our tortuous city Almaryha and seek asylum with you. We are not armed, and we have a guest you may be interested in."

At the mention of a guest, a thin and frail elf, slightly darker than the rest, came forward. He was weak and fragile.

Jyan demanded, "Who are you? I will not ask again!"

"I wish to speak with my family if you may. My parents are the King and Queen of Morhgrammir," the frail elf commented.

"Lies! The King and Queen are dead," Jyan exclaimed as he put the spear point to his throat.

"Then I must speak with my sister, Nekora. Tell her Grogham has returned and wishes to enter with my new friends here."

Jyan looked at the elf intently. "Grogham? Grogham is presumed dead.

"Jyan, do you remember when you were younger? You asked me for help in training for your trials? You left a few days before me. Remember? We trained each other."

Jyan recalled his memory. It was exactly as he described it.

"Grogham? Holy shit! What happened to you? Everyone thought you were dead."

Grogham smiled at his recollection. "I should have been. I was imprisoned and tortured. These elves helped me escape that hell hole. I know the ins and outs of that Kingdom, as well as the dangerous creatures that guard the city. Take me to my sister so I may press upon her the importance of wiping them out of existence. Give these people a chance. They have risked life and limb, some have died, getting me home. That at least earns their right to be heard."

"I will have Queen Nekora settle this. Everyone in line five wide so we can keep an eye on you."

The elves did as they were told. Hands were up showing obedience and marched the rest of the way back to Morhgrammir.

The guards reported back an hour later.

"Your highness, the band of elves are from Almaryha and claim to be refugee servants wanting asylum with us. They claim to have knowledge of the underground."

"Are they armed?"

"No, all of them are in ragged clothes. There is something else, your highness." The guard looked to the ground as his voice trailed off.

"Prince Grogham is with them."

Nekora's eyes watered as she pondered her situation. Tears welled and fell.

"Show them in. One false move and kill them."

The guard looked puzzled. Her father, the previous King, would have put them down immediately. Confusion ran across his face, but he did as he was ordered. He had questions. Did Prince Grogham join their ranks? Or was he rescued? What is his plea? One of innocence or guilt? That was something he left for the Queen to decide.

Two and a half hours later, the guards returned with over two hundred refugees in tow. They were all clad in slave rags and looked the worse for wear. They bowed in front the Queen and asked for asylum, returning intelligence in trade. Nekora listened to their story of retreat, survival, rescue, and escape from the evil dictator. Afterward, they produced all the documentation they could find in one grab on their city itself. It proved to be a treasure trove, indeed.

Prince Grogham slowly made way to the front, badly injured. Nekora ran to him and caught him in her arms as they embraced in a tight hug. Grogham looked upon a tired and worn sister. He'd just found out she was now the Queen, which meant something happened to his parents. His eyes watered both in relief and sadness for his family. He deeply regretted not being here for them.

"Get some rest, my brother. I will have the city healers tend to your wounds immediately." Nekora's eyes watered even more.

Grogham smiled as he wiped away her tears. "Do not fret, sister. I am back and alive. From what I hear, you are doing better than mom and dad ever did. My hats off to you, and you deserve your rightful place as Queen," Grogham replied.

CHAPTER NINE

After overhearing the conversation between the King and prince, Gareth decided to have a chat with the other slaves he trusted. He instilled hope, freedom, and the chance at a new life toward his closest friends that night.

"I overheard the wood elves are true, not a myth. If we can get to them, we may be able to seek asylum, we can finally be free," Gareth stated. "We can be in the sun, roaming on our own free will if given a chance."

"And just how do you propose we get out of here?" demanded Taryn, the slave to the jailer. "How do we know we won't wind up as some sort of slaves in this new Kingdom? Huh? At least we can survive here," he continued.

Gareth viewed Taryn with an evil glare. He only wanted to spread prosperous intentions, not mythical lies. Taryn should know better since he has seen and been with Grogham. A sense of knowing should have crossed his thoughts. Now Gareth had continued as if he never heard that. His expression lightened as he looked in the general direction of his colleagues.

"Exactly as we have been planning these last few months. We need that diversion and as much intelligence about this place as we can. Plus, now we have a bargaining chip." Explained Gareth as he looked toward the stairway to the underground cells.

"We may need those notes and Grogham to bargain for our lives if we make it," Gareth reminded everyone. "Grogham has assured me that his Kingdom is very lenient to their people. We do not know if he is lying, but this is a chance I am willing to take if it means freedom. Especially if we can become a member in their society."

Taryn gave a disturbingly questionable look. "You?" he fired back. "A chance YOU are willing to take. What about the rest of us? Did you not think to consort with us on the matter?"

Gareth could not take anymore. He fired back at Taryn. "What have you done to aid in this adventure?" He whispered so as not to be overheard and get his point across. "If you have a better plan, I am all ears!" he defiantly stated as he crossed his arms in front of his chest and stepped back. "Come on, Mr. Almighty, enlighten us with your wisdom."

Taryn felt the evil stares descending upon him from the others. They were all waiting intently for his answer. Taryn had none; he never thought of a plan before, so he backed down. "As I thought," said Gareth. "We need all the information about this place as we can find. Now, here is the plan. If you have anything better, I am up for discussion, but we do not have the luxury of time."

The group huddled. A plan formed. The first order of business was to create a distraction to the south. When the guards headed that way, the group would break the circular gate that closes off the tunnels and zigzag quickly but quietly to the Minotaur maze. The objective was to get through the maze and out to freedom. No one could think of a better plan.

They came to an agreement as they had already stolen a detailed underground map from the historian to plan the escape. The history of Almaryha was written on top of the map. The history must have been the ever-growing additions to the diagram. No one knew when they stopped adding, so they drew secret tunnels and wrote down the hierarchy on the backside.

Every nook and cranny were detailed to include secret entrances not otherwise noted on the maps. Everything was coming together; it was a matter of time before the items were discovered missing. Time, they did not have. If they moved out, it had to be that night.

Taryn grabbed a sleep ointment to slip into the jailer's drink so he could remove the Prince of Morhgrammir from his cell and out of the city as they planned. As much as he was in the cells, he never gave a second thought to the prince.

Gareth placed all the documents into a large sack while the group gathered at the underground gate, waiting for their signal to break the gate free and move to their first stopping point for accountability.

Trendel, the older dark elf, moved about the city through the shadows taking precautions to not get caught by the city guards. He slinked through an alleyway toward the southern end and sat atop the wall, pondering how to pull off his next move. He did not want to die, but that may come to be. He had lived out his life. As he pulled out a large slab of meat from his clothes, he heard a shout from below.

"You! Slave! Get back down here this instant!" the guard yelled, pulling out his crossbow and coming to bear on him.

It was fight or flight. He threw a palm-sized rock at the guard he had found on top of the wall and jumped down the other side. The rock was meant as a quick diversion to get the crossbow away from him. The ruse worked. The guard instinctively brought up his arms, and the bolt went whizzing harmlessly by. A warning bell sounded, and the guards all rushed the southern city hoping to get some action. The signal was given. No Gareth or Taryn in sight yet. No time to wait; it was time to go and go now.

Trendel ran as fast as his legs would take him. He ran in no specific direction. He just wanted the guards to be away from his colleagues so they could have a chance to escape. It was a matter of seconds before the Cerberus were upon him, tearing him apart limb by limb.

Prince Grogham, weak and unable to move from the bindings, was in a lot of pain. SMACK! Another hand across the bloodied and marred face introduced additional pain. His head was aching badly and vision fluctuating.

"Where are your mages located?" the jailer yelled. He stopped torturing Grogham as he listened to the bell. "I will be back; don't go anywhere."

He turned about and strutted out the cell door. He turned to lock it and made his way to his office, hanging up his keys. He grabbed his crossbow and ran out to aid the guards in whatever trouble was going about.

Taryn was waiting outside the jail when he heard the warning bell. Trendel was off. He had but a few minutes to get out. The jailer ran past him oblivious of his presence as he backed into the shadow. Taryn made his move. He ran to the jailers' desk and quickly found the keys hung on the wall next to it. He grabbed them and ran into the dungeon calling out Grogham's name quietly, pocketing the sleeping draught he had meant to give the jailer.

Prince Grogham stirred. He was bloodied and marred, hung in his cell, and too weak to move. Taryn quickly opened the gate and freed Grogham. He struggled to pick him up. Out the door they went. They made it out quickly. Luckily, the jail cell was close to the city entrance and exit.

They got to the edge of the gate and watched the remaining Cerberus running around the city, heading to the south. The group of slaves were waiting in the same area, and they all ran to the exiting tunnel. Four people stopped to help Taryn with the prince.

They reached the entrance to the Minotaur lair without being seen. The stalagmites and stalactites aided in their stealth.

"According to the map, the climb up the walls should be right about there." Aeod pointed slightly right of their current course.

Aeod was a slave in the historian's office. He would pay attention and learned about reading maps since he was a boy, without the historian knowing he was doing. It gave him something to do between beatings. Gareth nodded and pointed in that direction. They almost missed the climb as it was barely visible. Any passersby would have never found it. They made the painstaking climb up the maze wall, another step toward freedom.

Another alarm was heard behind them. From the top of the wall, they had witnessed six Cerberus running toward the Minotaur entrance and stopped, sniffing. They lost the scent. All the slaves laid low lest they be caught. A dozen or so elven guards, crossbows at the ready, moved forward. They also stopped at the entrance.

After a quick listen and viewing into the maze entrance, it was determined that the slaves did not go through. The guards looked about the entrance without officially entering the labyrinth. They scoured the area, even looking up the walls, which were impossible to climb. There would have been footprints. After a brief search, they returned to the city to face the wrath of the King. The slaves heard their voices, slowly getting farther due to the distance as the guards made their way toward the Kingdom.

"If they ran into the maze, they are Minotaur food."

"Where else would they be, you idiot? There is no other way in or out!" another guard exclaimed.

"You know this could be our heads…" the voice started and faded into the distance.

After deeming it safe, Gareth took the lead. The tops of the walls are wide enough for five of them to walk side by side. Before the trek, Gareth had memorized the way to the other side. Off they went.

"What about the dragon lair?" asked one of the other slaves.

"Wasn't there a dragon lair between the city and the Minotaur?"

Gareth pondered the whole trip. He saw nothing that resembled a dragon lair.

"I suppose there is none. There was that open area we passed through. It was a huge cavern. Unless they were on top of those large pillars, we have not passed through it." Gareth continued, "Besides, if we already passed it, excellent. I don't need that kind of shit right now."

Hours passed as they traversed the walls.

"Aeod," Gareth called, "there is a way to climb down the other side of the maze, right?"

Aeod looked perplexed. "I don't know. I never looked that far into the plan."

Gareth looked less than amused. He was hoping there would be an easy way down. A few more hours passed. The end was in sight.

"We are close now," Gareth said in a hushed tone.

He motioned for Aeod to come over and asked him to scout ahead to the end of the walls. He wanted to know for sure if there was an easy way down or would they need to jump. Gareth looked over the wall. It was a long way down. He watched all the Minotaurs scurrying around the maze, sniffing the air. He knew they smelled them. "Go ahead, try to find us," Gareth thought, smiling.

An hour later, the group made it to the end. Gareth told everyone to rest up a bit as he made his way to Aeod.

"What have you found?" Gareth asked.

Aeod was confused. "Well, I hope you have some rope. Well, a lot of rope. It is about a hundred feet down, near as I can guess."

Another disappointment. Gareth was getting used to it now. He viewed down the side. Sure enough, the slope was straight down.

"But there is some good news," Aeod started as Gareth glared at him.

"If you look to the other side of this entrance, there is an area right there." Aeod pointed. "Where we can slide down. It is our only option."

Gareth contemplated. "That would make another hour before we can get to the trail there." Gareth pointed to the small trail leading up the cliffside. Herock came before Gareth.

"I have traveled here years ago. There is one other way."

Herock explained that there was a small jump to a clumped mess near the center of the maze. From there, they would have to avoid detection of the Minotaur and make their way to this exit. He pointed to the exit that stood before them, separating them from freedom or certain death.

"One can hide from Minotaur. We are two hundred and twenty strong. We would be caught easily and used for food for months to them," Gareth countered. "Our only way is there." He pointed to the other side.

The group made their way back around. Gareth constantly looked down. He has seen many skeletal bodies on the floor. Like before, Minotaur going frantic as they sniffed and ran throughout the maze looking.

"It's like they smell us but can't figure out where we are," Aeod commented. Gareth nodded. He was just happy he was not the only one who thought the same.

They all saw a closed doorway that connected one side to the other. The door could have as many as three elves lined up across. The only place where wood meets stone at the top of walls. Walking on top of the door, acting as a bridge, was the only way to get past this section. Since the door was crooked, it appeared it was not shut all the way.

Gareth spoke, "Okay, I will go first to test it. If good, then all make your way single file. We need to get to the other side quickly."

They all waited as Gareth made his way across. One side was the continuation of the maze; the other side was a treasure room. Something he took note of.

The pathway was solid. He motioned for the rest of the band to come across and fast. The second to last group were the ones carrying the prince. About halfway, the door moved slightly from a gust of wind coming from nowhere. The group lost their balance and dropped the prince. The immense pain made balance and thinking skills problematic. A quick reaction allowed the group to remain footed and grabbed the prince as he was dangling from the edge. Grogham winced in pain from the sudden shock. It took a bit, but they finally got him up and continued without further incident. All but the last group made it with no problems.

The last group was not so lucky. An enraged minotaur, who had heard the commotion and saw the prince dangling from the doorway, quickly came into view and headed for the doorway in a full charge as the last group was crossing. The Minotaur forcefully kicked the doors open with a thunderous cacophony and rained elves. Thirty elven slaves fell to meet their doom.

The Minotaur let out a war cry as it quickly dispatched the slaves with its Great Axes. Screams were heard as each one was dismembered, blood spurting in all directions.

Four more Minotaur reached the area. Teary eyed, they had to move on. The Minotaur looked up but saw no other trespassers crossing the doorway.

Once at the edge of the maze entrance, Gareth looked down. A steep slope, not straight, but steep, nonetheless. He said he would go first and if he died, to look for another way down. Gareth sat on the edge where he could see the slope. Too steep to climb back up but enough to get down safely. He slid off, and away he went. He hit the slope with a thud and rolled a bit. After regaining his balance, he realized he was gaining speed and had to slow down somehow. He was at the fate of gravity now.

The bottom harnessed a sharp angle, causing him to roll into a large rock awaiting him at the bottom. His body slammed his left arm against the rock; the weight and momentum were far too much to avoid. SNAP! He heard the sound when his left arm went into the rock as he bounced over it. He screamed in pain.

Gareth grabbed his arm and held it. He rose and looked at the rock that gave him the surprise. He was wincing in pain and hobbled to the rock. He slowly moved it out of the way with his feet so the others would not hit it.

Gareth gave all clear signal as they slid down the wall one by one. The prince was the hardest and were hoping he would not suffer anymore injuries. Gareth felt bad. The prince had gone through so much. Gareth looked to the entrance and saw two Minotaur staring them down, anger beyond comprehension. It was then he realized they were safe since they have not left the confines of the maze. The group made their way up the cliffside.

Atop the cliff was a plateau. Gareth decided this was a great resting place. They all took turns on watch, stomachs growling and weak from the travels. They were not used to this kind of lifestyle. Each one on watch has kept a close eye on the Minotaur. None of them came out. Some spiders, snakes, and other odd creatures would come by, but they mostly kept to themselves. Scorpions and spiders would sometimes cross paths and fight. A little amusement for the watch until morning, or at least they thought was morning. After a brief respite, they continued through the tunnels and out of the cave.

It was late afternoon when each elf came out of the cave and immediately succumbed to the new smells. Each bent over and heaved as the rotten smell of dead cyclops, and Griffins reached their nostrils. They moved quickly to get out of the stench. As they peered down the cliff on each side of the plateau, they quickly realized that they were lost. The scenery and location were all new to each of them.

"So which way now, Aeod?" Gareth asked.

Aeod looked at the map and viewed his surroundings. "Not sure; it looks the same," Aeod remarked as he looked one way then the next.

"Look, castle off in that direction," someone commented, pointing to the east.

"Oh, good, so now we need to head…" Aeod trailed off as he held the map close to his face. "That way!" Aeod exclaimed as he pointed to the west, opposite the castle.

Gareth looked at him questioningly. "Are you sure about that?"

"Yes, a castle indicates the human city of Haversmith. The elven city is hidden. I overheard stories about the humans on the coastline and the newfound city of Morhgrammir in the valley, which means opposite direction. So, the elven city must be this way," Aeod directed. Prince Grogham nodded. Gareth was now convinced. "Okay, so it looks like trees below. We need to get under the cover of the trees quickly." They made haste as they descended the cliff's side, each step bringing them closer to freedom.

Once they reached the safety under the cover of the dense forest, they made a makeshift camp. Not much could be done since no one had anything to use for camping. This was an all-new experience for them.

The next morning, they woke, conscious about their surroundings, taking in the smell of the forest, which was far better than the dank cave from which they came. They took note of the sunrise and made directions based on the sun. The forest was dense, which made it difficult to navigate.

Prince Grogham was now under his own power. He felt better yet still aching badly. He remembered that pain dwindles from certain trees and was constantly looking, trying to remember what it was. A willow tree he knew but almost forgot what it looked like until they came across one and it sparked a memory.

He scraped some bark off the tree and pocketed it for later. He fashioned a bowl from hard wood he found and a sharp rock on the ground while looking for water. A while later, they came across a small stream. Every one of the elves practically dove into the stream to drink fresh water, some vomited from drinking so much so fast and learned the hard way.

All the prince needed now was fire. He had Gareth stop the group and make camp, careful about Gnolls. All of them were confused. He used two branches and rubbed them together to start a fire. The slaves all but forgot about the creatures as they gazed into the fire giving warmth and a sense of freedom. Once it was set, Grogham kept it low and put his bowl on top of a thin river rock he had laid atop the fire pit, hoping the water would get hot before the bowl turned to ash.

He immediately ground the willow bark and set it into the water. Once boiling, he carefully removed the bowl with a shirt and set aside. After a small cooling, he carefully, slowly, drank the water.

After a small rest period, Grogham felt less pain than minutes ago.

Thankfully, he had more bark for the next camp and some pieces to chew along the way. Before they set out, the prince told them stories of the infamous Gnolls and how tough they are to beat in combat.

"Gnolls are hardy and robust creatures that have canine features yet stand like us. They have hands to wield spears and are deadly accurate. Dexterous creatures that only a skilled combatant can best," he started. Grogham looked outwards, not focusing on anything as he attempted to remember the information he had overheard from past trial successors. "Their reflexes are uncanny, extremely intelligent for a beast."

Grogham continued, "Their quick reactions and strength made them a deadly adversary. Not coming across one is of the highest importance. I had heard that one elf was in a melee for over ten minutes before he killed it. That is a young fresh elf, I can only imagine the stamina it would take to down one. Since they travel in packs..." Grogham left it there for others to ponder. They got the picture.

As they concluded their packing, they made their way toward Morhgrammir.

They were looking everywhere, taking in the sights of greenery, dense foliage, the smells of fresh pine trees, and birds chirping as they flew with magnificent grace. The fear of Gnolls would inhibit the full experience.

"Ah, this is what I was waiting for," thought Gareth. He took in more of the senses and was highly elated at the sights and sounds before him. This gave him a sense of relaxation. A calmness he came to realize he took for granted.

At the next campsite, the group sat and kept their voices low. After the prince's description of the Gnolls, they hoped to never encounter one. Since he only heard of them, he described them with more ferocity to scare the others; more than anything, it gave him a chuckle to see their discomfort. All in all, the group was terrified.

After a couple hours rest, a rustle was heard to the south. Everyone was quiet and had the look of horror in their eyes. Current stories and terrified of being ripped to shreds by a Gnoll was fresh on their minds. No one dared to move. The sound grew louder, the tension was thick.

THUMP! A Gnoll landed in the middle of the camp.

A look of surprise and fear enveloped the entire group, even the prince as this was his first actual Gnoll encounter.

Gareth yelled, "Run!" Everyone jumped and ran in different directions. The Gnoll smiled as he went after the apparent leader, Gareth. Some twists and turns, under, over, and through the brush, Gareth made his way farther west. He had heard the others in a similar path. "Good, at least some of us have a chance of making it. How much farther do I need to go?"

Thwip—an arrow passed dangerously close to Gareth's head and slammed into the Gnoll's forehead, killing it instantly. A Morhgrammir guard had another arrow pointed at Gareth, who was amazed at how fast the arrow was reloaded. Gareth raised his right hand and surrendered. He could not move his broken left.

The rest of the group caught up and surrendered. They talked about the event and realized ten more elves were missing, presumably caught by the Gnolls. The thoughts of their demise horrified Gareth. Sadness overcame him.

Grogham, hands raised, approached the guard. He explained who he was and how he was rescued by the slaves. He wanted to talk with his parents. The guard did not recognize him and told him the king and queen were dead. Grogham told a story of memory allowing the guard to remember. The guard did not recognize Grogham. He did as he was told. The group was rounded up and held at arrow point until the lead guard came back from the city.

Two and a half hours later, Poko, the lead guard, had returned. He was side chatting with the prince, out of earshot from the others.

"There was a dragon attack on this Kingdom. Both the King and Queen are dead. Nekora is our new Queen. She will be delighted to see you again, my Prince. As I am so happy to see you are still alive. What of these intruders? Your highness?" Poko questioned, motioning to the slaves sulking about. It was an old rule to kill anything not from Morhgrammir; however, since Prince Grogham was with them, there was a story and a potential twist to the rule. It was for Nekora to decide their fate now. Poko only hoped the best for them. The malnourished bodies of the slaves hit him hard.

All the slaves stood and were escorted to the city. A line of guards on either side of the group ensured they went the right direction. Any sudden move would result in instant death. All former slaves were in agreeance and compliance with this rule. All of them were ushered into the new great hall where Nekora was waiting.

Nekora listened with great intent, occasionally glancing at her brother standing next to her, gaging his reaction. Prince Grogham kept his head low throughout most of the recollection; sadness, guilt, and exhaustion all catching up to him now.

"I can only imagine the pain you have been through these last few years. Please, get some food and rest. We will converse when you are better," Nekora stated to her brother. As for the rest of you, thank you for bringing my brother back. As you are dark elven, we must confine you for the time being until we can figure out what to do with you."

A great sigh was heard. "Yes, your majesty," Was all Gareth could say.

The guards ushered the group into a large open area outside where a makeshift fence line was used to encircle the encampment housing the slaves. The encampment was under constant watch by the city guards. "Great," Gareth thought. "We went from slaves to prisoners."

Grogham woke the next morning with a splitting headache but nonetheless moving. The city healers worked tirelessly to get the prince up to speed as quick as they could. Grogham saw the prisoners and became irate. He stormed to Nekora.

"Why are you keeping them captive? For everything they have done for me. Their lives were on the line getting out of a harsh environment only to be in a far worse situation that you put them in! All they ever wanted was a chance at freedom!"

"The information they have brought has been valuable and useful, not to mention rescuing you from your cell, which is why they are still alive," Nekora stated calmly.

"Besides, my brother, we do not know their true intentions. How do we know they did this to attack us from the inside? We have already been attacked from the outside. Suddenly, they show up with you and all this information? I have to ensure the safety of my people are first and foremost."

"I will talk with... what's his name?" Nekora asked. "The leader of the so-called slaves."

"Gareth!" Grogham interjected with irritation.

"Yes, Gareth, and I will discern their intentions myself. With their impeccable yet suspicious timing for getting here, it causes great concern since they are from the ones who declared war on us for no reason at all. If all is well, and their intentions are legitimate, then I will investigate releasing them into our society under close observation for security reasons until it is found that they have no intention of harming our Kingdom. I will decide their fate from there," Nekora explained as she walked out.

The next day, Gareth was led by Captain Poko to the audience chamber. Queen Nekora had her personal garrison surround the fugitive.

"We need to assess your intentions, and why you have decided to show up at our most inopportune time. I have people here who can tell if you are lying, so I highly advise you to speak the truth." Swords were drawn, bows and crossbows were at the ready, and pointing at Gareth.

"First question, who are you?" Gareth stood as tall and as confident as he could given the circumstances. The pain in his left arm has subsided a bit from the healing touch of the wood elves. But movement was still limited and painful.

"I am Gareth, former head slave to the city of Almaryha."

Queen Nekora looked at her advisers, who nodded in confirmation. She proceeded her questioning to find out where the city was located, guards, personnel, Armies, traps, and so on. Gareth gave up information with no hesitation or remorse. He even named all the others with him who had unique specializations. After everything was confirmed, and Gareth was found to be telling the truth about his band of slaves, Nekora decided to free them from captivity.

Satisfied they were not a threat to Morhgrammir, the Queen allowed them to utilize their trade expertise to help the Kingdom and enhance the city trade. Nekora took the most interest in the historian and kept him in the castle to work alongside the intelligence community. The first order of business was maps of the under-dark memorized by the high elven guardsman.

CHAPTER TEN

One week had passed since the refugees arrived. The under-dark maps were almost complete in detail. Morhgrammir was close to being back to what it was, plus a few additions. Fireproof materials made by the mages and alchemists covered the buildings. The covering had a nasty pungent smell but dissipated after a couple days. In the event of another attack, the citizens could go inside without fear of burning. A lesson learned unfortunate in the making.

Queen Nekora has settled nicely into her role as the Queen of Morhgrammir and is doing an outstanding job of leading her people. The morale is quite high given the circumstances. Prince Grogham was content in his role as prince and wanted nothing to do with the throne. He gave up his right since Nekora fit in better than their parents ever have.

"All matters aside, I am glad you are still alive, sis," Grogham stated. "You have done far more for our society than our parents ever have. I have never seen them so joyful. Even after losing our loved ones. They seem," he paused, "content. As if nothing ever happened."

"I have been trying to get them to understand what we have lost, but we need to focus on the present for our survival and our future. Letting them know that vengeance is upon us kind of put them in an up spirited mood," Nekora stated as she gave a quick chuckle. "I miss our parents, and I am glad you are, my sweet brother. But I must ask, what do you think of Thorn ruling as King? Or would you rather rule in my place since you are the true heir?"

Grogham sighed. "That overrated slimy Ox mule of a friend of yours?" he teased. "I am joking. I think he would do well. I will watch him to see if he is worthy to serve as King. I am too broken to rule a Kingdom. You are doing perfect. I will hereby bequeath my title as heir to the throne unto you. You have proven yourself time and again. I have never been prouder of any of my siblings. Even though you were adopted, you are still a Mancer," he continued.

Tears welled down Nekora's cheeks as she jumped up and hugged her brother. She never really cared about her real parents since they gave her up all those years ago. Besides, she was always treated with dignity and respect. She has also loved her life, which has dimmed her desire to find her true parents to nothingness. She was very happy here. She wiped away her tears and looked unto Grogham.

"Thank you, my dear brother," she said as she embraced him in a vicious hug. The grasp was so strong it made him grunt. "I am glad to hear you approve of Thorn, and I think you will be amazed at what he really has become. For one, he is the first of our kind to down three cyclops, one being a giant."

"I saw those on the way back home. While impressive, it does not judge an elf worthy. He has the combat skills required, no doubt; let us see about his judgments," Grogham stated as Nekora smiled and walked away to visit the people. Visiting the elves was the only thing she could do to get her mind off that night, and she hoped it did the same for them.

The next day, Nekora was perusing the under-dark maps. She needed to know the layout, inhabitants, traps, city location, guards, and so on by heart. Her eidetic memory helped tremendously. She was yearning to understand everything about Almaryha. Thorn walked in, smiling to Nekora.

"How goes the research?" he asked. "You sure are making more time studying those maps than you are with training these days. I have never seen you more dedicated."

"Well, it wouldn't be good if we marched into foreign territory with all the details currently in front of us and not knowing the ins and outs when we get there," Nekora stated. Thorn looked perplexed.

"You said we?" Thorn asked. Nekora let out a short quiet laugh.

"Yes, my special unit and I are departing in a week. I want to make sure we aren't caught off guard. It is not like a cyclops is going to sneak up on us because they are 'large and silent' right?" Nekora let out a huge laugh as she used her hands to make quotations while slowly walking toward Thorn, who was now feeling embarrassed.

"Just wait, you will see how true I am. Besides, why are you going? You should be here protecting the Kingdom, and we are to be married in two weeks!" Thorn exclaimed.

"Maybe I should go since I know the layout very well, and I don't know what I would do without you if something bad were to happen." Thorn laid his hands on her shoulders.

He was bitter and surprised at the same time. He wanted to be included in every facet of Nekora's adventures. He was overly apprehensive about her but knew deep down she would take him out in seconds. That was already proven on many occasions.

"I know, sweetheart, but I have arranged a proper and special marriage upon our return." Nekora ran her finger down Thorn's chest while putting her lips close to his.

"Besides, you are more than capable of running this place in my absence," Nekora said in a low sexy voice then gave him a quick kiss, turned, and walked back to the table where the maps lie in wait. "Plus, the Kingdom needs someone here to keep their spirits up. I am hoping you are the right person for the job," she stated with a smile. "Or do I have to find someone else?" she teased.

There was no doubt he was ready; she loved toying with him, even with the little things.

Thorn turned and walked out, confused, hurt, but he knew she was right. He despised her always being right but that comes with the territory.

Nekora knew deep down that her Kingdom was not safe so long as the Drow still live. She must remedy that immediately or make it the last thing she does. The latter did not sound too appealing so back to the city maps in case she missed some minor detail.

She knew the castle layout and location of every house, shop, and so on. What she was looking for was the King's and Queen's room. The directions and even the hidden walls all thanks to their newfound elven additions. She always worried about their true intent; so far, they have been nothing short of great. She decided to let fate run its course.

That evening, she settled down at the dinner table with Thorn and Grogham. They conversed about the day's events as usual during the start of the meal then discussed other matters of importance. Today, talks were mostly how the former slaves were working hard to fit in and prevent future slavery or lockup. Thorn had to explain to the new citizens how the Kingdom runs without slaves, which befuddled their minds but happy there are none. They are adjusting to and fitting in with society very well.

"Tomorrow, I will be adjusting the Kingdom. I will talk with the mages and alchemists to bring them closer to the city; any objections?" Nekora stated more than asked.

"What about a potential disaster to the Kingdom with an 'oops'? That is why father made them work so far away from the Kingdom, to keep everyone here safe from accidents," Grogham countered.

"I know them very well, dear brother. I talk and work with them daily. I know their habits and can promise no harm will befoul this Kingdom. Besides, it is another way to show trust. They saved us after all," Nekora interjected. "Had they not shown up that terrible night, everyone here would have perished. I think we owe them some respect and better living conditions, which will also persuade them to help us more. It is time this Kingdom grows in power. In fact, it is far past due," she finished.

Thorn chimed in, "I agree with the Queen. It is highly probable more elves would have survived had they been closer. It will build a comradery and could bring more attuned magical items that would give us an advantage should we ever come across another threat. Unlikely as it is, it is best to be prepared nonetheless."

"Then it is settled," Nekora stated. "The towers can go behind the stables. It is closer to the market and if an oops happens, it will be away from the community."

Nekora wiped her face and hands on her napkin. The servant helped her move the chair back, and she stood, placing the napkin on her empty plate.

"With that, gentlemen, I will bid you goodnight" Nekora turned and walked toward her room, leaving Grogham and Thorn at the table. Both sat back down. It was customary for guests to rise when the royalty stands from the table.

"So," Grogham looked at Thorn as he continued, "what are your plans for the Kingdom? If you are going to be a King, they normally have a plan set forth, rules, events, and so forth... My concern is, how are you going to protect this Kingdom? And my family?" he finished.

Thorn thought for a moment. He was always in Nekora's shadow and had not given this any thought.

"To be honest," Thorn started, "I have not given that any thought. I always followed Nekora since she is the Queen and above me."

"Yes, I know!" Grogham exclaimed. "But if you marry my sister, you will be the king of Morhgrammir. I want to know what your plans are when you become a king."

"Well, first and foremost, I will look into safety concerns, which I have been paying attention to. There are many weak links in this Kingdom that need addressing. However, once Nekora finishes her project, there will be nothing to be concerned with."

Grogham interrupted. "Okay, but what current threats are we addressing in this Kingdom? How likely are the dark elves to attack us again, now, or soon, while we are still rebuilding? Tonight? These are just a few examples of things you need to address immediately. Not in the future, now," Grogham finished.

Thorn thought it through. He was right. The Kingdom, while in the future will be protected, needed security. He would talk with Nekora tonight while it was fresh on his mind.

"Also," Grogham interrupted Thorn's thoughts, "and most importantly, how are you going to keep everyone's spirits up? High morale is a happier Kingdom. I especially want to know how you intend to treat my sister."

Thorn ingested everything he heard. He agreed that the morale had to be always high. "There should be zero concern over the welfare of your sister. I would die for safety," Thorn remarked.

"All very good points, Grogham. I will discuss these matters with the Queen immediately. Also, Grogham, if I were to become King, would you be my advisor? Would you mind? I say if because no one knows what will happen in the immediate future."

"I would be delighted. We will discuss this another time," Grogham stated.

That night, Thorn was lying on the bed. Nekora had her head upon Thorn's chest as he was stroking her hair. The feeling of comfort and was making her fall asleep fast until he spoke.

"I have some thoughts about securing the city and boosting morale. I know everyone is happy, but I was thinking we need to enact some sort of event to get everyone to push the memories back for a bit. What do you think?"

Nekora lifted her head from his chest. "Well, I think it is about damn time you started to help!" she exclaimed. "Do you have any idea how difficult it is to make every single decision around here? Once you become King, the pressure will be harder to bear. You know that, right?"

"Yes, I know. I am sorry, Nek. I just thought since I was not in an authoritative position, I could not make any decisions yet. I should have asked earlier. I am sorry," he said empathetically.

"Good," Nekora answered. "You can start tomorrow by designing a better entertainment program for our people. I was thinking games, shows, and have the community be involved instead of the regular entertainers."

Nekora laid back down on his chest and closed her eyes. Thorn did not sleep that night.

The next day, Nekora traveled to the mage building. She made her way to Ghorn's desk. "Okay, so I have a plan for all the mages and alchemists, but I need you and Jangir in attendance immediately."

Ghorn bowed and made his way to the head alchemist, Jangir. Both returned as instructed. Nekora looked at both and smiled.

"I believe we can compromise since I know all of you very well. The mage and alchemist buildings can reside close to the city. I have absolute trust in all of you that there will be no 'accidents' while at the new location. All of you can traverse the city much more frequently than before, as often as you like, mingle with the locals, and be part of us. A larger family. No longer a distant thought to those who are not familiar."

Nekora looked them up and down, finding it funny how they failed to hide their enthusiasm. Nekora unrolled a map of the Kingdom and pointed to the northernmost building.

"This is the royal stable. Your buildings can be relocated right here. She pointed to an open area behind it. I would love to have my friends near me for the rest of my life. Which reminds me, how is the research going with the magical shield to protect our Kingdom?"

Both smiled broadly. Ghorn produced an amulet with a diamond one inch in diameter.

"Place this on that table please," Ghorn stated.

Jangir obliged. Ghorn had everyone stand behind a blast protector as a safety precaution and cast a diminutive fireball spell at the table. The table was unharmed, but some books in the background and wall were burning. A quick cone of frost put it out.

"As you can see, the table was never touched. If we can figure out how to increase the protection umbrella, we can get this coverage across the city. We still have a lot of work to do, but progress is being made."

Ghorn was excited. Nekora did not realize her jaw was still open. She looked at Ghorn and Jangir in complete admiration.

"Diamonds are hard no doubt, but what would happen, for arguments sake, if a lucky strike were to hit the diamond just right and cause it to break?" she asked.

Jangir answered, "I thought you would never ask. This is where alchemy can aid in magic. With a solidifying compound we developed, we can make the diamond one hundred percent shatter proof."

Ghorn interjected, "It is that chemical balance that has allowed the shield spell to hold permanently. There is an invisible barrier that protrudes roughly three meters from a one carat diamond and a detection barrier slightly farther than that. If the detection barrier is breached, the protection and shield spell go off instantaneously to prevent any harm from coming close."

"We used a pendant to see if it would work with a living elf, so far, no one wanted to volunteer. I don't blame them," Ghorn stated with a chuckle.

Nekora responded, "I have witnessed the event; I will volunteer. This is something we could use to our advantage."

Ghorn looked to Jangir, who looked away then back to Nekora.

"Get to it!" she snapped happily. "I cannot believe this this is all coming to fruition."

"Here are enough identify scrolls to identify up to ten unknown magical items should you find any on your journey. One scroll for each item. These scrolls will reveal the true magic fastened upon them, so you know what they do. That is, of course, should you manage to find any magical items," Ghorn stated as he handed over the scrolls. He continued, "All you have to do is unwind the scroll, lay the magical item upon it, and recite the specific words. Unfortunately, the scroll will burn up after use, which is why I gave you ten."

"Allow me to demonstrate, your highness," Ghorn inquired.

"Please do, master Ghorn," Nekora replied.

Ghorn took the necklace used in the fire protection demonstration. He placed the necklace upon a different identify scroll and started concentrating.

Revelios Eetema

The scroll immediately lit up with a blue hue. A description appeared in the air above the item.

Shield

Protects item or person from any harm. Imbues a three-meter protection barrier along with an additional detection barrier. Once the detection barrier is set off, the protection barrier immediately deploys disallowing any harm.

Indefinite use until dispelled.

The floating inscription remained for a few seconds, long enough for the average elf to read, then dissipated into mist before disappearing. The scrolls hue turned a bright red then burned to ash in less than a second as it too turned from ash, to mist, and disappeared.

"Thank you, master Ghorn. These scrolls should come in handy if we need them," Nekora stated as she left to continue her duties.

Between Nekora practicing and increasing her spell power, the military training, and overseeing the new construction, Nekora was too busy for anything else. She stayed up late into the night studying the maps. She read them so many times that it had become ingrained into her memory. She kept fearing something was missed; she did not trust her instincts. Even captain Poko was fearing that they were missing something important.

Captain Poko started the conversation. "So, from what we know, there is a hidden passage on the eastern face of the mountain here. A long trek through perilous paths and cliffs, an open large cavern with a Minotaur lair and maze, followed by a dragon's lair, then through a courtyard guarded by three-headed giant dogs and spider elves, then avoid being hit with poison tipped bolts from the elven crossbows. Sounds easy enough," he said sarcastically while holding his head as if it were hurting.

"Well, look on the Brightside," Nekora said. "At least you get to adventure." Everyone laughed. "Besides. If all goes right, we can test our new formation. Shields from our warrior elite will help with the bolts, no doubt, but let us start answering questions. One, how fast are the Minotaur? If they are as big as they say, they will be no match for our elite warriors. We have the speed and tactics. Two, if the Dragons are sleeping, will we be silent enough to pass them undisturbed? Three, can we get the three-headed dogs, what did you call them, Gareth?"

"Cerberus, your highness," Gareth answered.

"Yes, can we get the Cerberus to fight amongst themselves? What about fresh meat thrown into the middle of a couple, they would fight over the meat and be otherwise preoccupied. Other than that, all that is left is for us to make the castle here," Nekora pointed, "and find their King and Queen. Alive for questioning first. Then we can kill them. Pay them back for what they have done to us and our families."

A plan formed. Preparations were underway as they readied for the upcoming travels.

Two days after the meeting, Ghorn came running to his Queen and bowed breathlessly. She was talking with her advisers on monster weaknesses and potential hidden entry ways into the Kingdom of Almaryha.

"We have done it, your highness!" he exclaimed excitedly. "May we speak with you immediately?" Ghorn said as he was jittery with glee and all smiles.

Nekora excused herself from her group and walked briskly with Ghorn. His smile was contagious as she smiled with him but not knowing why. He led her to a secluded area where Jangir was waiting for their arrival. In front of them was a table with various items on it and three small pedestals with a one-carat diamond atop each. Each diamond had been imbued with a shield spell.

"The size of the diamond was the issue all along. We used smaller and larger diamonds and found the protection umbrella was increasing and decreasing with the size. Our mathematician figured out the size protection per size of diamond ratio. The missing piece we needed."

Ghorn and Jangir was ecstatic. But Nekora showed concern and confusion.

"Carry on," she stated.

"A one-carat diamond will cover a three-meter radius. Or a six-meter diameter umbrella."

Nekora exclaimed, "The largest diamond ever found from what I heard was only three carats in size."

Nekora was puzzled. How can this possibly be good news? The Kingdom is huge; no diamond would ever exist in the size they need to cover the Kingdom. She felt hopeless. All was lost.

"Do not fret, your highness" came a voice from behind them.

It was Krem, the Kingdoms mathematician.

"The answer lies in abundance," he stated.

Now Nekora was really confused. Krem looked upon Ghorn to show her. Ghorn took two one-carat diamonds from the pedestals, leaving the middle one in place. He came back and turned, facing the diamond. Ghorn cast a flame spell. Everyone could see the six-meter circle untouched. Adding the two diamonds back to their respective pillars and positioning them three meters from each other near the opposite wall, Ghorn cast the fire spell once again. This time, the three umbrellas fused, increasing the protection area three-fold. Eighteen meters of untouched zone. Nekora understood and was elated.

"So, if we place pillars to match the size of the Kingdom, there would be a lot of pillars, we would be cramped," Nekora stated. "Can we obtain larger diamonds resulting in fewer pillars around the Kingdom?" she inquired.

"Yes," Ghorn answered. "The mountain range to the southwest harbors an active volcano. It harbors the pressure we need to turn Carbon into a diamond. The problem is the amount of heat is far too much to bear for an elf to safely traverse.

They would burn up before they even got close."

"So, a protection spell on the miners infused into necklaces or rings or somewhere touching the body would protect them from the heat. It is possible to obtain these diamonds. If we bring them back, we can tweak the sizing to meet our needs. I am sure larger diamonds exist. We just need to mine for them," Nekora thought out loud.

"We just need time," she stated. "Ghorn, can you assign some elves to head to the southwest and retrieve as many diamonds as they can carry? Ensure each elf is protected by allotting a handful of guards for threat protection."

They conversed and came up with a plan. One problem stood out. According to Jangir, one diamond had to be central and much larger than the rest for the umbrella to work on such a large-scale area.

Ghorn smiled as he reached into his pocket, "Got that covered," he said and produced a ten-carat diamond from his pocket, the largest diamond Nekora could possibly imagine. "Of course, this would have to be much larger. However, the theory remained. We will work on placement when the diamonds arrive, we need to know what we have to work with," Ghorn concluded.

The next day, they scattered around the Kingdom, looking at the spacing between buildings and so on. Some diamonds could be placed on buildings to reduce the number of pillars needed. A plan was formulated to get the shield up and running. It still depended on the diamonds retrieved from the mine.

"Okay, so pillars can be erected in several spots with a diamond on each one. We should be well protected once everything is in place." Nekora smiled.

The Queen was so happy. She could not ask for a smarter bunch. An idea crossed her mind.

"Ghorn, Jangir, Krem, I would like you three on my board of advisers. This way, we get differing points of view and ideas with additional resources."

They bowed and accepted their new roles. The Kingdom was growing immensely in power.

That night, Nekora spoke with the citizens. She stepped up on the newly built dais and looked upon her subjects with Thorn by her side.

"Elves of Morhgrammir, you have weathered through disastrous times. We need to focus on our future from here and now to strengthen our unity. Keep our loved ones, lost in an unfair governance of the Drow in your hearts, and focus on those of us alive today. I promise you there will be retribution to those who have wronged us that dreadful night. A team is leaving soon to destroy our enemies who have declared war upon us. Let us pray for success, then feast and celebrate life."

Nekora was deeply saddened for the loss of her parents but joyed at the return of her brother. She was confused with the gods. Why would they let those terrible Drow destroy her life, family, and home, then give her a lost brother back. Where is the other brother? These are questions that plagued her daily.

For now, she must put her focus on the feast, mingle with her elven friends, and celebrate life, their life.

"That was an excellent speech," Thorn stated to Nekora.

"Thank you. It seems to be getting easier each time. Now I know how my father felt whenever he had to address the Kingdom."

Nekora's head lowered as she mentioned her father. Thorn took her into a rigid hug and kissed the top of her head.

"Time heals all wounds," he proclaimed as he grabbed the back of her head and nestled it upon his chest in a gentle, reassuring embrace.

The following few days were filled with errands and ensuring progress was made. The Kingdom was around ninety-five percent rebuilt now, including the new modifications. Life could finally move forward in prosperity and harmony as it once was. Peace was once again showing promise. The excavating team was underway and should return by months end if they are lucky enough to obtain what they needed.

"Are you ready for your mission tomorrow, your highness?"

Captain Poko startled the Queen from her daydream of her prosperous Kingdom. He was so used to being silent for warrior training that he had forgotten he was not loud enough to snap the Queen from her dreaming.

"My apologies, I did not mean to startle you."

"It is quite all right, Captain. If you were loud, I would question my decision to make you leader of my special unit", she snickered. "While you are here, Captain, I need to go over these maps with you one more time. Should anything happen to me, you need to keep on mission. Is that understood?"

"Undoubtedly, your highness."

Poko bowed. He did not like her statement but understood her concerns.

The Kingdom would never rest, especially since the dark elves knew their location. They must be destroyed at all costs before they come back to re-attack. Since they have not through these times, the Drow must believe the Kingdom was destroyed.

Poko turned to head out of the hall. After about three steps, he stopped and turned to face the Queen. "Your Majesty, what if they are waiting for us to rebuild so they can destroy us again? You think that may be their ploy? Nothing would hit us harder than a reattack after we rebuild," Poko asked.

Nekora looked seriously at the captain. "Which is why time is our enemy this day. I have plans for our future, but we need time, a luxury we currently do not have. Therefore, we must retaliate immediately. We need to prevent them from obtaining the resources they need to re-attack until we are ready," she responded.

Captain Poko understood. He turned again to depart the premises.

"Oh, and Captain, do be ready before dawn. We must march early in the morning," she commanded.

"Yes, your majesty," Poko responded before exiting.

Nekora stood on her balcony looking over her city and people, still not believing the events that transpired. Thorn was lying in bed looking over his fiancée with a fascination and admiration he'd always felt since childhood.

Her naked, flawless body standing there, looking over her Kingdom. She turned and smiled at Thorn, slowly walking over to him. Her perfect supple breasts, thin muscular and toned body from years of training, shaved baby smooth, glistened in the candlelight. Thorn still could not believe that his dream woman, childhood best friend, was now his lover, soon to be wife. She was perfect in every way, and he wanted nothing more or nothing less.

Nekora looking over her fiancée with love. His rock-hard body toned and built with years of strength training and honing. She knew how deadly he could be since she trained him herself. She pondered her life with him by her side forever and always as she smiled before sliding into bed. They embraced for passionate love making that night.

The next morning, Nekora and her entourage gathered in the courtyard to say their goodbyes to the town elves. Thorn was saddened but knew what must be done. This was Nekora's chance to prove her strength, to show she belongs to the elven community as Queen. People already knew it, but she felt that she must prove it, not only to them but to herself. Nekora watched Thorn as she left, tears slowly slid down her face, hoping this would not be the last memory of him, and returning victorious with a fresh start to a new and more protected life for her elven nation.

Chapter Eleven

The eastern mountains awaited the greatest army to ever come across its location. Nekora was especially excited since it was the first time she was able to see outside territory. Always on alert, especially from all the stories she had heard from every warrior who ever stepped foot on their trails.

The first day was uneventful as they made camp for the night. For a large squad, they made excellent headway. They made lunch with a fresh boar found on their journey. As they packed up, growling was heard all around. Nekora knew what they were from the stories told by all. Gnoll's, finally, she would see one up close and personal. The squad fell silent, listening for movement to track by sound. Nothing else was heard. THUMP! A Gnoll landed in the middle of the squad and moved with a grace and fluidity never thought possible.

"HALT!" Nekora demanded forcefully. "Who are you that dares intrude upon my warrior elite?"

The Gnoll looked at Nekora, sizing its opponent and laughing in a gurgled voice.

"You realize that you are trespassing upon my domain and must now pay the toll."

The Gnoll smiled. Nekora looked at the Gnoll.

"What is the toll?" Nekora asked.

The Gnoll's smile broadened. "Death!" it yelled as it turned and hurled a spear at the same time toward Nekora.

Nekora twisted to avoid the impact and quietly cast haste upon herself to gain the advantage. She could not fight a Gnoll without an advantage. Now she sees the stories and believed they should have been hyped up more than they were. The toned-down stories were to keep the villagers from living in fear. All the guards drew their weapons, but Nekora put her hand up.

"I will take this one."

In one solid movement, faster than any warrior thought possible for a biped, Nekora whispered her magic words while drawing her bow and knocking an arrow. At inhuman speed that impressed each one of them, Nekora let loose the arrow. The arrow was straight and true, faster than any eye could watch. The Gnoll caught the arrow in midair, throwing it to the side, impaling it deep into a warrior's leg. The Gnoll brought its spear to combat readiness.

Nekora dropped her bow and arrows, realizing they were worthless in this fight. "Oh my god, how did the warriors do this?" She thought. The Gnoll threw a second spear to Nekora.

"The fight shall be fair, even though you are a woman, I will not kill an unarmed assailant." It growled. Nekora caught the second spear and brought it to combat readiness as she was taught. She smiled as she looked at the Gnoll.

"Shall we dance?" Nekora asked as she raised her eyebrows and slightly cocked her head.

Even with the haste spell, the Gnoll was keeping up with her moves, dodge, parry, thrust. The Gnoll caught Nekora by the legs with the spear and knocked her to the ground. Damn these creatures are fast! Nekora rolled before the spear impaled her in the chest. She back rolled onto her feet and flipped before being struck again. There was no resting. Fatigue was setting in. Nekora had to end this quickly. She started casting an acid spell before she was clocked over the head with the butt end of the spear. Spells take away from her attention. She had to think fast. A classic move came to mind. She felt the haste spell wearing off, so she had to do this now.

Nekora faked a move to side strike on the right. When the Gnoll started moving to block, she lifted the spear, spun around on her left side bringing her spear in to contact the Gnoll's rib cage on the opposite side. She dropped while spinning extending her leg out and surprised the Gnoll with a leg sweep, knocking it to the ground. She flipped up and thrust the spear into the heart of the Gnoll, killing it instantly.

Nekora dropped, exhausted and bleeding from the battle that seemed to go for days yet lasted near three minutes. The team camped so she could rest and set up watches throughout the night.

The next morning, they disassembled camp and made way to the eastern mountains. A few Gnoll encounters were quickly dispatched by the guards. On a one-on-one basis, Gnoll's were difficult to kill. But with many, Gnoll's are easy to take down. Nekora went through each move from her encounter and thought on what to do different next time. She had a new respect for the Gnoll's.

The squad made it to the base of Almaryha mountain. The cliff was higher than it originally appeared from home. The stench from the giant cyclops rotting corpse nearby was a testament to Thorns victories. Nekora wished it were eaten by now as she gagged on many occasions. The rest of the team followed suit, doing their best to get above the stench and stop dry heaving.

At the top, Nekora took in her bearings. She looked to the east as Thorn had described, the human Kingdom was barely visible, but the land was beautiful. She could even see the ocean in the distance. "No wonder the humans built their Kingdom there," she thought. So beautiful.

Nekora snapped out of her daydream to find the entrance to the secret caverns. She observed every detail and moved where the map, the one she memorized and left at home, said the entrance would be located. As it said, an illusory image covered the entrance. An illusion that was far too detailed. Someone wanted this entrance to never be found. They had found the illusory entrance and entered the cave. They descended into the dark and dank cave on their trek to enact revenge against the Drow.

The cave wound down with all kinds of nasty little critters crawling and slithering in all directions. A guard was attempting to touch one of the snakes slithering by.

"DO NOT touch anything. We do not know what ones are venomous, Nekora stated.

The guard's hand retracted quickly as he looked at his now determined enemy. There were creatures here that they have never seen before. The farther down they went, the weirder, larger, and creepier they became. "If these are just regular off-the-wall ordinary creatures, I would hate to see the guardians," thought Nekora.

The maps precision markings were detailed exactly as the cave twists through the mountain. The cave slowly increased in size until it reached the large opening into a gigantic cavern. The cavern was large enough to fit the entire Kingdom of Morhgrammir thrice stacked on top of each other. It was truly amazing.

Dim lights could be seen at the bottom of the cavern inside the maze. Looking at the pathway, the small footsteps leading down into the immense cavern leading to the Minotaur lair was wide enough for one elf to traverse in single file. The maze at the bottom appeared exactly as outlined in the map.

"Okay, so the trail is slippery; be careful and mind your footing," said Nekora.

Captain Poko relayed the instructions to his team. Looking at the trail, Poko instructed the lead guard to assign an order of march. Poko went first to test the trail.

The lead guard assigned an order of march to the men, single file to secure the ground level for the Queen. Every one of them made the landing, staring in awe at the immense walls with one entrance into the labyrinth.

The dimly lit corridors made just enough light for the Minotaur to see but well-lit for the elves. Nekora was in the middle as they went two wide into the lair. Even though three could fit, two were necessary to allow for movement in battle while possessing the ability to block and counter threats.

The Minotaur were no match for the elite guard as each battle executed successfully in a graceful dance. Nekora noticed the great axes were glowing with a blue aura signifying magical enhancement. With each impact there was a cacophonous roar as shockwaves filled the battlegrounds.

"The weapons are infused with a sonic enhancement, mainly to stun allies on any impact. Smart, but thankfully our warriors are trained so there should not be many casualties if any at all," stated Nekora to the lead guard. "Just stay away from the sharp side." It did not take an expert to realize their abilities.

When one got tired, another jumped into action, fresh. There seemed to be similarities in attack patterns, meaning they were trained the same. After the maneuvers were studied and understood, it was easy to bring down the beasts. Nekora gave directions through the maze; she wanted to check the armory. Not just for weapons and such, but for the possibility of clues leading to anything that might be of use to them.

As they neared the armory, and slain a multitude of Minotaur, the team spotted a pile of jewelry, gems, and gold, as well as empty armor and weapons fashioned for humans. She had the guys spread out the items and put the treasure in a sack after careful inspection. Only a few of the jewelry, armor, and weapons appeared enchanted. Nothing in the room was valuable aside from the treasure.

The team put the sack in a hidden alcove for later retrieval as they moved back on track through the enormous maze. The weight of the treasure would slow them substantially.

One after another, Minotaur died at the hands of the elves. The new scimitars worked even better than anticipated. The new king of the Minotaur was different, however. He had a new set pattern not distinguishable by the Elven elite. The last Minotaur, before the exit, was towering over the Elves. Even the other Minotaur were smaller in comparison. The great axes were swung with malicious intent, showering the corridor with rocks and debris.

It was amazing the walls did not crumble. As one Elf got tired and exited for the next fresh warrior, the Minotaur's axe came crashing down splitting the warrior in two. A quick upswing prevented a potentially fatal execution by another warrior as it blocked the attack.

Back and forth, the blades were in a dance of blurring designs. Nekora looked down at the barrage of sparks and clanging of metal. The Elven army was being slaughtered. As the fourth warrior was slain, Nekora finished her spell as a ball of ice came hurling at the Minotaur.

It was not fast enough. The ball hit the Minotaur square in the chest, and it froze like a statue. The warriors hit the beast with all their might, striking the ice statue until the Minotaur was no more. Nekora could see the amulet worn by the mighty beast glowing a soft blue hue in the darkness. She snatched the amulet and pulled out a scroll to identify the magic on the amulet.

Revelios Eetema

Nekora said just as Ghorn had shown her. As before, the scroll glowed a soft blue hue with a written description above it.

Amulet of Strength and Speed

When worn on the body, strength and speed is multiplied by a factor of three.

The scroll revealed the amulet increased the speed and strength of the wearer. That would explain the difficulty in defeating it. Nekora gave the amulet to Poko to wear. He needed him to survive and successfully finish the mission if she should fail.

The band did not move after the final battle except to sit and listen for approaching enemies. The vast cavern before them with huge spires ending in plateaus was cleared. The height of the cavern was unbelievable, and they could see starlight through the top gaping hole. The army retreated to the confines of the maze to rest, satisfied the Minotaur was no more.

Nekora broke the silence. "We will rest on the other side of this cavern to get our bearings and strength back and tend to our dead. I need everyone to be as quiet as they can."

Tears flowed down the Queen's face. She had lost her friends and protectors. Her eyes rolled into the back of her head, and she collapsed into darkness.

Nekora stood on a plateau, in a green grassland with tombstones around her. Am I in a cemetery? "Did I die in battle?" she asked aloud.

A voice answered her. "No, not yet. But you will with your current regiment. Your team is not strong enough to withstand the upcoming battle. Align with me, and you will become the greatest sorceress ever known." It was a beautiful female voice that talked to her, sending her an emergency message. She felt as if she needed more. More warriors and she debated turning back to retrieve additional units until her vision went blurry and swirled.

Nekora bolted upright, sweating. Captain Poko put reassuring hands on her shoulders to calm her.

"These battles must be too much for you to bear, your highness. Training is one thing. Warfare is a completely new experience. Your magic may have weakened you, your highness," Poko mentioned.

It took a bit to realize where she was. She remembered the maze and realized they never left the immediate area. Nekora looked weary.

"I just had the weirdest dream."

"Shh, you are safe, your highness. I will keep two of my top-notch guards to protect you while we scout farther along. You need rest," Captain Poko responded.

He was becoming concerned over the well-being of his Queen.

"No, I will go with you. But I feel as if we need more people. We will not have enough to take on the Almaryhan guards, let alone the Cerberus that roam the grounds. We need more!"

Poko did not say a word. He knew she was right. But he couldn't get his lost guards back. Nekora snapped around to look at Poko. The captain thought it odd; it was like she heard his thoughts.

The party pressed on. No one noticed Nekora, who was deep in thought about the events that unfolded. They pressed through another massive cavern with eight pillars ending in plateaus.

"This has to be the dragon lair," Nekora whispered softly to Poko. Poko looked up and nodded.

Captain Poko listened carefully as he moved silently. He gestured his guards do the same. Not a sound emanated from the cavern. There was no life to be seen or heard except their own. The experience was creepy to say the least. For now, they had to focus on moving ahead. Thankfully, the Dragons were out hunting. The cavern was clear.

The army eyed the opening to the next division. Nekora spoke softly as they were still in dragon territory.

"According to the maps, the city is in the next segment through there." Nekora pointed to the opening. "There is a lot of ground to cover before we can attempt to enter the city, which from what I understand is guarded by mythological creatures. Thankfully, stalagmites and stalactites as well as boulders throughout can be used for cover."

The army continued to the opening. As they peered into the vast cavern, all they viewed was blackness. Nekora looked back to her entourage and attempted to count the remaining elves. Poko saw what she was doing and decided to save her time.

"We are still sixty-eight strong, your highness. We only lost four to the Minotaurs', and the remaining injured are healing quickly."

Nekora looked at Poko and smiled.

"Thank you. We just may have enough to pull this off," she said as she slowly scanned the emptiness of the cavern ahead. But a dream interrupted her thoughts.

"Your team is not strong enough to withstand the upcoming battle." Nekora did what she could to push the negativity away. She had to be focused for the upcoming battle.

Flapping sounded from above and behind the group. The sound was coming from the last cavern they departed. The dragons returned, but they were worried that the animals making the loud flapping noises would come down the tunnel and rest in the city area. No one knew for sure.

Dragons! They all thought as they froze in fear. Nekora silently gestured the group to hurry; they had to find a hiding spot. They quickly descended the tunnel until they found numerous giant boulders around the open area. Each of the guards spread out so they would all be hiding. Voices were heard in the tunnel from behind them.

"What a boring night," one of the riders stated.

"Yeah, but it beats being here sometimes. I am tired of fearing for my life every day," another retorted.

"Have we ever got any intelligence on that city we destroyed?" another rider asked.

"No, but that could mean they are completely demolished since there hasn't been any retaliation. Besides, what could survive dragon attacks? I would love another round of destruction come to think of it," one of the riders stated. The rest of them laughed.

"Sometimes, I wish we could fly to a new zone. This area is definitely boring."

"Yeah, good luck with that!" one of them said in a high voice. They all laughed.

Nekora wanted to jump out and kill them. She was irate. Poko laid his hands on her shoulders to keep her down and put his finger to hush her. It was all he could do to prevent them from being caught. If they followed, they would certainly find their destination.

The riders were discussing the nights events as they walked by Nekora's army that has gone unnoticed. When all was quiet again, they started to breathe easier. Nekora was red, fuming with anger.

"Your highness, we need you on the playing field, level with the rest of us.

We need your leadership and guidance. Now is not the time to lose your temper. Remember what I taught you," Poko stated.

Nekora knew he was right. Damn how she was hating the role of Queen. I will eradicate each one of those wretched scum. Especially the riders. Oh, their deaths will please me to no end. Nekora started to smile again, a smile foreign to Poko. The captain regarded her.

"Are you okay, my Queen?"

Upon hearing Poko's voice, she snapped out of her illusionary dream and replied positively. She was content with the surroundings and everything going on;b she just needed to be prepared for the final battle. She was smiling at her imaginary victory. Oh, the torture she would love to inflict.

They regarded each corner as though something were ready to ambush them. Scouts reported all-clear up to the riders. Captain Poko was determined to come up with a plan to keep his army alive, but it was much harder to do without solid intelligence collections.

The next scout returned out of breath. Poko calmed him a bit to get information from him.

"What is your report?" Poko calmly asked.

"Three more turns and the tunnel opened up to an expansive cavern. Dim lights barely show the under dark city. I can only imagine this as being Almaryha," the scout informed, slightly relaxed.

"There was growling and howling, something much larger than a common dog is in the area. Too many sections for hiding. I am not sure we can..." Poko put his hand on his mouth to shut him up before the Queen heard him.

"You do not do the thinking here, do you understand? You just obey orders. The thinking is my job." Captain Poko was frustrated. His army was breaking apart. What happened to his training? He made mental notes to expand the training to include fear tolerability as well as a can-do attitude into his men.

The army continued to march for the opening. It was just dawning on them that no insects resided here at all. The first entrance was swarming with insects and reptiles of various shapes and sizes. Why would there be no sign of life? Poko wondered. No time to ponder the question. The quest was nearing its destination.

Nekora was anxious. She was finally going to see first-hand the myths of the fabled under-dark city. A fabled myth that aroused her curiosity since childhood. She quickly returned to reality when multiple booming barks were heard. Growling of immense volume made them sound close. Every guard was on edge, each drew their weapons, looking upon one another for clarity of their next move. This was something they did not train for.

"Captain!" Nekora said loudly and harshly.

Captain Poko was by her side quickly.

"I want three teams to spread and cover as much ground as quickly and safely as you can."

Poko nodded. He knew these Elves. He knew each could withstand anything coming at them, except for webs raining down on the team.

Driders that were on guard above viewed the incoming threat as they approached the entrance to the cavern. The lead called for his scout to redirect the guards and Cerberus to that location.

"I want these intruders surrounded and brought to the king!" he demanded.

A nod was all it took and off he went. The body and eight legs of a black widow spider with Drow form from the torso to the head made for a frightening scene. Each one of the dozens wielded a spear. Some had crossbows to take down from a distance or fleeing escapees. Either way, more Driders were on their way as well as the ground forces.

Immediately, Nekora thought the plan was a bad one. They looked up to see web netting heading straight for them as they tumbled out of the path.

"Torches!" Poko quickly demanded. Each Elf quickly lit torches to burn the webs or be caught. They melted the webs that caught elves not dexterous enough to evade the incoming sticky cage. The burly ones were considered tanks as they were extremely strong and difficult at best to compete with. Unfortunately, their strength came at a cost of dexterity.

"Oh, this is so unfair!" thought Nekora.

The burned webs had small pops as it burned like air bubbles but louder. The darkness enhanced the sound to make it seem more dramatic.

Four Cerberus were running to the desired location; the city alarm sounded as guards were seen exiting the gate and running toward them.

"This is it my Elves! Look sharp and defeat thine enemies," Nekora demanded.

Poko looked at Nekora, thine he thought. Where did that come from, she has never said that before. He filed it away for future questioning as well as her position. Poko was supposed to handle the military affairs. She was to advise him when necessary, not take over command.

The army spreading out happened to be the best plan they could come up with considering the circumstances. With the raining of webs, now devoured by fire, and the oncoming enemy of all classes, the spread army was able to survive much longer.

The first wave to hit was the Cerberus. While the archers were shooting at the Driders overhead, the ground forces would fend off the evil hounds. They had to be quick for the next wave of Drow guards were on their way, and fast.

All archers took a knee and quickly nocked their arrows. They went up in unison and arrows were fired in all directions, no one knowing which enemy to target. The head archer gave directions after what he saw. The ranged ones first. Start left and go right.

All archers reloaded their bows. Crossbow bolts were streaming at them at a hastened speed. They have never seen a projectile move so fast. Three archers were taken down. When they all recovered, which was very quick, they aimed and fired. A volley of arrows heading toward the first crossbow wielding Drider. A few arrows were easy to evade because of their slow rate. But thirty or so arrows? Impossible to evade. The first Drider came crashing down to the dirt.

"Only a few dozen left!" shouted the head archer. Now they knew how to kill those bastards.

The tanks moved ahead of the frailer Elves and quickly blocked the Cerberus from overrunning their forces. The Cerberus stood over six feet with three heads on one body.

"What in hells creation would make these evil canines? I thought the Gnoll's were fierce!" exclaimed one of the guards. Poko was too busy fending off his insatiable desire to NOT fuel one of these creatures. He did not plan to be food today. His shield came up to block one of the heads ready to ingest the captain when his sword automatically came from underneath the jawline and thrust up into its brain. The head limped lifeless. The other two heads descended upon Poko to avenge its third.

When one team fell their opponent, they moved to help their teammates. The Cerberus took a while, but they were finally defeated. Just in time, the hundreds of guards now arrived to play.

"No rest for the wicked, I suppose," Poko mentioned. Captain Poko was the only Elf in history to ever defeat a Cerberus singlehandedly. He thought back to moves from watching Nekora fight mock battles. Moves and countermoves he never even thought of and too proud to admit he learned something from the princess. Expect the unexpected was her motto. He did not know where she got it from, but he was glad she did. It has come in handy more than once thus far. A motto that has kept him alive.

Driders were falling one by one. The archers were tiring. Nekora took her place among her archers after the first one fell. She was accurate and deadly with her bow. The team knew she was good, but now they held a whole new admiration for her talents. No one knew where she got her luck from, or her incessant stamina, but they wanted it and were glad she had it.

Nekora shifted her focus to the oncoming guards. They were grouped together. Suddenly, she had an idea.

"Poko!" She demanded his presence. Poko came running to her.

"See how they are grouped together? This could not be any simpler. I need you to get your army positioned to surround the enemy, keep them grouped. I need a little time. Keep your army at distance; do not engagement them just yet."

Poko was about to interject but thought better of it. Then he realized he had to say something. He was captain of the guard.

"My Queen, I mean no disrespect, but this my army and I have a plan to eradicate them."

"First off, Captain, this MY army, not yours! You are to command them as I say, do you understand?"

Nekora was heated. She was not in the mood to argue, but she needed to rid the enemy and fast. She gave Poko the evil eye. All he could do was follow orders.

"Teams one and three, surround the guards but keep your distance. Keep them grouped!" he shouted.

The army split up evenly and did as they were bid. Nekora positioned herself upon a tall rock, so she had an overview of what was happening. She took in her surroundings ensuring no enemy would interrupt her.

Faerum nu destro

Nekora waved her hand and violently pointed her finger at the enemy as she murmured her mantra. A large ball of fire headed for the guards. They had no time to get away. The ball of fire entered the center of the group and exploded on impact. Eighty percent of the guards immediately died with the rest badly burned. Nekora stared in amazement at how well it worked. She smiled and was filled with overwhelming joy.

"This is the best day ever," she thought as she fell unconscious from a falling Drider. A large, hardened leg hit her on the head as it fell to its death. Blood started to pour upon the rock.

CHAPTER TWELVE

King Bron and Queen Kardya peered out their window when the alarm sprang. The king turned to look at his queen, concerned.

"The time is has come, my dear. We must destroy these foul creatures. I did not think the bastards would have the audacity to attack us. But here I stand, awakened to the alarm of battle. I would have hoped to be given ample time to dress and prepare for this outrageous onslaught!" he exclaimed as he changed his view toward the cavern entrance "Here I am, ready to watch our guards get all the fun. Besides, I was told the elven Kingdom was destroyed! Why did Baern not finish the job?" the king stated irately.

The queen looked dismayed.

"I thought you would be the first one out there, you have been training for this day for years. There is still time to try out your new poison mix." The Queen laughed.

"Relax, my love. My guards should make quick work of them. I need to punish Baern for not fully carrying out my direct orders."

King Bron was mad, but for now he wanted to watch his guards in action.

Bron looked to the ceiling and was always mesmerized at how graceful and fluid the Driders traversed the webs. Their movements were fluid and filled with ferocity, fast yet never faltering. He watched as they all moved toward the entrance, soundless.

The Drider Captain setup ahead of the rest and had them ready their webs to capture the incoming enemy forces. He watched as they hid among the rocks, waiting for them to move and make their calculated attacks.

One Drider noticed an Elven guard looking up at the webbing and make eye contact. He threw a web to cover his mouth so he would not alert the others and miss. His reflexes were too fast to be caught off guard.

"Above!" the guard yelled. The other Elves looked up; panic and fear overcame them. They had never seen a creation such as those hideous creatures. The archers quickly took defensive positions that shocked even the head Drider.

I am amazed they can think and react like that. What kind of Elves are they? A volley of arrows interrupted his thinking.

"Webs, now!" the Drider exclaimed.

All Driders were about to web the entire area when flames were seen being lit below.

"Wait!" But it was too late. Web nets were thrown just before the command. Dazzling displays of fire eruptions and popping sounds were seen and heard from the ground forces below. No webs held fast.

Smart. He loved a challenge. After his thought, more arrows came up, easily avoided but appeared to target one

Drider in particular. Amok, second in command went down with a body full of arrows. Basnik, the lead Drider was about to drop down and melee when a volley of arrows got him. He fell, lifeless.

The king watched in utter dismay. "How did they know? Those damned escaped slaves must have found their way. Guards!" the king yelled.

The guards came rushing in. "Are you okay, your highness?" one asked.

"I want every slave owner whose slave had escaped killed this instant!"

"Yes, your highness," was the only reply. Any further discussions would result in fatality. Off they went to find, and slaughter lost slave owners.

The king continued his watch as each of the Cerberus were killed.

"How can this be?" The king was infuriated now. He pummeled his hand into the window opening and stomped out to get ready for battle.

"Release all the damn dogs!" he yelled as he made his way to his closet.

Baern was on his roof, watching in dismay. "God damn rookie fliers! If he hadn't given away our position, this would not be happening right now." Baern jumped down and grabbed his hand crossbows. He was furious and outraged that his own homeland would be under siege. His hand crossbows were loaded with poison-tipped bolts, ready for nothing but death. It was all he could do to be away from his wrathful father and prolong his imminent death. He would rather die in battle than at the hands of his father.

Bron came out of the closet back to his window while securing the last of his buckles on his armor. He wore leather armor with fasteners and belts to tighten the armor to his body. The thick padding underneath allowed more freedom with no chafing and more protection than standard armor. He grabbed his crossbow as he made his way to the lower floor to retrieve his bolts.

The bolts were separate since they were soaking in a homemade poison concoction. Deadly with just a scratch. He stepped out of the castle to see a ball of fire erupt from atop a large boulder heading toward the gate. It disappeared behind the wall from his vision for a moment when a bright flash of orange, yellow, and red colors erupted outside the city. Another round of explosions above the field was seen and heard. The deafening roar from an explosion of that magnitude caused massive ringing in the ears, followed by waves of unbalance.

That must have been the fireballs Baern talked about. Speaking of, where the hell is Baern? I should kill him as a warmup. The king looked around everywhere and spotted him running for the gate entrance after he got up from being knocked over by the blast. He was just out of range, so the king waited to close in before engaging his son.

The Queen sat on her bed, not knowing what to do. She was not trained in warfare, only torture. All she could do was wait it out. She got up and walked to the window; the battle would cheer her up.

The Queen mused at making her own decisions for the battle. She would make a game of how to win the war. To her recollection, there were many of them. Fifty or more so, she thought. "They are very powerful together." How to split them up was her concern. She viewed the lay of the land and remembered the behemoth stalactites on the ceiling. She had a wonderful idea and sprinted to the alchemist's office.

"Rory!" exclaimed the Queen. He was nowhere to be found. He was busy fighting. She went over the scrolls around the office until she found what she was after. She unrolled the scroll and read.

EXPLOSIVE CONCOCTION

Black powder found in fuses mixed with a Nitrate together in a holding capsule.

Mix three parts Nitrates to one-part powder in a sealed container. Insert fuse into sealed container and seal hole. When ready, light fuse and distance or suffer the consequences.

"This is it!" she exclaimed and looked around for components.

She brought a small vial, some black powder, and a bottle of Nitrate to the table. She arranged them in order of build. The candle was lit at the opposite end to prevent inadvertent explosions.

"For one part of powder, mix three parts of Nitrate," she said to herself. "How much is a damn part?" She was infuriated. She looked at the vial and had an epiphany.

She grabbed the vial and a scoop of black powder, and carefully poured in the powder until it was one-quarter full. She had found a small glass stick and stuck it into the vial.

The vial was set into a holder at the edge of the table. With the stick inside, she slowly and carefully added a little bit of Nitrate and mixed it carefully. The vial was filling slowly, but she wanted no chance. The vial was filled to the brim with the paste mixture.

The Queen grabbed some string and covered it in the powder. She then pushed one end to the bottom of the vial and had another five inches hanging over the side. The cap had no hole.

"Đammit!" she exclaimed. A nail was found after a brief search, and she punctured the lid as close to center as she could eyeball. The string was routed through the hole from the bottom side and through. The lid slid down to the vial and attached securely.

The Queen grabbed the candle and dripped the hot wax near the base of the lid and string, securing the hole to prevent the concoction from leaking out and providing more pressure for an even larger explosion. As she grabbed the vial, it slipped out of her hand.

"BOOM!" came another explosion from outside. The sound petrified her. She could not move for a few seconds until she realized there was no immediate danger and the vial fell back into the holder without any damage. She was lucky this time. She gripped the vial firmly and ran out the door.

The Queen just made one container due to time constraints, so it must matter. She made her way to the bedroom to retrieve her bow and one arrow. She affixed the container to the arrow tightly and ran outside the balcony, which was close enough to the wall to make her shot. Seeing a lone figure on a rock gesturing, she knew it had to be her target. A mage of some sort. The Queen lit, knocked, and aimed at the ceiling above her target, where dozens of dead Driders hang lifeless.

Her arrow went flying and struck the lifeless Drider near the mage. A few seconds lapsed when a ball of fire erupted from the figure and the explosion from her concoction went simultaneously. A half-dozen bodies fell from the webbing as well as a few stalactites along the ceiling outside the wall. One Drider body fell onto the rock where the mage was standing. When the Drider lifelessly rolled off the rock, the mage was seen lying prone, limp with a hand hanging from the side, she thought she could see blood slowly flowing down the rock.

"YES!" she yelled and presumed the battle was going to turn. With no mages in the army that she knew of, her husband had the upper hand and would be victorious. She witnessed the army below separating to avoid falling debris. A few were not as fortunate.

Captain Poko looked everywhere for his Queen. He did not see her anywhere. The explosion rocked a new level of consciousness into him, and the tides were turning quickly. His army not fleeing but separating to avoid fatalities. He could not blame them, nor would he punish them for doing so. They need every available body alive, and he himself barely escaped the squashing doom.

"Where is the Queen?" Poko thought to himself as he peered around the battlefield. "We should have brought more troops."

Poko remembered seeing a fireball come from the largest rock in the cavern. It had to be Nekora. He sprinted as fast as he could to find her to make sure she was safe. Some elite guards saw him sprinting away from the battlefield and shouted, "Coward!" Some followed to see where he was going. Others continued as best as they could, stumbling from the shockwave induced by the blast.

The Elite guards had realized that they were split up and had to regroup if they had a chance to succeed. A thinning army against these many opponents was an impossible task. Especially now that their Queen was missing.

Poko found Nekora lying on top of the boulder. Her arm was hanging lifelessly over the edge, and blood from her head was running down the side. She was unconscious on her back and her body was limp, barely breathing. Her pulse was weak, and her head was bleeding profusely. Poko did what he could to stop the bleeding, but not much could be done.

He grabbed a wad of cloth from his emergency bag and applied it directly to the wound. The bleeding slowed, but it was deep. The wound had to be tied together with some string he did not have if she were to have a chance to survive. He was hoping she would come around and made a mental note of battle dressings for future incursions.

"Lesson learned," he thought with tears rolling down his cheeks.

Nekora's spirit was floating above the combat field, looking down at her body. She was quite concerned now.

I cannot die like this! She thought if she could survive a dragon attack, how could she die from this small affair? Nekora was crying; she figured her life was extinguished and awaiting the fate of the gods. What have I done? I brought my best warriors, my elite guard, here to die in this horrible place.

"Do not fret just yet, my child." It was a beautiful, singing voice that filled her head. She looked around but no one was around. She thought it must be voices in her head.

Have I died and gone mad? What kind of trickery is this? She watched as Poko climb the rock to help her and desperately attempted to get back into her body, but she was held back by an unseen force. A field she could neither see nor touch. Yet it prevented her from moving.

"Relax, and I will explain all" said the beautiful voice again. This time she witnessed a figure slowly fade into view behind her. It was a female Elf, the most beautiful elf Nekora had ever laid eyes upon. Her long red hair, flowing in the astral breeze. Her eyes so blue, they were glowing. Her slim body was wrapped with ghostly cloth flowing in the makeshift breeze, leaving no imagination to her ample breasts, and toned, flawless body.

"Who are you?" Nekora demanded.

"I am here to explain why you are here," said the apparition. Her movements were graceful and perfect, smooth, and ghostly.

Am I dreaming? Have I gone mad? Nekora pondered.

"Yes and no," she responded as if reading her thoughts. "You are dreaming right now, but you are far from mad or dead in case that thought ever crossed your mind. You are blessed in ways you cannot imagine. This will be difficult for you, but you must listen carefully. To see is to know, to know is to grow, and to grow is to be strong."

"Why are you talking to me in riddles?" Nekora questioned.

The apparition slowly moved to Nekora and put her hand on Nekora's cheek. "You are more beautiful than your mother. Now think about the words, and it will make sense to you. Once you understand, you will understand your importance."

Nekora jumped back but wobbled. The Astral Plane is not exactly the easiest plane to navigate, and she has never been there before.

"Tell her!" came a disciplined whisper, one that make a Gnoll tremble in fear. It was a male voice from what she could comprehend, but no other figures were visible. "Yes, tell her!" came echoes from more apparitions, a harmonious sound from different apparitions young and old, male, and female.

The female figure sternly looked around. "Enough! I am telling her."

The first male voice replied, "Time is running out, make haste."

The flawless woman peered into Nekora's eyes and said, "You must come with me, now."

She took Nekora by the hand and floated quickly to another zone, time, world. Nekora has never seen this. What was happening?

"Allow me to explain your heritage. Eighteen years ago, you came into this world. Your parents were deeply in love, and nothing could change that. Not even your grandparents," the apparition started.

"Your mother is Vera, the goddess of beauty. Your father is Lord Draykon, son of the dragon god Drahkan.

Your grandfathers Gammon, Lord of the underworld, and Kilmeth God of the Dragon kind never liked the idea of your parents getting together in the first place. They feared the offspring, you, and what you may become. They feared that one day you might wake to your hidden potential and overthrow the gods. Take your position and be more powerful than any god currently in existence.

"This union was never supposed to happen and has caused an imbalance in the life essence. The essence is what keeps the worlds in balance. You were taken by your mother and hidden away to this world where an imbalance already existed from your step Uncle. You were put here to bring balance back to this planet.

"As a baby, you were handed to a Wood Elf King that soon became your temporary father as you remember. He was to raise you as he would any daughter. Even though he knew your heritage, you would not be treated special. You were to be raised until you were ready."

Nekora was perplexed. "Ready for what? Why would my parents leave me and never check up on me? What do I do now? How can I help my friends? How can I bring this balance thingy back if I am here and not on the field?" Tears were welled inside her.

"You are what you have always wanted to be, Nekora. You are a supreme mage. To wield the arts, you must first find your center. You can wield any spell that you can learn. Since your father is the lord of dragons, your natural affinity is of the elements. But your heritage goes deeper than that. Being blood to the underworld, you can control life, death, and even poisons as well. But your mind must connect to the ether world, and your body must be centered. This world here," the apparition gestured around her, "is where all your questions will be answered. It is up to you to find them." The apparition stared into Nekora's eyes.

"Even though you were given away as a baby, you were never abandoned by your parents. Your mother always checked on you as you grew up. She is also where you get your beauty from. Your talents came from your father. How do you think you were so good at everything you did? Your archery, your spell casting ability? How do you think you did not perish in the fire from the dragon's breath? What you must do now is defeat your uncle. He has been the treacherous traitor in this world and had planned on domination in a few years.

"He is also the reason you had to be hidden. He was not to know of your existence at all. Eventually, he would have figured you were put here to defeat him and would have killed you early in life. Now you must rid this world of your reason."

Suddenly, the prophecies Nekora had to learn made sense. Every one of them. They are all about her, but she could not have been told lest she be killed as a child. All questions from earlier in her life were coming to fruition. She knew what she must do. But how was she going to accomplish those things from here?

The apparition continued, "Your actions have kept everything in balance, exactly as your parents had hoped. Since your father was constantly watched, he could not visit you. He was hurt and heartbroken. Always worried about you. Your mother knew how to escape temporarily so she checked on you from time to time. She gave reports back to your father so he would stand proud and relieved. But your life was not worth the risk of him compromising your location. The elders would have you terminated immediately."

Nekora wondered how she even beat the odds without this knowledge. First, her grandparents would have her killed for just breathing. Now her step-uncle would have her killed as a child had he known of her. A whole new admiration overcame her as she remembered her father. He must have been dying inside holding all this back. She was trembling from information overload.

The lady continued, "You are much more than you appear, Nekora. You are much stronger than you think you are. It is now time for you to complete your quest. Success or failure holds the balance this day. Open your mind, let yourself get lost. You will see everything clearly once you have mastered this. You already mastered the concept of time. Retrieve the hidden staff of Gammon; it will explain the rest of the story to you. I must go now. I cannot be caught here, or your life will be forfeited."

"How? Would I be able to see my real parents since I am so powerful? What do I do? I do not know where to start." Nekora fashioned question after question. The apparition started to fade. Nekora looked at her woefully.

"Who are you?" Nekora's voice was a whisper; she could not speak anymore from sorrow.

"Your mother."

CHAPTER THIRTEEN

"Your mother" was all Nekora could hear in her mind as the apparition disappeared. Nekora was pulled back into her body. Her back arched upward as her eyes opened wide and she gasped for air. She burst into tears as Poko held her in his arms for comfort, happy she was still alive.

Nekora welcomed the embrace, wishing it were Thorn, but she would take what she could get in this moment of confusion. She closed her eyes and opened her mind. She needed to find her connection.

She concentrated hard on making a connection—something, anything. She must find her center, she remembered, so she relaxed and let the blackness sink in.

Captain Poko was worried. Her pulse was fading. He kept her in his lap, holding her to comfort her. There was nothing he could do.

A few seconds later, Nekora felt a presence. She concentrated on that feeling as it grew in strength inside her. Butterflies danced in her stomach as she felt an immensely strong connection.

All seven black dragons looked up at the same time. They sensed an ancestral connection. One dragon silently conversed, "Who dares enter upon our domain?" Gilgamere more demanded than asked. "It is I, Nekora, princess of dragons and the underworld. I am awakened and in dire need of help to bring balance to this world." All the dragons roared in apprehension at the same time.

Every guard looked at each other as the roars echoed into the cavern. Fear overwhelmed them.

"The last thing we need is dragons in here now!" thought every guard. They looked around the cavern, terrified of being eaten.

"How can this be? A mortal among our ranks?" questioned Gilgamere.

"I am a supreme mage and seek your help, mighty dragon," Nekora stated.

"You must prove yourself worthy. We are one yet many. Seek you the staff of the overlords. If you can wield it, you are worthy. Find us when your task is complete." Gilgamere ended the communication. The dragons were now on high alert. For the first time in ancient history, contact has been made between elven and dragon.

Nekora woke again. This time she felt different. She felt a power alien to her. She closed her eyes again; this time, she found she could control her direction. She went after what she sought. The astral world, the ease of which to navigate was benign. All she ever had to do was think of what and where she wanted to go.

Poko was worried. Nekora fell in and out of consciousness. She needed medical treatment quickly if she were to survive. Poko was about to sound the retreat when Nekora started to glow. It started as faint blue, then shifted to purple, then to black. Soon, she was glowing with the three colors intertwining. The aura became stronger and stronger, then disappeared as she woke, refreshed, ready and even hungry for battle. The wound on her head disappeared.

Nekora drifted into the ether world. She had found the great library. The aisles appeared to go on for miles in every direction. Each aisle filled with books. She presumed the books to be the history and recordkeeping of every event in natural history. Every book she looked at was with her current world. She finally found the aisle containing books on magic. When she touched any of them, she was welcomed with a tremendous shock. The book somehow linked to her. She would then read, absorbing all the material within.

The blue aisle covered the resources associated with elemental magic. Air, Earth, Fire, Water, and Poisons. Each book had detailed instructions as to how to prepare for and cast each spell appropriately. She knew spells associated with the elements such as lightning, fireballs, firewalls, acid arrows, and necromantic spells such as contagion and other poisons. She felt stronger as each book was ingested, and all the elements were hers to control. She needed to hurry.

The purple aisle was filled with ways to enhance and bend spells to the wielders will. There was ultimate control over the magical arts; books about manipulating and bending spells to suit the caster. This is something she never knew mages could do. Her body was now consumed by a purple aura. As she finished the last book, the auras came together as one, twirling together in one multicolored display. It was all coming together.

The black aisle contained books on raising and controlling the dead, life, armies, warfare, evocation, and conjuration spells galore. She was thrilled; a whole new opportunity presented itself. As she touched and absorbed each book, her body became encompassed by a black aura growing much stronger with each book. She had to know all of them. At long last, her mission, her life was clear to her, she knew what had to be done. She could complete her mission and return to finish the other books later.

Nekora woke and began to stand. She was clearer now than ever before. Her uncle must perish, and everyone else who got in her way.

Baern witnessed the impacting event that had caused the intruders to disburse. A large smile crossed his face.

"I will retaliate with everything you are not!" he yelled. He knew the intruders would not hear him, but the yelling gave him a sense of satisfaction. He exited the gate into the battlefield. The first intruder he saw was killed by his bolt. Another, then another. One by one, the Elves were dying at Baerns hands.

"This should grant me a stay of execution," he thought as he took the army down one at a time. He viewed a figure kneeling high atop a rock. He appeared to be holding another victim. The victim stood and showed confidence and strength that startled him.

How is that possible? That Elf was squashed by a falling Drider unless my eyes played tricks on me. He took aim. The standing figure reached out her hand, a multicolored ray of black, blue, and purple sprang forth from her hand and hit him square in the chest. Baern dropped the crossbow and fell to his knees. He was weakened. Poko ran down and killed him on the spot. The other guards followed suit.

Twenty-seven elite woodland guards survived. The events have softened a bit to allow them to regroup. They formulated a plan to infiltrate the city and make headway to the castle. The first obstacle was the wall.

Nekora proclaimed, "I got that covered."

Next was to breach the city and take over the castle. They had to maneuver the hallways to find the King and Queen. After what Poko witnessed, he would never question Nekora again.

Nekora gathered about the loose rocky debris. Her eyes rolled back into her head as she twirled her arms in a circular horizontal motion with palms facing downward, she chanted,

Budro enak formas

She slowly raised them above her head as the rocks formed. With a thunderous sound from each impact, the rocks themselves merged into one. She increased her melody and spirit, voice increasing in volume as she continued her spell.

Mehan juro froketa
Han Juno destro!

She hurled her arms forward as hard as she could, releasing the pent-up energy welled within her. The massive boulder shot forth at great speed, impacting the wall with a mighty force, easily demolishing the barrier. The army gathered and entered the city with minimal constraints. Many villagers were crushed from the boulders impact. Villagers were easy prey if they got in the way; otherwise, they were left alone. There was only one thing on their minds, revenge. Nekora stayed behind.

Nekora's eyes rolled back once more as she intricately moved her arms and hands in a wavy fashion from top to bottom with a strong purpose, quietly voicing an incantation.

> In Septus Unike Val Almaryha
> Rizen todo ni sufres
> Caelum reparo, vengas detro

The ground shook violently. Nekora kept her focus, her aura strengthening. Rocks were falling from walls and ceilings, stalactites dropping like spearheads. The quake rolled throughout the caverns. It took a lot of dexterity to remain standing during the rumbles. She continued,

> Sin titolu des Bron Ja Kardya
> Rizen avenji demises
> In Gammon ni seerney.

All around, the dead were moving. They shifted to an upright position, slowly, and headed toward Nekora. Every dead creature on and off the battlefield rose to greet their new master.

Nekora had risen the dead. Her army was now enormous. The freshly dead guards were glowing, wounds still festered, and their hearts still but hunger to serve. All the dead guards, both woodland and Drow, Cerberus,

Minotaur, and Driders have stiffly risen from their resting place. They rose do one thing, serve their master.

She commanded the undead. A feeling of supremacy overwhelmed her. Her body tingled with anticipation of future events. She could be invincible.

"Find the King and Queen, bring them to me immediately!" Nekora shouted.

Each of them dispersed and did as they were commanded. They headed into the broken wall and toward the castle as she looked down and spread her arms outward forming a "T." Without raising her head, she looked up toward the gate and smiled an evil smile.

Nekora was elated that she could not only raise but control the dead; she somehow harnessed the power. The idea was exhilarating. She had no idea just how powerful she really was. She needed to fixate on her newfound skills. She needed to harness it, make it better and stronger. She yearned for more power. She smiled at the idea.

"I must open my mind, let in the newfound freedom," she thought. Her smile grew even wider as she opened her mind and raced to find her answers.

After some time, Nekora finally walked through the broken wall and into the main courtyard. Her armies have overrun the city and are now in search of the King and Queen. Poko ran to his Queen.

"Stand Back! I will rid this city of the undead." This time, it was Nekora who placed a calming hand upon his shoulder.

"Fear not, young Captain. These undead are mine. I control them."

Poko looked at Nekora with fear in his eyes. "What happened to you?"

Nekora smiled. "My mother, my REAL mother, is what happened."

Poko was confused, fear filled his entire body.

As the undead were roaming the outside, the lively guards entered the castle. Searching room by agonizing room. The thought of splitting up was quickly dismissed since they knew how deadly the king can be according to the slave reports. As a group, they cleared each section of the castle.

The army entered what they thought would be the bedroom but instead was the treasury. Nekora had caught up to the group as they descended the winding stone staircase. Each person took what they could carry. Captain Poko found some shelving with scrolls and books. There was a stick barely visible behind the shelving. He reached back and brought forth a staff. It was very heavy, much heavier than it looked. One side was shaved to a spear like point, the other had golden donut, housing a six-inch diameter ruby stuck to the golden mount with small, animated lightning bolts.

Nekora perked up and commanded Poko to bring her the staff. He did so. The rune markings were not only for power but told a story. Nekora began reading as the guardsmen collected everything in the room.

The writings on the staff stated, "Gammons Staff. For the wielder to control of the unworldly powers. A gift for the bloodlines. A power to a seeker, a danger to prey. Wield carefully for consumption will reveal all."

"The staff of Gammon," Nekora whispered.

Poko, wide-eyed now, looked to Nekora. "The mythical staff of legends?"

Nekora pointed the staff at a locked door.

Leet Destro!

Nekora yelled as lightning shot forth toward the entryway. The wooden door suddenly burst into splinters as the lightning bolt impacted with a loud crack and sizzling sounds. The thunderous lightning set forth a shockwave, knocking the wind out of everyone. All the guardsmen ducked for cover with the surprise attack and sudden loss of breath. Metal and wooden shrapnel was sent flying throughout the room before finally resting throughout in small pieces.

The Elves rummaged through the room, amazed at the ferocity of power the staff yielded and only found fragments of what used to be a door, the largest piece left was only three inches in length.

The treasurer hidden behind a false wall witnessed something impossible. This Nekora girl had wakened the staff. For hundreds of years the staff lay dormant. No one was able to activate its power. Yet here she is. He ran off to find the King through the tunnels hidden in the walls so as not to be seen.

"Oh my god, this is it. We are doomed. The prophecy is here, the city will die terribly." He was much in thought and forgot to stop before running directly into the hidden doorway. The treasurer fell with a thud. Rubbing his forehead, he got up and flipped the small lever to release the latch holding the false bookcase securely to the wall. The King turned and eyed his treasurer with his crossbow pointing directly at him, fresh poison dripping from the tip. He relieved a sigh and lowered his weapon.

"You almost died, you idiot! What is the news of my castle?"

"Your highness, the prophecy is here! She wields the staff of Gammon and is coming for you and the Queen!"

Bron looked up as if looking to the heavens. "Then I know what must be done."

Bron departed the room with haste and made his way outside the castle. He took care to not be seen by the roaming soldiers. He ducked to the right and crouched, now hidden in the brush.

Nekora looked at the staff; it glowed and hummed. The weight was that of a feather. The glowing brightened to a blinding light then quickly dissipated. The staff of Gammon was now solid gold, even the shape changed a little. The pointed end was now more rounded. The opposing end was no longer donut-shaped but half-mooned, a crescent with the ruby suspended with the lightning bolts seen earlier, dancing, vigorously shifting to different positions and silently crackled as they danced. The staff was a marvel to behold. A beauty with no comparison.

Knowing what this meant, Poko knelt before his Goddess and gestured everyone to do the same. He knew of the staff from many stories told over the centuries. He also knew that only a God or Goddess can successfully wield the staff of Gammon.

"Your holy ship," Poko barely squeaked in a raspy voice. He was filled with turmoil and found it hard to find words.

"Please, Captain, I am still Nekora. The one you trained and befriended." She smiled a comforting smile. The smile warmed him, and he felt much more comfortable, which was odd. Her beauty glowed as she innocently smiled.

"I must report back to Thorn," Poko stated.

Nekora looked over to her captain and smiled.

"And that you must, but he shall not know of me and my new livelihood for it will scare him off. I cannot lose him, not now as he is needed."

Poko understood; he bowed then made way to depart the city and head back to Morhgrammir. He ensured that no one would tell this tale, ever. Only Nekora could disseminate this information when she felt it right.

Nekora looked around, and finding nothing of value, she departed the area and started to the exit of the castle. Queen Kardya was hidden in the shadows, ready to pounce and kill this intruder.

Nekora felt the presence and turned to face the hidden Queen.

"Hello, Aunt Kardya. What brings you the pleasure?" Nekora stated as she reached out her arm. An invisible arm grasped the Queen from thirty feet away and brought her to the center of the grand entryway. Queen Kardya gasped for air. She could not speak as the life force was draining from her.

"What is the matter? Magic got your tongue?" Nekora hurled the Queen as hard as she could against the marble wall. The impact shattered her skull and numerous bones.

The Queen fell limp with a gelatinous landing. Nekora looked around the ornate entryway. Statues of former rulers lined the entryway to the back area where a giant throne was sitting. The elaborate paintings depicted the story of the city and how it became as it was.

Scientists engineered the Driders from spider and Drow DNA, merging them until the final being emerged as a spider body with eight legs and ended with the torso of a Drow warrior. Arms were attached to regular shoulders to wield spears and a large bulbous abdomen to throw webs, a dangerous concoction of materials.

The Cerberus, were altered magically to stand over common enemies, inducing fear before ripping them to shreds with their three heads attached to a canine body.

"What a sick and twisted group," Nekora thought as she headed for the exit.

As Nekora departed the castle, the King stepped out of the shadows, pointing his crossbow at Nekora. She smirked.

"We have come together at long last, Uncle. Give up now or die."

King Bron laughed. "You think I shall bow down to you? I think you have this backward. You should bow to me since I am King here. That staff changes nothing!"

Nekora replied, "Since we are on the subject, I am a Queen, therefor the rules do not apply. Now that formalities are terminated."

Before she could finish her sentence, a bolt came rushing in to meet Nekora square in the chest. Knowing this would happen, Nekora cast a shield spell she had been holding to deflect the bolt away from her.

Sheyna!

The bolt bounced off an invisible force field and lodged itself somewhere in the brush.

"Not a wise move, Uncle"

Ackin!

Nekora shot forth her right arm, conjuring an arrow of acid moving at breakneck speed. The arrow hit Bron in the stomach and splattered acid all over his body as it abruptly dissipated. The acids power hurled the King backward to the ground as it quickly ate through the clothing and light armor the King wore.

"What the hell (cough), was that?" the King demanded weakly.

It was now reaching into his skin as it burned. The King yelled as he was in horrendous pain. It smelled of rotten, burning flesh. The pain was immense and was traveling through his skin and into his body. Hissing noises sounded as it touched fresh liquid. Blood and acid mixed, generating vapor. King Bron, slowly, painfully laid to rest.

Nekora was beside herself. There was nothing left to do. Her vengeance was complete. All there was now, was to head back to Morhgrammir to live out her life peacefully. After her visit with the dragons, of course.

Nekora looked at her staff, reading the symbols as she left for the dragon caverns, trying to find other answers. Her mother stated the staff would tell her the rest of the story.

She sat on the steps and started looking around the staff, deciphering what it said.

STAFF OF GAMMON

Only a true blood may awaken the staff. To awaken the staff, is to awaken the power within. Enhances abilities to insurmountable power to suit the wielder.

"Huh?" Nekora's eyes squinted in confusion. "So, according to the apparition, Vera, who is my mother, whom is a goddess of beauty, and my father, Lord of dragons, makes me a Goddess or half goddess?" Nekora thought. She was perplexed, but she understood. She had always cheated in her battles to win; she used magic to enhance her marksmanship, and she was always better at everything she did, her ability to memorize the smallest of details. It all finally made sense.

Though Nekora had cheated in life, it trained her to read and redirect energy to suit her needs. The battle they had just won, she had easily found a way to redirect the energy so they would win from a losing scenario. Her ways had trained her for this moment. Now she felt bad. Her wonderous look turned to that of sadness as she never gave Thorn a fair chance to prove himself. But she knew if she had not used her powers, Thorn could have easily defeated her.

The undead were still walking among the ruins. Nekora took her staff in her left hand and waved it in a horizontal motion to dismiss them back to the gods. There was no reason for them to wander the area.

Ju tanak astou
Rit thok habirye
In Gammon ni seerney

They collapsed where they stood immediately. There was no more danger to come from this city. All the stories, treasure, and history were collected. Nekora stood and looked around at the layout of the city. She finally had a chance to take in the scenery. It was beautifully structured, no doubt. Most houses were topped with spiked roofs, dark in color to match the darkness in the cavern, almost masking the city had it not been for the dim lanterns showing the outlines. Even the castle was beautiful.

Too bad it was designed from Cretans. This could have been a wonderful place to live, quiet. She quickly removed that thought. There was no smell of pine trees, no bird singing, no friends or family. They would be dismal here. Before she knew it, she was at the entrance to the cavern. She turned and tried to think of anything they may have missed. Satisfied, she turned to the caverns and did not look back.

She caught up with Captain Poko as he was face to face with Gilgamere. The black dragon stood his ground, and from habit, did not let anyone leave the city. Nekora put up her hand, raising the staff as she muttered in the dragon tongue.

"Uhkno doJha Khrani Dohr Sahnge," she said in a stern voice.

Gilgamere took two steps back after seeing the golden staff of Gammon in Nekoras left hand. He talked with Nekora in here mind.

"So, you are the prophesied one. What are your orders?"

"Be free, my friend. Leave the Kingdom, my Kingdom, you attacked earlier this year alone, and you may wander, explore, and feed. Maybe find a better living place." Nekora thought back to Gilgamere.

Confused, Poko looked to Nekora and the dragon. Neither of them said a word, but both concentrated as if it was a staring contest.

"As you please, my lady." Gilgamere let out a mighty roar, scaring the army to death. The roar awakened the other dragons, and they flew out the cavern top. It was once again quiet.

"So, we couldn't get a ride, huh?" This time it was Poko who cleared the air. As he started speaking, it started raining gold coins and gems of many colors upon the army. Nekora had a wonderful idea.

"Get the ropes together high enough to reach the top of those platforms." We need to hurry before they come back.

Poko and the team fashioned a long rope chain to hang from the edge of the plateau down to where they were all gathered. As they were tying the knot to the makeshift hook, one of the guards peered down to them and called out, "Are you guys coming or what?" He laughed as he pointed to barely seen pathway up to the ledges.

One by one, each elf navigated the pathway up to the plateaus where the dragons previously resided. Mounds of gold and gems were piled high on each plateau. Each elf gathered what they could carry. Every item that was not a coin or gem was magical in nature. Nekora spotted them immediately. Hundreds of items glowing their faint blue aura, indicating magic enhancement.

Nekora did not have enough scrolls to identify all the items. She was reminded of the Minotaur treasure as well and had to remember to detour and take the bag.

The youngest guard came to Nekora with an empty bag in his hand.

"Your Grace, this was given to me to give to you should we need it. I had forgotten until now about it and I am so sorry to have disappointed you. The mage said something about being a bag of holding. Not sure what she meant since all bags are made for holding things."

Nekora's eyes widened. "It is not what it is for, it is what it is for." She smiled knowing it utterly confused him.

"Watch," she stated.

The longsword she found on the plateau was thrust into the bag, disappearing. The guard was amazed, the bag was not large enough for that weapon, yet it fit. She put everything she found into the bag, and it appeared empty, weightless. Only Nekora knew how to utilize its power. All seven plateaus were emptied of their riches.

"Quickly, we must leave before the dragons realize they had forgotten their treasure," stated Nekora.

"We will never have to worry about the dragons again," Nekora continued as she led the group to the Minotaur lair. The dead Minotaur lay where they stood after Nekora released her spell. The group had to climb over the bodies to get inside and work their way back to the bagged treasure. They grabbed the bag, any other loose treasure, and made their way to the mountain exit.

CHAPTER FOURTEEN

The human town of Haversmith was alight with energy. An enormous wall made of stone was erected to keep out intruders and local wildlife. In the middle sat the largest building, the castle, was surrounded by the army quarters. The town, market, and housing were bustling with activity this day and surrounded the castle with the market square closer to the ocean. Taverns were always busy. Gold, silver, and copper coins flowed from traders who made their way early to get the best deals and items before the festivity began.

Haversmith was known for their impeccable ivory made from the tusks of the local wildlife such as boars and elephants in the area. Ivory has a history of being medicinal and lucky to own. Due to the limited resources, Ivory was very expensive and usually only purchased by the rich. This does not mean the guilds around town do not try to get their own share in the profits. Guards are always on extra alert since thievery heightens during the trading event.

Traders arrive in Haversmith every quarter in hopes of finding their riches. Items included a vast range from spices to perfumes, silk to ivory, and everything between.

Hundreds landed here to make profits. It is also the only place large ships could safely dock.

Jagged rocks and mighty reefs encircled the island, making it highly dangerous. Many have tried, and many ships are lost to the sea along with thousands of gold items and coins. The humans cleared the eastern beach by destroying the reefs and rocks, making it safe for large ships to embark for their trades.

It is the ivory everyone was after. It sold for quite a bit more on the mainland. The hard part is smuggling the items into the mainland without being arrested. Fortunately for the traders, there were many hiding places around the ship.

Michael Crook, an extraordinarily rich trader, stood on the dock with his entourage as expected for every arrival. He was looking to the east, watching the incoming trader ship approach.

"Can these ships move any fucking slower," Michael said in a soft voice. His entourage was with him as they always were, each hoping to be on his best side.

Erick, his second in charge spoke up, "Well, they can only go as fast as the wind will take them. Besides, do you think there will be better garments in this shipment? The last two shipments were useless and should have been dumped overboard in the middle of the sea." He pointed out.

Michael was deep in thought. "We got word of special cargo, but no other details were given. This better not be a waste of my time."

The ship finally docked. Yelling was heard as they directed the ship to the dock safely. Ropes were thrown overboard as the ground personnel tied them up. Foam barriers were put into place for the safety of the ship and the dock. The gang plank was coming down, and the ship slightly rocked with the small waves.

Michael turned to his people. "Time to put on our trading faces," he said, disgruntled. He spotted a scrawny man gracefully walking down the plank.

"Michael!" he stated with a wide smile.

"Steven!' Michael responded with an equally large smile.

They met at the bottom of the plank and gave a quick welcome hug.

"Rumor has it you have special cargo for us this time. How can that out do any treasure you have brought us so far?" Michael patted Steven on the back. Steven slightly stumbled forward from the overly strong pat but quickly recouped his balance.

"Oh no, not yet, my friend," Steven responded, waving his finger. "We must dine on fine wine tonight before I unveil that which will truly catch your interest." They made way to the best tavern Haversmith had to offer, which was right on the docks.

"The freshest seafood anywhere, not to mention a mouthwatering roast," the Wicked Wench stated Michael as pointed to the larger building with smoke rising from the top.

"The smell is delectable, I tell you. If I remember correctly, the wine and food exceed the smell," Steven responded with a smile. "Besides, the ship food and wine are the nastiest thing you will ever experience, Blah!" Steven stuck out his tongue. They entered the tavern.

Michael laughed. "I will take your word for it. Server! Bring us your finest wine and roast!"

The server nodded and off she went. She always made Michael priority number one before anyone else aside from the royalty, which was easy since they never dine here. Michael tipped better that way.

Steven recounted the nasty storm they passed through, causing him to throw up in the middle of the ocean. "It was absolutely horrible, I tell you! The waves were huge. I thought the ship was going to plunge into the depths!" Steven started with his hand showing an exaggerated eighty-degree incline. "Nature was not kind to us on this trip," he finished as the server came by with a bottle of their best wine.

He also recounted the calm starry nights that could never be seen in the city; the times the moon was full, and the amount of light that was produced gave full view of the ocean. The best sunsets and sunrises. The stories went on and on. The problem was the stories were the same every time he came to visit. By the time he finished, large platters were set in front of them with the softest, best tasting roast anywhere.

The roast melted in their mouths with a rich beefy gravy made from scratch and was the chef's secret recipe. He never gave out his recipe and for good reason. However, small jars were always on sale at the trader market, and people snatched them up like hotcakes.

After Steven recounted his tales, he snapped his fingers. He had to do it a few times since the grease from the roast covered them. A quick wipe with the towel remedied that. "Hate the damn grease but love the food here!" Steven exclaimed. Two lads came around with bundles covered so as not to be seen by the wary folk.

"Where can we do business in private?" Michael asked the server. She took them to a private room where they could inspect the goods. Two lads opened the door and ushered the two traders into an empty room. It was then they uncovered the bundles, revealing the most beautiful and soft silk linens. Six of them were laid out for inspection. Michael touched each one after a quick washing of his hands and could not believe how soft and slick they were. Michael had wide eyes as he felt the softness begging him to lie upon them. Each contained unique patterns.

"All of these linens were made in Angut, a small village across the ocean. I want you to have first dibs before I bring them to market. You would not believe what I had to pay for them", Steven stated as Michael looked them over.

"How much are they selling for?" he inquired.

Steven looked at his friend. "They will go to market at five gold apiece. I will give a set to you for three." Michael produced an ivory statuette of an Orc, readying his axe to swing.

"Will this do?" Michael inquired. Steven smiled.

"You always know what makes me happy. Of course, please choose your set," Steven said and gestured.

Michael was drawn to the black linens with silver linings. The intricate star and cross patterns were soothing, and he figured it would help him sleep better at night.

"Do you think the chef will have bigger jars of his delicious gravy this time?" Steven inquired. "His normal jars are too small, and it does not last long," he finished. Michael laughed.

"I will see what I can do, old friend" he said as he put his hand on Steven's shoulder to bid farewell for the night. "Don't you have a date with the brothel?" Michael asked.

The two lads covered the linens and took them back to the safe room until the event was about to launch. Steven quickly glanced out the window. "Crap, I need to get there before all the good ones are taken!" he exclaimed as he ran out the door.

Michael paid for the meal and tip. As he walked home, he noticed a skinny figure running toward the castle. Thinking nothing of it, the master trader went home. Who am I to interfere with an assassin? Maybe it was an assassin. Was it a thief? "Gah, so long as he or she does not go my direction," Michael thought as walked back to his house. He kept looking back to make sure he was not followed or next robbery or assassin victim. He picked up his pace.

It was still early in the night as royalty got ready for the night's embrace. Two guards ran in and asked for the King's appearance for an immediate concern. One guard hastened to the chambers, where he knocked on the door. The King opened it.

"My apologies, your highness, but the scout has returned, and he says he has news of the utmost importance. I tried to get the news from him, but he will only speak to you," the guard stated. "He claims it to be an urgent matter."

"All right. I will be down in a few minutes," the king answered, frustrated. The guard bowed and headed off to the awaiting party.

"Can't this wait?" asked the Queen. She let her dress hit the floor. She was baring her naked body, prompting him to wait until morning.

"My dear," the king started, "I really hate this interruption, believe me. No one is more irate than I. But this business could mean we would be the richest couple on the planet. I have to take this, but I will be back as quickly as possible," he remarked, then kissed her passionately as he cupped her breast. He kissed her breast and set off to the main hall.

A few minutes later, the King arrived in casual garments. From the hastened nature of events, he deemed there was no time to properly dress in formal wear.

"Your highness!" the royal guard yelled, and everyone stood at attention, bowed, then back to attention. A skinny male bowed low and remained there until told to rise, which the King did quickly. The scout was breathing heavily. The king was tired and ready for passionate lovemaking. The Queen was already upset with him for not waiting until morning.

The skinny guy known as David stood t and waited for permission to talk. The news he had could turn events around for the Kingdom. He was elated and could hardly hide his anticipation.

"Well, out with it!" the King demanded.

"Your royal highness, it was my turn to scout the outer limits of our boundaries and decided to head to the mountains of Almaryha. I went up and peered over the Kingdom to take in the view in its entirety, which is absolutely beautiful."

"I don't have all night, scout! What is your report and this better be good to interrupt my night!" the King retorted.

"Oh, it is your majesty. I was getting to that."

The King was even more flustered now that he caused a delay in his romantic night with the Queen. The scout continued, "I was taking in the scenery when I heard voices that did not sound familiar. I hid in the dense foliage and waited. There must have been a hundred Elves looking for something on the small plateau. It was then something amazing happened. One of them disappeared through the stone and dirt!" The scout was elated. It marked an event in history that could broaden their horizons.

The King was pondering. "What do you mean, disappeared?"

"They walked through the dirt as if it were not there. Once they were all through, I waited for a bit and checked it out. There is an illusion of debris hiding an entrance. It was a dark narrow tunnel that wound downward. I think it may lead to the infamous city of Almaryha itself. I had to quickly depart since I heard one of them coming back."

The King's interest piqued. Hidden treasures magical in nature was thought to be down there. Mythical creatures that would make him look victorious to his people. Dragons that hoard treasure. The King's eyes glossed at the thoughts of the overwhelming wealth.

"Tomorrow marks the trading event. I will discuss this with my advisors in the morning. Scout, you are dismissed."

David bowed, turned, and was escorted out of the castle.

"Tim, get with your knights. I need to you collect all the information you can from that scout and any other person you may know of who has gone off in that direction. I want to formulate a plan that will take place exactly four weeks from today, after the trader's market event. I want to lead the party myself."

"It is true then. There are underground beings in those mountains. How have we not seen them before now?" the King contemplated as he went back upstairs to bed with his wife. He was too excited to sleep now.

"I'm back, honey, ready to rumble with..." his voice was cut off with the sound of light snoring. Now, he was truly mad.

Michael rose early the next morning. He was pleased at how well the linen he purchased offered a good night's comfortable sleep. He needed to thank his friend. For the first time in a long time, he was looking forward to the next four weeks of trading.

Michael was in the middle of setting up his table when the King approached him.

"Michael," the King stated.

"Your highness", Michael responded with a bow.

The King looked around; no one was around. "You can call me Bob." Bob and Michael were the best of friends since childhood. Bob was the prince, and Michael was the son of a lord. While growing up, formalities had to be adhered, regardless of how much Bob hated hearing his friend calling him by his royal standard. When no one was near, the King insisted Michael call him by his first name.

"Hi, Bob, sorry, no time to ensure eavesdroppers. Took no chances since we are in the open." They laughed.

"I have a proposition for you if you are interested, Michael," the King continued.

The king and master merchant walked the streets, catching up with each other. The King stopped down the roadway and turned to Michael.

"Our scouts have reported a hidden entrance to a cavern up on the mountains. If there is a cave with a hidden entrance, particularly an illusion, then that means..."

"Hidden treasure," Michael intervened. "If someone has to go through enough trouble to hide an entrance, then it may be worth looking into."

Both smiled. "I will go, but I get forty percent since I am doing all the work," Michael replied.

"You will get your usual twenty-five percent since I will lead the charge, and I will have my guards look the other way in all your dealings."

"Thirty-five percent and not a copper less, retorted Michael. King Bob smiled.

"You drive a hard bargain, sir, no wonder you are the master merchant." They laughed.

"I would like to look at the archives we have, so my men and I will be ready at your command."

"Actually, the prophecies are the only information we have to work from. Besides, what is the fun in going on an adventure knowing what to expect?" the King responded.

"Um, life maybe," Michael teased.

The royal guards always at attention of their surroundings, propped up when a ruckus was heard inside the Double Duck, a nearby tavern. They quickly surrounded the pair when six men came out in a brawl. The guards took the men to a safer area back to the docks as the others arrested the men for disturbance.

"Never a dull moment down here?" inquired the King.

"Never," replied the merchant.

They soon parted ways, and Michael got to thinking about the upcoming adventure.

Why would Bob want to wait until AFTER the trade event? Four weeks is an awfully long time to wait. Michael was deep in thought when he collided with Steven.

"Michael!" Steven exclaimed. "What happened? Crows got your eyes?" Steven laughed.

"Sorry, Steve, need to figure out a master plan is all," Michael responded.

"Oh!" Steven perked up, wondering what kind of treasures were at stake. "Anything I can do to help?" He continued tapping his fingers with anticipation.

Michael contemplated the moment. An idea struck his head.

"Steven, what do you know about Almaryha?"

"Just myths and legends, of course. You would have better information than I. Why? are you planning a camping trip?" Steven asked.

"Yes, in three days, myself and some trustworthy fellows are going to excavate what may have been found. No longer a myth, my friend," Michael said as he stared off into nothingness.

"How about explaining to the King that you need to scout the terrain so the knights would not be caught off guard from the unknown. Then after the scouting party, you will report with more accurate information," Steven gestured.

Michael smiled at the idea. He grabbed Steven by the head and kissed his forehead. "Steven you are a genius!" he exclaimed.

"I have my moments," Steven acknowledged as he wiped the lip prints from his forehead.

The next day, Michael went in search of Jordan. He was found finishing the presentation table when Michael arrived.

"Jordan, I need a favor from you. I need you to tend the table this event. An urgent matter has come up needing my immediate attention," Michael stated.

Jordan smiled. "No worries, Michael. Just be careful." Jordan was always the cautious one. He worried about anyone and everyone who ventured out and about. Too many tavern tales of monster wolves and such.

The next day, Michael was summoned to the castle. The King needed his friend's advice and counsel for this trip. Maps were strewn about the table with none of them showing an entrance except for the top hole, which extended thousands of feet down, making that option not available. The scout was there and pinpointed the exact location of the illusory entrance.

Michael memorized the map and entrance location. He intended to make way soonest to snatch and grab what he could before the King became involved.

"Your highness," Michael started. "There are rumors of creatures and mongrels that inhabit the city. Even the guardsmen are creatures according to the fables and myths. I would like to take some personnel with me and do a scout of the area. If there are any truths, we will uncover and be better prepared for the attack. Also, not to mention, mapping the inner tunnels."

The King pondered the idea. Even though Michael was his friend, he did not put the possibility of him being all truthful, either. He looked for any facial gesture for lies from his friend.

"After all these years, sire, you think I would steal from you?" Michael said as he noticed the King's expression.

"That is a great idea. Michael, take twenty guardsmen. I want as much detail on this as you can muster," he responded.

"Thank you, sire," was all Michael could say.

As Michael turned and fled the room, the King beckoned his first in command over. He whispered to the guard, "I want you to go with him. Make sure he does as he is bid and no more. I want a full report upon your return."

"Yes, your highness," said the guard as he resumed his post.

"So, where were we?" the King asked as he smiled and gestured to the maps.

Michael had a plan of his own. He knew the King would send a spy with him, so he had to play it cool. He met with a few of his friends at the Double Duck. They were friends he could trust without question. The server sent them to a separate room where they could talk privately.

"First order of business, we will be on a treasure hunt tomorrow. The entrance to the famed city of Almaryha has been found. At least, it must be or else why the illusionary entrance. So, if this is true, then there would be treasures galore. We could be filthy rich," Michael started.

"There has to be a catch," Gordon stated.

"You think there is a catch to everything, Gordon," Steven replied.

"I'm still breathing, right?" he retorted.

Gordon was always grumpy, but he had his moments. For one, Michael could trust him with his life. He was a bit older than Michael with long dark hair and a deep scar running the length of his left cheek. His nose was large from being broken on several occasions. His brown eyes were as sharp as an eagle on a hunt; he caught everything.

"Anyways," Michael began, "as I was saying, there are riches to be had, but we must be quick. Sleight of hand must be foolproof. The King will surely have a spy or twenty with us so we must be careful."

The server came by with a large roast and two bottles of wine. Everyone was waiting for her to depart, then Michael spoke up. He went over the plan with the guys and did a makeshift drawing of the mountain with the entrance location.

"So, when the guards are with us on the inside of the cavern, we need to have a treasure call. Something indicating treasure in sight," Michael started.

Gordon sat upright. "Since this is a cavern, in a mountain made of dirt and dust, what about a sneeze? The guards would think nothing of it."

Michael pondered, "But since there will be dust, there will be sneezing. I am not going to have the guards lured away for a false alarm."

Gordon shot up his arms. "Then throw in a sniffle! For fucks sake, how can you not make an obvious noise."

Michael retorted, "You may be on to something, Gordon. If you legitimately sneeze, then keep going. If you see treasure, stop and wipe your hand on something."

"Yeah and follow it with a word like 'that's disgusting' or something like that," Steven added.

"Okay," Michael continued. "We got that part. If the pile is large, then say you are bagging it to bring to the King, but on the way out, try to sneak some. Either way, we are getting rich from this excursion."

The plan was almost complete. Next were talks about mythological creatures that roam the caverns that should be easily dealt with considering the guards are with them. Assassins and thieves were among the current party.

Day three came. Michael and his good friends gathered about the small gate in the west. No one ever checked the gate, which is why Michael chose it. He wanted a head start so the King would not have to worry. All would be taken care of before the event was over. Off they went.

CHAPTER FIFTEEN

The night air was brisk. Once outside, they all began to shiver. None of them brought blankets or warm clothing to wear. This dramatically slowed their progression.

"Ah, what do we have here?" Michael exclaimed. "A rash of bandits here to take our treasure?"

Nekora looked upon the human group. She took note of the amount of people who stood before her.

"Do you think this wise, human?" She accented human with ferocity after a brief dramatic pause, a general provoking technique meant to cause a disturbance and feud between the two groups.

"As you can see, you are far outnumbered. It would be wise of you to turn around and go back to the garbage heap you call home. You have no idea who you are dealing with," Nekora stated. With that last statement, Michael smiled.

"And you underestimate the number of forces on our side. Actually, by a lot."

As if on cue, over fifty armed mercenaries came out of hiding and twenty knights. With the number of boulders and brush, it was easy to hide, especially with the darkness hiding their numbers. The humans did not realize that Elves could see in the dark.

"Why is it we cannot we have a good day for once," Nekora thought. She was tired of fighting, and all the magic casting was taking a toll on her physically and mentally.

The Elves had the advantage, owning the higher ground. They quickly drew their bows and swords and started firing. The humans figured this would happen; they quickly ducked behind the boulders. Three of the Elven army dropped as arrows came from above, not realizing the ambush of humans higher up on the mountain. Nekora raised her staff.

Shikren

Nekora yelled as she slammed the butt end of her staff into the ground. The mountain started to shake. It started slowly and softly, then increased in intensity until it shook so violently that all the rocks and debris came loose and avalanched down the side taking the humans with it. The humans above were now in sword fights with the Elven elite. They were no match for the elite guard as they were quickly slain. Their defenses were down due to the unforeseen quake. They did not expect the unexpected.

The Elves watched as the remaining living humans retreated down the mountainside toward Haversmith. No other danger lurked, so they decided to make their way off the mountain and make camp to rest for the night in the cover of the forest.

The terrain of the cliffside was treacherous, even for the most dexterous Elf. Once they had reached the bottom, they ran for the cover of the trees twenty feet in front of them. They all gathered around and looked up to ensure the humans did not follow suit.

No humans were seen. However, the dragons have returned. They flew down the hole at the top of the mountain. And couple minutes later, they emerged and perched at the top, looking around the land.

The dragons came flying in after the Elves had made camp. The roars were heard outside, frightening roars, increasing in pitch as the dragons relocated to the top of the mountain, causing fear into anyone or anything nearby. Gilgamere saw the humans running for the city. They viewed the would-be thieves with hatred in their hearts. Gilgamere roared to the others.

"The humans have robbed our lair! They will pay for this!" he exclaimed in dragon language.

All seven dragons took flight and overflew the groups of humans as a practice run to ensure maximum fatalities. Michael heard the commotion behind him and saw movement. The black dragons were hidden with the night sky, but he could see movement at times. He was frightened, and his breathing was borderline hyperventilation. He had to slow down. The roars struck fear into the soul.

The dragons could see just as well in the night as they could during the day. They took note of the movement below, trying to discern which had their treasure.

The dragons were heated. No one person was carrying a bag large enough for their treasure, so they figured every human has their treasure dispersed among them, distributed to hide what they have stolen. Treasure that belonged to the dragons, not the humans.

All the dragons assembled into attack formation with a lead dragon, Gilgamere, formed into a triangle with three dragons on either side. They flew toward the largest mass of humans and laid fire walls through the groups. All the humans were burning minus Michael, who was well ahead of the group. Michael remained still, hoping to see only movement and not heat.

Every human died quickly. Not only were they burning, but the immense heat was much hotter than regular fire, causing the humans to die almost instantly with a short moment of pain, then ash. One more fly-by and the dragons retreated over the mountains to their newfound home. Michael did not move until he was sure nothing was around. Once satisfied, he made his way back to Haversmith.

At the bottom of the cliff, Nekora's group had descended; a tranquility overcame them. The air was not as cold as above, but it was still and stale. The group made way to the nearest clearing, scouted for safety, set up watches, and rested for the remainder of the night. Flapping and angry roars were heard over the mountains.

"We should be well hidden, no fires tonight," Poko commanded his men in a hushed voice. Nekora was fast asleep. Casting spells of this magnitude was new to her. It quickly diminished her strength as fatigue set in. She fell asleep the moment they stopped.

The next morning, the group packed up and made their way back home. Half the day was uneventful. The grouped stopped for a quick lunch with the snared rabbits and vegetation collected along the way. Unfortunately, the food also brought others to the party.

Gnolls were enroute to their position. The smells of the Elven spoils wafted through the air downwind into their greedy and heightened sense of smell. Scouts returned, notifying the group of their imminent arrival. Nekora was ready this time. She knew their attack patterns from her last encounter. Plus, she had a golden major advantage.

One Gnoll jumped into the middle of the camp to surprise the party and catch them off guard, making for an easy kill. The group was counting on their arrival and quickly jumped the Gnoll, preventing him from causing further harm. Once the Gnoll landed, four elite guardsmen jumped toward the Gnoll from every angle, confusing it for a moment. Swords ran deep into the tissue, and it fell lifelessly.

A second Gnoll entered the fray, only to hear a calling whistle. The Gnoll turned and faced Nekora.

Nekora raised her left hand and chanted,

Boondo!

The Gnoll fell to the ground and transfigured into a rabbit. Nekora stood there, weak, as she was not fully recovered from her experience. The elite guard surrounded their Queen and guarded her.

Seven other Gnolls entered the camp, furious at the outcome from the first two Gnolls and decided to take them with sheer numbers. Nekora raised her staff.

Leet Gropen Destro!

Lightning flew from the staff at great speed. The power was immense, shockwave taking the air from the groups' lungs. The bolt struck through the first Gnoll and bounced to the next, each hit with a sonic boom. The impact pierced through all the Gnolls and dissipated after it hit the last one. All of them fell in unison.

"There, much easier." Nekora laughed. The group all nervously laughed with her. After a bit, the laughter died off and they regrouped.

Nekora spotted an amulet on the first Gnoll. Something familiar. She inspected the amulet, then with surprise, ripped it from the corpse.

"This belonged to my brother, Meeka!" Tears welled and flowed down her cheeks. She now had closure, and a new hatred for these foul beasts. She sat to rest before continuing the journey.

Captain Poko recommended that they keep camp until Nekora was strong again. Nine Gnolls is the norm for a group so they should be good for another week or so. Nekora only needed a couple days.

A couple days later, the camp was quickly packed up and they continued their way home. The group had to hasten the march since they lost time. Nekora was getting antsy and wanted back in her bed. She was tired physically and emotionally. It was time to relax in peace and enjoy her friends and family.

Thorn was busy ensuring the Kingdom was running smoothly. Ensuring everyone was happy was a lot of work.

He did not understand how Nekora's parents did it. As he was inspecting the remodeled dais, the owl call came through. Thorn immediately took position for the group to enter.

Leading the charge was Nekora, followed by Poko, and forty-four remaining Elves out of one hundred thirty that had left.

Thorn ran to Nekora and embraced her.

"I am so glad you made it. I was worried about you."

Nekora looked him over as they held hands. "No need to worry about me, my love. I am stronger than you, remember?"

"Not for long. I have been training harder. You would have to...." Thorn got view of her staff strapped to her back as his sentence trailed off.

"Where did you find that? Is that one of your uncles?"

Nekora touched her staff, recollecting the events that unfolded. "One day, I will tell you; for now, we celebrate life."

The day went smoothly. No further hindrances occurred, and the Kingdom no longer feared anything that may arrive unannounced, mainly dragons.

The next day, a huge celebration was about to begin, but the noise was low. As usual. Queen Nekora stepped up to the dais. Impressed as it was more stable and solid than the last one. She looked at Thorn with admiration then turned to her Elves.

Nekora started her impromptu speech. "As you all know, a couple months ago, we were attacked by the evil lizards of the Drow. They commanded the dragons, and they were forced to obey. Since that time, we have cleaned up, restructured, and rebuilt this city to what I believe is better than it was before. The new shapes give this place flair. The beautification is much better in my opinion, and every one of you have done nothing short of an outstanding job."

Nekora continued, "Today marks a special day. Every celebration we have ever enjoyed was done with low volume. Well, no more! We have rid the Almaryha city of their inhabitants and creatures. I have made a deal with the dragons, and they have departed to a distant land and the humans are too far to pose a threat. We can celebrate as loud as we want and make it as fun as we desire. No more shall we live in fear. We can live as wild and free as want to be! But first, we must give a moment of silence to those who have perished for protecting our Kingdom. A great many brave soldiers died so you could live. Let us pray for their passing into the afterlife."

After Nekora ended her speech, the Elven people gave a moment of silence, then shouted as loud as they could muster. It felt good to no longer fear any threats. Food and drink flew, and the Elves were finally having a great time.

Thorn regarded Nekora and whispered, "Shall we keep this celebration short and get back to work early tomorrow? We have so much to do and are so close to finishing."

"No, let them relax and celebrate. Let them have fun for a few days to release stress." She overlooked the party. "They earned it."

Thorn agreed and raised his glass to the townsfolk. "To our new lives!" Cheers erupted. Games began. This was the most fun the Elves have had in a long time.

CHAPTER SIXTEEN

Michael barely made it back to his home, tired and weary from his long dramatic travels. Never again is would he step foot outside the walls.

Magic was not supposed to exist, he thought as he lied in bed, contemplating the day's events. Worse yet, two weeks left for the trader event, and the King was going to notice thirty-two missing villagers plus his twenty guards. How will he ever explain this? How can he cover dozens of missing people? He thought about it as sleep overcame him.

The morning came. Even the soft linen did not help his slumber; his sleep was interrupted by nightmares. He knew he had to do something. Then an idea hit him. He would hire the Orcs to revenge against the Elves that killed his friends.

"Yes, I will make way immediately after breakfast," he thought.

Steven entered the Boars Nest to visit Michael. This was more Michaels style as it was more expensive and only entertained the wealthy. The crowds were much less "energetic," and it soothed him. The food and wine were much more pleasing and easier on the stomach. The seasonings used by the master chef was imported from the city of Malgan, where an unlimited supply of spice resides.

The chef has mastered the art of crafting different seasonings to suit differing tastes. He was the best seasoner by far. "Why aren't they ever at the trader event?" Michael pondered. He would buy them all up. Also, how does the chef get them? He does not know his town, after all. For a master merchant, he surely does not know the trades well enough to govern them.

"That is it! I will govern all incoming trades and regulate taxes on them. This can fund my revenge," Michael thought as a smile crossed his face.

"Michael! So how was the raid?" Steven asked as he sat next to him in the booth. Michael did not realize his friend showed up. He was deep in thought and barely touched his breakfast. The server brought Steven some wine and asked if he wanted breakfast. Steven obliged and listened to Michael fester over the night's events.

"We had those damned elves surrounded. They did not seem to be carrying much, but we had the show of force. We were destined to win. The battlefield could not have been laid out any better," Michael started.

"That's what happens when you have a merchant plan a warrior's event," Steven interjected sarcastically.

"That's the problem, Steven! I was a warrior in my past life, remember? I was the best knight in this lousy city before I gave it all up for riches and glory." Michael reminisced his past before he was snapped back to the present with Steven trying to get his attention.

"Michael, how long ago was that? Things have changed. You need the help of the warrior elite," Steven said.

"Steven, I know what you are saying, but there was not supposed to be anything there, especially Elves! How I hate those nasty creatures!" Michael slammed his fist into the table, breaking the edge in half. Everyone in the tavern looked his way, then continued about their business.

"Steven, can I trust you with a secret?" Michael asked.

"Of course, did I not keep your alternative motives a secret?" Steven replied.

"Yes, yes, you have, I guess. Otherwise, the King would have ripped my arms off for disobeying him."

"And that is why you owe me one now. This is great because soon you will owe me two." Steven laughed uncontrollably. He hated owing people but loved when people owed him. That made him feel powerful.

"Ugh, I would have your throat cut if we were not friends," Michael said with a sigh. The thought of it was appealing to him, nonetheless. "Besides, I need your brains to keep the King entertained on my absence."

"Your absence? Are you leaving again? How many people you need to kill before you realize how bad of an idea this is?" Steven countered.

"I am going alone this time and not to the mountains. I am going to the Orc encampment to the north."

Stevens eyes widened with surprise and fear. He had heard countless tales of the lawless Orcs and their quickness to act by ripping off limbs before asking questions. It seemed to sooth their appetite. Anything that moves is potential food to them, so he had heard.

"You do realize those beasts are far worse than these annoying Elves?" Steven countered.

"No, I think these Elves need to be taught a lesson. On the subject, since when has magic ever existed?" Michael asked this question with hatred as if Steven had kept strategic intelligence away from him.

"Why are looking at me like that? Magic does not exist. It cannot exist. You realize how many people would vie for power if they knew magic?" A thought occurred to Steven. "Why do you ask?"

"One elven bitch conjured an earthquake, which killed most of my men and possibly called upon black dragons to finish off my team. They died horrendously. They died for no reason. I want vengeance. I want her head!" He said the last statement loudly, slamming his fist once more upon the table.

No one in the tavern had seen Michael this upset. It made them all wonder what was going on. Was the trading event ending early? Did someone not clean the bathrooms? Was there bad food in the tavern? All of them questioned what could upset the master merchant to such a magnitude. Gossip spread like wildflower.

Michael glanced around, giving everybody the evil stare until they looked away and minded their own business. It was impossible to plan anything anymore with too many prying ears. Michael turned back toward his friend.

"I need to get this resolved or I will be finding a new place to live," said Michael softly to keep from being overheard. Steven nodded.

"I will go to them, white flag in hand as a gesture of peace. I will then offer them what they need to do my bidding. When the job is done...." Michael trailed off. He had not thought the whole thing through. The more he inquired, the more questions it brought. This was driving him mad.

"Either way, this has to be on the down low," Michael continued.

"I would agree, you are not looking too healthy. Are you feeling all right?"

"Do I look like I am all right?"

Both members departed the tavern. It was best to get away from the gossip mongers and clear his head. He needed a plan and needed one fast. There was only one person who could plan this adventure in short time with precautions, but he works for the King. A bribe might help him.

Upon departing the tavern, they both made way to the trading event. Numerous tents filled the courtyard with promising merchants all trying to make their mark and gold. The linen supply from Steven was going quickly. Their stock was fading fast. The medicine man was also making sales at an alarming rate. Michael was curious and made his way to the medic.

During the event, Charlie, the medic, had provided artificial supplements to substantiate his proclamation of the "Healing Potion." He even used one bottle as a tester to prove the effectiveness of the concoction.

"Come one, come all. I have a brand-new service that you just cannot believe. I did not believe it until I tried it. Holy cow! What a potion to have for any unhealthy occasion!"

Charlie exclaimed. He went on to explain how he had met this mysterious person far away in an unknown land. How it cost him too much to just get a sample to save his life. When he lifted the bottom of his trousers to show the crowd, they all gasped. The scar was barely seen. Others laughed and called him a con man. That was when Charlie sprang into action.

"You there, sir, may I have a moment of your time?" he asked the laughing man closest to him. "I will prove to you how remarkably great this stuff really is." Charlie grabbed the man by the arm, led him up to platform, and immediately made a cut in his forearm. The man reared back and was ready to kill Charlie. Charlie smiled and put a dab of the mixture onto a rag and mimicked putting it on his arm. The man reluctantly gave in. To his surprise, the wound immediately felt better and began to heal. The man's mouth was gaped in surprise and awe about this magical mixture.

Charlie turned to the witnesses. "This is the best healing potion around. You will not find this anywhere. Since it cost me four gold for a dab, I will sell you an entire bottle for only five gold!" Charlie exclaimed, holding his hand out to indicate the number five. "I need to procure more bottles so the more you help me, the more I can help you," he stated as he pointed to everyone in the crowd. "There is limited stock so buy now."

The crowd was eager to get their hands on the bottles before anyone else. They witnessed a miracle, and they wanted to be the first. The bottles sold out almost immediately minus the one kept for showing. Business was excellent this year. Thomas counted his gold and put them in his side purse. That was when he saw Michael coming down the pathway toward his booth.

"Well, shit, it was a good day," Charlie thought as he thought as he put his head down.

"Charlie, what have you got here? It looks as though you spiked your sales recently. Outstanding job!" Michael congratulated his acquaintance. Charlie smiled.

"Thank you, sir. I have a new potion that heals injuries. It is very new to the realm," Charlie responded.

"Where did you come by this new concoction?" Michael asked he picked up a bottle to examine. He threw his face away as the rancid smell immediately hit his nostrils.

Charlie laughed. "The rule is, the better it smells, the faster it will kill you."

"This one should give me back years of my life then," Michael responded, almost ready to throw up his breakfast.

"Oh no, as you well know, a merchant never gives up his sources," Charlie responded as he took the bottle away from Michael.

Michael laughed as he agreed. It was true, any release of sources jeopardizes sales and stock. He was on the right track to becoming a master merchant. How did he con people to believe such an item exists? Michael pondered. Either way, he was impressed.

Charlie watched Michael leave. He could not tell him that he got his stock from a trusted elven friend from afar. He could not betray Thomas.

Thomas was very busy in the mage tower at Morhgrammir. He was making vial upon vial of healing potions as Nekora called them and hid a few at a time to sell to his human friend. He wanted to be rich but could not show his wealth with a steep incline, so he slowly increased his funds to avert suspicion. Besides, he wanted everyone to benefit from their findings, not just Elves. It would help make the world a better place. Trade relations between other nations could be a possibility in the future. He started reminiscing about months past.

One day long ago, Thomas went on a hike to procure specimens for testing when he came across a willow tree. A thought occurred to him that if he utilized this tree bark with other medicinal plants, he could fabricate a juice that would heal. Maybe save Elven lives. He was now on a trek to hopefully find plants to aid in his quest. He would question his master mage and chemist about the idea later after he collected what he could find.

The first plant he came across matched the diagram in his book. It was called the heart of Gammon, a green plant with thin stems and broad leaves. Later in his travels, he collected an orange-colored root, a thick stemmed plant with small green spikey leaves and bright yellow flower blooms, and thick stemmed oily branch with thin pointed leaves for the base. With all these combined, he would be able to concoct something medicinal, he was enjoying this newfound interest as an alchemist.

He brought out his stone bowl and large stone handle. It was put aside as he lined up all his ingredients then started grinding them one after the other into a thick liquid concoction that had a rancid smell. He figured he would add water to thin it out a bit; water never hurt anyone. He put what he had in an empty bottle and sealed it.

On his way back, Thomas heard someone calling for help. He quickly and silently moved toward the noise but had to keep from being spotted. He saw that a human was caught in a bear trap.

Why was a human so far out here, from his city? One less human to worry about, he is Gnoll food now.

The cries were that of a non-warrior, helpless and scared, not the strong courageous deep voice yelling at himself for being careless. He thought the man

didn't sound like a threat. He could be in search of vegetation as well. Besides, Thomas had the ability to roast the human if he were a threat. He decided to chance a meeting.

It was possible that humans were not as bad as the King presumed. Or they could be worse. Curious about the human in question, Thomas made himself known.

Charlie spotted Thomas slowly coming out of the dense foliage that had been hiding Thomas from view. Charlie was scared.

"Is this it? Will I be slain by this elf?" was all Charlie could think. Not realizing his eyes were wide with fear, mouth gaped about to let out a scream.

"Are you friend or foe?" The question seemed stupider out loud than it did in his head. "I am such an idiot," Thomas thought, but he kept a stern facial expression.

"That depends on your point of view," Charlie replied. "To an elf, we are sworn enemies. Are you here to slay me where I sit?"

"What are your intentions since you are trespassing on our land?" Thomas countered, not ready to give up the upper hand.

"Look, I am just a simple merchant, not a threat, nor do I mean any harm. My King is sick and needs healing. Unfortunately, our healers are inexperienced. They do not know the arts and are trying in vain to keep the King alive. Please, release me and I will depart this land never to return. I will not say anything to my kinship, either."

The passion in his voice sounded truthful. Thomas relaxed his guard just a bit and kept a wary eye on the unknown human while removing the trap from his shin. The jaws had penetrated his skin and appeared to have pierced his shin bone. Thomas touched his vial then looked at Charlie.

"Look, we may have an understanding. I will let you leave without harm so long as you do something for me in return." Thomas knew the human was incapable of doing harm, so he towered over the merchant in a defiant stance.

"Anything, please how can I help?" answered Charlie.

"I need money, lots of it. You need healing items. Maybe we can trade?" Charlie looked perplexed but what else could he do.

"How do I know I can trust you?" questioned the merchant.

"Looks like you're the one needing assistance, not I," Thomas said as he produced a vial with dark contents swirling within.

Let me dab some of this on your wound or you will lose your foot from your shin," said Thomas.

As he opened the vial, a sharp acrid odor emanated. It nearly caused both to vomit. Thomas took out a "clean-as-can-be" cloth and dabbed the contents onto the rag.

The herbs immediately went to work and soothed the pain Charlie was experiencing. As this was ongoing, the two were in conversation about events current, past, and future. Charlie explained the internal sickness the King was going through and feared he would be dead in a moment's time. He was desperate to find a cure. The replacement was an evil heathen hell bent on conquering the entire isle. A note Thomas did not care for. His Elven family and friends would suffer.

"So, if this stuff works on you, try it on the King. If it heals him great. We can strike a deal," said Thomas.

"If this works on the King, I will pay you one gold for every bottle you want to sell me. We can both profit from this. I know I don't know you very well, but I am glad we encountered each other," Charlie smiled.

Thomas smiled. "As am I." The news was not good, he needed to do something to keep the humans from certain death should they want to march into elven territory. It was all Thomas could think of.

"Let us meet here again in two weeks' time. This will give the King time to heal or not; the potion is very new mixture and not tested enough to be sure of its viability," Thomas suggested.

"Well, it certainly has my vote. I can walk without limping. What is that called, anyway."

"Well, a friend of mine called it a healing potion, and I think it suits," Thomas replied.

"If you do not mind me asking, why do you want to leave so badly? It sounds like you love your friends, family, and home?" Charlie asked.

Thomas looked away, saddened from his memories.

"I was in love with the most beautiful Elven woman I have ever seen. She was extremely smart, bright, athletic, she could kick anyone's ass in a fight. As it turns out, her heart belongs to another. I cannot compete with that. So, I figure, we cannot be the only Elves in this land so I am doing what I can to earn money for passage out."

Charlie looked away. "I know the feeling, my friend." Thomas eyed Charlie wearily. "Look," Charlie continued, "we have a trader's event in three weeks. It lasts for a full month. How many bottles can you afford by then, you think? This stuff smells something awful, but damn it works great. I can sell these, enough to help you off this land."

Thomas went on about the event, and how he could smuggle Thomas onto one the departing ships to another land and start over. The money he could make would keep him comfortable for years.

"I believe I can get as many as one hundred bottles. There is a surplus of ingredients out here." Both Thomas and Charlie went over the plan. It was foolproof. Thomas realized that he left with more than a promise of luxury living away from the Kingdom; he also gained a friend. It was time to gather as many ingredients as he could carry. Time was now a luxury he could not afford. He also had to be vigilant on his extra bottles not being seen.

Charlie pondered the deal. "How can I make up for this?" Then a thought struck him. "If this stuff really works, I could easily make a fortune. No other concoction exists that I know of. Five gold a bottle would suffice a small profit." An evil smirk crossed his face. "Thomas, you just made me a rich man."

The event was upon him. Thomas was true to his word. He had brought the first twenty vials as a test to see if he could hide his concoctions and bring them to the meeting point without being caught. Since it worked, he promised the other eighty at two more meetings. Forty was about the maximum he could carry in a trip. A few here and there was all he could afford without drawing attention. Charlie paid Thomas. He had never seen so much gold in one place. It made him happy. Charlie viewed his contentment, and he too smiled at his purchase.

"I believe we can use these as a start. If I run out, I will tell them more is coming," Charlie explained.

"You will have another forty next week, followed by the rest in two weeks' time," replied Thomas.

Charlie was happy. He also explained that the King had recuperated enough to be fit.

"Do you think you can manage a few extra for the King to keep his health?" Charlie lied. He had to lie to save his skin. Now he is going to try to get a few extra for additional profit from Thomas. He liked Thomas, but business was business.

"Sure, would ten more suffice? It would be an additional week," Thomas explained.

"Yes, ten would be absolutely perfect!" Charlie pretended to be overjoyed. It must have worked; Thomas suspected nothing foul was afoot.

CHAPTER SEVENTEEN

Chief Torack, the Orc chief of the Wolf Clan, had awakened to the sound of his little one crying. He was getting tired of waking early, but his baby needed tending. The wolves needed to be tended to as well or they would turn against the Orcs quickly.

"Do not fret," said lady Alora, the chief's wife. "He is just hungry."

"He is always hungry!" exclaimed the chief. He rose with a stretch and mighty yawn.

Orcs average height was eight feet of solid muscle. Two tusks usually grow from the lower jaw just below the canines. Some grew outward toward the ears. Some grew straight toward the eyes. Orcs may be slow, but their shear strength easily made up for it. Once hit with an Orc, the body goes numb from a bone or seven breaking. It is then the Orcs finishes the body off.

Coloration and markings varied by family. It made distinguishing each family easier. The Orc chief had a broken tusk on is right side with a scar running from the top left of his forehead down across the nose and to his lower right cheek. The previous chief came close to taking out his eye.

Torack challenged the previous chief for being weak-minded and wanted his clan to venture out, expand their territory. It was soon after he learned the reasoning behind the camp positioning.

The brisk morning was welcomed by the chief. The other Orcs were out and about doing chores around the encampment. He viewed the campsite every morning to ensure all the Orcs were doing their duties.

This morning, some of the Orcs were grouped together having a discussion. More Orcs walked by the group to hear what was going on when they dropped whatever they had and joined in the conversation. The chief rolled his cloth on his forearms upward and walked toward the gathering.

"What is this? Why aren't you doing your duties?" Torack exclaimed.

"We are tired of boar. We want dragon meat!" the group exclaimed.

"Dragon?" The chief let out a hearty laugh. There have not been dragons around for centuries. The chief laughed, putting his left hand on his stomach. It was starting to cramp from laughing so hard.

Every Orc was looking at him as he was the only one laughing.

"So, our scout is lying to us?" asked Munik.

"Of course, he is lying," started the chief. It was then two Orcs escorted the badly injured scout from the medical tent.

"Sir. Ferrik went to the top of the mountains a few months ago. He just now returned with reporting a sighting of dragons on the other side of the mountain range to the south," said Dulin, the head chef.

The chief looked perplexed. "What do you mean months ago? Why am I just now hearing about this?"

The escorted scout showed up hanging from two Orcs shoulders with one leg twisted sideways and blood running from his head. His right tusk had been broken halfway down, and blood was running out of it as well. He felt worse than he looked. "Tell me what happened," demanded the chief.

The Orcs sat him on a chair and adjusted the bandages.

"Well, Chief," he started.

Ferrik had left the camp one morning. The Orcs were complaining because it was either fish or boar for meals. He went off to find a different delicacy for his tribe, an expansion to their territory since the families were growing rapidly. He figured there was more out there than just these for meats, so he set off. A crew of three went with him.

They headed south as a group. Each was hoping something good for once. Since the encampment was a day's journey from the woodlands to the south, then another week or so to the mountains, it would be a while before anyone saw anything decent.

The woods were eerily scarce this time. The large birds were not chirping.

"Do you think a large predator is nearby?" asked one of the other scouts.

Ferrik could not hold it any longer.

"Yes, I believe there is. Stay on your toes. We do not want to be caught off guard." Ferrik watched as the other two were cautiously looking around. "It's us, you idiots! We are the danger." Ferrik was tired of the idiocy but had no choice. "You guys go on. I am going up the mountain," he stated.

The other two went another direction, relieved that no larger danger was around. The boar hunt was underway.

When Ferrik reached to the base of the final mountain, the others were already heading back to the camp with several pigs for their food. If they delayed any longer, the food would spoil, and the hunts would have been a waste. Ferrik started his journey alone through the mountain range. So far, he only saw snakes, which helped him. They made great snacks. The last mountain had different sounds entirely. He made it to the summit at nightfall and wanted to see what the noise was. Something was different; he had never heard these sounds before. The sounds were low, but he had great hearing, better than any Orc.

The mountain was flat on the top. He could not see much since the clouds covered the moonlight, making the scenery much darker than usual. Total blackness on the north and southern ends and he could only see a few feet to either side of him.

He crept to the west, where the sound was coming from and saw huge nest. Climbing to the inside was easy. There were broken eggs and an empty nest with a few large white feathers scattered around. He climbed back out and looked for footprints. The wind was making noise through the branches of the nest.

An unusually small cyclops was heading for the nest. He had what looked like a brown baby bird in his hands and one on the fire. There were brown feathers spread all over. One bird was roasting on a spit between himself and the nest. The fire was small so as not attract attention to predators, but it also took longer to cook food. The smell was getting to the scout; it smelled so good.

Ferrik took aim with his bow and killed the child cyclops. He had tossed the body over the cliffside and took the bird from the fire. The meat was done it tasted so good.

"Oh my, I need several of these birds for us. Where are they? I see nests," Ferrik thought.

"Ah, much better than the damn boars and fish," he said to himself. As he finished the last portion of the bird, he saw firelight to the south. It looked like eight streams of fire coming from something he did not recognize. He could not make out the features from this distance, but it appeared the receiving end was not going to be happy.

"As long as those do not come this way," he thought. It was then he saw balls fire coming from the ground up killing one of those fire breathers. It was now official. He had to find those fire breathers.

He looked toward the nest. He had realized that he must have come across it. Since it was nightfall, and this happened a long distance away, he had time to run away and get as much distance between him and the nest as possible. He headed for the west to get even farther.

"Another campfire? Up here?" He took mental note so could report his findings. What he saw mesmerized him. "No way!"

A group of cyclops were roasting a Griffin on the spit. It was a fresh kill, and Ferrik saw what looked like a bird, but it was only half a bird. The back half looked like a cat of some sort. Their fire was much larger but so was the food.

Six of the cyclops sat around the fire. Each one was about as tall but more muscular than he was. He waited for the group to sleep before entering and taking the rest of the food provided there was some left afterward. All six cyclops were watching the events as they unfolded in the valley.

The streams of fire burned a large mass, even moving to cover the entire area. Soon, fireballs were coming from the ground, all hitting one unidentified flying creature. The streams went down to seven when it stopped suddenly. It was so far out. They could not see the objects.

Shortly after, there was white glowing conical movements from the cone of frost cast by the mages. The fire stopped spreading and it went dark, just the darker image of smoke was now seen as the portion of forest was destroyed. The cyclops watched, eating the Griffin like popcorn at a theater.

He found a place to make his camp out of the way. He looked to the south to see a massive fire roaring in the jungle. Cones of white liquid came from the same area and doused the flames after a couple hours. Ferrik waited a couple more hours before checking on the roast. He was furious; the entire thing was bones. He thought about killing the beasts in their sleep. He wondered what they tasted like but thought better of it.

Ferrik started his journey back to his homestead. He heard flapping as a fully grown Roc overflew him and landed in the farthest nest. It was not happy to find it empty and its squawking woke the cyclops. It was time to leave.

A Roc is a brown eagle like bird that can grow to an enormous size. Like the Griffin, they were aggressive, especially around their territory. He wanted to get as much distance between himself and the nest as possible. He knew the size of the bird had to be huge if the nest it occupied was that large.

"Could it be the birds were the ones that attacked whatever lives in that valley? Last I heard, none of them breathed fire. The half bird half lion, maybe that one? No, it could not be." Ferrik was deep in thought There must be some explanation. He thought about it long and hard before he was slammed hard against the ground, nearly knocking him unconscious.

A Roc had Ferrik pinned to the ground. It was trying diligently to peck at Ferrik's head and kill him. Ferrik, even though he was strong, was not strong enough to move the heavy weight of the bird. He dodged each attack but would not last much longer.

Ferrik found his knife and pulled it. He cut a deep gash into the Rocs foot.

The Roc let out a loud scream and lifted his foot for a second, just long enough for Ferrik to roll over. The Roc tried to pin Ferrik again but could not. Both were in combat stances.

The Roc pecked but Ferrik was faster. He dodged and tried to hit the beak with his only weapon, his knife. It harmlessly scraped against the tough beak. Ferrik lunged at the beast, but it jumped backward, hovering. Both talons came at Ferrik. One claw got him in the shoulder. Ferrik counterattacked the talon, gashing its foot again. Suddenly, the Roc dropped lifeless to the ground. A giant wooden spear protruded from its sides.

Ferrik turned, smiling to greet his brothers in arms and thankful that they made it to him. He was not greeted back with a smile from the giant cyclops that had speared their feathery friend.

"Oh shit! This is going to hurt badly," he thought as the angry look on the cyclops face told him he was not there for a social visit.

The club he wielded was relative to the size of a medium tree. Frozen with fear, the Orc watched as if in slow motion; the cyclops readying his club to swing. The Orc ducked, but the cyclops was aiming for his legs, not head, to get him on the ground. The club impacted Ferrik on the right leg and shoulder, throwing him off the mountain to the north.

Ferrik rolled and slid down the mountain, trying to desperately gain balance and stop the fall. The attempts were moot. He was now at the fate of gravity. The Orc watched as Ferrik rolled down the mountain. Multiple impacts to boulders and trees on the way down broke his legs, ribs, and both arms.

The cyclops gathered its feast and brought it back to his tribe. He assumed the Orc was dead.

The cyclops carried the predator to the camp and immediately started pulling feathers off the body. He cut the belly open once he finished and threw the gizzards into a large pan and put it on the fire. A large metallic rod was aggressively inserted through the anus and out the mouth and placed on the fire.

Ferrik groaned. The pain made the travel back to his camp extremely slow. It took several weeks to make it back, but he made it. Thankfully, the small river supplied water and he had stashed some food in his pack for survival.

The small river runs from an oasis beyond the Orc encampment to the mountains where the water is gathered into a large lake. It is gathered up and brought along by the cyclops in the mountains. Three sections of mountains had to be crossed prior to entering the northern woodland with deadly creature inhabitants, then desert.

Ferrik stuck to the river and crawled upstream. He stayed shallow as the cold water provided relief from his pain and made traveling easier. His weight felt lighter with him mostly in water until he reached the desert, which came close to the western side of his camp. The watchtowers sounded the alarm, and a group was sent to recover Ferrik.

"Thank you," Ferrik said. "I have news of the utmost importance. Help me get to Torack immediately."

"Ferrik, you are hurt and look bad," said Jungo.

"Yeah, reminds me of me when I was child and talked back to my parents," another stated, all four busted out laughing.

"Ha ha, funny. Now can you please get me to the chief?" Ferrik was tempered.

Jungo looked upon Ferrik. "It could have been worse, you know."

"Really, and how is that?" Ferrik answered.

"It could have happened to me!" All four were laughing so hard they dropped Ferrik.

"Ouch dammit! I swear I will kill you both if you don't knock it off this instant!" Ferrik threatened.

It took them most of the day to get back to civilization, as the Orcs called it.

They brought him straight to Torack. Torack heard the news, then told the four to bring him to the medical tent for healing.

They laid Ferrik on a makeshift stretcher in the medical center temporarily until they got him in his proper bed and after consult with the chief. As the small group left, they were joking again and laughing up a storm.

"I will get those mutant mutts if it is the last thing I do," he thought, not realizing the anguish glare he gave the entrance.

The medical practitioner came by to give him the once-over. He moved body parts, and everyone in the camp could hear his screams.

First, he moved the arms, then legs, then pressed his belly and chest.

"As I thought," the doctor said. "You have broken both arms and legs with a few broken ribs. It does not look like you will be going anywhere soon."

The doctor took some boards and reset the bones the best he could. He addressed the fractures with the splints and wrapped them with cloth. Ferrick was screaming in pain as this was done. "You will be like this for at least two months," the doctor said.

Ferriks eyes widened, then anger again set in. "Two months!" he exclaimed. "What if."

His belligerent demeanor was soon halted by the chief's entrance. "What if what?" the chief asked as he came to the bedside. Jungo and Hierjik came in behind the chief.

"Chief Torack," Ferrik started, "there is more food in the mountains. You should see the gigantic birds and half breeds up there." He could not remember too much from the last few days or whether he told the chief about the food and cyclops. He noticed Jungo and Hierjik going through his belongings.

"Leave my stuff alone!" Ferrik ordered.

Hierjik answered, "Just looking for what you ate or smoked lately because we want some now." They started to laugh again, but the chief waved them away.

"There are large birds with enough meat to almost fill this medical center. Flying creatures that are half bird and half cat," he stated.

"You have encountered Rocs and Griffins," Torack answered. "Those are most formidable opponents, and you want us to hunt that far away from camp?" the chief inquired.

"No, but if we move our camp farther south, closer to the mountains, it would not be so bad." Ferrik was trying to help the Chief but felt ignored. "The forest has a lot of food as well. We could live as immortals. Never have to worry about starvation."

"Why do you suppose we chose this spot?" the chief asked. "Is it because we love the sand so much? Is it because we want our inhabitants to starve to death? No, this spot was strategically chosen to keep us strong. The oasis to the north has an abundance of food as well. When was the last time you went north? The river is close by and has fresh water, the woodlands have differing foods as well no doubt but there are creatures in the forest that will kill us all in a moment.

"This spot is great for seeing around us, keeping our defenses sharp, fresh water nearby for drinking and fishing, and gives the hunters strength by going out and carrying the dead weight of the killed animals home. Keeps them in shape in case we ever go to war. You are skinny, that is why you scout." The chief stood.

"Our position is here," the chief answered. "Have you seen the giant spiders yet? Obviously not or that would have been the first thing you mentioned. There are deep underground caverns where cave spiders live. They make trap doors by the base of the mountain and wait for the vibration of food to come by. That is when they spring out of the trap door and snatch their prey, hauling them back into the ground. They are all around the mountain base," he said as he pointed to the mountains from left to right, "and you want us to live there? Did you see dragons?" asked the chief as he moved closer to inspect Ferrik's face as he responded.

"No," Ferrik responded feeling humiliated. "Dragons do not exist."

The chief had the look of surprise on his face. "So, you believe Griffins and giant birds exist, but dragons do not?"

"Get some rest," the chief stated. We can talk about this later."

The Chief departed the tent.

"Do dragons breathe fire?" Ferrik called out.

"Some do, the fabled dragons of Almaryha breathe fire and kill whatever they can. Afterward, they gather all the gold and treasures and bring them back to their lair. A lair is said to exist in this very mountain range. No one has ever been able to find the entrance however," the chief answered from just outside the tent.

The chief finally bid farewell and off he went.

"Did I see dragons that night?" Ferrik pondered before falling asleep.

Two months passed, and Ferrik was up and about doing chores by cleaning camp, then get ready for the days hunt. Jungo approached Ferrik. Ferrik had been ignoring Jungo the last couple months. His experience led him to believe that Jungo did not take anything seriously and jokes at every moment. That is a dangerous proposition to anyone, especially on a hunt.

"Ready for the fight of your life, my friend?" Jungo asked Ferrik.

"What do you mean, "fight of your life," and what do you mean "my friend?" We are not friends after that night you joked around and dropped me. That hurt badly. In fact, get away from me you weasel's ass!" Ferrik countered.

Jungo grunted and swatted his hand toward Ferrik. "No one likes liars neither," he said. "If we were not brothers, I would have you torn you apart."

Ferrik was furious. In fact, he was always mad. Nothing ever went his way, and he resented his brother for that. One day, he thought, I will be the hero. Ferrik continued his duties picking up trash around camp. He crested near the top of the dunes, and he looked out to the desert.

He viewed to the north and worked his way to the south. To the north was a giant scorpion five feet in length walking in a northerly path.

"I hate this place," he thought, then brought his hand up to shade his view by habit. The sun was behind him.

A figure appeared off in the distance to the southeast, which thwarted his daydreams of crushing his older brother with a boulder.

Michael was walking through the desert. He had strapped a white flag to a pole, which was secured to his pack in case he accidentally came across an Orc camp without notice. He was busy looking at a map and referencing objects, ensuring he was heading in the right direction.

Ferrik ducked behind the dune, ever watchful. The encampment was just inside the valley, hidden from view giving the Orcs the advantage. The human was barely distinguishable at this distance.

"I need to alert the elders," he thought. "But why would a single human be in this area?" The thought eluded his senses. He was bred for combat and scouting. The elders did the thinking. So off he went to console with the elders.

Michael was busy looking at his map. According to the map, the Orc encampment should be where he stood. He looked around him; dunes were spread as far as the eye can see.

"Been on this horrible route for three weeks now. The encampment should be RIGHT, FUCKING, HERE!" he yelled at the top of his lungs. He turned to face the direction he was heading and cursed the map maker as he started his advance. He should at least run into something. He brought the map up to his face once again when a large arrow pierced its way through Michaels left upper hip.

"Ahh!" he screamed as he tried to get the white flag in order. After, he dropped to the sand. "Peace! Peace!" he yelled twice. The arrow pierced his upper left hip and came out through his left ass cheek. The barb on the tip ensured it would not pull out easily and the thickness ensured quick bleed out. It was very heavy and large, normally made for big game.

The Orcs mounted their huge dire wolves and raced to Michael. The wolves themselves were five feet tall at the shoulders and stocky. Strong enough to run with Orcs and equipment on their backs.

"Who do we have here?" the lead Orc asked.

Michael did his best to cover the sun from his eyes with his hands so he could see the Orcs.

"My name is Michael, and I have a proposition," he stated as he gasped in pain. One Orc dismounted and walked up to Michael. He grabbed the arrow, snapped off the barb, and yanked it out increasing pain for each step in the process instantly. Michael fainted from the pain.

"Damn humans are so weak," the Orc that yanked the arrow out commented. The rest of them laughed. They heaved him onto a wolf and brought him to the camp.

After an hour or so, Michael woke. His hip hurt badly and was barely covered. The Orcs have not decided what to do with him yet, but humans have not been on the menu for a long time. He found himself bound to a stake inside a large tent. It was moderately decorated with hides and furs. Some random items, grabbed from invading parties, also strewn about the tent.

"I would like to talk with the leader," Michael stated in pain.

"You will, if we let you live that long," Ferrik answered. "Why are you out here? Do you favor death?" Ferrik asked.

"Where is my pack? I have a proposition for you, one that you may find pleasing," Michael desperately pleaded.

CHAPTER EIGHTEEN

It has been a week since Nekora has been back. The community was looking great. But today was a special day.

"My Queen, this gown is absolutely stunning," the bridesmaid commented.

She was not wrong. The embroidered cloth was pure white. It harbored a "V" down her chest, barely covering her breasts with lace and white studs. The train trailed the bottom of the dress for ten feet and was carried by her best friends. She insisted on wearing her crown but denied Thorn his crown as they were not yet married.

Thorn wore his finest attire. It was a black silk suit with a white silk tie. He figured the white tie would match the dress she was going to wear. His groomsman helped tug on the suit to rid any wrinkles that showed. Today was going to be a grand day.

The crowd was conversing, and there was minimal drinking since they wanted to watch the proceedings. All of them were elated that the little girl they all once knew and loved had grown to rule their lives. Each of them had given her advice on how to rule in one way shape or form, and they were anxious if their teachings were well-taken. So far, she had been grand.

The ceremony spot was held just outside the city borders. This was for two reasons. One, the beauty outside the territory allowed everyone to focus on happiness. Two, the flowers in bloom made for a perfect setting with the tall trees. The butterflies were twirling about from flower to flower. Everyone was in attendance, and they all looked amazing making this the best wedding in the history of Morhgrammir.

The priest began to speak. "There are times in life when a challenge calls, and you face it head on. There are times when life gives you a break and you wallow in the splendor of all that is. For these two," he gestured to Nekora and Thorn, "there has been nothing but challenge. Each one took it and succeeded, not allowing the troubles to overcome them. Thorn, the challenge of just growing up to be the best he could be, and Nekora, who faced her calling."

The priest continued, "Our past lives have been a blessing, a mercy given to us from the gods. They have tested our strength and resolve for each challenge we have encountered. Whether it be the trials of our young, to be tested into adulthood to the food we eat, not being spoiled or incorrectly cooked. It is this cohesion that exists, a bond between elf and their profession that allows them to excel to new heights.

"The cohesion that brings us together today to witness this holy bond between two elves in love. An extraordinarily strong bond that brings them together, and delivered unto us, under the trust of the gods to do what is fair.

The decisions made after this matrimony must be within the confines and expectations that the gods favor us, and fairness will prevail." The priest coughed to dislodge a food ration stuck in his throat, then continued, "It is not only this couple that will make decisions, but the Kingdom must work in unity to ensure our safety and longevity on this land.

"The longevity will be decided by these two elves. In the hopes that they persevere through life's challenges and ensure our safety, we shall aid them in comfort, keeping order, and maintaining vigilance." The priest paused, then turned to Nekora.

"Do you, Nekora, Queen of Morhgrammir, take Thorn to be your lawfully wedded husband, to have and to hold, in sickness and in health, until death do you part?" Nekora looked at Thorn in the eyes and a great smile came across her face. "I do," she responded.

The priest turned to Thorn. "Do you Thorn, Prince of Morhgrammir, take Nekora to be your lawfully wedded wife, to have and to hold, in sickness and in health, until death do you part?" Thorn smiled. He looked upon the people and an overwhelming feeling of happiness overcame him.

"Finally, my biggest dream has come true!" he thought.

"I do," he responded louder than intended. Nekora giggled as she knew how he felt. She knew for a long time how he felt; it was a matter of time before he found out who he was, and a test to see how badly he wanted her. She knew this time would come provided he was brave enough to ask, for she wanted this day just as bad.

"Then I now pronounce you husband and wife," the priest said. "You may kiss the bride."

Thorn and Nekora smiled at each other. They looked deep into each other's eyes. "I love you, Nekora," Thorn said. "And I love you, Thorn," Nekora said as they embraced.

Cheers from the crowd were loud. Now that there was no volume limit, the crowd went wild, and it felt good to get the feelings out. Thorn turned to face the audience and was surprised when the priest snuck the Kings crown on his head. Tears flowed down his cheeks. Tears of joy and happiness that he could not control.

"Don't be such a pussy now, Thorn. No need to cry like a baby," Nekora sarcastically remarked. "I told you it was a special celebration," she stated as they walked down the aisle and back to the castle to consummate their marriage.

The townsfolk followed. It was always customary for the King and Queen to enter first. It showed the citizens that the area was safe for them to enter. Business was conducted until later that night when the celebration food and games began. It gave the newlyweds time to "chat about events" as the townsfolk told their children. But they knew what really goes on and could not be happier with their new rulers.

Thorn helped Nekora out of her dress. It practically slipped off with her slim yet muscular and tone framework. Her breasts were complimentary to her figure, not too large nor too small. Her clean-shaven body, covered with a light coat of oil, glistened in the sunlight. She twirled as she became aroused by his stares with a jaw drop each time. She fancied him looking at her like the most beautiful thing he has ever seen.

Nekora aided Thorn with his outfit since it was tighter than it should be due to his large muscles and sculpted body. She loved the way his body felt, like a solid rock if it were not for the flesh. He was also well endowed, which pleased her to no end. She could not wait anymore as she jumped on him. He caught her in the air and twirled as he gently lowered her onto the bed.

They passionately kissed. Nekora's eyes rolled back as he gently kissed her neck with a slight nibble. A tingling sensation shot straight down her body, and she pivoted up a slight bit in response. He kissed her down to her nipples that were erect with delight, just waiting for their turn. The anticipation and feeling growing ever stronger as he moved farther down. She gasped in elation for the feeling of purest delight overcame her. He worked his magic with his tongue until she exploded. She could not hold it any longer and was trembling. He slowly made his way back to her nipples and softly suckled on them until she finally regained control of her body again.

She brought Thorn's head up to her face to kiss him, but instead flipped him onto his back. It was her turn to return the favor. She kissed and slightly sucked on his neck. His body tingled and goosebumps appeared out of nowhere. She suckled on his nipples as she grasped his large muscular pectorals and down his chiseled stomach. She took him into her hands and slowly stroked him until her mouth made it. She took him in and sucked, slowly going up and down until he exploded. His body was throbbing with delight when she came back up and worked his nipples, then up to his neck.

They laid in the bed for a few moments more until the feelings came back with desire for more. He flipped her on her back and was now gliding into her. He started slow, then worked his way faster until they both exploded at the same time. He remained inside her until he was done ejaculating. She laid trembling. He slowly moved out and laid next to her, running his hands down her chest, causing a convulsion of her muscles. They kissed for a long time after.

When they were finally able to stand, both got up and went to bathe, each cleaning the other and readying for the final day's events. Both were starving and, in the mood, to relax for a bit. They dressed in their finest clothes for the night, knowing that they could no longer partake in the events like they have before. So, they took their positions for the first time as King and Queen at the head of the table.

Everyone was standing until the royalty sat. Once the King and Queen sat, the rest followed with wine and food quickly flowing out of the pits and onto the plates and goblets. The festivities were now in motion.

Pigs were brought out, surrounded by vegetables that were soaking in the meat juice, giving extra flavor. Bowls of fruits were set on the sides. Goblets of wine were filled while everyone tore into the pigs with their bare hands. Each stripping a piece and eating it before going for more. The King and Queen had their own pig as was customary. It was believed that if the royalty was strong, the Kingdom was safe.

"So, have you changed the events at all while I was away, or did you leave them as they were?" Nekora asked as her goblet was being filled.

Thorn responded, "I had them changed; you will have to see and let me know if you approve."

"You are King now. You do not need my approval," Nekora responded.

"Sorry, habit. Not used to this yet," Thorn replied.

Nekora smiled and was curious as to what events would be presented.

First was the band, normal so far, but she saw elves lining up off to the side, which was different. The band started playing as the dancers lined up in front and danced to a choreographed theme. She sensed it was that of a hunt and was most surprised at their fluidity and ability to move the same way at the same time.

Most impressive, she thought her stepparents would love to see it.

Next up was a gymnast who moved around in incredible ways. The flips, rolls, the dexterity were impressive as she danced with the beat of the music. She had a thought, "My team needs to learn some of these moves. It might make a difference between survival and death."

"Not too bad so far," Nekora stated.

"Just wait, it gets better," Thorn responded.

"Oh," she remarked.

"More wine, your highnesses?" the server asked. Both said yes at the same time as she pulled more meat from the pig. The server poured the wine and moved on. Thorn watched Nekora's expressions as she watched the festivities. He did not care to be King; he only wanted her. After all these years, his love for her had never faltered. The way her red hair sometimes gets into her face, her movements so perfected it was as if she was guided. Her smile, everything about her he just absolutely adored.

Nekora motioned Captain Poko over. "The moves on that guy are fantastic. I have never seen that before," she commented.

"None of us have, your highness," Poko responded. "He just visualized moves and practiced them until he perfected them. I asked him when he was practicing one night."

"I would like him to train those moves to our elite warriors, they may prove useful," Nekora stated.

"Already on it, your highness. He will start tomorrow," Poko responded as he was waved away.

"How did you find this guy?" Nekora asked Thorn.

"It was easy; he almost beat me in a sparring session," Thorn stated.

"Almost?" Nekora questioned.

"Almost," Thorn replied. "I just applied what you taught me, and I won, barely."

"And what was that?" Nekora asked.

"To expect the unexpected, of course," he replied, tearing off another piece of pork as he took a drink of wine.

Both were watching the younger acrobat and visualizing themselves moving in that manner.

Nekora realized with the wrist flipping, the scimitars were in his hands. She did not see that before. Now she was truly intrigued. She called this one the death dance.

When the acrobat finished, he did so with grace as he went low, both scimitars swiped out, and he bowed at the same time at Thorn and Nekora. Nekora started clapping as did everyone else. It was a spectacular show.

Seven large targets were being brought out. Nekora was excited. The archery event was finally upon them. She missed being there. It was her go-to spot to clear her head and be herself.

Seven people came out with no bows or arrows, but axes and knives stuffed in their belts. Nekora was perplexed.

"Where are the bows?" she asked.

"Just watch," Thorn responded. Massive cheers erupted from the crowd.

When the sound died down a little, a whistle was blown. All seven jumped forward while pulling out their axes and threw them once upright. All of them hit center. A back roll as they gathered three knives and threw them, hitting the target near center while tumbling. An act that made Nekora stop drinking and gape. Since she was gone, she had no idea the prowess of her people; the others knew as they witnessed the practice and loved this event.

"Shit! The implications this could have on our army," she started.

"Way ahead you. This is being taught to all our warriors. I figured this would make you happy and increase our lethality," Thorn said as he clapped and cheered.

"So, everything you designed here, you did to show what our army will be capable of?" Nekora asked.

"Yes, it is to reassure our citizens that we will be the best, stronger than any other army in this land. Maybe even this planet. We are already stronger and faster than before," Thorn commented.

"Well then, you should have made this the final act," Nekora stated as Thorn pointed to the field.

One person stood next to the target with an apple in his mouth. The thrower blindfolded himself so he could not see. The crowd was quiet. Nekora was worried; what if he missed, what if the throw was made.

The knife twirled in the air and hit the hit apple dead center. Everyone cheered. Nekora was beside herself, not sure if she saw that right when the thrower removed his blindfold. Both the thrower and apple holder turned and bowed before leaving.

"Damn, you are going to give me a heart attack with these events," Nekora stated, holding her heart without realizing it.

Thorn laughed. "Don't worry, the practice it took for them to get this good was quite a bit. There is nothing to fear. I made sure of it myself. What a rush though, right?" he asked, laughing.

"How long before the army is proficient?" she asked.

"We are working them daily. I cannot put a timeline on proficiency, but I can assure you, they are learning quick," Thorn answered.

The archery event was next and conducted in a fashion that Nekora was accustomed to. That event never changed, at least.

The festivities were over. Everyone went off on their ways talking about the events and what they liked best. The cleaning crew stayed behind and cleaned the area. The market square was soon back to its old self.

"Smoke to the south!" came the alarm from the watch.

Everyone took cover as the warriors made their way to the south. Thorn flashed back to his time when he had to light the fire as he was severely injured. He asked if anyone was on their trials. That did not change since they need elves to be strong and vigilant.

"No one is currently on their trials. Javis has his in the coming weeks." Thorn gathered some of the warriors and made his way silently into the woods, the archers behind him as cover, a new tactic he'd invented given the circumstances around his adventure.

Nekora stayed behind, wondering if she could disappear for a short time and be in the ethereal planes just for a bit. She did not realize how habit forming this would become. She quickly ran to the castle and made her way to her empty chambers and began meditating.

She found herself quickly entering the planes and saw the smoke as a squiggled line across the southern emptiness. She willed herself to the smoke and found a mother and her younger Gnoll. She was scolding the younger Gnoll for using wood that was not dry and could attract enemy attention. The female Gnolls were scantily clad with her chest bare. The younger Gnoll was completely nude since they still grow.

The mother was quickly trying to douse the flames in the hopes that the smoke was not seen. She saw figures approaching from the north. It was Thorn and his escort. They remained hidden but watched as the Gnolls tried to douse the flames. He saw the scolding mother and images flashed into his head about his encounter with a Gnoll warrior.

Realizing this was a mistake and a training evolution for the younger Gnoll, Thorn left them alone. He would not dare attack an unarmed female and child. But that left the question of where the males were.

Nekora willed herself back to the library. She was in dire need to know more about magic. It consumed her. It was getting harder to hide every day. A feeling of danger overcame her. She willed herself back to the Kingdom. Thorn was returning soon. Nekora has no concept of time yet as it is different in the ethereal plane. Today, she checked just in time and went back to her body as she grabbed her scimitars on the way out.

It was then, seven male Gnolls leaped into the Kingdom. A smart strategy. They know we would not hurt the female and child so use them to get our army out of the city. Clever.

Nekora leaped into action as citizens were slain one by one. Spears were twirled and thrown with blazing speed.

"I forgot how fast they were," she thoughtfully recalled.

She and the rest of the army were unaware of their presence. An issue she needed to address immediately after the fight. The acrobat had amazing speed, much faster than the dance he put on last night. He killed the Gnoll quickly and with deadly accuracy. Nekora looked forward to learning from him.

Nekora cast the trip spell on hers, causing it to fall. She immediately leaped in the air and jabbed both scimitars down into the Gnoll. She then rolled and ran for the next closest one in combat with Poko. Poko came up, whacking the Gnoll in the groin area causing it to Keel over as Nekora cut its head off. Blood was spurting everywhere.

The rest were killed by the warriors shortly after. Nekora was fuming.

"How could they get within our borders unnoticed?" she questioned as she suddenly stopped, bent over, and threw up.

"Funny, I have never thrown up after a battle before. Could it be I have lost my nerve after Almaryha?"

Nekora was perplexed as to what was going on. She asked everyone to clear up the yard before the team came back. Nekora cleaned the blood from her face. She ran to the entrance after regaining composure and faked not knowing what was going on. The owl call came through, and everyone loosened up a bit.

Thorn and his team came back unhurt.

"What happened? What was it?" Nekora asked, already knowing.

"Just a couple Gnolls. Nothing to fret," Thorn answered.

Nekora decided to really play it out for the fun. It gave her a sense of satisfaction.

"Couple Gnolls? You know how much trouble they are," she started.

"Relax, it was a mom and kid. I wasn't going to kill the mom and kid, especially after she was already scolding the child," Thorn retorted.

"Mom and child? Where were the males? Did you slay the males?" she conveyed in a serious tone, knowing no males were around.

"That is what concerns me. A female and child, no male," Thorn said softly. "Makes me wonder what happened." It was then he noticed fresh blood on everyone's outfits, including Nekora's.

"What happened while I was away?" Thorn inquired.

Nekora looked sincere. "Oh, nothing, just some Gnolls who thought they could attack our Kingdom while you were out playing with other women and their children!"

She slowly increased her volume until she had hatred in her facial features. "How could you NOT see or sense Gnolls as you passed them?" she exclaimed.

She was right. As before, the King always had backup plans and ensured security through attention. Attention to detail was everything, including paying attention to one's surroundings, a basic skill he overlooked.

Nekora walked away, leaving Thorn feeling shameful for putting the Kingdom at risk. Thorn caught up with Nekora but did not speak.

"They were testing our reaction," Nekora stated. "The attacks will get worse before they get better. Our Kingdom is no longer safe here. We need more vigilance and guards on patrol. We may have to move to a safer location," she commanded.

Nekora desperately needed to get back to Almaryha. With the City wiped out, she could be there in peace as she transitions her spirit to the ethereal plain and not worry about interruptions. That is not possible to do here without raising questions. She longed to be back in that place; her mind dwelled there for some reason.

If she tried to project in Morhgrammir, everyone would try to get her back to consciousness. It was decided she had to go, and soon. First and foremost, she had to plan.

The next morning, the misty chill in the air gave a little relief to the warmth. As always, the chill and mist left quickly before heat and humidity took over, which the elves were accustomed.

Nekora was at the window of her room, covered in a warmer gown for the chillier morning. Thorn woke, staring at his bride, still lost in love.

"Good morning, sunshine," Thorn greeted.

The sudden noise startled Nekora. She turned and smiled. "Good morning, my love," she responded. Nekora looked back out the window before continuing, "I will have a full day's worth of Kingdom overviews. Perhaps we can have a romantic dinner tonight," she suggested.

Thorn got out of bed, naked, as he quickly went to Nekora and wrapped his arms around her. She discovered he was not covered and offered to share the blanket. He obliged, and they watched the morning activities together.

"That is okay. I have Kingdom security to look over today. We are testing some new methods for trials. Even though a lot of children succeed, we still lose far too many. Captain Poko should have something in the works by weeks end. Until then, the trials will go as planned until we can iron out the details," Thorn commented.

Both departed to dress and get on with their business.

Nekora went straight to the Magic office. She had not been there in a while and decided to check on their progress.

"Good morning, my Queen" said Ghorn. "Have you come to see our latest in technology?"

"You know me, Ghorn, only wanting what is best for my elves," she responded. "My elves" sounded foreign to her. She was getting accustomed to being the Queen, and she always did her best.

"Well, we are having issues with the diamonds. We are still waiting for the collection team to come back. Hopefully, they will have enough. It must have been farther than previously expected or there are no more diamonds in the mountains," Ghorn explained.

"Please don't say that master Ghorn. I would really hate to talk with the dirty Dwarves. They chill me to the bone," Nekora responded.

"Well, we will give them one more week then send a rescue party out if they have not returned," Ghorn said.

Nekora looked upon Ghorn. "If a rescue party is sent, ensure a few mages go for protection. If we lose anyone to the Dwarves, I will not be a happy elf. The longer the shield waits, the longer enemies have to destroy us."

"You think we will be attacked again?" asked Ghorn.

"I do not know, but you know when you get that feeling that something bad is going to happen?" Nekora asked.

"Oh yes, always just before a student blows something up," Ghorn teased. They laughed.

"Good, except for one thing. It has been a long time. Send out a rescue party first thing tomorrow. I want two of your best with the team. Talk with Captain Poko and tell him I want some of my elite units with you. This will help ease the loss just in case. I want my elves safe and sound," she demanded.

"Yes, your highness," responded Ghorn as she turned to leave.

Thorn headed toward the training camp.

"How is the training going, Captain?" Thorn asked.

"Going well; the guys are getting deadlier by the day. I had a chat with the armorer a couple months back and asked if he could make lighter yet stronger armor. So we helped him mine for mithril, and we are testing them out today," Poko stated.

"All I see is common leather. We always use those, Thorn said.

"Ah, but the mithril is thin and light. It weighs less than a tunic, yet it protects like plate armor donned by the humans. It is also worn under the leather. The weight allows our units to move freely without getting in the way and makes us more dexterous. The leather armor you see is also thinner, reducing more weight. The increase in movement aids in making the units faster and nimbler," Poko explained.

"Outstanding! Where is mine?" Thorn asked as he looked at Poko.

"I thought you would never ask, my liege," Poko responded as he gestured to the changing rooms.

Thorn and Poko headed for the rooms. The thought of combat overcame him as his thoughts of training came back. He needed to get back into the training pits. But first, he needed to test out his new battle garments.

Poko was right. The leather was thinner, reducing the weight by half, but the mithril armor worn under the leather was almost weightless. He put the mithril armor on then the leather over it. The thinner leather allowed him to move more freely and even breathe better.

"I would like a demonstration on sword against armor, Captain," Thorn requested.

"Of course, your highness," Poko replied.

Poko placed a small sheet of mithril on the table and handed a scimitar to Thorn.

"I am getting older, slower, and weaker, he commented. "How about if you gave it a whack?"

Thorn laughed. "I would not go against you in a real fight old or not. I have seen you in battle; it still haunts me." They both laughed.

Thorn raised the scimitar and struck the armor with all his might. There was barely a scratch on the metal.

"Impressive indeed. How long until everyone is outfitted?" Thorn inquired.

"They will be outfitted within two months," was the response. "We are training everyone to be quick, agile, and silent. Even more so than before. The armor takes a long time to process," Poko explained. The armor was the answer.

That night, Nekora and Thorn came together at the dinner table. They talked about their day's events.

"Ghorn is sending a rescue party to ensure our collection team is okay. They have been gone a while," Nekora started. "Two of the finest mages are going with them for protection." She explained the implications of the new diamonds to create an impenetrable barrier around the Kingdom. She also explained the size requirements and amount necessary to provide the protection plus more for individual amulets as a personal barrier, making the units indestructible.

Thorn responded, "Oh, finally a test of the new armor planned out by Poko and our armorer. Very impressive indeed." Thorn explained the testing he oversaw and the strength he witnessed firsthand of the new material armor. He explained how he swung with all his might and barely put a dent in the armor.

After dinner, the two went to their room. They both got undressed and slid into the covers, wrapped in each other's arms. They were laying there for a little bit when Nekora spoke up.

"Thorn," Nekora said as she turned to him. "I am afraid I have some bad news." She did not want to tell him just yet, but it had to come out sooner or later. She thought now would be a good time.

"What's wrong?" Thorn worried.

"I have to leave again, and soon. I need to go back to Almaryha."

A worried look came across Thorn's face. "Why, I thought all was done?"

"Well, there are things I need to go back for, you would not understand yet," she said.

"Yet, when will I be able to understand? You tell me." Thorn was becoming irritated. "How many warriors are going with you?" he asked.

"None," she replied.

CHAPTER NINETEEN

Two days passed. Nekora was making final preparations to get underway and make her way back to Almaryha. She had to get there before the humans regrouped and claimed the city, making it difficult to get into. Thorn expressed his displeasure of her going alone. He could not think of her in danger but was told by many who went that the forces were no longer evident.

The trek through the wilderness was not easily convincing. Thorn knew of the dangers lurking in the forest, but he did not know the extent of Nekora's gifts. She was dangerous enough, true, but he was still clueless of her magical prowess.

"Your highness," Poko said as he came up behind the King. "I have seen her in battle, she is more than prepared for this journey."

Thorn turned. "How did you know she was leaving? And did it not cross you to let me know of this?" Thorn was frustrated by all the secrets.

"She has confided in me, your grace, and she has asked me not to tell you," Thorn replied.

"I will not cross the Queen. I have seen her in battle, and I assure you there is no danger in the forest that would threaten her," Poko replied.

"Leave us, please," Thorn asked Poko.

The captain bowed and walked away. Once out of earshot, Thorn turned to his beloved. "Why won't you tell me what's going on. I know you are keeping secrets from me. I thought no secrets between betrothed?" Thorn stated.

"I want to tell you, but I cannot. Not yet. Not until I find answers. Believe me when I tell you this, when I do, which is after this trek, then I will tell you upon my return. I solemnly swear," Nekora pleaded.

There was a long, dramatic pause as Thorn watched Nekora gather a few things. She grabbed her weapons and donned her leather. Thorn looked at her like it was going to be the last time he saw her. He walked to her and gave her an embrace.

"Please come back safely. I don't like being apart from you," he whispered as he squeezed harder. After his release, they kissed one last time.

"Do not fret, my dear, after this I have no reason to go anywhere else again," she said softly.

Nekora lifted her bag. She secured her last items with some rations and survival items to her belt before walking out. She turned before exiting the door, gave Thorn a loving smile, and walked off.

Thorn was beside himself. He wanted to be there with and for her, but he had a Kingdom to protect. Considering the latest attacks, he needed protect his elves from a reoccurring attack. He made his way to the grand room.

A meeting was called and important benefactors for war were in attendance. Thorn had the Kingdom layout in front of him with watchtowers and other security areas clearly marked. Thorn looked at Poko.

"Captain, there is a large gap here and here," Thorn started as he pointed to two locations on the map. "Can we erect additional watchtowers here and here?"

Poko looked at the map. "We could, but there would be an overlap in views. Since the forest is lighter between these two areas, it was admissible to erect what we have. The additional towers would be unnecessary," Poko commented.

"Your highness," Ghorn spoke up. "We have plans in the works to erect a shield barrier that would magically protect the Kingdom from intruders. When it is finished, there would be no need for watchtowers. The Queen is foreseeing the events. We sent out a party this morning to check on the gathering group. Once we receive the diamonds, then it will be two days before the shield is in place."

"Diamonds? What diamonds? What are you talking about?" Thorn asked.

Nekora asked about a shield to encircle and protect this Kingdom. We found a way to get it done, but it requires specially crafted diamonds of large size to cover the entire Kingdom. No one except those who wear these will be able to traverse the barrier." Ghorn produced a necklace with a diamond on it.

"How much time before it is done?" Thorn questioned as he looked at the necklace.

"It all depends on the gathering team. Best case scenario is two weeks," Ghorn replied.

"Why was I not made aware of this?" Thorn demanded. "This changes everything."

"You were not privy to this information at the time. I am telling you now because you are the King. Nekora wanted this hushed," Ghorn replied.

"Could this be the secret she was keeping from me?" Thorn thought. "What else is changing that I do not know about?" he pondered. He decided to have a long chat with Nekora upon her return.

Thorn was satisfied. The security of the Kingdom was already at maximum. It was up to the elves to do due diligence and keep on their toes, to report anything suspicious. It was time to inspect the finished Kingdom.

Thorn was amazed at how the Kingdom turned out. The roofing was changed to a more modern spire look yet remained under the treetops. Single-story houses were now two-story. Shops spread horizontally for additional storage needs. A couple elves built their houses on top of their stores; soon all were building domiciles over their shops.

"Such an engineering marvel," Thorn thought as he walked through the Kingdom. He was elated to see the creative construction efforts of his elves at work. Though the market square was larger, so were the buildings making the pathways narrower with increased luster.

Flowers and shrubbery lined the pathways to most homes. The water mill was built around a fresh water well, and the burnt ash and debris were gone. Nothing was left to remind them of the fateful night. Additional guards were patrolling the area, ensuring no harm was going to fall upon the city, to keep an eye on outside predators that escaped the watchful eye of the treetop guards.

The King made it to the west side of the Kingdom and looked out upon the forest in the hopes that his friends would come back and soon. He kicked himself for not going with them but not much he could do when secrets are in place. He looked to the east, hoping his love would return soon.

Thorn continued to the southern boundary. The Kingdom was now officially complete.

The watchtowers were rebuilt, the buildings were rebuilt, and the area was clean once again as it used to be. The similarities in placement made him feel good as if nothing happened. But that was where the similarities ended. The looks and feel made him feel at home and comfortable.

The next day, the Ghorn was out and about with Jangir taking measurements for worst- and best-case scenarios. All the buildings were outlined with precision and in place directly where they were needed to place the diamonds. Everything was absolute. The only thing missing were the precious materials and the permanent spell inscription.

Once Ghorn and Jangir returned from their observation, Thorn wanted a test. He wanted to see with his own eyes the extent of the protection. This time, Jangir took the necklace and wore it. He ensured the diamond touched his skin by placing it between his skin and clothing. They walked to the newly constructed mage tower just north of the stables and found an open area.

"You sure you want to do this?" Ghorn asked Jangir.

"I am sure. I just hope it works this time," Jangir replied.

"Wait a minute, this time?" Thorn asked.

Ghorn smiled. "Last time it mostly worked."

Conus flamoye destro

A cone of flames sprang forth from Ghorns hands. It covered Jangir as he screamed in horrendous pain.

"Stop! Stop this instant!" Thorn yelled as he ran to Jangir who, with Ghorn, were laughing hard. They had planned to play this trick on Thorn should he ask. The expression made the trick worthwhile.

"That is not funny!" Thorn yelled as he grabbed at his chest, breathing hard.

"I thought it was hilarious," Jangir commented. Ghorn and Jangir laughed harder still.

"Do not fret, your highness. This was thoroughly tested and was successful one hundred percent of the time. Besides, you think I would be stupid enough to volunteer as test subject if it did not work?" Jangir asked.

"Who knows what you would do with all the chemicals you sniff daily." Thorn was not amused. Impressed, but not amused.

"Looks like the plan worked," Ghorn said to Jangir once the King was out of earshot.

"As expected," Jangir replied.

Both walked to the entrance of the mage and alchemist tower to research other ideas.

Thorn was in a foul mood. He really thought one of his elves was in danger, and the flashback to that fateful night now reminiscing through his thoughts. He decided to sit in a hot bath to sooth his emotions and relax.

"What kind of Orcs are you? Squash these measly elves and destroy the buildings. No one is to be left alive." Thorn ran down the hallways dressing in his armor and readying his scimitars for battle. The voices were not elven.

Thorn came onto the battlefield, which was his home.

"Not again," he thought. "Where in the hell did they come from without being seen, or heard. They step louder than an angry cyclops."

A quick glance revealed tree-branch-sized arrows impaling the watchtower guards. These Orcs were huge, taller than a single-story market, light to bright green in color and wielding double-edged axes in each hand. Some wielded a shield. Fires were once again clearing the area and elves were dying. Thorn sprang into action.

Thorn went for the closest Orc and leaped just prior to getting to the first Orc. His downward motion allowed for deeper and harder hits to cut through the thick muscle of these intruders. The first one went down quickly and loudly as he hollered for help in agonizing pain.

The second Orc came at Thorn with shield in front while down swinging the ax. Their movements were slow but brute. Thorn could read their movements easily, but to be hit was to be dead. Thorn rolled away from the brute. He came up and kicked the shield away and twisted to the right, bringing his scimitars to full flex, and contacted the neck of the foe. Its head went rolling down the pathway. The army was not fairing as well. For each Orc cut down, the elven army lost three.

The civilians did their part and helped to mow down the enemy.

"What have we done to anger the gods?" Thorn thought for a split moment before dodging a blow. Another swing parried by Thorn. When the motion of the attack stopped, Thorn quickly struck upward, causing deep gashes before the Orc could recover from his strike. The cut allowed a pause long enough for Thorn to cause many gashes, slowly killing the Orc.

A third, fourth Orc downed by Thorn. There seemed to be dozens in line. Thorn was hit on the back of the head and lights went out.

Thorn awakened to a throbbing pain in the head, bound by rope so he could not move. He was dangling over a rivers edge, a part of the river that ran deep. He felt a tremendous weight pulling him down. He could not see the stone bound to his feet.

"Where is the woman mage?" Ferrick demanded. His ax was set level to the rope holding up Thorn.

"What woman mage?" Thorn asked.

Ferrick was not amused. He had no time for games.

"Tell me where she is or you will die!" Ferrick demanded again.

"You guys are just pissing everybody off, aren't you?" Ferrick said laughing. The other Orcs joined in the laughter.

"Last chance," Ferrick stated as he brought his ax back to swing.

Thorn kept his mouth shut. He was concentrating on being loose from the ropes before he succumbed to a watery death.

Ferrick struck the rope and said, "Next" before Thorn hit the water.

Thorn was sinking fast. He could not get out of the ropes that bound him. He struggled hard to be free but was not successful. One last hurrah as he splashed his way out of the tub, breathing hard, and panicked. He ran to the window and everything in the Kingdom was perfectly fine. No attacks this day.

"OMG, what was that dream all about," he thought as two guards rushed in to check on the commotion.

"I am fine," Thorn stated as he put out his hand and doubled over to catch his breath. Thorn grabbed the nearest towel and wrapped himself. "Keep an alert eye to the north," Thorn commanded. "We may or may not be having visitors," Thorn stated as he sat in the chair by the window.

Both guards looked at each other quizzically before shrugging and setting off to deliver the command to the captain of the guards.

Thorn's breathing began to slow, he looked to the north. No sign of impending invasion.

That night, Thorn tossed and turned. Sweat beaded from his forehead. Suddenly, he bolted upright, wiping his face from the sweat. He looked over and Nekora was still gone.

"Another Orc dream," he said to himself. He suddenly got the feeling Nekora was in danger, and the gods were telling him.

But she did not go north; she went east. Did she lie and go north? Fear overcame him, and he closed his eyes. "She is not in danger. Poko made it clear she could handle anything. He was there after all." Thorn talked to himself. He laid back down but could not fall asleep for a long time. He worried about his love.

Nekora started off to the east. She traversed the dense foliage as quietly as possible but quickly. She did not want to ruin another Gnoll family regardless of their eagerness to kill. The first few days were uneventful.

The fourth day was an eventful day beginning in the morning. She had not been paying attention to where she was going or what she was doing. She was daydreaming about what and where she would go in the ethereal plane before stomping into a Gnoll camp.

Nekora quickly scanned her surroundings.

Sixteen Gnolls. "This must be the main coven," Nekora thought. "Well shit, my fault for not paying attention."

"A tasty morsel happens upon our lair?" one of them said. Both male and female members stood and encircled Nekora.

Nekora drew her scimitars. "You will do best to let me go on my way. I have no quarrel with you."

"But quarrel you have, yes?" one responded.

Nekora kept her peripheral and even watched for glimpses from the reflection on her scimitars. The staff was glowing on her back. It was too late; a Gnoll leapt into action.

Nekora took one step back to solidify her balance as she parried the attack. She remembered the Gnoll encounter earlier and their movements. She remembered the pattern. It did not take long before she had three Gnolls dead.

"You can either leave or let me leave, and I will spare your lives," Nekora said defiantly. Each looked at the other, and they all ran to the north. Nekora sheathed her blades and ran fast and silent to the east in case she was being followed.

The sun was just starting to set. The light was still there but fading as she came across the bones of the giant cyclops. The corpse was picked clean, but something was different. Something was amiss so she decided to investigate more tomorrow before she climbed the huge cliff.

She set her things on the ground but kept her scimitars sheathed as she stalked around the area, ensuring it would be safe. Nothing was there to note, so she started a low fire. She took some sticks and poked a few strands of meat from an earlier kill over the fire, keeping the stick wet so as not to catch it on fire and losing her meal. She felt she had to eat more to keep up her strength and alertness.

After she scarfed down her meat, she laid down to rest, projecting into the astral plane to investigate the area. Nothing but a few Gnolls downwind of her current position and some boars out and about, but nothing near for danger.

Nekora woke with two spears poking her sides. She cursed herself for not being awake earlier. Two Gnolls had their spears against Nekora, who put her arms up as a gesture of giving up. She stood upright two giant spiders grabbed the Gnolls from behind and vanished into the earth.

"That is new," she commented. She looked deeper and saw the faint outline of the edges of two trap doors. She also noted webbing across the ground where the Gnolls once stood. "That would explain the lack of decay and meat on the cyclops," Nekora stated. She started another fire and grabbed a stick. She put the stick to the web as it burst in sections toward the door when a giant explosion occurred followed by loud screeches and smoke pluming from the cracks.

"That was easy," she thought and laughed. She packed up her belongings and started the arduous ascension.

At the peak, she peered both directions. Not seeing or hearing anything out of the ordinary, she took the last steps onto the plateau where she gazed out toward Haversmith.

What a beautiful scenery. It would be much prettier without those wretched humans spoiling it with their castle she thought remembering the night she finally met the humans. Which reminded her.

"I better be more careful just in case the humans came back to take over Almaryha." She shuddered at the thought of fighting humans again for the city. It was hers now by right, but who would want to live in an underground dwelling? It has its advantages and disadvantages for sure.

Nekora bent over again; she was feeling nauseous.

"Ugh, I feel horrible," she said as she put her hands on her stomach. She stood after a few minutes and proceeded to enter the cavern. "I should not have eaten so much food."

Thorn put down his spy glass. He had used this device to track the cyclops movements and was now watching a small figure crest the top of the cliff side.

"That must be Nekora," he thought as he put it down. Thorn turned to the north and brought the eyepiece back up and looked through it toward the mountains.

"Are you expecting an assault from the north, your highness?" the guardsman asked. Both were atop the northeastern watchtower.

"Just have a feeling something is amiss," Thorn responded. "Keep a heavy eye in that direction. Just in case."

"Yes, your highness," was the response.

"Your highness. Who would have thought that one day I would be called that?"

Thorn thought as he descended the stairway from the perch with a smile.

All was going according to plan. The Kingdom was bustling with regular activity. Thorn decided to pay a visit to the barracks.

"How is the training going?" Thorn asked Poko.

"Actually, not too bad. The regiments are mostly armed and armored with the Mithral weapons and armor. They have been the first to undergo speed and throwing techniques. Then you have the lackeys, not by choice. They have not received their sets yet. Which reminds me, you have not been to practice at all. All Kings still keep their combat honed," Poko responded.

"What reminded you?" asked Thorn.

"Hmm?" Poko responded.

"You said, 'which reminds me,' and that was after you mentioned the lackeys," Thorn stated with an accusing look.

"Oh, that, no, it was the reference to," Poko paused a bit, "the combat training."

"Uh huh. Did King Kardin ever attend training? I have never seen him so why are you throwing me out there?" Thorn said as he watched the sparring lessons go on.

"Oh, do not think he never trained. He trained nightly. Only when you guys left the arena. He always wanted to make sure he was in top performance. Who wants a weak King that cannot fight for himself?" Poko stated accusingly as he started to leave.

King Thorn was beside himself. It was true he did neglect his training. He had no idea Kardin trained nightly. Maybe it was why he was so good. Thorn stared into the arena. "I really need to up my game. After all, Poko has a point, who wants a weak King leading the charge? That would look bad from every direction." Thorn caught up with Poko and wanted to know the old King's habits.

Two days later, the gathering party and the rescue party arrived at the western side of the Kingdom. The whole gathering team minus a few were carrying large bulging sacks. Only half of the gathering team and a few of the rescue party were missing.

"Where are the others?" Ghorn asked. "We were attacked and held prisoner," said Turnic, the leader of the expedition.

Nekora entered the tunnel. She wound her way down to the cavern and wanted to try a new spell she remembered that would make one fall as slow as a feather. Problem was, she did not know how long it lasted. The book she read never covered that. She ran and jumped off the ledge toward the Minotaur lair.

Fettis Flume

An explosion of light and dust blew outward from her, and she found herself falling at a slow rate of speed. When she was two feet from the floor, the spell ended.

So, it is either two feet from the floor or thirty seconds. Nekora made a mental note to write that in the book if she could, but for now, she needed to remember that info.

"Oh, what was the levitation spell?" she whispered to herself.

"Rizen," Came a voice in her head. Her mother's voice.

Rizen

Nekora said as she rose to the top of the Minotaur wall. Once at the top, she stopped say thanks to her mom.

Nekora wandered the top of the walls through the entire maze. She now knew the maze and what is available and where. She made her way back to the center of the maze where the treasure once resided. It was still empty minus the small faction of human warriors. She decided to eavesdrop on their conversation.

"So where are the jewels and coins. Those blasted elves from last month took them, didn't they?" One of them was irate. "My family heirloom was among them!" he exclaimed. Michael is going to hear of this. Our King will not take this lightly."

"There are more areas in this cavern. Now that all the Minotaur are dead, we have free reign. Though, I suppose a similar fate has befallen Almaryha. I will be pissed if there is no treasure to bring home," was the response of a second warrior.

Nekora felt so bad, she smiled, then softly enchanted a spell so they would not hear her.

In Septus unike val Almaryha
Rizen todo ni sufres
Caelum reparo, vengas detro

The ground started rumbling below. The warriors gathered in the center as rocks and debris fell from the ceiling.

"Quake!" came a yell.

"Shields!" another voice exclaimed. They all raised their shields to protect themselves from falling debris.

Nekora continued her chant.

> Sin titolu des mahses
> Rizen avenji demises
> In Gammon ni seerney

The dead Minotaur throughout the maze were moving. Each grabbed their weapons and roamed the maze, looking for intruders.

"That was a quick quake," one warrior stated.

"Yeah, just glad it was not worse," came a reply.

"Oh yeah, how could it be worse?" asked the other. "You see anything keeping the mountain from collapsing?"

Now all of them were petrified.

"I say we get out of here. And pronto."

"I do not like this one bit. We can just tell the King the place was ransacked."

"And get your head lopped off for insubordination?"

"Well..." a voice trailed off as two undead Minotaur crested the corner.

"Oh shit!" was the last thing heard before the screams of agony followed. Then silence.

Nekora made her way to the exit of the lair and into the dragon's lair, where she cast her feather-falling spell again. This time it was only ten seconds, but the spell ended when she was two feet from the ground floor.

"Okay, so it ends when I am two feet from the floor," she thought. "But is there a maximum time?" she whispered. Testing these spells have become fun for her. She could not wait to be a true master. She was already a master at archery and melee combat. As a master mage, she would be undefeatable. The thought drove tingles of overjoyed feelings coursed throughout her body and she was truly happy.

Finally, the hole that was missing has now been filled. The first hole was having Thorn. Now, she was almost complete, but this time she knew what the hole was.

She had made it to Almaryha once again. The absence of life made this place eerie. The carcasses were giving off an unimaginable stench, and she had to cover her nose and mouth to breath. She ran to the castle and searched every room. The King and Queen's room were on the top floor as usual. A thorough search throughout and she found a few magical items and the treasury filled with gold, silver, and copper coins. She bagged everything of interest including the fortune.

Thankfully, the room was not succumbed by the stench of the dead. She knelt on the bed and began to meditate to reach the ether world. She willed herself back to the library, her most desired place, and went through each book. She loved that she could take her time in the ethereal realm since time was on her side. Every hour in the ethereal was equivalent to one second in the real world so she had plenty of time.

First, she gathered the books on the undead and began to read at an extreme pace. She took in every paragraph. She wanted to know how to completely control them. It took her a very long time; there was much information she had to ingest.

"Once a mortal is slain, the spirit is linked to the body for all eternity. Even though the spirit can roam wherever it wants, it is bound to serve when called upon. A spirit cannot harm a mortal and thus inhabit its original form no matter what condition the original form is in. It also remembers its last duty and is bound to conduct further action as commanded by the summoner," she read.

Interesting. So, my parents are still linked to their bodies. She thought for a second as she skipped many pages then continued reading.

"The undead may not speak, only receive orders and must obey them. To not obey would mean permanent disembarkation from the world and thrown to a terrible place where the soul is tormented forever. It is a rule all spirits understand."

"To kill a mortal body of the undead, the head, arms, and legs must be severed, rendering the body useless and unable to cause any harm. The spirit is still bound but cannot take action."

"So now I know how to rid the undead should they ever attack my Kingdom," she thought.

Once she knew everything there was to know about the undead, she moved to the elements section. She studied the elements and knew how to manipulate the energy to her will. She could create a fireball out of thin air by inducing heat into a vacuum ball, which would ignite and explode on impact causing massive fire and sonic damage to enemies in an area. She already did this with acid to her step Uncle. Water, and even earth can be devastating.

Interesting, she was elated.

She continued throughout the books in every section. Since the ethereal was in a vacuum plane, she was able to practice spells until she knew exactly how to manipulate them. She had so much to teach her mages but only so much to protect her Kingdom. She even knew how to cast the protection spell her master mage was talking about, but his method was rudimentary at best. She needed a way to keep the elves safe so they could travel in and out without issues but prevent anything else from entering. She found that task daunting but favorable.

She'd had enough; it took her two weeks of ethereal time to learn the books. Every day she had to come back and feed her body, which she almost forgot a few times. Now she just had to get back home and put some changes into effect and actions into place. It was time to be the most formidable protector in all the lands.

Nekora departed the castle with one last search. No other items of interest were found, so she left this place for good. Upon reaching the Minotaur maze, she forgotten about the undead Minotaur's roaming their home, so she dropped the spell. She cast her levitation spell and walked above the maze then her feather falling spell to get down. She then cast her levitation spell with a forward motion so she would reach the top of the cavern cliff and enter the tunnel leading out of the mountain.

From the top, she looked to the east and saw the human city she swore to attack one day. She turned around and looked to her Kingdom. A massive plume of smoke was seen. Nekora's heart dropped as she went into shear panic.

"No!" she yelled as she cast feather fall to descend the cliffside and ran to the Kingdom.

CHAPTER TWENTY

Michael's extremities were numbing. The ropes used were fastened very tight, and his tailbone started to hurt from sitting for such a long period time. He was getting restless.

"Where is the chief?" he cried out.

A moment later, Chief Torack came into the holding tent. He peered in Michael's direction then gazed upon the two guards holding spears with the butt ends to the ground.

"Why is he still alive?" Torack asked. "I am hungry," he continued.

The two guards looked at each other and remarked, "Ferrik has forbidden us to kill him until you heard what he had to say."

"Oh really," Torack replied as he gazed at Michael.

Michael stared him down. He would not show fear or cowardice as it would immediately result in death to the Orcs. He explained his intentions.

"Chief, I think I have something worthy of your ear. I am Michael, master trader in Haversmith, and I have a proposition for you. You see, a couple months back, a research team including myself went to the eastern mountains in hopes of finding the lost city of Almaryha. However, A group of elves beat us to it," he said.

The chief grimaced. "Why would I waste my time on elves. They are too skinny."

Michael continued his story, dismissing the interruption from the chief. "My team encountered them at the hidden entrance, and they ambushed us. They must have seen us coming," Michael lied. "We tried to reason with them, but a female, mage let loose many boulders upon my team as they laughed." Michael kept a straight face and was very convincing.

"What do I care about meddling humans? You have your own battles; we have ours with those disgusting dwarves." Torack looked at the two guards. "Kill him, then prep him for our meal."

"Wait!" Michael exclaimed. I have brought you gifts as a show of no ill intention. If you set me free, then I can get more, much more. As I was running for my life that fateful night, I overheard the mage say the Orcs are next. They have specialized scimitars that are magical in nature." As Michael finished, another guard had entered midsentence. He dumped the contents of Michaels bag onto a table filled with gold coins, gems, pearls, ivory statuettes, but the chief focused on the adamantine ore. He shoved the rest onto the floor.

"We have no use for your treasures, but this," he held up the ore and felt the weight. "This is Dwarven metal. How did you come across this?" Torack questioned.

"I have mounds of it back home. I can get you whatever you need if you spare my life. Plus, the Elves have their

Mithril, which is lightweight. Their scimitars are exquisite. Not to mention their bows, which are more powerful than ours." It was all Michael could do to keep himself alive at this point. He relayed only what he had heard, hoping they would bite. Torack rubbed his chin while pondering.

"You have mounds you say? If we let you go, you will make adamantine axes for my group and have them brought here. Where is the Elven city located?" Torack concluded.

One of the guards cut the binding ropes. Michael produced a map of the immediate area and pointed to a spot close to where he thought he saw the lights one night. "They should be right around here," Michael stated as he pointed.

"You know, Chief, we have a trading event quarterly; we just finished this quarter, but you are invited to the next one. I will ensure no harm comes to you or your merchants, but you must have something worth trading for," Michael stated.

"Your life for starters," started the chief. "If you bring us our weapons, we will take care of your pest problem," he finished.

"Agreed," Michael said without hesitation. "If I can borrow a horse to get back, I can have them here much quicker," he stated.

All the Orcs laughed. The chief wiped tears from eyes from laughter then looked down at Michael. "Do you see or hear any horses here?" They all burst out laughing again. "You better hurry. Your thirty-day countdown has already started," the chief said.

"Thirty days! It will be that long just to travel. I need at least sixty to fashion the weapons," Michael retorted.

"Not my problem. You better get going," the chief said. "And if I were you, I would be running."

Michael was not in the mood but at least his life was not forfeited. He started running as much as he could and made haste back to Haversmith.

The chief and the other Orcs were watching him run. They were saddened by the loss of a meal but were happy about receiving strong weapons. With adamantine axes, they will easily cut through the Dwarven armor. They despised the Dwarves.

The chief looked to his group. "Shall we extend our territory into the valley?" All the Orcs erupted in cheer. Now that the chief knew the approximate whereabouts of the Elves, he could expand his territory. It was a time saver, and he hated scouting.

Since no other enemies were anywhere remotely close to their camp, the chief gathered all the male warriors around the table where the map sits, unrolled.

"The human said the Elven Kingdom resides somewhere close to here. We will spread out and cover as much of this area as we can until we find the Elven Kingdom. Everyone will run to the raging sound once found. Is that clear?" the chief briefed.

"Yeah!" was the cheering heard from every male Orc. The females were to stay and tend the camp while they were gone.

"We leave at dawn," the chief commanded.

Every Orc went to their wife to have the last night together.

Michael had about enough of this desert heat. He tried to stay hydrated, which was a difficult task. There was no shade, just some clothing he wrapped to keep his skin from frying. The problem was overheating. He had to get back quickly.

The mountain region was finally in sight. A small river crossed his path about a quarter mile ahead.

"Thank the gods I can cool off a bit. That will help keep me going," Michael thought as his breath was wheezing from the heat and sand.

He quickly ran toward the river and dove in headfirst, hoping it was not a mirage. He found himself covered in mud and water as the shallow river offered little depth to completely cool. Michael rolled around until he was soaked. He then drank as much as he could and quickly set off for the mountains.

He reached the mountains on his second day from leaving the wretched Orcs. David was still near the mountain edge and in sight. He stayed to wait for the return of Michael as he promised. Michael collapsed near the camp. Fatigue was setting in, and he was sore. David almost felt pity.

"Rough day, dear?" David teased.

Michael stared him down as if to kill him.

"Relax, it was a joke. Now we can relax on the rest of the way toward home."

Michael shook his head. "No, we must hurry. There is very little time," he said.

David looked at him. "For what? What did you do?"

Michael stated, "We need to have fifty adamantine axes back to the Orcs in three and a half weeks' time. We need to move, now!" Michael was adamant.

David quickly cleared camp. Michael jumped into the back of the wagon, and they made haste. The two horses were galloping down the trail back home.

Two weeks after Michael left, the Orcs rallied together. When morning came, the chief blew his horn and all warriors assembled. They took a quick assessment then departed toward the southern mountains.

"What about our axes?" Ferrik asked.

"Our weapons are more than sufficient to defeat the Elves. We do not need the adamantine yet, only for the Dwarves," the chief responded. "Besides, I have not had a good war in a long time; this may just fill the void," the chief stated with a smirk. Some boar and scorpion legs were on the menu each night. Scorpions were very large in this territory, and the legs were delicious. The stingers were usually mounted on staves to provide a poisoning effect when a victim is punctured.

Nightfall came upon the war party. They crested the top of the mountain and peered down into the valley. They spotted a dim light in the distance.

"Well then, now we know where they are," the chief announced. "We will make camp at the base of the mountain, he said as they all hurried down to the base near the forest. A quick scream interrupted their run.

"Where is Gulkan?" asked Ferrik.

"He was right behind, then I heard a scream. Nothing here, though," said one of the warriors. Another scream was heard in the distance with the disappearance of another Orc.

"Be on the ready!" the chief yelled.

All the Orcs drew their weapons and looked behind and in front of them. It was possible that arrows took them down but to make an Orc disappear. That was the mystery. Ferrik noticed a black line in front of him. The line was getting thicker.

"There!" Ferrik yelled just as a large spider lunged out of the ground to snap him up.

Ferrik was quicker and swung down with his ax, killing the large spider in one swing.

"So, this is the infamous ground spiders I have been hearing about," Ferrik thought as he turned it over. Two large fangs were open as this spider was ready to kill. Poison was dripping from the end of its fangs. Another scream and another disappearance.

"Move farther inland, into the forest!" Ferrik yelled. All the remaining Orcs obliged. They quickly ran into the forest and away from the spider line.

"How many did we lose?" Torack inquired.

Ferrik was nearby and answered, "I think I heard four but may have been six.

I lost count."

"That is still too many. We set up here with watches rotated through the night," the chief said as he unrolled his fur mat to use as a bed.

A band of Gnolls came upon the group of Orcs. Judging by their massive size, they decided against fighting. Seeing they were heading in the direction of their rival Elves, they decided to watch the war from afar. They knew that their dexterity was no match for the shear strength of the warriors. They backtracked to warn the herd and remained far enough to not get caught.

The next morning, the chief rose before the rest. He looked around and saw nothing but trees. He had no idea which way he was facing. Guk woke soon after.

"Which way, Guk. I am testing your navigation skills," the chief lied.

"Judging by the tracks we made getting here, that way is to the mountains, so the Elven city is this way." He pointed in the direction the tracks were heading.

"Very good; maybe you can be the navigator while I devise a strategy," the chief stated as he walked off thrusting the map into Guks chest.

"Shit, any moron can read footprints," Guk softly whispered as he perused the map with the chief out of earshot.

"Rise and shine, turd balls. We should reach the Elven city within a few days," stated the chief as they all woke grumpily.

The camp was quickly torn down and they made quick headway for Morhgrammir. Minor disruptions hampered their movement. Some angry boars that had charged the group were quickly killed. The bodies were prepared on the way to be eaten later. Unbeknownst to the Orcs, the Gnolls had been tracking them, yet remained far enough away to not draw attention upon themselves. They knew a fight would be futile. All Gnoll camps were moved between the group and the Kingdom.

It was day three. The Orcs came into full view of Elven guards who sounded the alarm. The Orcs were happy; they wanted to test the warrior instincts of the Elves, not catch them off guard. The Orcs gave the rage yell as they ran toward the Kingdom.

Thorn was busy at the time preparing for his voyage to the Dwarven city. He was finishing his packing when the horns sounded. He immediately donned his leathers and scimitars.

Ghorn heard the commotion and peered out his window to see the Kingdom under attack by the mighty Orcs. He estimated over thirty Orcs invading the Kingdom. He sounded the alarm so that all mages would gather and fight. As he made headway to the door, he was met with an extraordinarily large arrow in the chest that was lit on fire. Ghorns clothes immediately went up in flames. More lit arrows came through killing a few more mages, setting the building on fire. The fire blocked the exit for the rest of the inhabitants.

"Dammit, Nek! I need you here now more than ever," he thought as he scampered out the doors. The Orcs were already inside the Kingdom. The Elven dexterity was no match for the brute strength of the Orc clan. For every Orc slain, six Elves were killed. The odds did not favor the Elves.

Women and children were executed. The newly built domiciles were burned as families and the Kingdom was destroyed. Thorn saw what he thought was the leader and ran toward him.

"If I can destroy the leader, the rest will leave as they will be lost," Thorn thought. It was a chance he had to take; he no clue how to take down an Orc.

Thorn ran to the chief, leaped into the air, and came down with both scimitars in full attack. The chief saw this and smiled.

"At last, the King has come out to play," the chief said. He swung his mighty ax, which collided with the scimitars and drove them harmlessly away. The chief came down and hit Thorn on the top of his head, knocking him out cold. Blood started to run out from the wound.

"Ha ha ha, is that the best you can do?" he chief laughed.

He quickly bound the King in ropes and threw him in the middle of the market with other unconscious Elves.

"Where are these so-called mages?" the chief yelled.

Ferrik looked around. "Not sure, they could already be dead, or they are out of the Kingdom."

More attacks came from every direction. The army fought them with precision and grace. Elven arrows would pierce the skin and embed themselves in the muscles of the Orcs, causing nothing but irritation to the Orcs as they removed the arrows and snapped them. Knives were flung with precision, catching many Orcs in the eyes, the only weakness found and penetrating the brains. They fell lifelessly to the ground. The army advanced.

Arrows caught many of the Elves in the chest. The shafts of the arrows were a half inch in diameter and the speed made dodging impossible. Many impacted chest cavities, killing over half the Elven army quickly.

Many Elves were in melee combat, scimitars flashing rapidly, cutting the Orcs. A quick dodge and one mighty swing that connected was all that was needed. The Orcs were too tough for the dexterous Elves.

The Orc skin and muscles were too tough for the newly fashioned scimitars. When a few Elves handled one Orc, that Orc was easily defeated. The numbers were what is saving them, but the numbers were also depleting quickly. The fight moved on.

Once the fighting was done, the surviving Elves were bound and tied to a stake in the middle of the market square. Thorn was among them. He was bleeding profusely from the head where the butt of the ax impacted.

"Thorn looked at the clan defiantly and asked, "Why are you doing this? What have we done to instigate this attack? What have we done to you?"

The chief laughed heartily. "Oh, you have not done anything to us. It is what you have done to the humans. Where is the female mage?"

"You see that building on fire over there?" Thorn asked looking to the north. That was the mage tower. If it is a mage, you were looking for, you have killed them."

Poko was quiet. He knew Nekora would enact revenge for them. But he did not want to make matters worse by letting the Orcs know that the mage they were after still lives and is not within the confines of the Kingdom. He reminisced that fateful night and remembered the humans face quite clearly. He knew exactly who hired these mongrels.

"Ah good, then our duty is done. There is one thing left to do." The chief brought his hand up, then down. Flaming arrows were released impacting the wood at the Elves feet, catching them on fire. Once the clothes were up in flames, the Orcs turned and headed back home. All that was left were the screams of the Elves burning to their deaths.

The Kingdom of Morhgrammir was decimated. Rubble was everywhere, and the smell of burned bodies filled the forest. No one was left alive. Two days after the Orcs left, the Gnolls infiltrated the Kingdom only to find it empty. It was a ghost town. The pack looked everywhere for anything they could salvage. During their sweep, Nekora entered the Kingdom with ferocity in her eyes.

She squinted as she watched these Gnolls roaming her Kingdom. Her bow came up, and she shot one after another. Hatred consumed her. She killed every living Gnoll, believing it was they who ransacked her Kingdom. It happened before. She should have known they would be back in greater numbers.

She made her way to the market square. Numerous bodies were unidentifiable. She looked at each carefully, looking for anything that would give away their identity. She was looking for Thorn.

What she had found confused her. Axes of great size and weight were found next to crumbling bodies.

"Gnolls do not wield axes," she thought as she looked deeper into the mystery. It was not Gnolls that did this. The army would have easily eradicated them. She studied the size of the ash piles and saw that some of them were larger than others. She made it to the dais where several bodies were piled in an evenly spaced manner.

The center pile was where she found the King's crown. Tears welled and flowed as she cried uncontrollably. "Thorn! No! What has happened here?" She screamed as if an answer would come to her. Her legs wobbled and she sat next to him, weeping for her loss.

A moment went by before she had the strength to stand. She found a necklace that belonged to Captain Poko. More tears welled. She knew they suffered a great deal.

"I will get revenge for you if it is the last thing I do!" she exclaimed, looking at all the piles. First things first, she had to find out who did this.

She made her way to the mages tower, everything inside was burned to ash. Her entire Kingdom was burned to the ground.

"Who would have the strength and audacity to do this?" she thought. She came across a large muscular body in the eastern outskirts lying face down with two axes gripped in his hands. She rolled the body over and saw the tusks of the large face.

"Why the fuck are Orcs attacking my Kingdom?" she yelled. The only Orcish encampment she knew of was north over the mountains. She could not comprehend why they would make this trek, destroy her Kingdom, then leave in such a short amount of time. She ran to her room in the castle only to find everything burned. Luckily, she had her prized possessions with her including her bag of holding that held the Kingdoms fortune.

Nekora went back outside the castle, grabbed her remaining gear she left in the market, then started north with the look of fury in her eyes. She cast her spell to raise the dead and was followed by a large skeletal army. She commanded them to follow her. Every skeleton and corpse on the battlefield rose to greet their new commander and do as she bid. Nekora was went on a warpath to meet her enemies head on.

Five days after the battle, half of the Orcs had returned home. The other half burned with the Elves.

Michael showed up that day by horse and wagon, earlier than expected. He produced a set of adamantine axes to the

Orc chief to verify it was what he wanted. The chief looked over the axes and was impressed by the professionalism and craftmanship.

"These will do," said the chief.

Ferrik came up to the chief and chatted with him out of earshot of Michael.

"Don't you think that fight was a little too easy? From the accounts of the human, we should have had a tougher fight than we did," he stated.

The chief looked to Ferrik. "For us, it was easy. They would have given the humans a much harder time, even beat them in a fight. It is all about perspective. By killing the mages before they came out of their building, we have saved everyone here. It could have been much worse, but we were lucky," the chief commented. "We still lost half our troops."

A warning horn was heard from the southern watchtower. Ferrick came by investigate.

"What is it?" he inquired.

"I do not know; a mass is heading our way. They are too far away to discern," the guard stated.

"Weren't all the Elves killed and burned?" Ferrick was irate now.

"Yes, sir, but this is not a few," the guardsman answered.

Ferrick made his way to the chief.

"There is a massive army heading our way from the south," Ferrick stated to the chief.

"What army? I thought all the Elves were killed and burned as I ordered." The chief was angered.

"This may be a retaliation army but from where? Who? They are closing in fast," Ferrik responded. "Not a lot of time to gather our forces."

"That is not the point, Ferrik! There should have been no survivors. We are already at half potential!' the chief yelled. He made his way to the south tower to look.

"That is definitely a huge army. Prepare for battle!" the chief yelled.

Michael was starting to gather his belongings and throw them on the cart.

"You are staying!" exclaimed the chief. "It was your idea that got us into this mess."

Michael slumped. He had to get out; he would not survive a battle as he was not a warrior.

"There must be hundreds of them. Who and where did they come from?" the guardsman asked.

Ferrik just looked and watched as they got closer.

Nekora was at the head of the band, quickly traversing the desert sand to get to the Orcs camp quickly.

"Kill them! Kill them all!" she yelled.

The skeletal army ran in front, weapons raised. They had a short way to go, but she wanted them dead yesterday. Four hundred thirty-six skeletons ran ahead to do battle.

Nekora conjured up a storm.

> Hespera jeet coluses
> Leet destro campaya

Black clouds quickly formed over the encampment. Large lethal lightning strikes struck the ground inside. The Orcs ran in fear for their lives.

"Where the hell did this come from?" yelled the chief.

Ferrik looked at a lone figure behind the army. "That must be a mage."

At the sound of mage, Michael's heart sank. He knew it was her. Before he could reach his horse, the skeletons came through the camp, running, killing everyone in their path including women and children. Nekora ran for the camp and reached it shortly after the wave of undead. Both sides were in a fierce battle. Nekora spotted the human.

"You!" she pointed her finger and made her way to him. Michael froze in fear.

"You hired these goons to kill my people after you dare attack us first!" she accused. "You will pay the ultimate penalty," she cursed. Michael regretted everything.

Nekora called over two Orc skeletons and commanded them to hold him until last. They did as they were commanded.

Half of the Orcs hid nearby. Mothers, children, and a few non-combat males hid away from the city to survive. They had to keep quiet to survive. As long as the mage left before they were spotted, the odds of survival were great. Many warriors followed. They wanted no action against a mage, especially this one.

Lightning struck nearby. The shockwave was felt as a thunderous crack, the sound deafening Michael. Another bolt, then another, between the lightning and Nekora's army, the living Orcs were dying at a quick rate. Blood spattered all over the place. Nekora did not flinch when blood spurted over her. She was in an anger trance, destroying everything and enacting revenge in the same manner, which had befallen her. She had no care in the world at this moment.

The skeletal army stopped moving and awaited further command. The thunder clouds disappeared, and all was quiet minus the ramblings from Michael. "You are the one responsible for this! You alone slaughtered an Orc and Elven nation. Now you must pay the price!" Nekora stated.

She looked upon the two Orc skeletons holding Michael. "I want you to rip him apart slowly. Make him pay for what he has done to you."

"No! Please! I will give you anything! Please spare my life," he pleaded as he wept.

Nekora walked away. All she heard was the painful screams as Michael was slowly torn to shreds. There was nothing left for her now. She decided to head east; her army followed.

CHAPTER TWENTY-ONE

Nekora reached the jungle area that separated the desert from the forest.

She realized her undead minions were still following her, so she dismissed them. They all fell in place. She followed closer to the shoreline to stay away from other villages or Kingdoms, particularly Haversmith. She did not blame the humans for the actions of one, but she did hate them for their barbaric ways. Too much was coursing through her thoughts.

After the adrenaline overload, wave of spells, and flood of anger simmered, Nekora doubled over and vomited. She knew something was wrong but could not pinpoint the problem. She has never been sick before, but then again, she never had so much gone on at the same time, which reminded her, she was starving.

After a quick meal, she was off and running again. Renewed energy coursed through her, but she was dragging at the same time. Something was wrong. She also gained a lot of weight, so she thought better than to eat so much anymore. Exercise was not working.

Walking along the shoreline, Nekora collapsed. The pain in her stomach was too great to bear. She thought she was dreaming or dying as images of light were glowing in front of her. Her eyes closed.

Light elves found Nekora lying on the beach. Her stomach was bulging, but she was not moving.

"Get her to the Magister," Elannah commanded.

"Yes, Mistress," was the reply as two light Elves lifted Nekora with magic. They brought her to Moonglade, their Kingdom within the trees. Light Elves were not actually lit, but possessed a glowing aura only seen by the magical persona that appeared to be light to those around them. They served Jeyin, the god of light and believed in justice over everything else. The mistress kept her hand above Nekora's head as light waves connected her hand to her forehead. She read her memories.

"This one is broken. She once had a happy upbringing, but recent events have clouded her judgment. She is dangerous, and..." the mistress paused for a moment. "She is with child. Complications will kill her and her child. She does not know. We must save the child," the mistress concluded as they picked up their speed.

A scout brought the Magister to the Kingdoms edge, awaiting the arrival of the new Elf. The mistress brought the Magister up to speed about what happened and what was to be.

"This one is far too gone to bring back to the light, but maybe we can save her child," the mistress commented. The Magister thought a moment.

"She is definitely strong. We will have to pull her child from her. She does not know she is pregnant and must not know about her child lest it be brought up in a clouded society," The Magister stated. "I will send this child to be raised as a Paladin; the strength wells within her. If we can keep it on the path of light, it will be a prominent force to be sure." With that, the Magister turned and left. Nekora was brought into a room and prepped for the removal process.

Nekora lied upon the bed, unconscious. Light entrailed her body keeping, her sedated while the medics cut Nekora's stomach open. The doctor reached in and grabbed the baby Elf, separated it from the mother, then began to sew the wound closed.

"It is a baby girl!" the doctor exclaimed. The Magister was all smiles.

Send her to a nurse maiden for care. We have a lot of planning to do," the Magister commanded.

"What about the mother?" Elannah asked.

"We will keep her sedated and fed intravenously until she well enough, then put her back where she collapsed," the Magister responded.

Nekora's wound was closed. Nutrition was forced into her body to keep her alive until she healed.

A few days later, the wound was barely visible from the divine healing. Elannah and a couple accomplices took Nekora back to where she had collapsed weeks ago and left her there. They knew she would wake soon and remained within sight of her in case an emergency arose.

Nekora woke with a huge headache. She grabbed her head then bent over feeling nauseous. The light Elves spoke among themselves.

"She will feel better with time. It will be as if nothing happened. Come, we must return." They departed back to their village in the trees.

Nekora stood slowly. Her head started to spin, then began to feel better. She looked around trying in vain to recollect what happened.

"How long was I out?" she thought to herself as she made her way to the river for water. She looked back but did not see the smoke from her Kingdom anymore. She remembered she was on the other side of the mountains, so she would not be able to see it anymore. She felt as if something was amiss. Since she could not comprehend anything, she continued her trek toward the northeast. Hatred once again consumed her as images flashed into her memories from the human deceit. She must make the Orcs pay for their actions. They have destroyed her Kingdom, her love, and her friends. Revenge was the only thing on her mind, and she did not care if she succeeded.

The forest was damp. She made her way west toward the Orc encampment. She had hoped the forest edge would conceal her entrance, but she was not so lucky.

The desert sand was slowing her progression. She was not used to traversing sand, only hard dirt and rocks. Scorpions challenged her but were no match. Upon killing them, she had an idea. She raised ten scorpions from the dead and commanded them to march forth. She had cast invisibility on herself. Invisibility never truly made one invisible, just a translucent blur that could be detected if one looked hard enough.

Nekora had a hard time keeping pace with the monstrous undead scorpions. It took every ounce of energy to keep up in the sand, and she almost lost concentration, a few that would have dropped her spell. The longer she held it, the weaker she got, so she dropped the spell until she saw the first sign of the camp.

A few hours went by, and Nekora finally saw a glimpse of a watchtower. She immediately cast haste at the same time the scorpions reached the camp.

In the watchtower, one of the Orcs saw a line of scorpions heading in his direction. A behavior unlike a bug, so he rang the bell. The surviving warriors came to the eastern tower as he pointed to the scorpions.

"They have never amassed like this. Something is wrong." As he finished his statement, the scorpions were much closer and looked to be on a mission. The threat was real.

"Attack!" the guard stated. The scorpions were moving incredibly fast. They were at the camp quicker than anticipated. A fight brewed. Many of the surviving Orcs were slain by the scorpions; they would not die.

"What is wrong with them?" one guard exclaimed. One shot to the head killed one of the scorpions. The guard was the first to kill one.

"Aim for the head, that surely kills them!" he exclaimed.

It was about that time when a wave of sand blew through the camp, blinding the Orcs. The scorpions were slaughtering Orc after Orc. Two-thirds of the Orc population were dead when the final blow killed the last scorpion. Nekora dropped her spell and became visible.

"Orcs! You fucking creatures will die this day. Retribution will be paid for what you did to my Kingdom, my friends, and my loved ones!" she yelled in pained hatred.

"Ha ha ha, and who will kill us? You? I must admit, the scorpion trick was smart, but you are outnumbered. Surrender, and you may live," the new chief responded.

Nekora smirked. "I thought as much," she stated softly. Nekora raised her staff.

Leet Destro!

Lightning shot forth, hitting the chief square in the chest. The shockwave was so intense it knocked the close Orcs off their feet. The chief, on the other hand, exploded with blood and guts flying everywhere. She turned to the rest of the Orcs, now too afraid to move.

Sande te forma
Roku des handes
Smaten mi enemes

The ground shook, knocking the Orcs off their feet again. This time the sand rose high in the air and formed a giant rock hand, which came down and squashed the remaining Orcs. Nekora released the spell and boulder shaped hand dissipated back into sand. All the Orcs were flat with blood and guts spewed over the encampment.

Nekora smiled and turned to leave.

She wanted away from her land, to find a ship to take her away. Her revenge was complete, and she was satisfied with the results.

As she walked, she thought about the humans and how shallow they were. She figured if she did not do anything about them, they would attempt to reign more terror across the land. She stopped and looked around. There was nothing left for her here and decided to leave them be. There is no point fighting for no home or family and friends. She kept walking eastward.

A few days passed. She hunted many animals for food while staying as close as she could to the freshwater river. Her arrows were running low as some of them broke during the hunt. A boar would run into a tree, snapping the shaft in two before it stopped dead. She had no idea how to create arrows so during her boredom times, which were many, she would manipulate magic to create arrows out of thin air. She even tried to cast a returning spell on them.

She did manage to create a fire rod that would move forth from her bow and dissipate after a massive explosion on impact. It did no good for her hunting, but it satisfied her newfound love of destruction. Her thoughts dwelled on Thorn, then to her friends and parents. She missed her family a lot, and tears would well up every time she thought of them. She was alone in the world.

After two more days, Nekora found a port. She reached into her magical bag and produced a gold piece for passage to the next land. It was the first coin she grabbed and did not hesitate to give it to the captain. He took it and smiled.

"Welcome aboard the Trinity, madam."

Nekora smiled and followed the first mate to her room. Being a woman, they had to keep her away from the horny men. She was under the captain's security until they made landfall. A couple hours passed, and the ship finally began moving. Nekora fell asleep.

Night had fallen. Nekora made her way topside. The ocean was smooth, and the night was brisk with a clear night sky. The stars were bright, aiding the moon in lighting the way across the sea. The sound of the boat gliding across the water was all she could hear. A few footsteps went by behind her, but otherwise, it was a quiet night. She went back to her room and began to write about her journey.

The next two days were calm with smooth sailing. Nekora was given food in her quarters and came out at night to get fresh salty sea air and take in the scenery. It was beautiful; something she never got to see before. She went back down to her bed and laid down.

Nekora was woken with a clamoring of voices, all of which was yelling. She floated in midair before being slammed down into her bed. She was immediately floating again but landed on her feet this time. She put her arms up to prevent future liftings.

She made her way outside. The roaring of wind almost slammed the door in her face, but she caught it just in time. Waves were crashing over the bow of the boat before lifting again, changing the view from the ocean to the sky. Men were fighting ropes and loose debris on the deck. She went back down, hoping the ship would not sink. The thought made her nauseous, and she keeled over the nearest bucket and vomited. The rocking seemed to last for days but was only a few hours. The storm passed quickly leaving smaller waves to deal with the ship as it moved on.

Nekora lied on her bed, not feeling very good. She could not take much more.

A week later, the Trinity docked on the mainland in the port of Kaleigh. Nekora donned her leathers and drooped her hood over her head. Among the citizens of Kaleigh were Elves, Dwarves, and Humans, all living and working together. There were fights, but they were harmonized. She was confused but kept going.

A quick stop at the local tavern was what she needed, and she ordered food. The waitress brought her a roast and some potatoes with a glass of wine to wash it down. Her eyes rolled into the back of her head. She was surprised at how tasty the food was. Her Kingdom's food was bland compared to this. She ordered two more roasts to go and sat waiting before three male humans walked up to her.

"What do we have here?" the leader asked.

"Looks like an adventurer," another stated.

"Don't adventurers carry a lot of money for their travels?" asked the third.

Nekora looked them square in the eyes.

"You do not want to do this," she stated.

"Oh, I thinks we do. You see, you are passing on my turf, and must pay the toll," the leader stated.

"Oh yeah, and what might that be?" Nekora asked.

"How much you got?" the second man asked.

"Now knock it off, Mikel. You will not cause any riff raff in my tavern. You understand?" the waitress demanded.

"Oh, we ain't causin' no trouble. Were we miss?" The leader looked upon Nekora. Nekora took her bag of food and stuck it in her pack. She loosened her cloak just a little and started walking out the door where the three men had gone just moments before.

The waitress stopped Nekora and put her hand on Nekora's shoulder. "You can stay here a little longer. The alcohol will wear off, and they will be bored and leave."

"Thank you," Nekora responded, "but I need to leave before nightfall."

Nekora walked out the door. The three men came out from behind loose barrels outside. She put her left foot in front before she stopped.

"You still have to pay the toll," the leader demanded.

"Yes, we are thirsty and hungry," the second commented.

In just a few seconds, Nekora slipped out her scimitars from her loosened cloak. She killed two of the men immediately and stuck her scimitar up to the third man's neck. After a brief pause, the man talked.

"We was just fooling around. Please don't hurt me." He started to cry. He knew he was no match, especially after seeing her speed.

"I promise I will not hurt you," Nekora responded.

The assailant sighed a deep relief, and Nekora sliced his neck open.

"I will kill you instead," she stated then ran off toward the gate and to the mountains she saw in the north.

Nekora heard whistles behind her.

"The guards must have found the bodies," she thought as she smiled. She maintained her course to the mountains.

"Even the creatures are different here," Nekora thought as she looked upon an unknown animal. It walked on all fours like a boar but much taller. It was covered in fur with two curled horns on its head. It looked fierce so she kept her distance. The animal just chewed on the grass and left her alone but watched her with distrust.

Several hours later, she made it to the mountain's base. She looked hard for signs of hidden spider doors. Finding none, she decided that she must make camp. She found a hidden area near a small pond that seemed deep. The water was fresh and refreshing. She unrolled a large canvas to create a small tent that she carried, which was made from a horse hide. The tent was small, but she traveled with minimal gear that was necessary for survival. Her bow and scimitars were laid inside. She undressed and walked toward the pond. After a quick drink, she walked into the pond and began rubbing the dirt and grime from her body. She felt good.

After a brief cleaning, she got out of the pond and grabbed her clothes and brought them to the pond. She washed them and hung them on a strong, low-lying branch. She made a small fire and sat by it while her clothes dried. She grabbed some food she had bought from the tavern and heated it up on the fire. The meat was tenderized and seasoned perfectly. It was a taste she would kill for to have again. Asking for the spices was an afterthought.

Her clothes dried quickly with the heat. She got dressed and went to her tent, which was next to the fire that she put out. It was too hot for a fire, but it recooked her food and dried her clothes just like she wanted. Nekora laid down and fell asleep.

The next morning was a little brisk but felt nice. Nekora packed up her belongings and started her trek up the mountainside.

She passed a caravan on the trail. There was a total of three wagons and six horses. They were letting the horses relax before continuing. Nekora just walked past them with her head down and hood up. One of the humans ran toward her. "Hey, wait up a minute," he yelled.

Nekora hastened her pace. She did not want to get into another confrontation. The human was relentless and ran up to her. She turned around defiantly.

"What do you want?" she demanded.

"I am sorry, miss. I was wondering if you wanted a ride. It would be much faster, and we have the room," he offered.

"And what do I have to give for this? Another toll perhaps? Must I lie with you?" Nekora was stern.

"Oh, gods no, that is not what I meant," he responded as he backed off a bit to give her room. He sensed her dangerous posture. "I was just trying to be nice. No charge and no favors. Just a free ride to Ponteville. That is where we are going." That is the farthest north you can get before you reach a massive graveyard from centuries past. It used to be a huge bustling city nestled between the Agora Mountains," Robert recalled.

"According to legend, the brothers were always at odds. Being twins, they fought for who had claim to the throne. One of the brothers believed in might over intelligence, so he forced his more intelligent brother away. He came back to overthrow his ruthless brother in an epic battle between the two cities, Agora and Ponteville. The war lasted for years as each side was not willing to budge an inch. Their father died trying to get them to work together," Robert recollected.

"It wasn't until a couple centuries later, the bodies were found by explorers researching the fabled myth. What they found horrified them beyond belief. To make amends to the gods, they buried the bones where they laid. Agora had become the largest cemetery in the world. The abandoned buildings were searched, and anything of value was brought back to Ponteville. It is said that Agora is haunted, no one has ever laid foot there again."

At the mention of the graveyard, Nekora perked up. "Where is this site exactly?" she asked.

The man thought for a moment. "Well, it is a three-day ride to Ponteville, then another two days north. Why would you want to go there?" he asked. "Nothing but abandoned buildings and gravestones."

"Reasons," Nekora responded as she pondered her situation.

Three days ride or eight days walking. Then another two days ride or five days walking. She brought her hand to her chin.

"Abandoned buildings? Gravestones? Sounds like a good place to start over. No one would visit," she thought.

"Okay, I will take the ride too." She thought a moment. "What was the name of the city?"

"Ponteville," he answered.

She walked back to the wagons with him. There were a couple families with him on this trip. She wondered if they were running from something. The two boys about eight years of age smiled at Nekora.

"Welcome," they said together. "We are hoping to hear different stories. Our parents mean well, but they are boring," one of the boys said in a low and slow voice.

"Hey," the mother said, lightly smacking him over the back of the head.

Nekora laughed.

"What's your name?" asked the strange man.

Nekora looked at him skeptically.

"My apologies, I am Robert. These are my twin sons Andrew and Blake, and my wife Rebecca," he stated proudly.

"Nekora," she answered.

"That is a fascinating name," Robert said as he got the horses ready to leave.

"Where are you from, Miss Nekora?" Andrew asked. He had blond hair with deep blue eyes. Andrew had dirty blond hair and brown eyes. Rebecca and Robert had darker hair with brown eyes, so she pondered where the boy got his blond from.

Nekora looked at them and smiled. She always wanted kids of her own. She feared it was not in the cards for her this life.

"Morhgrammir," Nekora responded.

Both boys looked confused.

"Where is that?" Andrew asked.

"A long way from here. Across the ocean," she answered as her memories swarmed her head. She felt a sadness rekindling in her, and tears were starting to well again.

Robert saw the dismay. "Okay, that's enough chatter. Andrew, Blake, come up front and help me drive this thing home."

"Okay, Papa," they responded.

Rebecca looked at Nekora with sad eyes. She felt bad and knew deep inside she had gone through a terrible ordeal. "For what it is worth, I am sorry for your loss," she said.

Nekora smiled as tears flowed down her cheek. "It's okay, it was a long time ago." Nekora forced a fake smile. Before long, a male voice began to sing. He was not very good with song, and Nekora cringed. Rebecca laughed.

Rebecca leaned toward Nekora and whispered, "He is not very good, but we let him be. It keeps him busy, and the kids entertained. The less I must deal with them for a time. I can relax even if for a moment." They both laughed.

Her bow and scimitars were hidden from their view. She did not want to scare them after their generosity. The problem was her comfort. She could not get comfortable hiding her arsenal.

Rebecca saw her stirring. "Just lean back and relax. It is going to be a few days yet, might as well get comfortable."

Nekora smiled. "I am not used to traveling by carriage. I usually walk everywhere I go."

It was late that night when Nekora snuck off her cloak as they were sleeping. She wrapped her weapons and set them aside. Now she could get comfortable, but her back was hurting from leaning forward for so long.

Nekora felt the rocking and took in the sound of the wheels on the dirt, and quickly fell asleep.

"Whoa!" Robert yelled as the carriage quickly came to a halt. He turned toward the occupants and quickly shoved his sons in the back and gave the quiet signal with his finger over his lips. The family did as they were bid. Voices were heard outside. Nekora reached for her scimitars out of instinct. The voices did not sound friendly.

"Pay the toll old man!" the first voice demanded.

What is it with tolls around here? Is this whole land like this? Does no one get along here? she asked herself. Frustration was setting in. What is it with humans and their desire to screw each other over?

Nekora realized she had a lot more to learn. What she learned at home did in no way shape or form prepare her for this. She was ready just in case.

Nekora looked at Rebecca; she noticed the fear in her eyes and realized this must be a natural thing. "Shh. I will be right back. Do not take any offense to what is about to happen."

Rebecca had a quizzical look on her face but agreed after seeing Nekora take her scimitars and sheathe them behind her back. She quietly snuck out the back of the carriage and peered around the corner of the wagon toward the front and saw four men on horses. Nekora's hand reached in and found her bow. She strapped it behind her back as well as the few remaining arrows she had left.

"What is going on, dear?" Nekora came around the corner to face the perpetrators. One of the horsemen saw Nekora and belittled the man for being with a different race. Nekora had the element of surprise at her side. She quickly grabbed her bow and two arrows.

"You scum! How can you betray your race and lie with an elf? The toll is triple for you!" he demanded.

Robert was confused. He looked back as Nekora had an arrow knocked and released faster than he could think. The arrow was dead center between the rider's eyes. Before they could comprehend what was going on, she released her second arrow. One of the horsemen charged her with a longsword in hand. Nekora dropped her bow and quickly pulled out her scimitars with inhuman speed. Robert figured she practiced quite a bit and let it be.

The second man charged her as well. Nekora dodged the attacks by going low, severing the horses' legs, causing them to crash to the ground. They were now fighting on her terms. The men tumbled and got up quickly. One of them had a limp from the impact, but otherwise, ready to fight.

Nekora quickly cast haste on herself and went into a blur of whirling steel. She quickly killed the remaining two men with ease, then sheathed her weapons and picked up her bow. She made her way back to the rear of the carriage and began grabbing her belongings. She feared they would not want her anymore knowing how much of a danger she could be.

"What are you doing?" Robert asked. "That was incredible!" he stated aloud.

"I am sorry you had to see that. I must go. I don't want to put you or your family in danger," she remarked.

Robert smirked. "Danger? Nekora we could use your expertise on the rest of the trip. Bandits inhabit this area frequently, and we can use your blades. Besides, you saved my family. I am now in your debt," he stated.

Nekora felt better. After collecting her arrows, she paused for a bit to think, then put her belongings in the back of the carriage and enjoyed the rest of the trip. The boys were excited. They saw the whole battle through the crack in the canvas and started telling tales. Each one out exaggerating the other. By the end of the trip, Nekora fought off three dragons and a mage according to the boys. Nekora laughed hard.

CHAPTER TWENTY-TWO

Ponteville was a huge city. The walls went as far as the eye could see and was centrally located between two giant mountains. The path across was blocked and travelers had to go through Ponteville to get through the pass. Races from all over inhabited the giant city. Nekora was in awe at the sight.

"I had no idea such beauty existed," she stated with her mouth wide open. "Beautiful, isn't it?" Robert asked as they reached the gate.

The guards let them through with no checks. Nekora was not sure what to make of that.

"Do they just let anyone in this place? How do they protect the citizens?" Nekora asked.

Robert chuckled. "Hardly; they can spot danger a mile away. They are well trained. Besides, I know them personally."

The roads and pathways in the city were made with stone. The buildings were solid wood with impressive features. She had never seen a spiraling rooftop before. The tiles on the roof looked promising to keep the rain out of the buildings. Her cities leafy rooftops kept rain out, but they did not look as impressive as these.

"The Double Dagger. Goose Farm. Smith's Weapons Depot. You people have interesting names for your buildings. Our buildings did not have names, we just knew where to go to get what we needed," she said as she looked around.

"I wonder if Haversmith has the same buildings," she thought.

The carriage passed a few streets, then made a left. After a couple blocks, they were in an open field where crops are growing. They pulled up to an older-style home and stopped.

"We are home. I will let the family out, get the items in the house then I can walk you back to town if you wish," Robert offered.

"I am fine. I can find my way back. Thank you for the ride," Nekora said as she turned to walked off.

"Nekora," Robert called. She turned to look at him. "If you want my advice, trust no one here. There are thieves and assassins that congregate in this city. One wrong move or inappropriate eye contact can get you robbed or killed."

Nekora smiled and nodded as she turned to leave once again.

This land was full of surprises as she walked down the dirt path to the street.

Nekora backtracked toward the Double Dagger. She was more curious than anything but hoping the food was good. She made a right at main street and looked around. She could not help looking like a tourist.

People were sitting along the street that looked as if they had not bathed in ages.

"They must not have homes. I wonder why," she thought as she entered the Double Dagger.

It was bustling. She felt an immediate danger as she walked in, but the food smelled delicious. She found an open table in the back and sat, waiting for a waitress to take her order. Fights quickly escalated then dissipated when others broke them off each other.

"Such a rough town," she mumbled to herself. The waitress appeared.

"Just keep to yourself and you should be fine," she whispered to Nekora.

Nekora ordered a roast and wine with potatoes, her favorite dish so far on her journey. She set a silver piece down for the waitress, and off she went to get her order. Nekora watched the scenes but remained in the shadowed booth. She did not want to draw attention to herself.

Numerous fights broke out. Most of them were over bravado, a petty excuse to cause a fight, but it was not her place to intervene. She felt darkness, an emptiness she could not explain. But she fought the urge to separate the ruckus.

Her food arrived shortly after contemplating her urge to teach everyone a lesson. The travel was testing her patience. Her temper has gotten much shorter than it used to be. She missed the serenity of home badly. The food was tolerable.

It was not as good as the last town.

After her meal, Nekora snuck out the front door. She was just glad she was not caught up in the controversies inside the tavern. It was then a kid bumped into her. He kept going, and Nekora watched him, stunned that he had no manners whatsoever. The she caught a glimpse of what looked like her satchel.

A quick check revealed her satchel was indeed missing, so she ran after the kid. He ducked, dodged, and weaved around the crowded streets. A large man came from her side and pushed her down to the ground.

"Stay down and leave if you know what is good for you," he spoke.

Nekora could not comprehend the actions, the audacity of this man.

"That kid stole my satchel!" she exclaimed.

The burly man just scoffed and smiled. "I did not see him with a satchel. I just saw you ready to beat up a child." He laughed and walked off.

The hatred inside consumed her. Nekora jumped to her feet and hit the guy in the back of the neck, knocking him down, almost unconscious. She reached down and grabbed him by the throat.

"You will tell me where he went, NOW!" she fumed. "If you don't, I will slowly break every bone in your body."

The man went to grab her, but she was much faster. She grabbed his hand and broke his fingers instantly. The man snuck out his knife with his good hand and stabbed her in the left side. Nekora did not see that coming.

She released her grip and fell to the ground. Blood was slowly coming out of the wound. He went to slice Nekora's throat when the guards came around the bend. He grabbed his hand and ran into the alley way. The guards came up to Nekora.

"It is a good thing we showed up when we did. It looked like he was going to kill you," one of the guards stated. He was heavily muscled with a beard and mustache and large nose that appeared to have broken a few times. The armor was chain mail with the crest of Ponteville, a black raven with its wings spread wide. "Why don't you go after him?" Nekora exclaimed. "He was protecting a boy that took my satchel!" She was getting furious.

"First we need to get you to safety and to a healer. After you are safe, we will go after him. We know what he looks like now," the guard replied.

They walked a few blocks before turning right. They headed into a wooden building with a totem over the door.

"Here you are. We will post a lookout for the assailant," the guard said. After he finished, the two guards turned and walked out back toward where they came.

"So, I am guessing you had a run in with the thief's guild members," the occupant stated as she lifted the shirt to look at the wound. "Well, that is a deep one, isn't it."

"I need my satchel back. It has all my money. I don't know how I will be able to pay you," Nekora winced as the medic touched wound.

"Just get back to me when you get your money back. I doubt it, there are many people in the guild, and they do not take retaliation lightly. I am Carrie." She offered a hand in a friendly gesture.

"Nekora," she replied. "Is this whole city filled with evil?"

"You are obviously an outsider. To answer your question, yes and no," Carrie stated. "To the people who live here, being robbed or killed is a very rare thing. They need the population for this city to survive. For an outsider? Well, let us just say you have become a main target. No one knows you, and you do not know the city. The perfect heist," Carrie answered.

"Do you know where they hold up?" asked Nekora.

"Even if I did, I could not tell you. They don't take kindly to snitches," Carrie answered.

"Well, if you tell me, I promise you they will no longer be a problem. The guards don't seem to care too much about the crimes," Nekora observed.

"If you ask me, I believe the guards are on the take. They do not get paid much being a guard, so they make deals with the guilds. The thief's guild pays extra for the guards to look the other way."

Nekora was flabbergasted. How a city survives on such insolence is beyond her. Carrie finished stitching the wound.

"Give it a week or so to heal before you do anything rash. This is the best I can do for now. Take some of this whenever you feel pain." Carrie handed her some roots. Nekora took them.

"Thank you," Nekora said sadly.

"Hey, if you promise not to tell, I can point you in the direction of the thief's guild," Carrie stated softly.

Nekora headed out and turned right. She was heading to the north end of the city. Three blocks up, she turned left and headed down the alleyway for a couple buildings before coming to a grate. She quietly and painfully moved the grate out of the way. She quickly descended the ladder and replaced the grate back to its original position. The tunnels were dark, but she could see just fine.

Jacko was yelling at the boy. "Why would you bring me an empty satchel?" A hand came down and contacted with the kids face. He flew backward about five feet before stopping next to a column.

"I promise you, Jacko. I saw her grab a silver coin from it. I thought it had more," the boy cried. His face swelled up red and was very painful. Jacko turned the bag upside down and shook it.

"Do you see anything coming out of the bag?" Jacko harshly asked. "Oh, I see, you put the rest in your pockets, didn't you!" Jacko accused. He produced a knife and threw it, lodging the blade into the center of the boy's chest. The boy quickly died.

"Search him!" Jacko yelled.

The others did as they were told. No coins were found on his body. Jacko examined the satchel.

"Good material; we can sell it for a few gold." He examined the bag before throwing into the night's pile. Nekora peered around the corner just as Jacko threw the satchel on the ground.

"Seven people. Jacko must be the leader," Nekora thought as she watched. She quickly ducked in the shadows as one the thieves rounded the corner. She was prepared for a fight; she thought she was caught. The thief kept going on his merry way, oblivious to his surroundings. Nekora quietly unsheathed her scimitars. She walked around the corner, both scimitars lowered but ready to raise in an instant.

"Jacko!" Nekora yelled.

"Who the fuck are you? And why are you in my home?" he inquired in a harsh voice.

Nekora smiled. "Today is the day you can celebrate death."

Jacko laughed. "Unless you have an army outside the walls, you will be one to die."

Nekora felt the darkness creeping into her nerves. Her heart was beating faster than normal, which slowed her surroundings. She gave him an evil smirk.

"Shall we dance?" she asked as she leaped toward Jacko.

Three thieves appeared from both sides with weapons in hand. She dodged and parried the attacks and quickly killed the kids. Jacko witnessed her skills and knew he was outmatched. He ran for the far door to escape. Nekora was having none of it. She threw her scimitar which lodged the door shut. He could not remove it.

Jacko removed a glowing throwing knife. It was magical in nature. The weapon came flying at Nekora, but she was faster. The knife impacted the wall then returned to Jackos hand.

"That's new," Nekora thought quickly.

She leaped toward Jacko, who dodged her attacked. She reached out and grabbed her lodged scimitar and removed it with a hefty yank. Jacko threw the dagger, and Nekora batted it out of the air. It returned to his hand. Nekora went into a flurry of strikes, cutting into the flesh of the guild master. Jacko fell on his back and raised his hand.

"I yield!" he cried out. Nekora smiled.

"Yield to what?" Nekora asked.

"If you spare my life, I will grant you immunity to being a target," he begged.

Nekora thought a second.

"No, I will make my own immunity." She thrust her scimitar deep into his chest.

Six other thieves surrounded her. She brought her weapons up ready to kill.

"You are surrounded. Drop your swords," the guy who stabbed her demanded. She smiled.

"I will gladly drop them when you are dead."

Gusten Amora destro

A gust of wind exploded out from Nekora in all directions, sending each person into the wall where the impact killed them. Nekora's eyes turned into a red color. Her vision now had a red hue, sharpening her vision in the tunnel. After a while, no other dangers were near. Her vision returned to normal, and the internal darkness rescinded. Her eyes went back to their original color. Nekora looked around.

There were numerous gold, silver, and copper coins strewn about. Thousands of them. Trinkets and treasures with magical items strewn about. Nekora collected her satchel. She started collecting all the coins and magical items and threw them into her bag where they were warped into a holding cell in an unknown place. Only she knew how to activate the portal in her bag, which saved her from losing her fortune. She grabbed the returning throwing knife.

"This may come in handy," she thought and placed it into her belt. Nekora strapped her satchel and swung it under her cloak so it would not be stolen again. She made her way out of the underground and back into society. Nekora made her way to the inn and paid for a room after she paid the healer. She needed to do a little research, so she paid for three nights. The innkeeper showed her to her room on the second floor. She peeked out the window and saw no ledge. No one would get in without her knowing. She accepted the room and hid her belongings.

After she was done, she ordered dinner. The chicken was very good, but the vegetables were bland. She ate the whole plate, then walked down to the counter. "Is there a map of this land I can view?" Nekora asked the innkeeper.

"Yes, they are usually hung up in just about every building. We do not have one since it allows people to come in and not buy a room. It slows business, but I am sure the Doves Paradise has one. They are just down the street," he spoke.

"Thank you," Nekora said and walked out the door.

She found it. The Doves Paradise signified by two doves facing each other and kissing, making a heart shape. She walked in.

The place was a spa. Steam rolled out the inner door into the lobby when someone opened it to leave. The attendant looked to Nekora and smiled.

"Can I help you?" she asked.

Nekora smiled.

"Yes, I would like to look at a map of the land please. Yes, of course; it will be five silvers. You can enter here, and it is in the next room," the attendant answered.

Nekora produced five silver coins and headed into the next room. The map was huge; it almost covered the entire wall. She examined it. The steam was getting to her, making her sleepy. It relaxed her body.

"I really need to visit here more often," she thought as she continued to examine the map.

She found the city of Ponteville.

Robert said it would be another two days north. Nekora followed a northern route, but it did not end at any establishment. A mysterious empty section was due north in the mountains.

"That must be it," she said softly. Nekora sat on a log and relaxed for a bit before leaving. "For five silvers, I am going to enjoy it."

After a brief respite, Nekora departed the building. She walked out feeling invigorated, then headed to her room at the inn, where she slept soundly through the night.

The next morning, Nekora decided to take a gold and ten silver coins with her and stuffed them into her pocket. Her weapons, including her staff, were hidden from view. She hoped they would be there when she returned. She did not trust this place at all.

Today was a wander day. She wandered all over the city to get a feel for what building was what and a layout of the city. She quickly found the barracks and fighting grounds to the north. To her dismay, two people were in the arena; the rest were just talking and laughing on the sidelines. This was the worst training she had ever seen. The guards, however, were heavily muscled.

"They must rely on brute strength over tactics," she assumed. One of the guards noticed her watching the sparring. He stood and walked in her direction.

"Hey, you. Yeah, you. Having a good look? Do we turn you on, sweetie?" All the guards laughed at his exploits.

Nekora felt rage welling from within, but she subdued it and contested his accusations.

"Actually, you guys are pitiful. I was just watching a couple dead men pretend to spar," Nekora retorted.

"Really now. How about you get into the ring, and we show you just how pitiful we are," he challenged.

Nekora smiled. "I would not want to embarrass you guys. I mean, how would you look if you were beat by a mere woman?" Nekora replied. She was loving this. She missed her training sessions back home.

The other guys laughed. He was already embarrassed. "Look you, piss off if you know what's good for you," he threatened as he grabbed for her shoulder.

Nekora quickly shifted her weight and grabbed his hand, twisting it until he fell to the ground. She held him there as he was screaming in agonizing pain.

"Come on now, you going to let a girl whoop your ass? How about a sparring session?" she countered.

"Okay, okay," he cried. "Just don't say I did not warn you."

Nekora hopped the fence. A different guard threw a staff at her, which she caught. This guy was the biggest guard she had seen yet. He must lift homes for warm up. The staff was splintered in her hands. The weakened weapon gave her a disadvantage. His staff looked new and strong.

"Do you seriously have to give me a broken weapon to claim your victory?"

she asked. "Why don't we level the playing field and get me a respectable staff?"

"Why don't you shut your face? You were the one challenging us, you get what we give you," he countered.

"Okay, don't say I did not warn you." She smiled.

At first, Nekora only countered the attacks. She wanted to see their skill set. But he just swung the staff like an ape in all directions. The impact of staff on staff hurt like hell, he was strong. But she was dexterous. The guard came straight down, and Nekora easily parried the attack by putting her staff at an angle, causing his blow to slide away without effort. She then came up with a blow between the legs. The guard grabbed his crotch and became furious. An onslaught of wild swings came her way, which she dodged and parried easily. The other guards were leaning into the yard in anticipation. They were awed by her skill set with a staff.

Suddenly, Thorn came to mind. The guard reminded her of Thorn on his first day of training. The guard saw the opportunity and thrust his staff into Nekora's chest, knocking her back ten feet and taking the wind out of her lungs. A large bruise immediately appeared.

Nekora tried to breath and stood, yet it was difficult. Her chest was in a lot of pain.

"I have never lost a battle before. And I am not going to start now," she thought as she was gaining her breath back. The guard lifted his staff in triumph with his other arm. He was celebrating his victory.

"Oh, sunshine," Nekora stated as she came in from behind smacking him several times in the back and sides.

The guard coward and turned to face her. She was in a defensive position. The guard swung the staff as hard as he could. Nekora raised her staff to block the attack. It snapped in two. She smiled.

Nekora went into a frenzy, twirling her two parts like her scimitars causing the guard to back up and get off balance. She smacked him in the stomach and chest multiple times with a final smack across the jaw knocking him out. Blood slowly came from the scratches the splintered ends caused on impact. She threw down her staff.

"Now that is how it is done," she stated as she walked off the arena. The other guards were in awe. They could not believe what they just saw. Unfortunately for Eric, the beaten guard, he would never live it down that a girl defeated him in combat. Laughter erupted from the arena.

Nekora felt her chest. A large bump was protruding from between her breasts. Luckily, the breasts were hiding the welt. She looked down her shirt and saw the flesh a dark black, purple, and blue. Though she was in a lot of pain, she was happy she taught him a lesson. Unfortunately, it also taught her a lesson.

Continuing through the city, Nekora stopped at some shops and even watched a blacksmith. Thoughts of home clouded her mind. That night, she made it back to her room. Everything was still in place.

In the morning, Nekora set out to the north. The trails were tricky with loose dirt and rocks. She slipped many times trying to get up the mountain. Her weapons were stowed away, but she struggled a little with the staff. Being made of gold, the staff was awkward. It seemed to shift in her grasp making it more difficult to climb. The farther she climbed, the colder it got.

She made it to the snowy summit and looked around. There was nothing but mountains as far as she could see.

The north looked the worst. Off to the right, she spotted a wagon trail traversing through the mountains.

That must be how the armies got to Agora. She made her way to the trail. The wind blew fiercely, adding to the already frozen temperatures. Nekora shivered and was worried about misplacing her footing. One false step and she was doomed.

After a couple hours, she had made it to the trail. The wind picked up even more, causing dirt and snow debris to smack her in the face. The piercing chill was hurting her nose and forehead, so she looked for cover. All she could find were boulders along the side of the road, so she made her way to the closest ones and ducked behind them to keep warm.

Minutes turned into hours, and she wondered just how long the storm was going to last. There had to be a break sometime. It did not seem to let up, only get stronger. She was starting to wonder if this was a good idea. A quick gander back toward Ponteville seemed the best answer.

Suddenly, the wind died. Nekora took advantage and made her way farther into the mountains to her hopeful new home. Screeching was heard overhead. The sound was terrifyingly loud. Nekora looked up and saw nothing but cloudy skies. A cave was seen a few hundred feet ahead, barely visible, and small but protection, nonetheless. She ran for cover. The screech was heard again, louder this time. Nekora quickened her pace and made it to the mouth of the cave. She turned around just as a large Roc swooped up to prevent impacting the ground. The massive bird was furious at losing a meal.

She heard voices deeper in the cave. They sounded familiar. Nekora went to investigate. The storm was not letting up anytime soon.

She went deeper into the cavern. It twisted and turned in a familiar fashion. She came to an open alcove that descended hundreds of feet. To the left was a maze. It was all too familiar.

"Oh, hell no," she stated softly. She made her way down to the maze and went inside. She knew the Minotaur's were dead; she'd killed them a long time ago. She reached the last corner, and Thorn was there to greet her.

"Thorn!" she yelled with tears in her eyes. She ran to him.

"You killed us, Nekora. You left your Kingdom to die." He brought up his bow and fired. The arrow hit Nekora in the chest between her breasts, and she fell.

Nekora woke in a sweat. Her chest was hurting badly so she looked around for her roots. Immediately finding them, she started chewing a piece, and the pain slowly subsided. Her room was still dark with a hint of sunlight threatening to come out. She walked to her window and looked outside where a few citizens of different races were roaming about. Looking to the north, the skies looked clear.

Was it a warning? Nekora quickly dressed and went down for breakfast. Her hunger was satisfied with eggs, bread, and cheese. She washed it down with water.

Now familiar with the city, Nekora made her way to buy the items she needed—a belt to hold her staff, some rations, and a cloth mask. All she could think about was her dream, so she prepared for the worst just in case. Nekora looked around carefully; she felt as though she was being watched.

Her intuition was correct. Upon turning a corner around a building, she caught a glimpse of a tall man walking toward her. She walked out of sight then ran to a spot for cover. She hid under the building. The man was running behind her. He turned the corner then stopped. He looked around and continued forward, passing Nekora in her hiding spot.

"What the hell is wrong these creatures?" Nekora thought. She could not get a break the entire trip. She should head back home. Someone might still be alive, and they can start over. At least she would not be in as much danger anymore.

Nekora looked up to see the man bent over looking at her. She screamed when she saw him. It scared her. She was not expecting someone to stare at her.

"Stay away from me if you want to live!" she threatened.

The man laughed. "Please do not be frightened. I am Ulrick. I am a professional scout looking for fighters," he started. "I saw your match with the guards yesterday and was meaning to catch up to you. I have an offer you cannot refuse."

"I do not want offers. I am leaving this city as soon as I can," Nekora stated. She came out from under the building.

"Oh, but you haven't heard what I have to offer," he countered.

"Whatever it is, I am not interested," she replied. "Besides, I try not to fight if I can help it."

"But you have a rare gift I have not seen in anyone for decades," he stated.

Now that Nekora was upright and dusting the dirt off her clothes, she got a good look at the man. He was clean-shaven, dark hair, and very tall with a slender build. His clothes were of silk and very expensive. He had a large nose with a scar running down his right eye. The blade must not have gone deep since he still had use of his eye.

"Please leave me," Nekora stated.

"I will, but first, I can make you rich beyond your wildest dreams. The matches I hire for full contact fights, death is the only way out. You have the warrior in you. A powerful one at that. Being you are a woman, no one will bet with you until you fight. One fight, and you can have more gold than you can dream of," he said.

The smile on his face was welcoming; he practiced that look for certain.

"No. I have all the wealth I need. Leave me be or suffer the consequences," Nekora threatened.

"Okay, okay, I will leave you be. But, if you change your mind, ask for me in the Goose Head Inn. Millions of gold coins are waiting for you to claim them," he commented as he walked off.

Nekora scoffed. "I already have millions," she said softly and went back the way she came.

Nekora enjoyed her last day in town. She spent a few hours in the spa. It helped her chest feel better, and she could even breathe easier. She wanted to remember how to make a spa like this; it was far too enjoyable not to. Upon leaving, the attendant stopped her.

"Doesn't the spa feel amazing?" she asked.

"Yes, it does. I am going to miss this when I leave tomorrow morning," Nekora replied.

"Aw, going to miss your smiling face, Nekora. How about a massage? Free of charge," the attendant asked. "It will loosen your muscles and make you even more relaxed," she stated.

"What is a massage?" asked Nekora with a confused look on her face.

The attendant laughed. Come, let me show you. She reached out her hand and took Nekora's. They went into a private room.

Chrissy, the attendant, had Nekora take her clothes off and lie face down upon a tall bed. She then started massaging Nekora's muscles and almost put her to sleep.

"I could get used to this life," she thought.

CHAPTER TWENTY-THREE

Nekora slept in. She has not slept in since she was a child. Her latest massage comforted her to no end. She still felt relaxed and did not want to get out of bed yet. The sun peeked into her room through her partially shut window. Her eyes opened as she got a fresh whiff of eggs and bacon. She quickly removed the blankets, stood, and faltered but regained her balance. She was in a cloud. She got dressed and finally made it downstairs.

"Good morning, Nekora. You slept in today. Someone came looking for you while you were sleeping. He looked shady and was not the most pleasant fellow. I told him you came in last night for dinner then left. You might want to keep on your guard," the waitress commented.

Nekora looked confused. "Who would ask for me by name?" she thought as she began her breakfast order.

The waitress returned a few minutes later with scrambled eggs, six bacon strips, fried potato slices, and tall glass of cold fresh milk from the dairy down the road.

"Did you happen to see what he looked like?" Nekora asked as the waitress put her food down.

"He was about this tall." The waitress raised her hand well above her head. "He was very slender, long nose, and deep eyes that seemed to go back into his skull. He looked sinister if you ask me, and bad news to boot."

"Ah, yes, that ugly man approached with a deal to make millions. It would only cost me my life according to him," Nekora chuckled.

The waitress gave her a funny look.

"I already told him no; I am not going to be his puppet fighter," Nekora finished as she poked her fork into the eggs. "I love your breakfast here."

The waitress smiled and walked away. Nekora has had enough antics in this crazy city, but she loved it for other reasons. Either way, Nekora was filling her stomach to stop the growling.

Nekora washed the food down with a giant gulp of her still-cold milk. It was refreshing and gave her a chance to sit back and watch the tenants do their thing.

A few minutes later, the tall man walked into the tavern. Nekora crouched low and watched him look around the tavern. He spotted her and smiled. His demeanor was neutral as he strutted toward Nekora.

Nekora had no trust in him, regardless of his demeanor. She sat in the corner with her back against the wall, farthest from him and in a fashion to see her surroundings. She wanted no surprises.

Ulrich sat in the opposite corner in hopes of maintaining her trust. He smiled that disgusting smile with black teeth and smelled as if his clothes had not been washed in over a month.

"Greetings, Miss Nekora. You did not show up at the Golden Goose. I thought maybe you got lost," he started.

"Get away from me. I told you a I am not going to be your puppet!" Nekora retorted. "Besides, what could you give me I don't already have?" she asked.

"Well, now, the infamous question." The man stated as he waved his hands into the air. "Since you could be rich beyond measure but that does not interest you. So, what else could you gain besides wealth? Hmm? Notoriety, power, recognition, respect, and that is just to name a few," Ulrich answered.

"I do not need, neither do I want those. I want you to leave me alone! And you stink!" Nekora was irate.

Ulrich's calm demeanor turned dark instantly. "You have no idea what you are worth, child." He dropped his head.

Three people turned and blew darts in Nekora's direction. She instantly slowed time by hasting herself as three darts were moving in her direction. She blocked two but the third one got through, hitting her in the shoulder. She tried to remove it, but it was too late. The tiny content inside the dart was delivered. The spell dropped and Nekora went unconscious.

Nekora awoke, dizzy and nauseous. Her hands and feet were bound, and she was gagged. She could tell instantly she was in a box on a carriage traveling in an unknown direction. The darkness made her head sway; she had no idea which way was up. For the moment, she concentrated on her surroundings. All she could hear is a few voices and the wheels of the carriage.

"You think we could all be rich?" asked one voice.

"I do not know, but Ulrich said this is the one to win," said another voice.

"But she is a girl. How is she to survive against the barbarians?" said the voice.

"Not sure. I think Ulrich has a few screws loose now. He has been desperate since he has lost everything on the last fight. Well, almost everything," the second voice answered. "Besides, if she does pull through, what would the odds be?"

"Astronomical, I am sure, which is why I would bet on the sure thing," the first voice retorted.

Nekora attempted to lift herself in the ethereal plane to get a look at her surroundings. It was futile effort. Being bound and gagged caused her to be uncomfortable, and she needed the comfort for the spell to work, as well as freedom to move her hands in intricate patterns.

A horse clamored up toward the carriage and dislodged her thoughts. It was feint at first then got louder by the second.

"Now you know what to do, right?" Ulrich's voice was heard. Judging by the timing, he was the one on horseback.

"Yes, sir!' was the answer from both.

"Good, all we need is one fight, then we can survive forever. If I were you, I would put everything on this girl. I have seen her fight. She is faster and stronger than she appears," Ulrich stated.

A few hours passed, and she finally heard different voices.

"The ground is even. We are nearing a town, but which one?" Nekora thought as they went through the gate.

Moments went by. Nekora heard the shouts of other citizens. The carriage stopped. She pretended to be asleep to draw away any suspicion. She felt herself being lifted and carried. They dropped her onto the ground.

"Careful, you morons, or you will be the one in the pits!" Ulrich exclaimed. He did not sound happy.

Ulrich opened the chest. Inside, Nekora appeared to still be asleep. He had his goons lift her and chain her to the wall. Nekora opened her eyes and struggled, but they were stronger.

"Just wait until the chains are off!" she thought as she gave Ulrich the evil stare.

"I know you hate me now, but listen," Ulrich started. He nodded to the goons to remove her gag.

"No, you listen, you dolt! I will kill you for this!" Nekora yelled. "Where am I?"

"I lost everything on a sure bet, but only because the fighter got too cocky. He celebrated his victory too early and was killed. I lost everything that day," he stated. "Welcome to Bulbodock." He smiled and bowed.

"And you will keep losing. I will not be your puppet to manipulate to your will. I am glad you lost everything; that is what happens when you gamble," Nekora retorted.

"You have no idea," Ulrich responded. "You will make me richer than anyone alive. And you will do this willingly," Ulrich stated. "If you do not, then I will have to kill you."

Nekora gave him an evil smile. "You have no idea what you just unleashed into this world," Nekora accused. "You will soon find out." Nekora gave an evil laugh.

"That's the spirit!" Ulrich was pleased. "There is my warrior!"

Nekora had a plan worked out. If all else failed, she would still be victorious. This will be the most epic battle yet. There was no way she would be anyone's slave.

Two days went by. Nekora remained in her cell by choice. She had the best plan drawn up in her mind. During her alone time, she would go out of her body and look around her surroundings. Nearest she figured, she was northeast of Ponteville. She wanted the town to the northwest, but this one would do for now. She knew exactly what to do.

Nekora was brought out of her pen and into the pits. Ulrich insisted she be put in the main event as this would be a show of epic proportions. The game master agreed for a larger than normal price. But this would be an exhibition show only. He could not forgo the fighter's placement for the last week. Ulrich agreed.

When Nekora entered the arena, everyone laughed. The odds went up dramatically. It was now one hundred to one odds against Nekora. The other fighter was much stronger, muscles bulging as he moved. He was a trained and tested warrior in the pits, also the crowd favorite. Ulrich bet five hundred thousand gold pieces on Nekora.

The announcer stepped up to the podium on the side of the stadium.

"Welcome, everyone, to this comedic event to say the least. Not sure how this was arranged but nonetheless, it is my pleasure to introduce to you, on my right side, Steel Blade! The man who put the rage in outrageous. On my left, a newcomer, Nekora!" He turned to Ulrich. "What kind of stupid name is that?" he said softly so only the people next to him could hear. They all laughed except Ulrich.

"As we all know, the battle is to the death. There can only be one victor. Good luck to you mighty warriors," the announcer stated. A gong was heard from somewhere around the arena. Nekora could not see it.

Steel blade grabbed his sword and shield and held them aloft. Nekora smiled as she opted for a quarterstaff. They gave a metallic one so she would have at least a little chance of defending herself. She cast the haste spell then slammed the butt end of her staff on the ground, which shook a little. She then went into combat mode. Steel blade made multiple attempts to strike at Nekora, but she was too fast. She had parried every strike but did not strike back. She wanted the confusion to wear in and the people booing her. She smiled, exactly what she wanted. She then countered a strike and went into a flurry of blows. Steel Blade was too tired from all his earlier attacks. He regretted his decision to come out swinging as he was out of breath.

"Just like an idiot. Attack with too much effort to wear themselves down. You will be my puppet today," Nekora stated. The comment angered the warrior.

He struck again and again until he could no longer hold up his sword and shield.

"What's wrong, oh mighty warrior? No stamina?" Nekora said as she went into another flurry of blows with the last one striking his head, knocking him out temporarily. He slowly moved and tried to get up. Nekora started walking away. The crowd was silent.

"Sorry, Nekora, but one of you must die," the announcer stated.

"Oh, I am sorry I was thrust in here against my will to break your rules. Release me at once!" she yelled.

The announcer smiled upon her. "After you have slain Steel Blade" The crowd booed. Every person voted for Steel Blade.

Nekora went back to Steel Blade and thrust her staff into his chest. Then went into a chant.

> In Septus Unike Val Bulbodok
> Rizen todo ni sufres
> Caelum reparo, vengas detro
> Sin titolu des enemes
> Rizen avenji demises
> In Gammon ni seerney

Nekora slammed the butt end of the staff against the ground. The ground shook violently, knocking everyone on the ground. The warrior's past and present who died during the battles have been woken. They climbed out of their graves. Steel Blade rose during the precession.

"Kill thine enemies, my puppets!" Nekora yelled. The armies of undead stirred. When they came across the living, they would speed up and kill them, sending them to their afterlife. Each slain victim rose to defeat the people of the city.

Nekora's eyes went black. She was in the deepest hatred she had ever felt, and it felt good to enact revenge upon those that do harm to innocents.

People were running and screaming for their lives. Just like that, the city of Bulbodock was under attack by their own people. The guards attempted to kill the undead, but they were far too overpowered and outnumbered. The skeletal remains were too fast and strong to defeat against the much weaker denizens of Bulbodock. For every person killed, another joined Nekora's army. They were bound by supernatural law to aid their master.

Nekora went to the betting cage. Inside, she had found millions of gold pieces locked away in a vault plus thousands more from the betters. She went to work ensuring every coin and anything of value was placed into her satchel. She investigated the satchel and saw the storage she had was getting full. She smiled.

Anything and everything of value was stricken from Bulbodock. Precious heirlooms, coins, gold decorations, everything was taken by Nekora. She decided to head back to Ponteville to gather her belongings left in her room when she was taken. This time, the army goes with her. It was proving to be much more difficult to survive in this world, now she had a powerful army, and nothing could stop her. The thought of ruling over the entire land appeased her appetite for power. This sense was alien to her as she never wanted power, but thanks to Ulrich, she now had all the power she needed.

By the end of the day, every soul left in Bulbodok was turned into her grand army. The ones who fled were fine, and she was hoping they would spread the word of her power, hoping that no one would dare counter her. She was tired and just wanted to be alone.

She found many horses tied up in the stable. She took them all and made her way back toward Ponteville to reclaim her belongings. Most precisely, her staff. Nekora was a one-woman army with hundreds of soldiers. The non-warriors were weaker, but she will take what she can get. The sight of undead is enough to deter many living souls, and she was counting on that fear to survive.

Few days passed. The undead were easy; they did not have to eat or drink, and they could walk forever. She loved it. However, nearing her destination, she had the army remain where they were. She did not need a panic just yet.

A day away from Ponteville, Nekora had the undead wait just out of sight of the city guards. She went in alone by horseback.

She reached her tavern and went in. The waitress gave her a hug.

"I thought we would never see you again. When that awful man drugged you, we tried to get you free. He was just too powerful with his minions. I am so sorry, Nekora, just happy to see you back," she said.

"That is okay. I am here for my things," Nekora stated.

"Of course. Your room is still there; we never rented it out. At least not yet. We had to wait a bit to see if you would make it back."

Nekora smiled, and her eyes went back to normal as she talked with her friend.

"I am sorry to have to ask this, but the manager wants the rent since he had to put up with keeping a room open. He had to turn away several people and could have made money from it," the waitress said with her head down. She was embarrassed to have to ask after everything Nekora had been through.

"How much do I owe you?" asked Nekora.

"Twenty-five silver" The waitress responded. "I would have kept it free for you after your bout with that heathen, but I am not in charge here."

Nekora smiled. "No problem." She reached into her satchel and gathered a gold. "Give him this, you can secretly keep the change if you want to." Nekora winked.

The waitress smiled. "That's seventy-five silver coins! Way too much for a tip."

"Pay for my meal then if it makes you feel better," Nekora said.

The waitress ran off as Nekora found a table. She was starving and craved their food.

The waitress came back with a lot of food and some wine. "On the house," she said with a smile.

Nekora ate her meal, then went back to the stable where her horse was kept. She studied the maps of the surrounding area and found a pathway to the dead city of Agora out the main gate to the right. A small roadway led to an empty plot of land.

"Agora," she thought. Nekora made her way out and gathered her troops. She turned right, toward her new home as she thought.

It was two days travel before a small roadway was found. She recalled the map and remembered it was far to the path. Once upon it, she ordered her minions to stay close and remain near the path but out of sight in case of travelers. They could do nothing but obey.

Nekora was the only person on the road toward Agora. The road winded like a snake, up and down the mountainside. She rested when she found small plots of land near a riverbank. Her army remained on guard as they needed no sleep. It took five days to get to her destination, but she found what she was looking for.

The snowy ground coverings made for a slow walk. Nekora released her horse and it reared, turned the other way, and ran quickly. A storm was upon her. She could not see but a few feet from her but kept on going. She took in the sight and saw a large faint outline of what looked to be a building. She turned to the left and started making her way to it for shelter. Once inside, it opened into a massive room. The room was dark and full of cobwebs that have been around for centuries. Her first thought were the nasty Driders she encountered in Almaryha but quickly dismissed the idea. She had the remaining undead wait outside for now. She forbade them to enter her domain.

She snapped her fingers.

Fume

All the torches lit one by one from front to back. Inside was a broken-down figure, a statue of the hero Robert told her about. She could not remember his name, but his brother was the founder of Ponteville. The ground was tile with gold being every other tile fashioned in a checkerboard manner. Some of the marble tiles were destroyed by objects that have fallen from the ceiling. The throne was an ornate, old silk chair with oak trimming making it sturdy. Gold outlined the outer trimmings, but the silk was ruined. She would have to fix that.

Silken de runet
Fahsen ogen raynew

A circle of glitter started in the center of the throne and worked its way outward until it surrounded the chair. A flash of light solidified the magic and the throne stood there, looking brand new.

"A little work and this place would be perfect," Nekora thought.

She made her way around the building and found the grand bedroom with a deep golden bathtub. Everything was covered in dust and fallen debris. The kitchens had everything she needed except the food to cook with. She would have to order from Ponteville.

The two-story building was fashioned for the ultra-rich, but she did not care for such amenities. She longed to be back home with her family and friends. There were other buildings outside showing the once prominent city.

"I will bring this city back to life," she thought. "I swear to my death, this city will once again prosper and will be a dominant city on the map." The view outside was clearing up with the storm moving away. She could see her vast city, much larger than her Kingdom back home. The vegetation was dead, but she contributed that to the extreme cold. It was time to make a move for survival. She found her new home.

Oh crap, my horse ran away. What am I going to do now? She was furious. No transportation meant she was walking to Ponteville. A trek not to be taken lightly.

Nekora screamed as loud as she could. No one was there to comfort her. She ran downstairs and sat at the dining table. It was large enough and had chairs for a dozen people. She ate her rations and drank her water. She needed people to help her run this place.

"How am I going to sell this idea to have people to run the markets?" she thought. Nekora walked around the market area; the place was huge. Even the buildings were made of stone and a lot of gold inlays throughout. "Damn the last ruler was rich," she said aloud. Nekora walked down an unoccupied path for a couple days with her army in tow. She hunted for food and boiled snow for water. On the third day, she came across a giant cave. Her instincts had brought her here, but why? She needed to find the answer, and it lied within the cave.

The pathway wound down for miles. Occasionally, she would catch something glimmering, then it would fade into the walls. She finally stopped and wiped away some dirt that was causing the intermittent glow. "Gold!" she yelled unexpectedly. "No wonder they prospered."

She went deeper. At the bottom she saw a gigantic pile of gold, silver, gems, jewelry, magic items, and even trinkets, magical in nature. She also felt doom. Something was wrong; something was off. Nekora thought she should come back another day when it was warmer. The spring would help her. She needed to find a cart.

Back out the mouth she went. She made her way toward her great city. Since the others abandoned this Kingdom, it was now hers as she claimed it. Her new home of Nekorapolis.

Food and water were easily found. After about a week, she made her way to Ponteville to purchase some spices and find some people to help her get her Kingdom on the map. Off to hire some workers.

Her first stop was the Golden Goose, where she enlisted the aid of the waitress and promised her a manager position with one gold/month salary until she can get the tavern running on its own, then she would pay Nekora back in taxes. The waitress agreed. Next was her favorite spa owner, Chrissy. She declined but had someone else in mind to help Nekora.

"I cannot turn my back on my city, Nekora; you must understand. But I will support you in any way I can," Chrissy stated.

"I understand completely and will take any help you can offer up." Roger offered up his services for the same conditions as the waitress. He always wanted to see Agora.

Nekora had the personnel required to make her Kingdom thrive once more. She ensured they knew it for its new name.

Nekora purchased six wagons and twelve horses to help the new tenants move into their new home. Every home needed attention so it would take a while before the markets, inns, and taverns to open for business. It was fine, hunters came along for the trip and experience. Nekora struck a deal for spice trades between her and Ponteville. Things were starting to look up.

Spring has sprung. Everything was cleared up, the snow was moved, and businesses would be opening soon. Nekora took a wagon down the cavern and collected as much gold rocks as the cart would carry. She enlisted the aid of smiths to turn the gold rocks into coins. As far as her satchel, she had enough room for the pile of gold coins, gems, and trinkets at the bottom of the cavern.

"This must have been the treasury," Nekora thought, but the coins were fresh. Something caused the hairs on her neck to raise. She cautiously continued down to the bottom until she reached the pile.

"Why are you here?" Nekora heard the voice in her head she looked around and saw nothing. She carefully peered into each corner and looked behind every rock.

"I know this presence, Nekora, yes, why have you come?" Nekora froze.

"How does this voice know me?" she thought.

Nekora looked around, she saw nothing but boulders.

"Do not worry about me and my actions. I have come to claim this treasure." One of the boulders stood, and its wings flexed.

"Gilgamere!" Nekora exclaimed. "What are you doing here?"

"This is my home, and that is my treasure you are about to steal," Gilgamere said into Nekora's head.

"I did not know this was yours. But now that I do, I will leave it alone. It is your claim, not mine and I am sorry." Nekora thought back to Gilgamere. "I am reopening Agora. I am calling it Nekorapolis now. It is my new home and would love to have you as a peaceful neighbor."

Gilgamere stooped and investigated Nekora's soul as she felt it.

"You are telling the truth. You have helped us before. We will be your allies this day and all days forward" Gilgamere stated.

Nekora felt a chill throughout her body. The thought of having dragons as allies made her feel invincible.

Some trades were coming in. Word of mouth had spread like wildfire as more and more caravans were incoming. Nekorapolis sprang back to life.

Everyone wanted to get their hands on the golden items crafted in Nekorapolis and had to have high quality items for trading. Everything was moving per plan.

In the winter months, trading came to a stop. No one wanted to travel the treacherous roads during snowstorms and ice roads that would cause a wagon to slide down a cliff. During the winter, the tenants moved back to Ponteville, their original home, but with much more money in their pockets.

Nekora stayed behind and looked after the Kingdom. She paid her servants well and hated the thought of slavery. Her Kingdom presided over all else, and she is the Queen of her new Kingdom. She made friends and enemies along the way. But her parents looked after her and helped her prosper during trivial times. She always gave thanks to her parents for always watching out for her. She dedicated golden alters to them.

Many more prospecting tenants were looking for a new life, a prosperous life that Nekora could provide. She had more homes built, markets grown, her Kingdom was expanding during the non-snowy months.

Word of this new Kingdom has reached Haversmith. Rumor has spread all over the world about a new prosperous Kingdom with unlimited gold.

A scout from the mainland brought news to King bob in Haversmith.

"Your highness, I bring the most urgent news. There appears to be a new Kingdom called," he paused for a moment trying to recollect the name. He said it slowly, "Necropolis? Either way, it is said to be flourishing and bountiful with unlimited gold. From the merchant, it seems legitimate." The King thought on this. "Show me where on this map."

The scout perused the map of the mainland provided by the King.

"This is the main port for traders here; this road here goes to this large city Ponteville. He said it was north of here but no mention of it on the map." The scout showed the King.

"There seems to be a small road that winds through the mountains here into an unknown clearing. The city must reside about, here." The king pointed.

"I shall destroy this city and claim the gold for myself. We could use that gold," the king thought as a wry smile crossed his face.

"Get a legion of troops together. We shall go there and lay claim to our portion of this gold. Our Kingdom will prosper and be the best in the world." The king laughed.

"As you say." The lead guard went to gather the troops.

"Your highness, what of our protection from the elves? I am sure they are responsible for killing our trade master Michael. We have not seen him in months," asked the scout.

The king looked upon the scout as if to ask why he was still there.

"This Kingdom will be fine. We have not had any attacks in years. Besides, it is time we relocate to the mainland and become a much larger, more fearsome force to be reckoned with. Jacoby, send word to our host Kingdoms. We march immediately before the winter," the king demanded.

"Yes, your highness," Jacoby said as he carried out his orders.

"Gentlemen, mark this day in history. The day Haversmith expands to the mainland. We will become the richest, mightiest Kingdom in the world," Bob stated.

There was cheering from all directions. All the warriors plus the king made their way to the boats. Ten boats were full of warriors and rations. They set sail for the mainland.

CHAPTER TWENTY-FOUR

Ten vessels overall. All of them setting sail to the mainland. Their target, Necropolis, as they say it.

The king was in the lead barge, leading the way to greatness.

"Your highness, how are we going to get all the gold onto these ships? Especially with all the warriors," asked Roland, second in command.

"We are not," replied the king. "We are going to relocate to the new Kingdom and put-up mighty defenses. We will have a new way of life and will control trade. When we have established our residency, then we will send for the rest of the people in Haversmith and have them move out this way," the king responded. "It is a win-win situation."

"What if we are not successful?" Roland asked, Leary of the plan.

"Then we shall die. All that matters is the gold. He who has the gold controls the world. We will triumph since it is obviously a new Kingdom, and we will prosper in unmeasurable wealth," the king replied.

Roland was rethinking his role in this. He did not have a good feeling. But if he told the king, he would be hung. Better to be safe than sorry.

The winds were not in favor these days and took longer than a couple weeks to get to the mainland. Once they finally reached the shore, they were greeted by their allies.

"Is there a reason you pulled us all the way here, King Bob?" asked King Gerald from the northern Kingdom of Farah.

With that question, there was a lot of murmuring happening. King Bob put his hands up to quiet the kings down.

"There is news of an uprising in the north, a new Kingdom of Necropolis. It should be between the mountain pass near Ponteville. We need to put an end to their reign and keep our Kingdoms safe from harm. Rumors of dragons are known to reside there, and we need to ensure this land is protected," King Bob lied. "There have not been any dragon sightings in centuries. The mainland is safe enough," King Harold replied.

"You are lying and for what reason?" asked King Jillian.

"Now, now, my dear friends and colleagues. My scout has reported this to me only a few weeks ago. If we dawdle all day on what is, and what could be, it may be too late. If we conquer that Kingdom, I will reign over all the land and ensure your Kingdoms never go dry." King Bob lied again.

This time, the kings took the matter to consideration. Even if a rumor were true about a new Kingdom, even if a rumor were true about dragons, they would be in extreme danger if nothing were done. They all agreed, however, they could not agree on who would run the new Kingdom.

King Bob stated the march was his idea, the information was his, and has every right to rule that Kingdom.

"Besides, it opens up a kingship in Haversmith, known for their exquisite ivory," King Bob said.

More murmuring went on before they all agreed. After the battle, they will decide who got to rule Haversmith.

The march was on. Over two thousand soldiers marching to the north toward Ponteville.

Nekora was eating dinner. It would be a month or so before her friends would come back and get the Kingdom ready for the spring trades. The spices she hoarded made a huge difference in the meat, and even the vegetables were much better tasting. The flapping of huge wings was heard overhead.

"Good luck on your hunt," Gilgamere Nekora thought as he flew south.

Gilgamere flew farther south than normal. He did not want to rid the lands in the immediate area for food, so he searched in different parts of the mainland. Some areas took a couple days to get to, but he was scattering his hunt to retain food.

Before he got to the water, he noticed thousands of people with torches marching northward. They were heading toward Ponteville or Nekorapolis. I must warn Nekora about this after I eat.

Gilgamere took flight farther east and struck down a wild horse. He had not had a horse in a long time, so it was a welcome treat. Once he got his fill, Gilgamere lifted off the ground and headed home. He flew into his cave and slept until the next morning.

Nekora was awake. She was standing at her window, naked, looking out at the view with a hot beverage in her hands. She absolutely loved this view and could not get enough. After a few minutes, she went back into her room and got dressed. Her clothes were warm sitting by the fire, and it felt so good on her skin. Unfortunately, the warmth did not last long once she left the confines of the fire. She went downstairs where breakfast was being served. She loved to eat with her servants at the table. The company felt good.

After she finished, the women took the plates and utensils to be washed.

Nekora went outside where Gilgamere was standing on top of a roof looking south.

"What are doing out of your hide hole?" Nekora asked in a jesting manner.

"There is an army of around two thousand strong, heading in this direction. I would take precautions. This Kingdom is not fortified," said Gilgamere.

"No, but I have an army about half of theirs and kill when commanded, no questions asked," thought Nekora to Gilgamere.

"I have thousands of warriors at my disposal and hopefully a few dragons at my side?" Nekora cautiously asked.

Gilgamere looked to Nekora and roared. "The other six dragons went their separate ways. I do not know where they went, but if I did, I would ask for their help," said Gilgamere.

Nekora frowned. All those years ago and she thought the dragons would stay together. She felt bad, yet happy with her decision to let them go free.

Gilgamere took flight. "You must build fortifications. These humans are stronger than you think."

With that, Gilgamere vanished. Nekora was left to worry about her Kingdom being destroyed. She took a horse to Ponteville to gather the people.

Once in the city, Nekora got to the first person she could find.

"I need help building fortifications for an impending attack. Not sure if they are coming here or Nekorapolis," Nekora stated.

The guy shook his head and had her follow him to the builder's guild. She requisitioned them to build a fortified wall around her Kingdom. They would not move since the cold bitter days would kill them, but in the end, it took Nekora to part with thousands of gold pieces to hire them. They agreed and said they would make their way tomorrow morning. It takes time and resources to gather enough stone and bring them through the mountains.

Nekora agreed. "Thank you, but please be quick about it. I paid you handsomely for your help," she said.

"No problem, Roger is on the hunt for what we need."

Nekora went back to her home. During the winter months, the undead were awake to render guarding duties. The army included the fifteen hundred warriors from long ago, making her army over two thousand strong. She let them rest for the other three seasons, but this time was different. The warning from Gilgamere caused her to hesitate before sending them off to bed.

A few days later, the builder's guild showed and started working the wall. She ensured the undead army stayed farther in the woods and out of sight of the guild members. The wall was going up slowly. Too slow for her liking.

"At this pace, the army will be here before the first set of stones are laid!" Nekora yelled.

"Perfection is a quality that cannot be wasted with time. We must ensure your Kingdom is safe or else what am I but just another builder. Besides, you did not mention a time constraint," Roger noted, rubbing his fingers together indicating more payment.

"For fucks sake, you are worse than the thief's guild!" Nekora accused.

She threw a few more gold his way. "Get it done now!" She was very worried.

Gilgamere appeared that night. He landed on top of Nekora's castle.

It is too late; the wall is half built, and the army is here. I will aid you however I can. I have sent word to my brethren to help us. If they get here on time, we should be good. He spoke.

That is all I can ask for, my friend. "Be safe," Nekora thought. She looked to the south through her window with her fire burning warmth into her room. She saw the faint discoloration of orange in the distance and knew she only had a couple days. The cloud layer was below her window so she could get a good assessment on how much time she had. Time was not on her side.

Bob halted his military. The fog was dense, and he had no idea where the entrance to the pathway lies. He sent out a few scouts to check up ahead. During the downtime, the catapults and giant crossbows were examined.

The giant crossbows measured twelve feet across with arrows made from tree stumps. It was a design from ages ago when dragons existed. Six crossbows were being hauled by horse. They would be positioned in different directions, mostly toward the open areas to protect against dragon attacks.

The catapults measured fifteen feet in height that could hurl small boulders. The cusp was metallic so it could handle flaming objects. Eight catapults, pushed by men as horses could not be afforded, were in tow as the last line. They would be pushed forward to attack the gate and walls.

Gerald rode up beside Bob. "Bob, you are sure we are in the right spot? My scouts have never reported any pathways here. Besides, the cold is upsetting the men. They are not used to this weather."

"I know it is in this area somewhere. I sent some scouts to recon the area. They should find it soon enough. We will be on our way if this fog lifts." A flapping was heard to the north, a quick scream then silence.

"That did not sound good," Gerald stated.

"Must be the dragons I heard about," Bob lied. "To arms! Look to the skies and below! Protect the machines! Ensure nothing gets through the lines!" Bob commanded his men.

"Dragons? Get it through your thick skull, there are none." Gerald was gone. Bob remained silent and gave orders for everyone to do the same. "Keep an eye above," he whispered. Soon the command was spread throughout the encampment. Torches were put out to keep the light low so they could not see from above.

The army sat there, listening for any noise out of the ordinary. After a tense moment, nothing was heard. They resumed camp without light for the remainder of the night and into morning.

Nekora saw the silhouette of Gilgamere from the light background as he swooped down and grabbed unsuspecting personnel and flung them to their deaths. It was a glorious view, and she was just glad to have his aid, for now. By all rights, he could terminate their friendship at any time. Her father, being the lord of dragons, could be helping her situation. Either way, the defenses needed to be built and quickly.

A scream was heard as her undead army killed the scout. Nekora's spell kept the undead moving, and anything that died now belonged to her. The scout rose and had become part of Nekora's army. He came by to give accounts of the armies below.

"This may be easier than anticipated. Still, I cannot relax just yet. From what I hear, the humans are pathetically difficult to kill," she thought as she went back inside. Every undead was awake and roaming the grounds for security and protection. Nekora fell asleep.

She was awakened the next morning with Gilgamere outside her window.

The army drew closer. "The wall is not yet built. Your defenses are weak," he stated.

"Gah! If I only knew how the magical force field worked. I can't remember!" Nekora was mad at herself. Her old mage friends knew the incantation for erecting the force field. Here she was with diamonds galore but no spell to go with it. She did not have time to traverse the ethereal and look it up again. She forgot what she learned since she never used it. A lesson to keep in the books. The fires were getting much closer.

Nekora was mad at herself for not paying more attention. She figured her home would have never been destroyed as it was. Too late now. She was hoping this would be over before the Ponteville inhabitants come back to get their markets ready for the season.

The next morning, Nekora looked out her window. The wall was almost complete but still needed additions. The gate was just barely on; it would slow them enough to get her army in position. Two thousand five hundred undead versus the human two thousand. If they were as tough as she heard, she may not make it out alive. Her fate was in the gods' hands now.

The team from Ponteville was on their way to Nekorapolis. Numerous rations and trade items were in their carts on their way for the opening of the trade season. King Bob halted the caravan.

"Where are you going?" he demanded.

Chrissy was among them. She wanted to see how the new Kingdom was flourishing. She answered the King. "We are on our way to Nekorapolis to get ready for trading, your highness."

"You know there has been a terrible incident from Necropolis, right? It seems the ruler of the new Kingdom has waged war against our land. They are vying for power, and we are here to stop it," the king lied.

"No, that is not true. Nekora would never do such a thing. She is a sweet woman. An elf that cares for her people," Chrissy said in tears, not wanting to believe what she was just told.

"Your highness, the scout has yet to check in. He should have been back hours ago," a high-ranking soldier said to

King Bob. "He is the best scout we have and has never crossed our country. He is either dead or he joined the enemy, and I highly doubt the latter."

"There, you see, proof that she does not want her information known to others. If your men join us, we will see to it that you are taken care of for life. You are from Ponteville are you not?" the king asked.

"Yes, but that does not prove your accusations, King," Chrissy accused.

"Careful, missy, another accusation like that will cost not only you, but your cities lives. You would not want to be responsible for that would you?" the king interjected.

Tears flowed down Chrissy's cheeks. Reynold put his arm around her for comfort. The king looked to the men in the caravan.

"Gentlemen, if you join us in deterring the threat to our country, we will reward you handsomely. You will have enough gold to retire yourself and your family," the king bluffed.

"Say what you will, we already have enough gold to retire. We are just helping our friend, Roger retorted.

"So, the rumor of unlimited gold is true then. Soon it will be mine," King Bob thought, then put on a fake smile. "Well, then, if you would not help your country in her defense, then you must leave this area immediately lest you be tried for treason," the king commanded.

The caravan turned around, but three men remained to join the King in his duties.

"Your highness, why would Nekora, the nicest elf in all the land, be responsible for invading our territory?"

asked Nigel. Nigel had befriended Nekora when she first came to Ponteville. He has never seen a mean streak in her personality until word of it just now. Though he was skeptical, he did not want to stand by in case the country was dominated. He joined the army on a just in case basis.

The army marched early morning. They were a half day from the gates of the once known Kingdom of Agora, now known as Nekorapolis. At the front line, the king made sure everyone set camp out of range from archers.

"The wall is new," remarked Nigel. She might be planning to take over the country, but how? She has no army. It was then he saw a lot of movement on both sides of the camp. He brought the movement to the King's attention.

"To arms!" the King cried out. "Enemies approaching on both sides of the camp!"

The humans yelled the sound of war, giving them the adrenaline necessary to survive a fight. Both sides were engaged in combat. The King took a closer look. He could not believe what he was seeing.

"Skeletons? She must be a witch to control the undead," the King thought with a worrisome look.

The king turned to Nigel. "Did you know she controls the undead?" he more stated than asked as he charged into battle.

Nigel was confused. How can she do this? Why would she do this? There must be more to this story than he is being told. Nigel made it a duty to find out the truth. There must be more to this.

Nekora watched as the first wave of attacks on the sides were spotted before she wanted. The one thing about the undead is no tactics were ever understood. They just mindlessly go in and attack per orders. She was, however, interested in how the outcome would result.

For each undead killed, three humans were killed. Nekora could not tell if they were warriors or just peasants. She was not sure how to calculate her odds just yet. Since the warriors were killed by the undead, they rose to aid Nekora increasing her numbers. The clothing suggested those men were just peasants or farmers but still powerful for a human. Warriors came in to reverse the odds. She decided she needed help from Mother Nature.

She could not summon a storm just yet until the preliminary battle was over. All her concentration was used to ensure the undead rose when able. "Gods, why are you forsaking me? What have I done to deserve all this unfair judgment by these damned humans? All I ever wanted was a peaceful life."

There was no answer, only silence. Nekora was feeling saddened as the humans were destroying her army. Nekora lost her original five hundred army members, gained another five hundred, then lost those as well. The humans were proving to be tougher than she originally imagined.

"Oh, Nekora, what have you done?" Nigel asked in thought. His eyes did not lie.

He saw the truth in the King's story. But nothing added up to Nekora being a tyrant. If she had this ability, she could have taken over the nation a long time ago. Instead, she occupied an abandoned city. Nigel was going mad trying to make sense of it all.

"Do not fret, young lad. You still have your whole life ahead of you," said the guard commander. He noted the worrisome look on his face and could ill afford someone who's head was not in the game, especially after fighting the undead.

Nekora sized up her adversaries. She needed guidance as she was not accustomed to a full out assault. Gilgamere was nowhere to be found; her friends were still in Ponteville, at least she hoped they were, and siege engines that looked like they could decimate her new Kingdom.

Enough was enough. Nekora has an investment to guard. She started summoning her storm.

King Bob and three other kings were in the large tent going over plans. There were no maps showing the outlying buildings, so they had to make decisions from the start. The sky turned dark. Twirling clouds getting blacker by the minute. Rain was coming down hard with lightning close at hand. The head guard noticed a lone figure waving their hands erratically. He pointed the figure out to the kings. King Bob watched in fascination.

"She is a witch, just like I told you. If we do nothing, she will destroy everything we worked for. Archers, aim for that witch!" The gold would be all his.

Dozens of archers took point close enough to land their arrows. The head guardsman gave orders.

"Knock." All archers loaded an arrow into their bows.

"Ready." All archers pulled back their bow and took aim.

A rain of fire caught them all by surprise. Every archer was on fire plus the head guardsman. All of them were yelling for help. The King had a bewildered look. Then he looked up.

Seven dragons were encircling the invaders.

"To the crossbows!" he demanded.

The men turned the crossbows to face in the general vicinity of the dragons. It took two men to wind the string back, and two men to lift and load the large heavy bolt. The iron tips assured penetration through the scales. While the bows were loading, more lines of fire cut through the main build-up. Hundreds of warriors perished.

It was now a waiting game. The crossbows were at the ready, the dragons were too high up. The black scales camouflaged them in the night. All Nekora could do was hope. She looked upon the battlefield with rage on her face.

Why are they so impetuous? "I will kill every single last one of you all for your non-invoked attacks!" she yelled at the top of her lungs. Nekora's eyes turned black, her hatred has fully consumed her once again. There was no turning back.

Chrissy made it back to Ponteville. She went to Nekora's favorite waitress crying.

"Nekora is under attack." Chrissy could barely speak.

"What! Why? How?" So many questions crossed her mind.

"I do not know. King Bob from Haversmith said she was going to conquer our lands and he was sent to stop her." She sobbed.

"Haversmith? Where have I heard that before?" The waitress pondered a bit. "Nekora talked about that city. It is on an island far away. Why did they travel this far? Did Nekora do something to the city before she left?" So many questions went unanswered. "But Nekora is the sweetest elf I have ever known. I have seen her bad side, but it was justified. She was attacked. Oh my god, poor girl. She is all alone, and I am not there to help her" Tears ran down her cheeks.

"I always swore to myself that I would do what is best for Nekora. I must go. I know a back way into the city. Come with me if you want to help her," she stated as she darted out the front door.

The tavern owner stood in her path, "Where do you think you are going, Rachel? You have work to do," he commanded.

"I have to help my friend. She is in dire trouble and needs our help," Rachel stated.

"Is this the wench that won your heart and took over the sacred city of Agora? I forbid it! Now get back to work! All of you, listen up. If you so much as think of heading there, I will never serve you again," the owner demanded.

"Your food is not as good as you think it is, asshole! I am leaving, with or without your consent!" Rachel demanded as she ran out the door with Chrissy.

"I think you just lost your job, Rachel" noted Chrissy.

"That is okay. I hate working for him, anyway. I can cook food better than he can anyhow," Rachel said as they ran toward the north gate.

Though spring was right around the corner, the weather was still cold. Snow still lingered on the ground. Chrissy and Rachel ran down the path until they were out of sight of the guards then they turned left.

"This path was only marked on one map. I have that map hidden in my room, but I know it well. I remembered it when I was reading it last night since we now work in Nekorapolis," Rachel started. "The way is more treacherous, but also shorter. We should be there in a days' time, not two days."

"I had no idea there was a second entrance and exit. I thought there was only one," Chrissy commented. Technically there is. There is a small pathway to the eastern end of the market, coming out near my tavern. I saw the other side of it before I left in the winter. It is why I kept looking at the map, try to make heads or tails of it. Be careful, the trek is dangerous, loose gravel, and sharp edges," Rachel said.

Chrissy nodded. She trusted her friend and was anxious to get back to help Nekora. Both women worried for her safety. They only hoped to arrive in time.

Tents were blown up with the powerful lightning strikes. Fires seemed to burn with the rain in a downpour. Warriors and kings alike were burning and dying on the battlefield.

Nekora was exhausted. She had cast far too many spells for her mortal body to handle. Her eyes widened; an idea had struck her. It was only a matter of time before the enemy came through the non-finished gate.

"Any lord, my mom and dad in particular. Grant me this day the power of an immortal. Please help me to become what I am supposed to be. Terminate this human body and end my mortality, so that immortality may take form. I beg of you. Amen," Nekora pleaded.

She fell asleep.

Heavy sounds of artillery were heard. The crossbows down range were fired as one bolt struck one of the dragons. The other six saw the artillery and quickly swooped down before they could reload. Fire was released onto the bows, destroying them instantly. One of the bolts went higher than the wall, through Nekora's window, and lodged itself in her right lower back. Nekora screamed in pain.

"Why? What have I done to anger you? What did I do wrong?" Nekora yelled at the gods. She tried to dislodge the huge bolt, but it was too heavy.

All Nekora could do was lie in her bed, unmoving and in great pain.

The undead sensed their master in agony. Several of them waited inside the gate for a frontal attack. Nothing was forthcoming yet. Many others were still in the courtyard, unmoving.

King Bob looked in anticipation. "Raul!" he yelled. Raul came running and stopped with a salute.

"Yes, your highness," he answered.

"I want you to take to higher ground. Map out buildings and troop movements," Bob commanded.

"I will do as you command, your highness," Raul stated and turned to run up the hillside closest to the walls.

Raul looked, there was no movement at all. Only buildings that appeared empty and dead bodies everywhere. He ran back to report.

"Sire, there are dead bodies everywhere, buildings are empty. Nothing seems to thrive in there," Raul reported.

The king looked less than amused. He ordered and assault on the walls and gate. He was down to around a thousand soldiers, a lot, but still something felt off.

Soldiers used ladders to scale the wall and rammed the gate open easily.

Every soldier piled inside yelling their war cries. They were met with nothing. Confused, the soldiers sheathed their swords and looked around. Dead bodies, the smell of rot penetrating the rain.

The undead moved quickly. They surrounded the army and slaughtered the teams. Flashes of blades were seen outside the gate. The lightning allowed brief glimpses of the battle. King Bob was furious.

"Everyone! Get in there! Attack!" he yelled.

The rest of the army went in. Every living body that was slain was resurrected. Nekora's army was stronger now than ever before. King Bob, with his army, had been defeated.

The undead laid to rest. They awaited their next command.

Rachel and Chrissy showed up a day later. The smell of rot and decay filled their nostrils causing them to regurgitate their lunch and dinner. Human bodies were everywhere.

The lord of death came to visit Nekora in her chambers. He was less than amused to see her in her current condition.

"I now have a puppet on the mainland. You will forever be my handmaiden. You will do everything I tell you to do. In return, I will grant you immortality." His thoughts pierced her mind like he was talking directly to her. Nekora was weak, growing weaker.

"I agree," she stated.

"Then, by the nine halls of hell, you are hereby granted the gift of immortality. You will cleanse this land of filth and rule with a fair hand."

Nekora passed out. The pain was too great for her to bear.

Rachel and Chrissy entered the main building. The castle was magnificent on the inside. They decided to conduct their search starting with the castle then fan out as needed. They had to find their friend. Each one calling out Nekora's name. They were afraid she might be dead.

Up the stairway they went, each looking into the rooms along the corridor. None of them have ever been inside the castle so they had no clue where to go.

A large set of double doors were partially open on the southern end of the corridor. Rachel had an eerie feeling.

"This is it," she said softly. They opened the doors slowly and saw Nekora lying on the bed with a large bolt through her right lower back.

Both women cried as they attempted to remove the bolt. It was heavy, but they succeeded. No more blood came out of the wound. She was no longer living.

Both women cried and laid by her side. Soon, they got up and left. They decided to go back to Ponteville and swore never to return to this sacred place. It was cursed to live there.

Nekora opened her eyes. Her vision was much sharper, her hearing far greater, and her breathing fuller. She felt energetic. She stood and looked out the window. Her vision picked up heat signatures, and she quickly disposed of the living. All living things, including plants and wildlife, died in a two-mile circle around the castle. Clouds remained permanent above, the land turned black.

CHAPTER TWENTY-FIVE

Nekora remained motionless. Her hatred had permanently consumed her. Her black aura twirling around her beautiful figure. Blackened eyes have replaced her once shiny green ones. Her newfound senses were astounding. Her razor-sharp vision could see much clearer than before. Her hearing and smell were phenomenal; she could hear a pin drop and smell a living mortal from over three hundred meters away. Two figures caught her eye.

"This place gives me the creeps," Jenkin stated as he wearily looked around the field. "Everything is dead here. Rachel was right, this place is cursed."

Neither Jenkin nor Roger were combatants. They were professional beggars from the human city of Kalvania who had recently visited Ponteville in hopes to find work. They had run across Rachel, who told them stories of a once-friendly elf that had died from humans attacking her city. She talked about going back one day to retrieve the golden statue and display it in Ponteville as a reminder of their history and in remembrance of Nekora.

"It is all a superstitious fairytale. If what they say is correct, then the gold should be all over the place. I don't see a damned thing around here," Roger commented, looking for anything of value. "Everything is blackened. Wait a minute." He stopped and walked toward a statue. Roger gave the statue a gentle shove, but it was quite heavier than it looked. "Aha!" he exclaimed.

Both men wiped down the statue. The black covering appeared to be ash, but there was no sign of a fire anywhere. They wiped it down and saw a golden glimmer shine through.

"We found it!" exclaimed Jenkin. "Now how are we going to bring it back?" he asked, confused.

"We will come back with a wagon, maybe a couple more guys to help load this on the cart and off we go," Roger responded. "I wonder if this is the same statue Rachel talked about."

"Good idea, we will have to split the earnings but still better off than we were," Jenkin stated. "Now let us see if the statue is movable first," he said softly as he wiped the base.

Both men tried to move the statue. It budged a little, showing there was nothing holding it in place but the weight.

"I don't think a hurricane could move this thing. It took all we had to move it that much," Roger stated holding up his finger and thumb separated by less than a quarter inch. Jenkin saw a small pathway to the north heading toward the mountain just beyond Rogers fingers.

"Curious, where does that trail lead to?" Jenkin said pointing to the mountain. "A small path leading to the mountain. A cave maybe? Could there be riches in the cave? Maybe we can hire some people and bring them back? This just might be our lucky day!" Jenkin was excited. "Come on, Roger, let's follow this pathway. Besides, this might be the place they mined for gold, which means we can make more than enough to hire people to help. Hell, we would be able to buy our own cart. A fancy one that can hold tons of weight. We are going to be beyond rich!" Jenkin grabbed Roger by the shoulders and looked him in the eyes. "We will never have to beg for food again."

Roger looked warily into the direction Jenkin was indicating. "It is possible, but do you see anyone here?" Roger gestured with both hands to the city. "They moved on, Jenk. Use your head, even if there was a cave, it would be empty. Why else would this place be abandoned? Have you ever heard the stories of the Drow dragon riders? Don't you think if there was gold in this supposed cave, it would be guarded? I do not know about you, but I am not a knight. I am also not going to fight a legion of Drow. They are the fiercest." Roger was cut off. Jenkins held his finger to his lips to be quiet.

Jenkin started toward the path. It turned sharply to the left behind a mass of foliage and trees. Jenkin put both arms out and lowered them, signifying to Roger to get low. Jenkin told him to wait a minute as he disappeared into the brush around the corner. All was silent. The breeze and swaying leaves were the only thing heard. Roger became antsy and stood to leave. He was scared. A body jumped out of the bush next to Roger. He screamed and fell to his back on the ground. He coward with both hands covering his face.

Laughter was now the only thing Roger heard. He peered through his fingers to see his friend rolling on the ground in a huge fit of laughter. "Did you see the look on your face?" Jenkin exclaimed in a raging fit of laughter. Roger got up and took a swing at Jenkin.

"You asshole! You scared the shit out of me!" Roger accused.

Jenkin caught his breath. "Oh man," he stated as took in a deep breath." That was the funniest thing I have ever seen." Jenkin looked to his friend who was finally getting back to normalcy, sitting next to him. "Yes, I have heard the stories. You must know that those stories are in a different land, not here. If there were dragons and/or Drow, we would have seen them all these ages," Jenkin explained. "Besides, listen," Jenkin said as he put his hand to his ear. "Nothing, if there were anything here besides us, we would have at least heard chattering, or someone giving orders. Relax, my friend; we are alone."

Roger calmed down. He hated his friend for what he did. This place gave him unpleasant feelings without Jenkin messing with him. He was right, though. He would have heard someone or something by now with all the noise they were making. Both men stood and restarted their trek to the cave.

Nekora heard the entire conversation from the balcony. She called forth the nearest undead. "Make these two an example of future greedy trespassers."

Two skeletons stood near the area and did as they were commanded. Both skeletons ran to the path and split on either side of the foliage. They sprang out the dense foliage in front of the men from the sides with a sword and shield up and ready for battle.

"What the fuck?" Jenkin yelled, halting his progression. "She did not say anything about skeletons!" he exclaimed as they started running for the trail back out of the city.

Both men ran as fast as they could. The skeletons were hot on their trail, running behind them ready to kill. Shields were facing forward, swords raised. The mouths were open, but no sound emanated. Dirt flew up from behind the bones as toes dug into the earth and flung it behind them, adding traction to their motion.

Four zombies stood in front, blocking the path out of the city. The surprise stopped the men in their tracks. A couple seconds later, the skeletons attacked, severing each of their heads in place. The bodies fell lifelessly to the ground.

Nekora watched the events unfold. An evil smile spread across her face. She pulled out her world map and began planning to eradicate every single human civilization from the map.

Many years passed. Nekora was bound and determined more than ever to eradicate all humans from this world. She devised a plan to use the undead in her attacks. But they can only hunt humans, no other species shall be harmed. Much research had to be done to customize her spells.

"First, I need to do some reconnaissance in these cities and plan for action," Nekora thought as she pointed at each human civilization. She figured her best route would be to start at Farah. She would then trek to each Kingdom in an orderly fashion around the map and end up back in Nekorapolis. A bending counterclockwise journey seemed to be the best route.

The first Kingdom nearest to hers was Farah. It is a large Kingdom in the northern area with mostly human inhabitants. Nekora decided to make this her first visit; maybe she could find a map or learn the layout of the city. She had to see how it was designed and the current guard predicament. She had to visit to find the best way to attack.

Nekora wandered the cemetery. She found numerous bones from the war that ended the civilization, but nothing stood out to her as a riding companion. She departed to the battlefield outside the Kingdom limits to where the dead humans laid. She found a half-decayed horse that was very large and black in color. Parts of its flesh was missing. Bones from the horse's ribs and legs could be seen. Half the face was bone as well and it appeared to be a tall stallion. Nekora raised the horse as her mount.

> In Septus Unike Val herios
> Rizen mi hotas
> Sin titolu des humanas
> Rizen a mi mountes
> In Gammon ni seerney.

The death horse woke and stood. Its eyes were glowing red from the spell indicating it was being controlled. Nekora could barely reach the stirrup. The horse was huge and muscular. She was in luck. A war horse on top of the other boons. She had her own mount now, a way to visit each city.

Before departing, Nekora rode into the Kingdom and commanded the undead to protect the Kingdom. "Kill any and all living things that come unexpectedly but leave them so they would be useful this time," useful meaning the ability to come back as part of her army. The corpses put themselves in a way to view every inch of the city and collapsed.

Nekora set off on her journey. It would take years to investigate every city and take notes. By the end, she would have enough information on how to take each Kingdom by force. Her focus was to eradicate humans.

She was clothed in gray attire to match the mist. It disguised her presence to mere mortals and kept her warm as well. The chill followed her but did not cause her any discomfort. Her scimitars were attached to her back as well as her bow and a full quiver of arrows. She no longer needed the arrows since she could conjure her own, but she had to make it look like part of her outfit. A bow with no arrows would look suspicious.

Before reaching the southern 'T' junction in the road, she came out of the mist and turned right. Knowing the condition of the horse, she knew she had to remain hidden from view lest she be reported, and her plans thwarted. So, she stuck to the northern terrain and followed the road out of sight, her cloak flowing in the wind, giving a ghostly sway and ominous look.

Nekora stuck near the northern edge. With the slow trot along the path, it took her over a week to get to her first city. She had all the time in the world now. Her immortality gave her an infinite life. She wanted to enjoy the sights before getting to her destination. Nekora took her time.

Prince Thagren was still waiting for his father to return. He ran the Kingdom while the King was away on business.

He had no idea what business the King was conducting in Ponteville, but he had learned the hard way not to ask. Given the number of warriors he took, he wondered if his father was going to conquer the city. He had no idea why. It was a dismal place to his recollection.

The prince often tried to remember the face of the girl at the inn. He could not remember her name, but the long flowing blonde hair and blue eyes were riveting. Her face will be forever etched into his brain. He was brought back to reality from his daydreaming as his guard opened the door.

"Your highness," he said as he bowed.

"What is it today, Fred?" the prince regarded.

"Your presence is requested in the great hall. A visitor has asked for your audience," the young guard stated.

"Very well, I will be there momentarily," the prince answered.

Fred bowed and turned to leave. He entered the great hall and told the prince of Ponteville that he would be there momentarily.

Prince Thagren entered the hall and saw his friend. A smile came across his face as he greeted him.

"Tolin!" Thagren said.

"Thagren!" Tolin returned the greeting. They clasped wrists and embraced in a quick hug.

"What brings you here?" Thagren asked. "It is an awful long trek just to visit." "My horse did," Tolin answered, waiting for Thagren to react.

Thagren looked at him with a blank stare. "That is getting very old. You need a new line my friend. Wine?" Thagren started pouring two glasses.

"You know I can't resist a good wine," Tolin said. He continued after a brief silence, "The reason for my visit is I have not heard from my father. Last I heard, he was leaving to meet yours. That was over three months ago. He has never been gone this long. Rumor has it, they met to invade Agora, the city in the north. If they did," Tolin looked down, "then they could have awakened an evil. That was a sacred city full of curses."

"My father never told me where they were going. In my studies, Agora is rich in gold. Anyone who goes there never returns. Sources say it is the horrible weather that kills them; I say it could be an evil curse. Either way, we need to find out for sure if they went there. Are you absolutely positive?" Thagren asked.

Tolin looked away for a moment, then back to his friend. "Yes, A scout came running back to our city. He was crazy and drunk talking about skeletons and the dead rising to defeat their armies. Plus, a dragon. Now, I thought dragons were extinct. But then I thought about the possibility of them hiding, which is believable. I figured I would ask you if anyone returned from your army." Tolin trembled, remembering his father, and hoping that his father was still alive.

"Whatever it is, Tolin, we need to find out for sure. Can you ride with me to Agora? We need to find the truth," Thagren asked.

"I am not going anywhere near that place. Gold filled or not, I like my life, thank you. I want to survive for my wedding next month during the summer solstice," Tolin stated.

Thagren looked at his friend with a huge smile on his face. "You lucky devil! This calls for a celebration! Slave! More wine! And tonight, we shall have a feast!" Thagren exclaimed in excitement.

"Thank you, my friend. I humbly accept your invitation," Tolin said.

"Invitation, who said you were invited?" Thagren stated with a smile on his face as he took a drink of wine.

Both men cheered.

Two miles down the road, Nekora dismounted her undead war horse. She told him to wait where he was and walked toward the road. She continued her trek to the gate.

"State your business," the guard stated as Nekora approached him.

"I am here for shelter and food. I have traveled far," Nekora replied.

"Go on then, don't cause any trouble," the guard said as he waved his head toward the city. A female traveler posed no threat.

"Thank you, kind sir," Nekora said somberly.

She walked down the main road, taking note of every place. She found the local inn and reserved a room.

"I apologize, but I am new to the town. Is there a map I can borrow for the night so I can find my way around?" Nekora asked the innkeeper.

He looked at her with distrust in his eyes. Seeing she was not a threat; he reluctantly surrendered the city map.

"Don't ruin or lose it or I will have your head," the innkeeper threatened.

All Nekora could do was smile and nod. She went to her room and began studying the map.

The city layout was easy to learn. The main street led to the castle, with inns and taverns on either side. Streets ran from the main along the way and wound around the castle with houses and markets. The cities cemetery was kept to the north in a large open area. Daylight shone in her window, and she rolled the map.

"Thank you, sir," Nekora said as she returned the map to the innkeeper. Nekora turned to walk back to her room and sleep. She woke at nightfall. She went downstairs and out the door to the tavern for food and drink.

After her meal, Nekora decided to continue her stroll through the city. After Ponteville, she always kept an eye and ear out for something out of the ordinary. She did not trust the human population.

She made it to the cemetery. It was huge and filled with loved ones.

"What are you doing out here?" came a voice from her left. A figure was angrily walking toward her with a shovel.

"Take no fear, I am here to pay respects to the fallen," Nekora responded.

"This time of night? Which grave you planning on robbing tonight thief?" He yelled the last part as he called for the guards.

"I am sorry to disturb you. I have no idea what you are talking about, but I am no thief. I will be on my way then, goodnight, fine sir," Nekora stated.

"You will stay here until the guard gets here. He will get the truth out of you," the watchman said. "I am tired of you guys stealing the corpse to play pranks on others."

Nekora was taken aback. "That is disgusting," she stated. "I..."

"I said stay here!" The watchman brought his shovel down. Nekora dodged the attack. He attacked again, but Nekora moved out of the way and came in close. She grabbed his throat with abnormal strength. The watchman dropped his shovel and tried to scream, but no sound was made. He attempted to remove the grip on his throat but was unsuccessful in his attempts. Nekora brought his face closer to hers. She could smell the potent stench of alcohol on his breath.

"Now you listen here, you twat! I am not stealing, nor am I doing anything illegal. I am here to pay respects then leaving. If you want to live, you will take your shovel and go back home now!" she commanded.

The watchman nodded. He could not talk. His head movements were limited by Nekora's grasp. She threw him to the ground and stood over him. The watchman grabbed his throat and shovel and limped back to his home. Nekora looked around. Seeing no other adversaries, she continued her count.

Prince Thagren and prince Tolin were in agreeance. Their fathers have been missing for some time now, far longer than usual with no word from either party. It was time to send a rescue mission.

"They could still be alive," Tolin stated. "Maybe they are prisoners."

"Who would they be prisoner to? Agora has been abandoned for centuries," Thagren responded.

"Whether they are prisoners or dead, something happened up there. It is up to us to find out what," Tolin remarked.

"I agree. We need to set out before snowfall. It would be too cold to survive up there otherwise," Thagren stated.

Both decided to leave the following day. Thagren would have an army and follow Tolin to Ponteville so he could gather his troops. They would be ready for any attack or rescue. If their fathers were alive, time was of the essence.

The next day, they set out. Thagren took two hundred warriors and left the other two hundred back to guard the city. They set off to Ponteville as planned. Tolin sent a bird ahead with a note telling his forces to be ready to march as soon as they got there.

A scout looked in every direction. He saw a lone horse to the north and decided to investigate. He got close enough to see the bones protruding from the animal before it charged off to the north out of sight. The scout's eyes were wide with fear, and he sprinted back to the prince as fast as he could.

"Your highness!" the scout called out. "Your highness, we must turn back!"

"What is this? A coward?" Thagren asked.

"N-n-no, sir. But I saw an omen. A large war horse, one that looked like your father's. It was skin and bones and charged off to the north! I saw it in the mist before it left," the scout stuttered. He was in fear.

"Well, then, sounds like the horse is malnourished. We need to fetch it immediately," Thagren started before he was cut off.

"No, sir, the horse's bones were outside the body. It looked like an undead horse. An omen. A bad omen. We need to turn back. It is a sign that something bad is going to happen," the scout explained.

"Gods, you are a superstitious lot," Thagren accused as he looked around, seeing fear in everyone's eyes. "Now listen to me. There has never been, nor will there ever be, undead. They do not exist!" Thagren was upset. "The scout did not get a good view. The mist clouded his eyesight. We keep moving to Ponteville. Your eyes betray you. It makes you see objects out of nothing to make sense of what you see. Tricks of the mind is what it is called."

By the end of the day, the group gathered around and made camp. Tents were the first thing up as others went out gathering wood for a fire. A hunting party set out to find food.

Thagren called out for the scout that found the horse. He entered the tent accompanied by two other guards.

Thagren faced him with his hands behind his back. His large nose and green eyes gave him an ominous look. He had seen many battles for sure, most of them at home as he tried to prove to his father that he was no coward.

"What exactly did you see? It has been a half day, so maybe your memory is much better. Did you see my father's horse?" Thagren asked.

"Yes, your highness. It was wearing your father's tack for sure. But the bones, I was not hallucinating, sire. It was half bones as if it were decomposing, yet it walked. That is exactly what I saw, I swear it," the scout said as he looked down.

"Now see, how can I believe you when you lie?" the prince accused.

"No, I am not lying. Oh wait, I forgot, my mind is playing tricks on me," the scout said sarcastically.

The prince punched him hard across the face. He connected with the jaw and caused the scout to pass out. "Don't you ever mock me!" Thagren yelled. "Take him to the prisoners tent. When he wakes up, torture him until he dies."

"Yes, sir," the guard responded. He took the scout out of the tent with a smile. He loved to torture people.

"And find me a new scout. Someone I can trust," Thagren commanded.

Two hours later, the scout woke. He was bound with rope and could not move.

"Let me out of here!" he yelled.

A guard entered the tent.

"Ah, you are awake. You should not mock your leader," he said with a smile.

The guard pulled out a knife.

Nekora gave the departing party a few days head start. She laid low until the third day. Late that night, she went to the cemetery.

> In Septus Unike Val Farah
> Rizen mi minos
> Sin titolu des humanas
> Rizen a mi ermay Destro sol humanes
> In Gammon ni seerney.

The ground shook violently. It was as if a large earthquake hit the city. People were running and screaming as it finally stopped. Many houses and buildings fell. They were not designed to withstand earthquakes. In fact, no earthquake had ever hit this city before. Panic was everywhere.

Nekora smiled. The cemetery was coming to life. Every person who was dead, was now rising to do her bidding—kill only humans. She wanted to make sure her spell worked, so she perched atop a large building to watch the action unfold. But first, she had to secure the area; no one could leave.

Nekora went to each gate that was already shut and barred.

Solidie bolte
Na reparum o muvey

The securing bars be it wood or metal were fastened to the gate. No amount of strength could move them. It was as if they were bolted to the doors. The guards were unaware of the exits being jammed shut.

The undead rose from their resting place. They ran into the town with the already frightened people and killed all the humans where they stood. Her magic was so powerful; after a minute the dead came back to life to be part of her army. She was happy, her revenge was coming.

After a couple hours, the undead were halfway through the city. The people scrambled to get out but could not move the fastened bars from the gate. Screaming could be heard all around. She commanded half of her minions to take the castle. They did as they were commanded.

Nekora laughed as she looked at the crowd. Not one has ever thought to climb the gate. There were many avenues of escape and she watched all of them. No one ever thought to make way over the wall.

"Damn, humans really are stupid, after all," she commented as she gave her evil smile. While the humans were dying one after another, she made her way to the castle.

The castle was filled with undead roaming around the courtyard and inside. Nekora slowly walked into the castle and used her senses. She smelled a grotesque amount of blood and decay. But something else was there. She followed the scent into the dungeons. Many humans and other creatures were locked inside. They were screaming as bloodied masses attempted to break in but could not get through the bars. Nekora continued.

She found one cell where none of her minions were attacking. There was a figure inside.

"An elf!" she thought. Nekora went to see the prisoner.

"Why are you in here?" Nekora asked.

"I was framed for stealing a deer," the elven prisoner responded.

Nekora felt the heart rate from where she stood. She had powers she never deemed necessary but had made her stronger and more intelligent.

"Why aren't they attacking my cell?" the prisoner asked.

"I told them to only attack humans. You are elven, and therefore are not a target. Come, I know you are telling the truth. Humans are evil creatures. They are plaguing our lands," Nekora stated.

Nekora cast her acid arrow at the lock; it hissed and sizzled, then melted. The door hung open.

"Do not fear. You are safe and are free to leave," Nekora stated.

"But why? Why are you attacking them? Not all humans are bad. I have human friends," the prisoner started.

Nekora interrupted her sentence. "They bribed Orcs to destroy my Kingdom, and they killed everyone I loved including my family. They destroyed my love for this world. When I found a place to restart, the humans waged war immediately. They wanted my gold. Nothing was going to stop them, so I killed them all. Now I know that all humans must die," Nekora retorted angrily. "Go now, before I change my mind and kill you."

The elven prisoner departed quickly. Nekora noted a feint golden aura about the elf and had seen it before. She could not recollect where she saw it. None of the undead warriors even looked at her. Nekora knew her spell worked as designed. She made her way back to the ground floor and searched for the armory and treasury.

After a few hours, Nekora found the armory. There were a few magical weapons, armor, shields, and even some jewelry. Nekora put all the magical items in her bag of holding and continued. An hour later, she found the treasury, which was locked as she figured. A quick acid arrow and the lock was no more. She entered the treasury.

The mountain of platinum, gold, silver, and copper pieces was the tallest she had ever seen. It took her a long time to bag the coins, but the whole time she was trying to make sense as to why the king wanted her gold. He was set for a few lifetimes. Millions of coins of each size were shoved into her bag. Even though the bag was magical, and all was shoved into a portal, she felt the inner storage filling up. It was almost full to the brim. She had to find another storage location for her treasure.

Nekora dropped her spell. Every walking corpse dropped where they were. She cast a fireball against a small gate to the north, and it exploded in flames that died after a minute or two. Splinters were everywhere. Nekora departed the city and headed back to her horse.

Upon reaching Ponteville, Prince Thagren received a message via pigeon.

It read, "Prince, the city is under attack. Dead walkers destroying our city. Need urgent help. Everyone is dying."

The prince crumpled the paper and threw it in the fire. He looked to his city; it was too late. "We would not be there in time. We must continue our mission then head back to the city."

All was lost. He knew it, and he felt it. The only thing he had left to do was to find the attacking party and kill them. He knew his family was dead. Revenge was the only thing on his mind.

CHAPTER TWENTY-SIX

Nekora traveled to the next city. She was on her horse, galloping to the southeast and offset the main road out of sight. She was pleased with her spell-casting ability and how she could induce fear. Her hatred for humans was now solidified, and nothing was going to change her mind.

A large buck was seen off to her left. She stopped her horse and dismounted. She has not had a good meal in a long time, and she craved meat. She grabbed her bow and arrows and stalked the deer. Her ability to move with little to no sound aided her ability to close enough for a shot. She knocked an arrow.

Puntera, Sooth, Gan, Proto

Nekora let loose. The arrow went straight and true. The buck looked up while chewing just as the arrow slammed into his heart, killing it instantly. She pulled out her arrow and began cutting open the deer. Nekora gathered wood for a small fire and finished cutting up the deer into slabs of meat. She found that the more she ate, the stronger her spells were. That explained why she was fatigued after casting spells. She needed an abundance of energy to keep up her casting.

She seasoned the meat and put it on the fire. She flipped it once after the first side was cooked. Once the second side was done, she pulled it off and began eating.

"This is so good but needs more seasoning next time," she thought as she devoured her meal.

She added more seasoning to the rest of the chunks and cooked them until they were done. She wrapped the meat and put them in her regular bag for later. After she finished, she put the flames out and moved on, leaving the deer to feed other predators. She had to move before they found her.

Before mounting her horse, Nekora opened her map. She took note of the trails leading to next city of Killicut. A massively large Kingdom in this land. She figured it might be the major Kingdom, capital, of this land. It would definitely prove harder, so she left this one for last. She had planned to bring her undead army to invade after she conducted a reconnaissance of the Kingdom. Knowledge was crucial in her war.

She looked beyond and had to alter her original plan. She went to the southwestern corner and decided to work her way clockwise instead. Killicut was farther than the original last city, but she had to do some major planning for the final attack. Finally, she would be undisturbed in her own Kingdom.

Nekora set off to the city of Cowlay. It was located on the western shoreline of the mainland. She needed a new map showing what the mainland was called. After a brief pondering, she realized she never knew, and it was not marked anywhere on the map. Time to upgrade.

The trek would take months to travel, but she had all the time she needed to conquer this land and rid it of the human plague.

Tolin and Thagren met the army outside of Ponteville. They quickly turned and traveled along the roadway toward Agora. Any deer or boar was quickly hunted down and retained for camp. Wine was replenished at Ponteville. They placed barrels into a cart pulled by two horses. Catapults and large crossbows were pulled by horse as well. They planned for the impossible to ensure victory.

"Tolin, if all goes to plan, we could be heroes. Very rich heroes if the gold is still there," Thagren started.

"Yes, but what if nothing is there? What if they went a different direction? I wish I had more information," Tolin responded.

"Either way, we have a win-win situation. We find and rescue our fathers and/or we get rich. Sounds like a non-losing scenario to me," Thagren commented.

Tolin sat in thought. "Gold is fine and all, but you know what the priests say about greed. It is one of the seven deadly sins. It makes me cautious. Especially if the stories of the undead are true. We have heard it twice now. You think it is coincidence?" Tolin remarked.

Thagren thought a moment. "You mean the priests that lecture over something that does not exist and take money away from the feeble minded? You know the gods do not exist, right? Or are you one of the feeble minded?" Thagren asked. "Besides, what do we know about the undead?"

Both men looked at each other. No answer came to mind.

"How could you kill something that is already dead?" Tolin asked.

"That is the question of the hour. However, if they did exist, wouldn't we have seen them by now? How many centuries has Prolen been around? There would have been stories and wars if they existed," Thagren responded. He looked worried. "Maybe we should brainstorm just in case."

The princes called for a halt and camp set up. Everyone took their places and did their jobs setting up camp. Fires were started with meat immediately cooking. The camp was smelling good.

"I did not realize how hungry I was until I started smelling the cooking meat. I am famished," Tolin said.

"Same here, Tolin. Let us go over what we know," Thagren responded.

Tolin and Thagren peered into the fire. Nothing was said or coming to their minds.

"So, what have you heard? Besides they are the dead walking." Thagren broke the silence. "I mean, if the stories are true, someone would have seen them and explained how to kill them again."

"I do not know, but I bet they can see. How else would they be able to attack?" Tolin answered.

"Good, now we are getting somewhere," Thagren said.

Tolin looked at his friend as if he was crazy. "Getting somewhere? You a comedian now? We know they have arm and leg functions." Tolin stopped.

Thagrin perked up. "You are a genius Tolin!"

"What do you mean? I just made some supposed observations based on stories," Tolin answered.

"Hear me out," said Thagren. "We know they can walk and/or run, and high probability they can see, right?" he continued.

"I think so," answered Tolin.

"What allows those bodily parts to function?" Thagren asked.

"I don't get what you are asking," answered Tolin.

"The brain! The brain allows for those extremities to function, right?" Thagren observed.

"Well, of course, but if they are dead, then the brain is not functional, so again, what are you getting at?" asked Tolin.

"Well, even though they are dead, the nerves and muscles are still attached. The brain will use the eyes to see and coordinate the arms and legs as appropriate to get to their prey. Somehow, the brain is functioning. How I cannot say, I do not know," Thagren admitted. "What if we sever the brain from the body?"

Tolin did not think of that. It sounded obvious now. "We need to test that theory," Tolin said matter of fact.

Thagren looked at Tolin as if he were going to call him names then gave a stern look. "And just how, do you think to test this? Do you see, any undead out here?" Thagren shook his head, pointing around the area.

"Well, there is a strong possibility that we may not have a choice if we keep going to Agora. We may be overwhelmed and out-manned," Tolin suggested.

"Well, that is a chance we have to take. It is too late now to turn back, unless, of course, you are going to chicken out," Thagren stated.

"No, I am no fowl. However, how are we going to tell this to our troops? On one hand, they must know their potential enemy and the potentially obvious way to destroy them. On the other hand, they would leave knowing they may be facing an unnatural foe. You know how superstitious they are. And we know how they would react to something they know nothing about. Hell, we don't know anything about them or even if they exist," Tolin responded. "This can drive you nuts just trying to make sense of this!"

"Keep your head, Tolin. Odds are, they won't," Thagren answered as he walked out.

There was much on Thagren's mind, but Tolin was right. They had to let their troops know what they may be dealing with. Two eyewitness accounts were more than coincidental, especially from two different sources. One of them was killed on his command. Thagren and Tolin agreed; they would have to chance the reaction of the troops.

"Well, they will either take it well and be ready for a fight of their lives, or they will cower and run home to mama," Tolin said as he laughed.

"Only one way to find out. All leaders meeting in the planning tent now!" Thagren shouted.

Word was quickly getting around, and all the leaders were coming to the planning tent. Once there, they all sat awaiting orders. Thagren and Tolin were standing before them, pacing from side to side. They were whispering to each other to get a plan of action and get this information to the troops. Tolin stopped and faced the generals.

"Gentlemen, we may be faced with an unnatural foe. Something only a few have seen, and one that has barely survived. It is imperative that you know what we face," Tolin started.

"Sir, we know what we face, and we are waiting to finally get a challenge," Jorge interrupted. "Our troops are in high spirits and awaiting the chance to kill them," he stated.

"Oh, and just how did you come across this information?" Thagren asked.

Jorge responded with a smile. "it is only obvious that the disappearance of your fathers, followed by your armies, so the rumors must be true. The word has spread like wildflower. We cannot wait to kill them. Good time to test our prowess, especially against an enemy that dangerous."

All the guardsmen cheered. Smiles came across both princes' faces.

"Well, that was easier than I thought," said Thagren.

"Yeah, I did not realize they knew all along. We need to keep our voices lower or out of earshot from now on," Tolin answered.

One of the leaders approached Prince Tolin. He put his hand on his shoulder before he walked out. "Don't worry, sir. We will rid this place of those nasty Drow!" He laughed as he walked out.

Both princes looked at each other in a confused manner.

"Drow?" Tolin asked.

"I guess they thought we were going to war with them," answered Thagren.

"Well, I can't wait to see look on their faces when they finally realize it is not Drow we are after," Tolin stated as he looked toward the army. Both men laughed.

"I guess we will test their bond," Thagren stated as he turned to walk off.

"Yep, I guess so," Tolin stated softly. He sipped his wine and looked at the sunset. "I guess so."

Nekora sprinted through the night. It cloaked her presence and kept her from being spotted. Twice during the night, she would build a small fire and reheat her meat. She would then pack up and depart toward her destination.

Nekora came to a quick halt. The horse reared as a figure appeared directly in front of her.

"You are on a toll road and must pay the toll to proceed by the order of the Marshal," said the shadowy figure.

"Judging by the deceitful appearance, I would say you are here to steal from the people," Nekora accused. "I would highly suggest you move out of my way and let me be, or I will have your soul as well as the twenty others around you."

The figure laughed. "I would say pay the toll or you will be the one who dies."

Nekora quickly grabbed her bow and knocked an arrow. Before she could release, twenty other figures emerged from the shadows. All of them had short bows trained on Nekora. She dropped her bow and put her arrow back in the quiver.

"Well now, since you made this more difficult than it should have been, the price has now doubled. The toll is now five hundred gold," the figure stated. "Or we kill you and take everything you have. He lowered the torch. The illumination crossed the horse. The face with bone and flesh was now visible as he yelled and dropped the torch.

"What the fuck!" he yelled.

The others slowly backed away, their eyes betrayed their fear. Nekora smirked.

"Now you pay the toll for disrupting my travels," she stated.

"W-w-what is that?" he stuttered.

"Your life!" Nekora shouted.

Butero sercolu

A powerful wave of sound encircled Nekora and expanded ten meters out, knocking the thieves to the ground and collapsing their lungs. Each one died slowly. Not before Nekora took their money. The weapons and everything were of no value, so she left them where they landed. Her trek continued.

The next morning, Thagren and Tolin reached the southern road toward Agora. The mist was heavy here.

"Scout!" yelled Tolin.

A body ran toward the prince. "Yes, sir," he said.

"I need intelligence on our target. Since we have no known printed information anywhere on this fucking map, we need to have it mapped with wall and guard locations. We will camp here and wait for your arrival," Tolin said.

"On it," the scout said as he ran off toward the city. A sign was seen on the right side of the road.

Welcome to
~~Agora~~ Nekorapolis

Agora was crossed out and Nekorapolis was written in blood. He was confused and decided to send a bird to the prince.

Tolin received the note. He looked at it and read the inscription.

"Thagren, what does this say? How do you even pronounce that?" Tolin asked.

"Nekor - Nek - Necropolis" Thagren answered. "Well, close to that at least."

Tolin retorted, "Necropolis? That is a stupid name for a city."

Thagren laughed. "Well, I guess we can add this to the map."

The camp was quickly erected. All that was on everyone's mind was the up-and-coming battle. Talks of courageous acts in previous battles were frequently talked about and was all that was heard throughout the camp. Drunken stammering coursed around like wildflower.

"Should we tell them? I mean, we tried earlier, and we know how that panned out," Tolin asked with a short laugh.

"Nah, I think whatever it is we may or may not face could not be any fiercer than the infamous Drow. So, if they can keep it together, I think we can wipe out our nemesis. Besides, I am curious about the rumors about the gold that is found up here. Now that we are here..." Thagren stated.

Two guys came around wrestling and knocked over the table. Food and wine spilled all over Thagren.

"Enough!" he yelled.

Thagren wiped the wine and food from his clothing. The wrestling continued. The prince jumped in and separated the two.

"Enough or I will have you both beheaded!" Thagren threatened.

Both men stopped immediately. Thagren yelled at them for insubordination, then to vacate the vicinity immediately before he killed them. He knew he could not afford to lose anyone, not yet, but the threats were real enough and caused them to stop their ruckus. The rest of the night went well.

The scout moved quietly up the road. The sign, written in blood, disturbed him. He could not shake the image from his head. His mission came first. He must obtain the intelligence so the armies could be successful. Their mission outcome was in his hands, and the pressure was overwhelming.

He arrived at the wall and took notes. The city was empty, and the fog was thick. He silently moved around the city taking notes. He also noted the dead bodies lying all over the grounds, the rot and decay was overwhelming his senses. The grounds were black except the golden shine of a large statue. The statue was of the first ruler wielding a sword and was very heavy. He smirked at the thought of gold being all over the city.

Someone else has been here. Everything is covered in ash except part of this statue. He thought as felt it. Time to get back to work.

He listened and stayed in the shadows as he was taught just in case the inhabitants were still there. Every now and again it sounded like rocks moving. He looked in the direction of the sound, but nothing was there.

"My imagination is fucking with me," he thought as he scanned the area. He listened intently and scanned the perimeter. "No one here," he said to himself. "I can return with this great news."

He started back to the gate. Something was off. It was not arrayed as it was when he first arrived. The bodies were tighter together.

"Impossible, how can dead bodies move?" he said softly. A thought occurred to him. Someone was there. How else would these bodies move? He looked and only saw one set of footprints from each skeletal figure. "No fucking way!" he yelled just as the skeletons rose.

The scout ran toward the gate but was blocked by undead bodies. He turned and headed toward the large building. Skeletons blocked his way and surrounded him. He yelled for help, but he also knew he was too far from the group. A skeleton stabbed him in the heart, killing him instantly.

The skeletons went back to their original position and dropped, watching the yard for other intruders.

Three days later, Tolin asked about the scout. "He should have been back by now," he said to Thagren.

"Yeah, I agree. I fear something bad may have happened." Thagren agreed.

The midafternoon sun was beating down. Both princes came out of their tent.

"Everyone, gather around!" Tolin yelled.

The armies gathered. Murmuring was heard more about rumors than anything else.

"Quiet down, scoundrels," Thagren yelled, "and listen up!"

"Tomorrow morning, we march toward the city. Our scout has yet to return, meaning something has gone wrong. We have waited long enough and must move forward. Be ready at dawn," Thagren said.

Tolin and Thagren went back into the tent. Everyone else went back to their business. Tomorrow started a glorious event.

The sun started to shine. The camp was packed, and the army was ready to move. They all lined up and headed up the road toward the city.

Thagren faced the group. "Jefferson!" he yelled.

The first groups general trotted up to the calling prince. "Yes, sir."

"Send a scout to check up ahead and report the condition of the city. I do not want him seen by the enemy. Also, any sign of trouble, he is to head back immediately. I want to know what we are getting into," Thagren commanded.

"Immediately, sir," Jefferson said as he fell back to his group.

A minute later, one of the men trotted up ahead and disappeared in the mist. The armies marched slowly up the road and passed the welcome sign. It did not look welcoming at all. They watched the road for any sign of danger. The farther north they got, the blacker the ground became. The sight was disturbing.

Two hours later, the rider reappeared.

"Sir, the city is up ahead another hour and a half. The land is disturbingly blackened, and no one is in the city. The walls are crumbled. No signs of life at all," he reported.

"Thats good, easy pickings then," Thagren remarked.

"No, sir, NO life is up there," he stated.

Thagren was confused.

"No life at all. No insects, no birds, sir; it is dead quiet," the scout reported.

"Very well. Thank you," Thagren said while trying to process what he heard.

Tolin gave the signal for Thagren to listen. He did as he was requested. Even down here, no sounds emanated past the sound of hooves. Not a single animal noise. Even the breeze had a silent whirring through the leaves, but nothing else. This disturbed not only the princes, but the army was starting to have second thoughts as well.

A black crow flew into the courtyard of Nekorapolis. It squawked a couple times and flew off. The undead rose and formed in the main courtyard. A large skeleton clacked two bones together. They all merged into the main yard as he hissed. The group walked to their nearest hiding locations and waited.

The army finally reached the outer perimeter of the city. Wildlife was neither seen nor heard. They halted in front of a massive, yet crumbled wall. Tolin took the first group and slowly entered the city. He was looking for any signs of life; he was also looking for the missing scout.

"Arod!" Tolin yelled. He was quickly quieted by the first general, reminding him of the possible dangers lurking in this cursed city. He gave the general the "seriously" look, then continued his trek. The group split up to find answers.

Thagren watched from behind the safety of a non-crumbled section of the wall. He heard movement, but only dead bodies were seen, motionless. He scanned the area thoroughly. Thoughts of the rumors were discerning. At least he knew his army was on board. Regardless, he was confident that the undead did not exist, and they were going to be rich.

"Arod!" Tolin yelled again. Tolin and his group scanned the immediate vicinity. Dead bodies were strewn about the courtyard. He called his general over.

"Sir, I see no sign of the Drow. They must have fled when they saw us coming," the general remarked.

Tolin looked quizzically. "Drow? You think we are looking for Drow?" Tolin asked. It was the generals turn to look confused. "That is what we were talking about in the tent," he stated. Tolin brought his palm to his forehead.

"No, we were talking about undead. The undead are supposed to be here," he said to straighten the confusion.

"All I see are dead bodies. They are everywhere. Now they are supposed to be walking and fighting?" the general said, then went into loud, hysterical laughter. It was quickly cut short when a sword was thrust through his throat, then removed quickly. Behind the general, an army of skeletons came through the mist. Rumblings of bones were heard around the group. More bodies were rising with weapons in hand.

"RUN!" Tolin yelled. "Back to the others!" The group quickly made their way back but were halted by the wall of undead. Screaming could be heard all around. Tolin saw feint flashes of bodies moving quickly from one spot and out of sight. His breathing increased and panic set in. Looking around him, Tolin could not remember which way to the gate. He needed help from his friend and quickly. Right now, retreat was the answer.

Thagren listened. He thought he heard screaming from far inside the city. The mist grew much heavier, decreasing visibility at an alarming rate. He turned to his soldiers.

"The first group is in the city. From the sounds of it, they were unsuccessful. We must go in but be extra cautious. There could be" His words were halted. A body half-flesh and half-bone severed the prince's head. More shapes emerged from the mist. A massive army of undead walked out menacingly toward the army. The first general unsheathed his sword.

"Charge!" he yelled and ran toward the bodies. When he got closer and saw that they were undead, he panicked. That moment of pause allowed the skeleton to thrust his sword into the general's heart. The rest of the soldiers saw the death and ran forth until they too saw the undead. Some soldiers retreated while others went in courageously.

Many undead were dropped. One after another, heads were flying everywhere. The humans were also dropping like flies. The epic battle went back and forth. One scout, Milo, was hidden in the shadows watching the entire battle unfold. He witnessed Tolins death as well as his group. He was on his way out when he heard and saw the second unit coming in with swords raised. He watched as both sides dropped members. Fear froze him in place.

"I must get out of here," Milo said softly. "I need to warn the other cities. I need to warn everyone that evil has presided here. They must know how to kill the undead," he whispered as he watched. He took mental notes with the only effective attack against the undead is to cut off their heads.

Milo slowly moved through the shadows and out of sight. He kept to the darkness away from the battle. He heard a warrior yelling something but could not hear it clearly. He turned to watch the swordsman flex and gain power as they were taught and went into a frenzy. He killed three skeletons before he was killed. Milo dropped his head and closed his eyes.

A couple seconds later, he opened them and turned to move forward. When his head turned, he was face to face with a skeleton. It seemed to be smiling at him. "Oh no," he said uncontrollably.

The skeleton's dagger pierced his heart. Milo went down.

An hour later, it was once again quiet on the field. The only noise heard was a soft breeze blowing through the trees and brush. The princes and their armies rose and received instructions to protect the city at all costs. They were forced to obey. Nekora's army of undead has grown two-fold.

Nekora galloped hard and fast to her next destination, Cowlay. She could see the feint lights up ahead as she slowed to a trot. A mile from the gate, Nekora told her horse to stay. She maneuvered her cloak over her head and walked the rest of the way.

The sun was rising. Light was quickly coming as Nekora reached the front gate.

"State your business," the guardsman said, not wanting to be on duty.

"I have traveled from Ponteville. I wish to sleep then board the next ship," Nekora lied.

"Go on in," the guard said. He was tired and did not care at this moment. He watched Nekora go down the street then returned his focus to the road. The second guard came out of the side door.

"For fucks sake, Jack; you finally finished with her?" he said in non-caring tone.

"Yep, you're just jealous because she did not like you," he accused.

A few seconds later, a redhead came out of the side door and ran off up the street. She made the first left then vanished out of sight.

"Some of us take our duties seriously," the first guard said as he spat in the middle of the entryway. "Your turn now. I am off to take a nap." With that, he headed through the opposite door and disappeared. A few minutes later, Jack heard loud snoring.

"Why do I always get the fun ones," he said as he viewed the outside. "I bet all the other cities are having more fun than we are."

Nekora found the inn. She grabbed a room and slept through the day. That night, she made her way around the city.

The walkways were paved with bricks. Though it seemed smoother, an occasional brick would be higher than the rest causing people to trip. Nekora paid more attention to the road than where she was going. She took mental notes of the city, most particularly, the cemetery which was located outside the perimeter.

"One thing the humans do is make squared roads. Who walks and immediately changes direction? Why don't they make their roads with curves, a more natural walking style?" Nekora asked herself. She missed home and wanted to go back to her family and friends. She missed Thorn with all her heart. Tears fell down her cheeks.

She was so engrossed in memory that she failed to notice two city guards patrolling the roads. Nekora bumped into them and almost fell, catching her off guard. She quickly regained composure.

"My apologies," she said and continued her walk.

Both guards looked at each other and smiled. "A female?" they said at the same time. Not seeing anyone nearby, they turned and grabbed Nekora's shoulder.

"Not so fast, woman! Where are you going this time of night?" one of the guards asked.

"Nowhere in particular. Just couldn't sleep so I figured a walk would help," Nekora responded.

The first guard put both hands on Nekora's shoulder and she watched the second go behind her.

"You know, there is always something suspicious about a lone walker in the night. But we can give you a warning, if you comply with us," the first guard said, smiling.

Nekora heard the second one behind her snicker. She looked up. The light barely caught part of her face as she smiled.

"Oh yeah? And what would that be?" she seductively asked.

"Well, come with us to find out. Or we can arrest you," he responded.

Nekora quickly removed her cowl to show her face. The guards saw the ears and gasped.

"You're an elf!" he yelled.

"Yes, what's the matter? We like fun times too," she remarked as her foot implanted into his groin as hard as she could. The guard doubled over, and she glimpsed the second guard about to tackle her. She pulled the sword from the first guard before he impacted the ground and spun around, sword slicing through the air. Seconds later, the second guard's head fell to the ground.

Nekora stabbed the first guard and put the hilt into the first guard's hands. The second guard had his sword out. Now it looked like they got into a fight. She replaced her cowl over her head and moved into the shadows just as a shadowy figure ran away on the rooftop.

CHAPTER TWENTY-SEVEN

The following night, Nekora made her way out the gate. She acquired a map with a detailed outline of each city and the mainland. With all the newfound information contained in the map, she decided to head home and conduct a proper plan.

For two weeks, Nekora galloped toward home. She was wasting time but was good with it, especially if it meant her attacks being perfectly played. Her army was enormous; she had the numbers. But more could never hurt.

Nekora heard a roaring overhead. A large shadow passed her in transit. Looking up, she saw Gilgamere flying overhead. He was out hunting. She could not get over the majestic beauty of the dragon as it soared overhead. Her thoughts stopped shortly after her horse stopped immediately. It reared and bucked, knocking her out of the saddle.

Giant webs covered the ground and trees up ahead. Numerous cocoons in different shapes outlining wildlife were seen in various spots. Some looked like they may contain humanoid figures. Nekora stood. Her horse ran off to the west.

"Where in Prolen am I now?" Nekora said, trying to remember her maps. "Nothing notated spider country," Nekora sighed. "This is going to set me back plenty. I hate this fucking land!" she yelled at the top of her lungs. The ground trembled beneath her feet. She barely felt it. Every hair on her body stood up.

The black widow spider was slowly moving in her direction. The fangs were moving crosswise as if cleaning them. Nekora knew they had great eyesight and wondered just how hard they would be to take down as she grabbed her bow.

Nekora knocked an arrow. "Puntera, Sooth, Gan, Proto!" she said aloud out of fright. This spider was three times her height and just as long. The black body moved with purpose and the front antenna came up. She got a glimpse of a red hourglass shape marking the underside of her abdomen. This spider was highly poisonous.

The arrow flew straight and true. It lodged itself in the middle of one of its eyes. The powerful impact caused the spider to move backward. It tried to remove the arrow. Nekora knocked and let fly a second one. It impacted another eye with the same results.

The spider reared, and webbing shot forth. Nekora ran to the right causing the web to miss. "Webs!" she yelled as an idea came to her mind.

Fumen! A large fireball impacted the web next to the spider. It exploded next to it causing it to disintegrate into hundreds of pieces. Large chinks were sent flying in all directions, some landed near where she stood. Nekora sighed a huge sigh of relief but was soon cut short.

Thousands of smaller spiders, roughly one foot tall, emerged and made their way toward Nekora. The babies were out to revenge their mother. Nekora sent another fireball, which hit a few of the spiderlings. She had to stop them.

Fumen Wallas!

A wall of fire erupted on top of the leading spiders. Sizzles and loud pops were heard as all the spiders near the front caught fire. The previous fireball caught the rear webbing on fire. More pops were heard as the fire quickly engulfed the entire area, killing every spider in the area. The animals that were still alive but wrapped burned to death. Sounds of pain were heard for a long distance.

Nekora watched as all the spiders burned and ran. The huge area engulfed in flames. She looked down for a spot to sit. One of the spiders was free and was near her leg. Nekora jumped back and ran in different directions. The relentless spider right behind her. Nekora finally stopped, turned to face the spider, then jumped on top of it.

Nekora's light weight was not enough to crush the exoskeleton. The spider could not move; it was pinned to the ground. Nekora took out her scimitar and stabbed the spider in the head near the eyes, killing it instantly. She found her horse a couple hundred yards away. She mounted, then resumed her course to the north.

Upon reaching her home, she was overwhelmed by the additional undead she has obtained while absent. She tried to figure out if living in Nekorapolis was even worth the strain.

She took inventory of what she had and written down—a list of what she needed. Parchment to write up a spell book. She also needed food and warm clothing for the upcoming winter. Firewood for warmth, she left her trees alone, to grow and cover her once beautiful city. She added books with a question mark so she remembered to peruse the inventory, and if anything sounded good, she would get it; if not, she would not bother.

Two weeks passed, and the cold winter started its journey. Nekora made last minute preparations, then decided to take the northern route to save time. Once again, she commanded the undead to protect the city.

Her ambition was to purchase items to survive the coming winter and see her friend. The trek proved more difficult since she took the northern passage, which was a much colder, more dangerous route. The ice-cold cliffs made the trek a little uncomfortable, but that was the least of her worries. Icy ravines with jagged bottoms at the bottom of icy cliffs threatened lives should anyone lose their footing just once.

Nekora pondered her situation. She had defeated a few cities and was content with that sending a message to the humans. She decided to forgo the eradication of Killicut for now and try to live her life in solitude. Content with her decision, she decided to wrap herself to protect her against the deathly shill and sleep.

Nekora continued her trek. She was carefully treading the trail with her vision fading due to the storm overhead. A howling could be heard from her left. The hills to the north could not be seen as the storm turned into a blizzard. The howling sounded closer. Nekora quickened her pace. A dire wolf, the size of a war horse jumped at her from the trench.

Her eyes popped open suddenly. She was still wrapped in her blankets and was warm. A gentle snow was falling, and the sound of howls in the distance seemed to get closer. Nekora had to move.

She quickly packed up camp and moved on. Her gaze went to the clouds, watching as they slowly changed to a dark silhouette. She had to hurry. Her decision to take the northern route was made since it was a week shorter than the southern traditional route, but it had other more dangerous options. She was ready for anything.

The howling got louder. The wolves were getting closer. She looked everywhere for an alcove to use as defense. A couple hundred feet ahead, she found one. She put her back to the stone and grabbed her bow. Knocking her arrow, she conjured her magic.

Puntera, Sooth, Gan, Proto!

The runes became a deep blue, and she scanned the horizon. From behind her trail, a dire wolf was sniffing the ground, looking for her. She found it odd that the creature did not growl but instead whimpered. It slowly made its way to her, limping on her front right foot. Closer examination revealed a large gash in its shoulder. Nekora lowered her weapon.

"He is not after me to eat, he needs help!" Nekora thought as she put her weapon away. Nekora put her hand out and the wolf backed away. It was the size of a small horse and looked very young. Did it get lost? Was he dismissed from the pack? Nekora pulled out some meat and gently threw it, so it landed harmlessly in front of him.

The dire wolf looked at the meat, then to Nekora. It skittishly limped toward the free meal and sniffed. Not smelling anything foul, it ate the meat. Nekora slowly walked up to it. The wolf fell to its left side, unconscious. She immediately went to work cleaning the deep wound and bandaging it before it woke.

"What the fuck did this wolf fight to get such a wound? Bears? Other wolf packs? Humans?" She made a small fire while trying to match the wound with the animal or humanoid that made it to keep them warm and cook up her last rabbit. She had a while to go, but food was still abundant. Nothing was hibernating just yet but was getting close.

The last of the seasoning went onto the meat. She put it on a flat rock and gently laid it upon the fire to cook. The radiant smell emanated from the pit. Nekora realized she was famished. She ate half the rabbit and kept the other half for the recovering wolf.

The wolf's nose started moving. He was sniffing the air before his eyes opened. Nekora reassured the wolf that everything was okay and stroked his fur. She fed him the rest of the rabbit, which he gratefully accepted. Looking at the wolf, Nekora realized he was only a puppy, just reaching maturity. She could not help but wonder what had happened to him.

The wolf immediately stood, growling as if to warn her to stay away. She backed off a bit, afraid to make him any worse. The wolf lunged as Nekora ducked. He went over Nekora and ran a few feet, fighting another wolf. Nekora realized that he was protecting her, not attacking. The rumble went on for a bit then the trespassing wolf departed, bleeding profusely. The Dire wolf turned back to Nekora with head low and tail tucked under. She smiled a reassuring smile. Nekora made a new friend.

During the rest of the trip, Nekora would shoot an animal with her bow. The problem was keeping the Dire wolf from eating it all the time. She was getting hungry. Foxes and rabbits galore along the trail. If she killed more than one, she was able to eat, whichever the wolf decided not to munch on.

Traversing the last hill before Ponteville, The Dire wolf stopped. He would not advance another step. He knew he would be killed should he continue, so Nekora went on without him. She shopped for items that helped to keep her alive throughout the winter.

While in Ponteville, she made it a point to stop to see her friend Rachel. She had not heard from her in a very long time and decided to catch up on stories. Rachel was engaged to be married with one of the guards and was living quite well with the money she made in Nekorapolis. Nekora was happy for her. At least one of them was living a good life. She updated Rachel on the near constant attacks against her city.

"Why don't you move here, Nekora?" Rachel asked. I would love for you to be my maid of honor at my wedding. Plus, you will be safe with friends here."

Nekora looked down. She was deep in thought, then looked to Rachel. "I would love to. However, Nekorapolis is the only place I can truly call home. It has almost everything I need, including peace and quiet when the humans aren't attacking my city."

Rachel nodded. She knew what her friend was going through and would stay in Nekorapolis, but she was not a warrior. She could not fight bandits day in and day out to protect the city. She was also glad she left the city when she did. She wanted no part in life threatening deals. They said their goodbyes, and Nekora made her way to the market.

Nekora purchased a cart and horse. She filled the cart with essential supplies then headed toward the southern route. She missed her wolf companion but decided it was for the best. The wounds were healed before they reached town, so he should not have too much of a hard time on his own. She missed cuddling with him, however.

It was a few days out of town when the horse reared. He sensed trouble and it showed. Nekora tried desperately to keep him calm. Out of the corner of her eye, she saw her dire wolf friend pacing in the forest edge. He seemed too afraid to come, and she did not blame him at all. She knew if he did, the humans would kill him for sport. Another facet of humankind she absolutely abhorred. During the night, she would walk to the forest edge and feed her friend.

Nekora heard her horse neighing behind her. She saw humanoid forms around her cart; they looked like they were trying to steal it. She ran after the cart.

Ackin!

An arrow of acid fled her palm and hit the driver on the side. He screamed in agony as the acid immediately ate through his clothes and skin. He jumped off the wagon and started rolling. She ran to the cart and jumped into the driver's seat, stopping her horse. A commotion was heard in the cart, and she turned and saw another attacker a little too late. He drove a knife deep into her back. Before she passed out, a blur of white crossed her view and the sound of screams and gurgling then blackness.

Nekora woke feeling groggy. She was in a lot of pain from her stab wound. Last she remembered; she was in the driver's seat of the cart. She is now lying by a fire with an unknown male human sitting across from her. She attempted to sit up, but the pain was too overwhelming.

"Shh, it is okay. You are fine now," said the unknown male figure.

"What happened?" asked Nekora. "Who are you? Where am I?"

The man started to laugh, then spoke. "Save your breath, little one. You were injured. From the decimated bodies, I assume bandits. Your wolf friend here finished off the others it seems by the looks of their wounds. You are safe now. No one is going to hurt you." Nekora saw a silver sigil with a cross on it.

Nekora passed out again from the pain. The knife barely missed her lungs and only caused superficial wounds that were not life-threatening. She woke again, but this time she was lying on some wood. She heard the sound of wood on dirt and rocked gently with an occasional bump that sent pain up her back to her head. Her vision fluctuated from the pain waves.

"Where are you taking me?" she asked.

The man turned and looked at her. "Look who is finally awake. I am taking you to Ponteville to get your health back. I thought you died on me, since Ponteville was the closest city, I thought you came from there. Look, we are almost there," he said.

Nekora's head hurt too much. She could not do anything but go along for the ride. "Where is my wolf?" she asked.

"He stopped following a little way back. Large animal if I do say so myself. I hope he doesn't run into poachers," he stated in a calm demeanor. "They will kill and stuff him just for the fun of it."

Nekora closed her eyes. She focused on closing the wound, but it proved too difficult. The rocking shot forth waves of pain. She had to wait for regular healers.

"Why are you helping me? Humans have always fought with me for no reasonable cause," Nekora asked.

"I am Erick, a healer. I help everyone. Do not blame one race on the actions of others. Most humans are better than you give them credit for. A few bad apples should not sway your judgment," he responded. "Besides, you should focus on resting. You will be fine now, just try not to do anything strenuous for a while. Give the wound time to heal."

"Focus on resting, he said. I will rest when the last human falls," Nekora thought. He made it sound like humans are normal, but so far, she has been in three combats all from human greed and defiance. She was not going to risk any more.

A few days later, Nekora felt better. She always healed quickly and loved it, but she hated the pain. Every time she was injured, it added more fuel to her fire. She needed to get back home and plan. Only one city to go if she felt up to it.

Two months later, Nekora finally made it home. Her undead army still protected the city. Her newfound army added to her collection. Two thousand strong, she was more than ready for Killicut. "A few bad apples should not sway your judgement.".The thought resonated in her mind. "Don't blame one race on the actions of others."

Maybe I should lay low. He is right, even elves have a few bad apples, not all of them are bad. Nekora dismissed the idea of destroying Killicut. She kept to herself. She only went to town for items she needed to survive. Nekorapolis was a lonely place; her mind started playing tricks on her.

What if the human citizens are plotting her demise? What if they are marching right now to take over Nekorapolis? They could be marching up the road at any moment. These thoughts day in and day out for over ten years were driving her crazy. She decided to withdraw into the ether realm.

The ethereal plane, a place Nekora had not visited in years, was now open to her once again. She began reading books and studying the information contained in the ethereal library. She had all but forgotten this place, and it was refreshing to be somewhere familiar. Last time she saw this place, her Kingdom was destroyed. She missed Thorn terribly.

Nekora put down her book and rubbed her eyes. "Thorn, I miss you very much. I wish you were with me again. I wish my family and friends were with me one last time. I miss you all," she said in a whisper. Tears flowed down her cheeks as she set the book back on the shelf.

Nekora woke to a startling sound. Voices? In my city? She sprang from the bed and peered out the window. The lack of light kept her from being visible. Six figures were in the courtyard. They were trying to get her statue loaded into a cart.

"Thieves!" she said in a low but harsh voice. I will deal with them promptly. Nekora rose her undead army. They began to move to the living figures.

"Movement!" the warrior exclaimed.

"What the fuck are these?" a robed figure said as a fireball erupted from his hands.

"Peace out!" said the smaller figure dressed in dark clothes. He ducked into the shadows.

It appears to be a party of differing races. Have they combined forces to kill me? Nekora stated as she disappeared from the window. She grabbed her staff and headed downstairs.

"The mage has to be the first one to go," Nekora said to herself as she traversed the steps to the lower level of her castle. "If it is one thing I cannot stand, it is thieves!" she said a little louder. She did not care, she had to rid her city of them, and fast. They were stealing her decorations.

The rogue stopped in his tracks. He thought he heard a voice and listened intently. Hearing no other voice, he was satisfied, then continued his journey to the castle.

"If I am right, this place used to flow gold like a river flows water," he said. No one heard him speak; he was out of earshot. The rogue kept moving, watching every corner for an ambush or other attack.

"The intelligence collection was right. There are many undead in this place," said the robed figure as he enchanted.

Fumen Wallas!

A large wall of fire erupted between the undead and the party. Many undead burned from the wall and fell. The dwarf was hit in the back with a small knife from a skeleton.

"Gwarn," came a voice behind the group. A light followed and Gwarn the dwarven barbarian glowed. He felt much better and yelled a battle cry.

"For Killicut!" he yelled. He was fully enraged now and ready to continue his path of destruction. He beheaded the skeleton that attacked him, then continued his onslaught.

"From what I understand, aim to remove the heads or set them ablaze!" It was a female voice.

"A female? I have not heard a female voice since." She paused to think. "Rachel!"

An explosion sounded. Jeanette lit another arrow and knocked it. She released at a group of undead. The arrow hit the chest of the central rotting corpse. The fuse disappeared into the bag tied to the end of the arrow and another explosion rocked the courtyard, killing several undead.

"Why behead, when you can explode?" asked the ranger smiling. Her smile faded when a throwing axe lodged itself into her chest. She crumpled to the ground.

"Jeanette!" yelled the mage, but it was too late. He had to concentrate on healing the others; he could raise her later. A mob of undead were traversing upon the healer.

Litten fumare
Eti flacera
Stro di eneme

A large red cloud formed above the undead. Flames appeared in jets, streaming downward, striking the undead, killing them instantly. The flames consumed a large area and exploded outward when they hit the ground, igniting anything and everything flammable.

"What I would not do for a Paladin right now!" the healer exclaimed.

"Just worry about your…" The mages voice was cut off with a slash from the corpse behind him. The mage did not see him. The healer watched the head of the mage roll away and saw a band of undead behind the group.

"Behind us!" he yelled. It was too late. The undead army came at the party from every direction and killed the party quickly.

Nekora was fuming now. Why would her friend go against her? Did she succumb to their lies and pity? "She will learn the hard way what it means to defy friendship!" Nekora was close to the doors leading out to the courtyard.

The doors opened before Nekora reached them, and she ducked behind the closest pillar. She heard the battle slowing outside, so she knew her minions were keeping them at bay. A shadowy figure ran to the other side of the pillars, taking care to stay in the shadows.

"Rogue," Nekora said in a whisper.

Curious, she was wondering what they were doing here. Following this little guy may give her answers.

"Could they be here to bargain?" was her first thought. Then she remembered they were trying to take her statue. She was curious, indeed.

Outside the castle, the remaining party members were silent. Nekora was not worried; she had the numbers, and the screams solidified her thoughts. She followed the smaller figure.

He had made his way around the bend to the right and down the corridor, then the first left.

He is heading toward the treasury. Her eyes squinted in anger. She kept following.

The large ornate door made of silver, gold, and jewels was locked. He checked and found the doors to be far too heavy for the party to bring. It also piqued his curiosity. He produced a set of lock picks and began to work on the lock.

Another scream was heard in the yard. Nekora smiled. She watched the rogue intently as he kept working the internal mechanisms. Within a minute, the lock was open. Nekora was impressed and thought how much of a shame it will be to kill him.

The doors opened and Roderick, the rogue, viewed a mountainous pile of gold, silver, and copper. Gems worth a fortune also lie in wait. Nekora forgot about her treasury until she was reminded just how beautiful her collection was. The rogue's eyes went wide with fascination and grabbed his large sack.

He took silver, gold, and mostly gems. He knew what he was doing as he picked the ones worth the most. Nekora stood in the doorway, but the rogue did not notice her presence.

Ackin!

She yelled as an arrow of acid was targeting his gut. The rogue instinctively rolled and Nekora missed her target. The rogue dropped his sack and brought out his daggers.

"Ha ha ha, you think a pair of daggers is going to kill me. I am immortal little halfling. You will die for stealing my treasure," Nekora said in her evil tones to scare the halfling.

"I am Roderick, the wise old woman! Even immortality has a flaw," he said as he went into a defensive position.

"Fool, you shall now die," Nekora said.

Leet Destro!

Lightning shot forth and scathed the rogue's arms. He was fast, but not fast enough. While tumbling, he removed a throwing knife from his belt and flung it toward Nekora. She dodged the throw and became more furious. Nekora held her staff tight.

"Let us see you dodge this," Nekora threatened.

Fumen wallas!

A wall of fire abruptly appeared over the rogue. He rolled to the left, but the fire was still upon him. Seeing a clear area, he rolled forward to get out of the wall. Fire consumed him, and he rolled on the ground to put the fire out. He quickly shoved his arm forward and a small bolt flew from his wrist impacting Nekora in the left shoulder. She screamed in pain. The rogue took the advantage and disappeared into the shadows out of sight and quickly left the building with his bag. The smell of burnt skin and hair was all she could smell.

Nekora pulled out the bolt; it was dripping with her blood. She threw it on the ground. The metallic clanking was all she heard, no footsteps, nothing.

"This rogue is very good," she thought. "I will kill you for this. You and all your kind will die, this I swear!" Nekora yelled. She ran toward the main door and saw nothing. No moving shadows, nothing. She headed back to her room.

Roderick looked down from the ceiling. He was in a lot of pain from the burns he sustained. When Nekora left the room, he slowly, painfully, made his way back to the floor and into the shadows. He snuck out the main doorway and looked for his friends. The courtyard was clear; his entire party laid in a pool of their own blood. He had to get out of there to warn the rest of the world of the evil that resides here.

Roderick snuck to the wagon, sat in the driver's seat, then reigned the horses to full gallop. He held onto his bag to prevent it from falling over. He smiled.

Nekora watched as the wagon went full speed out the gate. The rest of party was a mixture of humans, dwarves, and even elves, not to mention the meddling halfling.

Nekora left her building to find the party. She found a stout dwarf wielding two large axes, a human with a sword and shield, a robed human figure with a wooden staff, a human in robes with a silver sigil and a cross. "This is the same person that saved me. Why would he attack me? Human Lier!" she fumed in her mind. Lastly, a female elf with a bow and six arrows remaining in her quiver, all of them lying in a pool of blood. She removed an arrow and found a bag tied to the end of the bow.

She looked, and not one of them was Rachel. The markings and looks of the ranger were alien to her. She stood and looked to the departing cart. "Don't think for one minute you will be safe from my wrath," she said, then headed back to her castle. She proceeded up the stairs and into her room, then made her way to the table and unrolled her maps.

Killicut, a large city in the middle of the mainland. Since Killicut was the capitol of the mainland, she figured the treasury would be larger than hers. More gold to store in her treasury. She studied the layout of the city just in case. The outlining area made sneaking into the city difficult. The words "For Killicut!" echoed in her mind repeatedly. It was time she completed what she should have done years ago.

A large expansive forest surrounded the city with grasslands between. She measured and found it to be a few hundred meters of open land, being out in the open ruined her surprise attack. She had to discover a strategy.

Months went by. She studied the map off and on until she came up with a tactic that had a high margin of success. It meant she would lose many warriors, but if parties attack her city, her numbers will rise until she finally had enough to spare. All she needed was to get to the gate.

Nekora studied each map. Six cities occupied the mainland with a seventh being built. She waited for the smoke to clear before making any moves.

The next six years proved challenging. Numerous attacks on her city were made. Everything from small parties to large mobs; a couple armies even attempted a hostile takeover. All of them intent on her gold. She was getting tired of it but loved growing her army. It was time for an all-out assault. Between the massive army she started with to the new members of her team from the deaths of attacking parties, she was finally ready to make her move.

She gathered half her forces. Three thousand undead followed her out the gate. She made a last-minute decision to bring an additional two thousand, leaving one thousand bodies to protect her city. The best part of having undead was that her army grew with each dead member. She made her way toward Killicut.

CHAPTER TWENTY-EIGHT

Rachel could not bear it anymore. Their prince should have returned by now. She feared the worse. He called every warrior to arms for a raid, but everyone was too tight-lipped. No one knew where they were going, not even the warriors.

"My darling," Rachel started. "Where are you going? Are you just going to let me worry the whole time without knowing where you are? What if something happens to you? How am I going to get you back home?" She started crying.

Ronald took her into his arms and cradled her against his chest. "Fear not, my love. I will be back before you know it. Besides, the prince did not tell us where they were going. He was very hush hush about it," he said.

Rachel cried in his arms. Tears flowed down her face and onto his chest. She did not want to lose her love. He bid farewell and departed the city to meet the prince with his garrison outside the city walls.

Rachel had not heard from him. It had been five years, and no one has come back. She had to know what happened. She remembered her friend, Nekora. Could she have known where they went? Rachel packed her bags for her trip to Nekorapolis.

Nekora left town and raced toward Killicut. Her army close behind her just in case. She knew that if she took the capitol, it would send a message to the others to leave her alone. Far too many inhabitants died during her war; no more sacrifices needed to be made. She was tired and wanted rest.

At the end of her road, a mass gathering of humans with pitchforks and torches were waiting. They had the look of hatred in their eyes. Nekora brought her troops to a halt farther back in the mist to keep them out of sight.

"Who are you to declare yourself ruler of the lands, elf!?" It was more of an accusation than a demand.

"I demand you step aside and let me pass, peasant, or you shall suffer the same fate," Nekora retorted. She slowly rode forward so they could see her horse. "A witch!" the human exclaimed. "As you can see, we have the numbers.

Surrender or we will take you by force," the human stated in a scared, raspy voice.

"I surrender to no human filth," Nekora answered. "This is your last chance."

Nekora waved her hand. A throng of undead, including those who lost the previous raid, were advancing into the scene. "If you so much as move against me, I will have you torn from limb to limb!" she shouted.

The peasants were frightened. As the wall of skeletons and half rotting corpses of their friends and family came into view, they could only stare in awe. No one could move. Some, with a smaller constitution, were puking at the horrid stench that had overcome them.

"Last time, leave or die," Nekora gave the ultimatum. She did not care so much for humans, but she was loving this game. She got a thrill watching them tremble in fear.

The humans slowly backed away. Every weapon was dropped, and the peasants turned to run. Nekora smiled. She raised her hand, paused for a moment, then dropped it rapidly. The undead warriors ran toward the humans, weapons raised. The air was filled with the sounds of struggle, pain, and death.

"The larger the army, the better," she thought as she smiled her evil smile. The army made a rest stop in the immediate area so she could give the souls time to return. Camp was made at her direction.

Nekora walked down the road toward the east. She needed the quiet now more than ever before to think. She had close to six thousand undead in her army including the new recruits. In the past, the humans have given her a run, especially after they figured out how to kill her minions. She pondered how to ensure a victory when a female voice was heard in front her.

"Nekora!" It was Rachel.

"What in the world is she doing here?" Nekora thought. She looked back and saw that her camp was too far from sight.

"Nekora! Thank the gods you are here. I have a problem and I was hoping you were still my friend, and I am in dire need of your help," she said out of breath.

Nekora looked upon her and smiled. Rachel was the only human she would ever consider a friend. "What is it? What is wrong?" she asked.

"I have not heard from my love in quite some time, and I was wondering if you knew where the garrison from Ponteville went?" answered Rachel. "Please tell me you know where they are and that they are all right, Rachel pleaded.

Nekora looked down. She knew it was that army plus another that had attacked her city. She saw the carnage in the dirt and ash where many fights took place. She now has those members in her army ready to fight off other human habitations.

"I do not know, Rachel," Nekora lied. She hated to lie but knew it would upset her. Eventually she would find the truth, but today was not that day.

"Please, I need your help. Can you think of any potential areas they may have gone? I have traveled a long way to see you. Can we rest at Nekorapolis?" Rachel asked.

"I am leaving right now to reclaim my rights. No one is at the city. Head back and rest. I am sure he will show up soon," Nekora stated.

Rachel's eyes widened. She could not believe what she was seeing. A half horse, half skeleton. It stopped behind Nekora and neighed to grab Nekora's attention.

"What happened to you?" Rachel started crying again and ran off to the east.

Nekora was left standing there. There was no reason to kill her. She would explain everything later. For now, she had to plan to take over the capital city.

Rachel fled along the pathway. She kept looking back in fear that she was being chased. Nothing but fog all around her. She was frightened but ran as far as she could and camped off the path just in case. Trembling, Rachel made a small fire behind some large boulders to cover the light yet provide heat for warmth and cooking a small rabbit she had brought with her.

"What in the world allows dead horses to walk? Why were Nekora's eyes so black, they used to be a beautiful blue? What happened to my friend?" It was then she realized that what she faced was pure evil. Nekora had been possessed. She fell asleep and dreamed.

Rachel wandered the city of Killicut. Everything was a blur. She kept trying to focus her eyes but was unsuccessful. She made her way to the gate when she saw her friend, Nekora, with an unimaginable number of undead with her. She was readying to destroy Killicut.

Rachel ran out to plead with Nekora. Numerous hands tried to grab her and prevent her from leaving the safety of the city. All of them either missed or slipped in their grasped. She was moving slowly and tried with all her might to get out there quickly. She arrived in front of Nekora.

"Nekora! Stop! Please do not harm these people. They have not done anything to you," Rachel pleaded. Nekora looked up and Rachel saw Nekora, half elf, half skeleton, hidden behind the dark robe. The look of nefarious intent on her face. Anger, Rachel feared, Nekora could not shake.

A skeleton arrived from Nekora's left side. It swiped and lopped Rachel's head clean off. Rachel's vision twirled as her head spun in the air. It hit the ground with a thud.

Rachel woke screaming and breathing hard. "Was that a vision? Is my friend really going to attack Killicut?" Rachel had to do something, but she had no clue. A story her mom told her came to fruition.

The light elves are very fervent. They seek to protect those who need it most and are the true protectors of the realm. These Paladins fight with the might of twenty warriors and with the gods at their side. The golden auras to protect the innocent and punish the guilty. To see one is rare, to watch them in battle is rarer still.

The idea struck her, and she knew what must be done. She ran home as fast as she could to pack and grabbed her fastest horse. She had to get to Moonglade, and fast.

Nekora decided to head back. Ah, yes. Another large city to the southwest that will give me more than enough troops to take over the capitol. Nekora looked up. "Kalvanya," she whispered.

The next morning, Nekora made her way to Kalvanya. Her troops followed behind, ready for any action. The undead were fast, very fast. They ran much faster than any human is even capable, and they do not tire easily. Nekora was focused on her efforts.

Rachel made it to Kaleigh. She explained her urgency and dumped a bag of gold coins on the captain's desk. He smiled "Welcome aboard the Trinity," he said.

The rough waters were difficult to navigate but were not near as ferocious as they were years back when Nekora had made passage. Rachel made the best of it as she fended off numerous groping hands from the crew. She decided to wait in her room.

They landed in Haversmith. Rachel took out her map and looked for the light elven establishment. She made her way to the stables and hired a fast horse. Her gold was dwindling down quickly, but she needed to get to the city.

Rachel quickly navigated the northern shores until she found the huge forest. All she saw were trees. The foliage was dense, and the trees were huge. She had never seen trees this big before and awed at their sight. A lone figure wearing silver and gold plate armor stood before her. The sudden appearance startled Rachel and her horse as it reared, almost bucking her off the back.

"Who are you and why are you here?" the figure asked defiantly.

"I am Rachel, and I am in desperate need of your help," Rachel responded.

"We are not to be toiled with, my dear. Your cities warriors are there for a reason, they are the ones you seek for help", the figure stated.

"That is why I am here. Our warriors went missing. Other cities have been destroyed, and I fear an evil sorceress may be involved," Rachel stated.

The figure stared at Rachel momentarily. She felt the truth in her words and brought her to the city. Rachel was once again in awe. She never imagined such beauty could emanate from a city, but here she was. Large and modern, yet reserved buildings towered in the air.

All the elves were going about their daily business with children playing in the yard. The sigil of a humanoid figure poised with sword high in the air and sunbeams gleaming to the edges, emanating from the sword, were seen adorning the city's main hall. The same sigil on the warriors' plate mail and shield. Silver background with golden figure and sun beams. It was majestic in its beauty. The arms and legs were silver with golden highlights. The figure brought Rachel to the city council where the magister awaited her.

"Tell me, child, why have you come?" the magister asked. Rachel looked around then began to speak.

"Many years ago, I made a friend, Nekora, an elf trying to find solitude and happiness. I could tell she was sad but always faked smiles. I felt bad for her, so I befriended her. She made an abandoned city her home, Agora. It was decimated by the Ponteville army centuries ago from a jealous brother. I was hired to run shops in town in hopes to reopen the dead city," she started.

"Yes, we know the tale. Why is this relevant?" the magister interrupted.

"Then, a nasty winter storm happened. I ended up staying in Ponteville. I quit my job in Agora and have not heard from anyone there since they left from the deep winter freeze." The Paladins looked at each other.

"That was a horrible winter for sure. We remember as it had extended across the world. A weather that deviated from the norm," the magister stated.

Rachel paused before starting again. She was waiting for the magister to finish. "My lover was in the Ponteville garrison and said he had to meet with the prince. In fact, all the warriors had to meet him outside the city. This was months ago. He did not come back home."

"Perhaps he faltered and died in a glorious battle," said Volhara.

"No, I fear something else." Rachel went on to explain what she saw in Nekora and how she had changed both physically and emotionally. It was not the same elf she came to know and love as a sister. Then she explained the horse, then finished off with her dream.

"There is something going on, I just know it. Something bad, something evil,"

Rachel said as tears flowed down her cheeks. "I miss my friend." She started crying.

"Head back to Ponteville. We will send a bird to Killicut and ensure they are ready for a battle. This is between the city and Nekora," said the magister.

Rachel felt defeated. She realized there was nothing they were going to do to help her. She cried as she rose and started departing the pavilion. "So, you will do nothing as my home is destroyed. I come to you, begging for your help, but you shun me?" she said while crying.

"No one is shunning you, my dear. We will do everything we can to find out what is going on. You must go home and rest now," the magister recommended. Rachel departed the pavilion.

"Volhara, you must investigate. If half of this story is true, then it will not stop until the entire world is overthrown. If it is nothing, then return here. If it is what we fear, then send a bird and we will send reinforcements," the magister commanded.

Volhara bowed. "It will be done," she answered and left the pavilion.

Rachel made it to Haversmith. She reached into her pocket to grab some coin and hire a ship back to Kaleigh when an arm grabbed her wrist.

"I will get this." The armored warrior in silver and gold released her arm. Rachel started to cry in joyous appreciation, relieved that they were going to do something. Rachel hugged Volhara out of impulse.

"I am Volhara, priestess of light, and I need a ferry to the mainland ASAP," she said, holding out a sigil. "This person is under my responsibility," she stated. The sigil was that of an armored figure with their sword high in the air. Sunbeams emanated from the sword to the edges of the large coin-shaped object.

The ferry master bowed. "Right away, madam." He rushed off. Volhara removed her helmet. Her long blonde hair flowed like a wave. Her blue eyes penetrated the soul in peace. Her body frame appeared to be chiseled with a face of mass beauty. Rachel looked again; she looked familiar.

Once again, the Trinity sailed across the ocean. "Thanks to yeh, I have enough gold to build another ship," the captain said to Rachel, laughing. "You must really need something bad if you brought back a Paladin. I have not seen one in ages."

Upon reaching Kaleigh, Volhara told Rachel to head back to Ponteville immediately. If what she said was true, then the danger was too much for her to bear. Rachel nodded her agreement and headed toward Ponteville from the eastern route. It was much farther, but she did not want to chance another meeting with Nekora. Volhara obtained a warhorse and sprinted toward Killicut.

Nekora took her army southwest. She reached the gates of Kalvanya, which were, of course, closed. An onslaught of arrows flew toward her and her army. They made no difference in the undead advancement. Arrows proved useless in battle.

"Ready the catapults!" yelled the king of Kalvanya. Seven catapults were in place and loaded with large solid fiery balls soaked in oil. "Fire!" came the command. All seven released their ammunition and sent them flying into the middle of the battlefield. The impact from the balls exploded and a sticky substance went flying everywhere, catching everything on fire, including the field.

"Ugh, why do they always use fire, so annoying," Nekora said to herself. She raised her staff.

Pera atuke melave
Forma helago jutike Krista
garn oneva!

The once bright sunny day turned dark and ominous. Clouds, immediately followed by thunder and lightning. Lightning struck inside the city toward all metallic objects. Armored warriors were hit and thrown to the ground. Archers took cover, but many were hit from the lightning. The cacophonous roar deafened the warriors.

Nekora gave the command to attack and the undead ran toward the city at full sprint. She raised her staff once again.

Leet Destro!

Lighting shot forth and hit the main gate. The gate splintered into millions of tiny pieces as the lightning disintegrated it. The undead made way into the city. Warriors met them at the entrance. A fierce battle ensued with a blur of metal from all the sword swinging. The undead were overwhelming. The battle started retreating to the inner courtyard.

King Boden swung his longsword. It connected to the skeletal arm wielding its weapon and severed it. Boden swerved, bringing his shield across bashing the head of another. They kept coming. The King swung again and met the skeletal head, removing it from the body. The skeleton collapsed. The king relayed the instructions to his warriors. He backed away.

"Behead them! Removing their heads severs their actions! Chop the heads off!" Boden yelled. The warriors did as commanded. The tide quickly turned as numerous skeletons and zombies started dropping. Boden looked around. He had already lost over half of his garrison and retreated for the castle.

Nicholas, the head guard, was out of breath. He was not used to fighting anymore and quickly lost his stamina since he had become complacent with his practices. He never thought he would die like this. He heard a female voice scream over the sounds of battle.

Fumen!

A fireball whizzed past Nicholas's head. The intense heat melted his hair to his skull. The smell of burning hair emanated throughout the immediate vicinity, and Nicholas felt severe pain. The left side of his face suffered third degree burns.

He screamed in agony and was quickly silenced when a sword impacted his throat. The skeleton pulled his sword out and moved on to the next living being.

The fireball impacted the nearest residence. The explosion knocked all the humans off their feet. The skeletons quickly killed them. The house debris went flying everywhere and caught the neighboring domiciles on fire. Innocent families died from exposure to the flames, heat, and smoke. Women and children were burned alive.

The remaining families saw what happened from their windows. They quickly evacuated and ran down the street to escape the battle. They took their chances over their house exploding or burning. Dozens of skeletons ran after them, and all that was heard was screaming followed by gurgling, then silence.

The King ran to the altar. He was out of breath and covered in blood. He put the tip of his sword to the ground to help him slowly get to his knees, but they gave out. He fell to his knees, and he held on to his sword for balance or he would have gone all the way down.

"Lord, please hear my prayer. I do not know what I did to deserve this, please help me. My Kingdom is under attack and evil is prevailing. My warriors cannot keep them at bay, and I heard innocent families dying. I have prayed to you daily. I do not ask much of you, but I am asking for your help. If you are there, please help me cleanse this city from evil so we may prosper once again. We need your help. So, shall it be." The king dropped his head after the prayer.

Nekora made her way to the cemetery. She cast her raise spell while her army focused on the humans. The ground trembled, then shook violently. All the dead corpses in the cemetery rose to greet their new master. Soon the battle was over. Nekora's army had grown significantly.

Though she lost many undead, she gained a multitude more. She now had well over seven thousand minions and decided to head toward Killicut.

Volhara arrived at Killicut in the afternoon. The heat was close to unbearable. She was escorted to the castle for an immediate audience with the King.

"Your highness, I am Volhara, priestess of light. I apologize for the urgency and am grateful for your ear," she started. "A few weeks ago, we received word of a possible evil sorceress in this land. I hear she is on her way here and would like you to prepare for the worst."

King Renaldo laughed hysterically. "An evil sorceress? Here?" Then everyone started laughing. "If I would have known how easy it was to get a Paladin involved..." He was interrupted by a scout. The scout whispered in the King's ear, then gave him a piece of paper.

"It seems we have lost Kalvanya and a few other cities to a supposed sorceress. If this is true, then the rumors are true. We may be in dire need of your help," the King stated.

Volhara looked at the King. "Where is Kalvanya?" she asked.

"Two weeks ride to the west. We need to prepare this city for an imminent attack," the King commanded.

"I will assess the situation. If she has an army of the undead, then she is highly educated in the arcane arts. God help you. Set up maximum defenses and ready everything with fire. If they breach your defenses, they must be beheaded, or they will not die. I pray the gods protect you", she said as she turned to walk out.

Volhara marched toward the stables. She obtained her war horse and galloped to the west along the path. "Please be wrong," she said.

Nekora gathered her forces and marched to the east. She was satisfied in the odds of her finally getting revenge for the human actions. Her rally almost complete, then, and only then, would she finally be in peace.

Nekora rested a mile later. She needed to gather her thoughts and plan her action against the largest city in the land. There would no doubt be thousands of people, but she was mostly betting on children and defenseless women. She unrolled her map to peek at the city outline, a last look before her dreaded two week-long march.

Volhara galloped as far as her horse would go. She would then rest for a few hours then off again. She would camp overnight out in the open. She feared nothing. Her mind kept playing tricks on her during her travels. Something was off. Morning came fast.

"Is this truly an evil sorceress?" she thought to herself. If so, what edged her on? If I can find the answer, I can turn her back to the good.

Necromancer, she figured, was just a term coined by the magister since she is dabbling with the undead. That would make sense, and arcane artist working with undead would be a necromancer. Though it seemed correct, something about it was unnerving. "How do I deal with a necromancer?"

"Why is this troubling me so?" Volhara thought. Her dreams were made up of clouded confusion. It was time to pray. She needed to be clear-headed.

Volhara knelt on a piece of fabric with her sword, pointed down, into the ground. She began to pray in the morning dew.

"Lord, I beg you this day, help me to see clearly. I need your guidance if I am to help rid this land of evil." A flash of flames crashed her thoughts. The explosion startled her, and she opened her eyes momentarily. She closed and continued, "My lord I beg of thee. Clear my head so I may be victorious in battle. I must be strong and clear in my journey to its end. Aid me in this, so I may fulfill my vow as a protector of the realm, Amen."

More flashes interrupted Volhara's actions. She would stumble. She looked to the air. "What are you telling me?" she yelled. She looked forward and concentrated on her objective.

Nekora marched. She kept going until she was midway to the city. Something inside told her to stop, so she did. She looked around. Not seeing anything, she was curious as to why her emotions were so strong. She readied a shield spell in case of ambush. All she could smell was damp air, dirt, and foliage. No enemies that she could detect.

Nekora had her minions scour the area. She decided to rest in this place for the night. Nekora felt a voice trying to talk to her, but it was blocked. She decided to reach out. She knelt and closed her eyes.

"Mother, am I doing the right thing? I have been treated as filth, and I believe it is now the time to enact revenge for the death of family, my love, my Kingdom. I would really like your view on this. I feel it is right, but I would like reassurance. I do not want to be the enemy, just to live in peace," Nekora said aloud.

She felt a presence but could not pinpoint it. She finally dismissed the attempt and concentrated on her revenge. She lied down and dreamed of all the wrongdoings caused unto her, as she felt in her earlier life. She felt differently now; she had changed. She also wondered where it all turned.

Volhara woke the next morning and mounted her war horse. The horse was rested and fed. She needed the horse's strength to continue her quest.

"Halt!" said an unknown voice in the morning shadow. Volhara stopped and looked. She felt a presence and detected an evil aura. She drew her sword and shield from the horse. A skinny man in dark leathers came into view. He sported a large mustache and goatee, salt and pepper colored, with a leather cowboy hat and a large crossbow.

"You look the part of a wealthy warrior," the bandit stated. "I think you need to share some of that wealth with the less fortunate."

"Turn and walk away. I am not your concern," Volhara answered.

"Ah, but you see, that is where we differ in opinion. You see, I have the crossbow. I can kill you in an instant, but why the needless bloodshed? Just hand over your fancy armor and coin and you will be free to pass. I give you my word," the bandit said. He was fixated on the gold and silver plate mail, shield, and sword, that Volhara donned.

"How about you leave, and we forget this ever occurred?" Volhara stated.

"Nah, I need money to live, you see. You have a lot, so why not share with the less fortunate?" he spoke. As he finished the sentence, he let loose the bolt.

Volhara raised her shield. The bolt impacted and went through the shield and pierced her left arm. She ignored the pain and galloped toward the bandit who was in the middle of reloading. She swiped her sword cleaving him in half with a flash of light on impact. When the body fell to the ground, she dismounted and removed the bolt from her shield.

"That is a powerful weapon," she commented as she broke the crossbow. She called upon her deity to heal her wound. She laid her hand upon it, and it immediately sealed up on its own, no scar tissue. She also burned the bolt to remove the blood from existence.

It was believed that dark sorcerers could use the blood in a demonic ritual and control the person it belonged to. Destroying the blood removed any doubt.

The thought of forcibly working with an evil sorceress did not sound appealing at all.

"Better to be safe than sorry," she said. "Now, for you. Lord hear my prayer.

Lead this lost soul to his destination. Be merciful as he is a soul in need of guidance. He knows not what he does." She mounted her horse and rode off toward the west.

Nekora moved on. The farther east she went, the stronger the feelings. Why am I feeling this? Must be danger up ahead she speculated. Either way she kept on guard.

Volhara searched her thoughts. "Necromancer. What does that mean. Why is it plaguing me?" She finally understood. She knew it was her destiny to meet and destroy this being. She was the chosen one to stop the spread of evil.

Nekora continued toward Killicut. The pathway opened into an expansive open grassland, encircled by a dense forest. She cautiously viewed the scene before her and readied her spells just in case an ambush occurred. She was always ready, but this time, it felt different.

She rode out into the field. No birds sang, and there were no sounds other than a gentle breeze through the leaves and the hooves of her horse. A lone figure stood at the other end.

Nekora eyed the figure. The overwhelming aura of silver and gold was too bright to view. She partially covered her eyes. It stood on the grassland with sword and shield at the ready. Nekora galloped toward the figure.

The figure changed posture. The sword went up then down, then across in a horizontal motion. Flames exploded in front of her and burned the undead warriors immediately behind Nekora, dropping them instantly in a flash of light. The figure stood there defiantly.

"Mother! Stop!"

Milton Keynes UK
Ingram Content Group UK Ltd.
UKHW040709050124
435493UK00001B/360